OPEN

WATER

OPEN WATER

WATER

Maria Flook

THE ECCO PRESS

Published by arrangement with Pantheon Books,
a division of Random House, Inc.

THE ECCO PRESS
100 West Broad Street
Hopewell, New Jersey 08525

Published simultaneously in Canada by
Penguin Books Canada Ltd., Ontario
Printed in the United States of America

Library of Congress Cataloging-in-Publication Data

Flook, Maria
Open water / Maria Flook.
p.   cm.
ISBN 0-88001-485-7 (paperback)
I. Title.
PS3556.L58306   1997
813'.54—dc20   94-17114

Designed by M. Kristen Bearse

9 8 7 6 5 4 3 2 1

FIRST ECCO EDITION

Acknowledgments

My thanks to Tony Jackett, captain of the *Josephine G.*, and to M. G. Moore, captain of the *Blue Moon*, for their technical advice; to Kim Witherspoon, for her wisdom and support; to Daniel Frank, my editor, who has helped me from page one, and whose particular vision schools and entices my own; to John Skoyles for every faith and freedom.

for
Judith Grossman

OPEN
WATER

He came home to Newport with a fractured wrist. He returned to his stepmother's seaside house and took the same upstairs room with the narrow bed and noisy mattress baffles he had slept in for years. His stepmother had saved him from Social Services when he was orphaned at thirteen and he owed her the visit. He denied it was his final courtesy. Yet, her cancer had advanced. He knew she was sick. Willis had come home to nurse her, but because of his fracture, she assumed it was the other way around.

Willis had received a general discharge from the Navy after a short assignment at the Naval Supply Center in Norfolk. He never shipped out. He worked on a terminal in the bowels of a warehouse, cataloguing dry goods and food supplies for the carriers. He started to do some wagering and some simple pilfering. It wasn't much, just what he could get into his partner's Plymouth once or twice during weekend liberty. Mostly it was cases of cigarettes, which he sold to Richmond Vending.

He reclined in his childhood bed. Even small movements jostled his wrist; its torn nerves were chattering beneath the heavy plaster cast. He tried to manage his pain but it was a strange, invisible geography. Its terrain shifted.

Pain migrated from its formal nucleus and wormed in all directions, into icy spinal ravines and flash fires of its thermal dimension. His pulse mimicked the trouble spot in the jelly of his retina.

Rennie came into the room. Her long white hair was loose and she had tied the satin strings of her bed jacket in a lopsided bow. She switched on the lamp so that Willis could see what she offered. A pellet in a silver wrapper. A morphine sulfite suppository. Willis sat up and took the foil almond from her hand. He peeled open the foil and pinched the smooth insert; its glycerol coating responded to the heat of his fingertips. He placed the suppository on the night table.

Willis said, "How long have you known me?"

"Forever," she said.

"I'm serious," he said. "I'm asking, how many years have I lived here with you?"

She sat down next to him. He was making a speech.

Willis said, "In all those years, have you ever known me to put anything in my ass?"

"This is a legitimate, broad-spectrum painkiller."

He was holding the crook of his elbow where the edge of his plaster cast ate into his biceps. "Where did you get these things?" he said, matching his thumb against the waxy insert.

"It's a prescription. With refills. I've got a whole inventory left over from surgery. You know, we're letting nature take its course. They hand out the whole candy store when it's terminal."

"Maybe you'll need these for yourself."

"I can share."

"Yeah, well. Don't be offended if I decline," he said.

"You're just acting embarrassed. Pain isn't so shy, is it?" she told him.

He agreed with that.

Rennie said, "Willis, let me remind you, this is not an oral medication."

She switched out his lamp. He followed his stepmother's no-nonsense silhouette around the room as she adjusted the venetians, slivering the moonlight.

Rennie had arranged her big Fresnel lens on his windowsill. A long hull of beryl-green glass, clear as mint tea. The scrap was from the original lighthouse at Bullock's Point and Rennie thought the broken shard held luck. The lens was usually displayed against the living room fanlight window, where it refracted normal sunlight and circulated green medallions across the carpet and chairs. She placed it in Willis's room for his recovery. Even weak moonlight filtered through the lens, shooting tines across the wall. Then she left him alone.

He rested for several moments. In the dark, his arm seemed to quadruple in size. The new plaster cast had hardened into an aching zone, imprisoning pain's trigger points. The delicate flesh on the inside of his wrist was prickling with fishhook sutures where he couldn't scratch. The fact that there was an available method to relieve his pain made his pain worse.

He waited. A wolf spider edged across the maple headboard and darted inside his plaster cuff, a recurring apparition. He knocked his cast against the bedpost to chase it out. He pushed down his briefs and inserted the medication, sinking the morphine pellet through the taut, resistant sphincter. Within minutes, he felt his hips liquefy, his spine warmed and ascended in fluid notches until the drug reached his gnawing wrist and Willis slept.

For the first week, pain vanished, returned, vanished again with every application. He peeled the foil from another crayon bullet and tamped it into his rectum. It freed

Willis from his wall of thoughts. When the drug had less effect, he doubled the dosage. There were side effects. After two weeks, his pelvis felt hollow as a coal chute and he had lost his center of gravity. He tried to wean himself from the morphine. The pain returned. Without the rectal suppositories, Willis never slept. He got out of bed in the middle of the night and searched for Rennie's vial of Seconal in the mirrored cabinet above the sink. Glossy capsules spilled across the porcelain like little slivers of pimento.

The rainy March weather revived the fleas; the humidity moistened egg casings and the insects emerged, dotting the curtain hems. Rennie had to call exterminators in. The men powdered the floors, but the fleas held on. Every night Rennie came into Willis's room to count his bites. She wanted to know if they were the same welts or new ones. She examined his legs and circled each individual swelling with a ballpoint pen. She rolled the tip of the pen over the back of his knee, tugging the skin. The tiny indented circle made a pleasing sensation until she lifted the pen and started again somewhere else. She moved up his legs, marking his buttocks and the small of his back. He turned over and she inked the sharp knob of his collarbone and spotted the ladder of his ribs where the insect bites flared. He listened to her count them out, drawing nineteen dime-size rings the first night, twenty-four the next. In a week's time, the painful histamine domes were subsiding. To make sure, Rennie took a pair of Willis's white crew socks from his drawer and pulled them up high on her ankles. She walked room to room in Willis's socks. She returned to his bedside and stood back, in the center of the oak floor. She told Willis, "See anything?" She showed him one foot and then

the other. Willis tried to look for the vermin but it didn't
show up. He couldn't keep his eyes focused on her tiny
figure any longer. The morphine had lifted into his line of
vision like a furry blindfold, a cashmere turtleneck tugged
up to his hairline.

◌◌◌◌◌◌

Holly Temple watched Rennie hopscotch in Willis's crew
socks. Rennie's silhouette bounced across the lace panels
from one window to the next. Holly couldn't figure it out.
She decided that her windows faced someone's sickroom. A
nurse was dancing before her charge, perhaps indulging her
patient's final request for the evening.

Holly had just moved into one side of an oceanfront
duplex. The duplex was really a single-story cottage halved
by some extra Sheetrock and carpentry. The house next
door was a weather-beaten two-story with a third-floor gar-
ret, part Greek Revival and part Victorian. The turn-of-the-
century house had seven-foot-high windows dressed with
lace curtains; tattered antique cloth hung in loose tails.
Large velvet sofas, their furred backs against the windows,
looked bleached by many seasons. Big wavy privet and
boxwood, wild and unmanicured, cinched the ground floor.
Its airy front porch looked over the water, same as Holly's,
but it had more height, and Holly suspected it had the
better view.

She had not yet unpacked her things. She still felt
anesthetized from having been forced to start over. The
duplex looked west, over First Beach. The water was
smooth until it hit the shore, where it churned and spread

out like sugar lace. Holly stepped up to the window and let her breath cloud the pane. She moved back and watched the mist crawl off the glass. She rubbed the window with the cuff of her Angora sweater, leaving a few blue hairs sticking to the glass.

Her divorce had just come through.

Holly was pleased to have the divorce. She wasn't happy about the charge of arson.

One week after her husband, Jensen, had left her, Holly went over to his new apartment. He invited her inside, then he decided he didn't want to talk. He went to his job and left her standing in his tidy new living room. The telephone started ringing. Holly saw the red light bloom on his answering machine and she waited to hear the caller. It was Sarojini, her husband's new Hindu love connection. Sarojini, again. Her husband had met his Eastern item when she was buying up three Carvel franchises in Rhode Island and southeastern Massachusetts. Jensen took the exotic visitor around for site inspections. Holly remembered that she herself had left several embarrassing messages for Jensen on the machine. She had begged him to reconsider. She had even held the telephone receiver to the Panasonic while it played an old seventies classic, "You Are the Magnet, I Am Steel."

Holly jerked the answering machine loose from the telephone jack in the middle of Sarojini's lilting message. She walked outside her husband's apartment and shoved the answering machine into the trunk of her Toyota. She picked up an empty coffee can from the backseat. She looked for new russet coils of dog shit, but the smouldering coals in a neighbor's backyard grill caught her eye. She scooped them up and went upstairs to the strange apartment. She deposited the red nuggets, fiery eggs of charcoal dead center on the quilted surface of her husband's double bed. For half a day she watched the bed smoldering. She called her husband at his Carvel Ice Cream franchise.

"Just one thing," she said.

"And what's that?"

"Guess what I'm doing? I'm burning the bed."

"Holly, I'm real busy. I'm taking a delivery. I don't need this—"

"You better get your ass off ice and drive right over here. It's smoking."

He didn't believe her.

"It's starting to smell funny. I bet I'm not supposed to breathe these fumes," she told him.

If he had believed her, she might have doused the bedding, but she waited. She dialed her mother's number in New Jersey where her mother had moved with her new husband. The telephone kept ringing. Holly wanted someone to acknowledge her gravest moment: she was moving from a stale, familiar loneliness into a *fresh* state of loneliness; its virgin landscape was electrifying. It didn't require a witness, after all. Holly sat on the edge of the mattress and watched the sheet's floral pattern curl in ashy petals, then the ticking charred and the fumes increased. She fanned the blaze to hurry it along. She started to cough and opened the window.

The fire department arrived in time to shove the mattress onto the fire escape, where it burst into flames, fully involved. In minutes the bed was consumed, the batting disappeared leaving only the meticulously knotted springs. Holly stared at the grid of wire and imagined their love-making sifting through, like sand and soul.

Before the police took her down to the station to record her explanation, Holly picked up some familiar kitchen utensils Jensen had lifted from her. She recognized the salt and pepper shakers, two halves of a ceramic house which when shoved together made a complete cottage, the chimney perforated with tiny holes to deliver the spices. She shoved the shakers into her purse.

At the station house, even the matron wouldn't take her side of it; she told Holly that "female hysteria," "PMS," or "whatever she wanted to call it," wasn't an excuse for arson. The senior officer explained the severity of her actions. Because Holly had set fire to a furnished apartment in an *occupied* dwelling, Holly could be charged with arson in the first degree. Holly set the blaze but did not leave the scene; this might have meaning in court.

"What meaning?" Holly said.

"That detail could go either way," the officer told her.

The officer wanted to know about her husband's insurance. "Jewish Lightning. Italian Lightning. In East Providence it's Lisbon Lightning. The what-have-you. It's an insurance scam."

"I've heard of that, but we don't pay insurance," Holly told him. "They don't sell insurance for people like Jensen and me—"

"Sure they do. It's common to have insurance for personal property. You don't have to be a homeowner. People can insure their possessions."

"I'm saying," Holly said, "they don't insure everything. Do they?" She rolled her gaze over the abrupt shelf of her breast and down the tight valley of her lap; she crossed her legs and rotated her white ankle. Her small foot, in its braided leather pump, was an irresistible attraction and the officers waited for her to drop her foot and cross her ankles again. The matron filled in the lines, telling the sergeant, "She gets married. Her husband turns out to be a textbook case. She goes berserk."

"Textbook?" He had to run it through his mind. There were a million different textbook cases. "Give me the example."

"Gash hound," the matron said.

The violence of those two words surprised Holly. Then she wasn't surprised. "That's right," Holly spoke directly. "What insurance policy do they have for that?"

She wasn't getting a lot of sympathy. They arranged the answering machine and the salt-shaker house on the table and tagged them. This was too much for Holly. She started crying.

After a short course of psychiatric evaluation ordered by the Superior Court for the County of Newport, Holly's charge was reduced to "malicious burning." She would face trial before a judge. Her court date would run almost concurrent with her divorce proceedings.

The *Newport Daily News* ran a story about her: SPURNED WIFE IGNITES THE NEST.

She still had six more months of probation. Her probation terms involved biweekly sessions with her probation officer, Dr. Kline, a psychiatric social worker. All winter, Holly had been out of work, collecting unemployment. If it weren't for her courthouse visits, her life would have had no external structure. Holly's regular job was during the tourist season, when she worked changeover Saturdays at Neptune's Hide-A-Way, where she cleaned summer cottages. The tiny beach cottages were named after perennial flowers: Hollyhock, Cosmos, Zinnia, Larkspur, a string of two-room efficiencies, eleven all in all, where Holly had worked summers her whole adult life. Five months a year, she took charge of the eleven units, cleaning and setting up for the new clients each weekend. Between changeovers, she went into the cottages to add soap and towels or to ration out complimentary packets of sugar and nondairy creamer. She found surprises. A jar of pee in the freezer. Somebody's pregnancy test abandoned. She found a set of glossy-red car doors. It was difficult to make up the beds with car doors in them. Doors often appeared in the rooms when people stripped down their four-wheel-drive vehicles before riding the back shore.

Holly worked changeover Saturdays in almost the same way people attended to their sabbath rituals. The tiny chapel-white clapboard cottages, in a zigzag line to the sea, were like pristine grottoes which Holly kept straight. Every autumn, when she closed up the shacks and Salvatore removed the screens from the windows, storing the hand-painted flower signs, Holly felt vulnerable and melancholy. When the string was boarded up, her duties suspended, she couldn't stop thinking of the place. She pictured the salt cellars where she had left them in pairs, the neat stacks of cobalt Fiestaware plates, the green iron stains ringing the drains in the tiny porcelain sinks, the striped Hudson Bay blankets folded at the foot of each bed. In the winter months, she felt a little lost and guilty, as if closed off from her house of worship.

Her husband, Jensen, had often stopped in at the units on changeover days, wanting something. She didn't like to rough up the bedclothes that she had already smoothed. "I'm not doing these sheets twice because of you," Holly told him. Neptune's was one place where she had the authority to turn him away.

In February, her unemployment insurance ran out and Social Services located a position for Holly at a local prep school. She was hired as a kitchen assistant at Saint George's School. When Holly started her new cooking job, she tried to think that she had everything in control; she had her divorce and a decent employment future. She told her co-worker, Robin, "I'm single again. I lived to talk about it."

Robin told her, "Congratulations. When it happened to me, I started singing in the shower. Are you singing yet?"

Holly couldn't say if she felt free enough or lost enough. She knew that she would have to feel unabashedly free or perilously lost to encourage a breakthrough. When her marriage deteriorated there had been corresponding environmental signs in the apartment house where she had lived with Jensen. She watched lines of sweet ants scroll across the kitchen counter and onto the pantry doors, a disturbing message in a pulsing script. Silverfish twisted in the porcelain sink like tiny bouncing drops of mercury. Then, on the day she received the official court document, Holly came home to her building after work to find that where there had once been a grassy front lawn, there was no lawn. It was a gaping pit. A sinkhole. Heavy asphalt crusts were turned over in scalloped rows around a circular trench, a breathtaking saucer. The hole seemed to be expanding as she watched.

The sinkhole had torn open the street, gouging a wide trench in the building's foundation. A bearing wall was tilting. Newport public works crews arranged fluorescent red sawhorses at each corner of the lot. The DOT trucks pulled to the curb and men unloaded a backhoe. Blue lights surged on and off in a pleasing split-second unison. A police officer explained to Holly that it wasn't an actual geological sinkhole, it was a *bubble*. A water main had erupted underground and pumped enough water into the sandy loam until the street collapsed, the asphalt erupted in a jagged funnel.

Her apartment house was condemned.

Holly's landlord came out of the building and handed

Holly a padlock still in its plastic blister. "This lock goes on the U-bolt as soon as you get your suitcase," he told her.

"Please don't tell me this. How long do I have to be out?"

"Your guess is as good as mine. They say it's the whole infrastructure. It depends on insurance. When they get moving on a claim, we'll be okay. Just pray they don't decide that it's an act of God. An act of God won't bring a dime."

"An act of God?" Holly enjoyed the sound of it. It implied an absolute finality. Perhaps the moment she had torched her love pallet it had been an act of God. Holly telephoned her friend Robin at Saint George's and made arrangements to sleep on Robin's foldout sofa as long as she brought her own linens. The officer permitted Holly to go inside her apartment to get some clothes and toiletries. She tugged her Wamsutta loose from the mattress and walked with an armful of bedding down the stairs and across the front courtyard. The sheet snagged on the turf and her toe caught in the elastic hem. The sheets' private floral pattern splashed open and the city workers turned their faces in the opposite direction. She balled up the linens and shoved them into the passenger seat of her Toyota. She went back inside and took her good dresses on pink satin hangers. Why she bothered with the dresses she didn't understand. The party dresses looked quite homely in the harsh sunlight, and the city workers rested on their forks and shovels to gawk at them. She went inside again and walked through the apartment, careful to choose her steps on the precarious flooring. Yet the floor didn't feel any different. She knew that sometimes there were warning signs, bridges might heave and wobble before collapse, otherwise there's no hint and structural integrity gives way all at once.

She examined her possessions gingerly, as if everything was part of the doomed whole. She decided to leave most everything behind until another time if she wanted to come back for them. An almost physical urgency took over and she snapped the padlock through its U-bolt. She had to remind herself to shove the toy-sized key deep into her pocket. She might have just as easily thrown it over her shoulder.

The night Holly moved into the duplex, her ex-husband was scheduled to be on a plane to Kanpur for a visit to his new fiancée's homeland. A fragile tissue copy of her final decree, with its embossed seal, fluttered on an end table near a warp in the storm door. She placed a giant seashell ashtray on the court document so it wouldn't sail around the room like something bewitched. Holly imagined Jensen's Indian bride, her tiny red pencil mark. All evening she saw Sarojini's ruby dot in the twilight. It was the commuter air traffic from Warwick Airport, one jetliner after another. Each bright speck throbbed and receded. In its anonymity, she was convinced that one certain jet in particular was the one that lifted her ex-husband off the continent. Then, another aircraft angled past, and she decided that *it* was the one. She wasn't wholly relieved to have met the finish line, which was, of course, also the starting line, but she was pleased that the sinkhole had forced her out of her apartment. She stood facing the dark Atlantic, whatever was out there, on her own terms. Of course, the local authorities were keeping track of her. She wasn't exactly under surveillance, but she was ashamed of her predicament. Shame itself was a cold eye out of nowhere.

Her psychiatric counselor, Dr. Kline, looked a lot like

the virginal TV actress Eleanor Donahue, the eldest daughter in the series *Father Knows Best*. The striking similarity between the actress and Dr. Kline had a paralyzing affect on Holly. Holly never wanted to open up. At Holly's last visit, Dr. Kline said, "How are you this week?"

"Same old same old," Holly said.

"Still feeling guilty?" Dr. Kline asked.

"Not exactly."

"You don't feel responsible?"

"From this minute on, sure. I'm a responsible citizen."

"What about the fire?"

"*That* fire is extinguished."

"What about the next fire?"

Holly played along. "Another fire? I don't see that happening." She told Dr. Kline, "What happened, *happened*."

"What did you learn from it?"

"Life goes on," Holly said. "On the other hand," Holly continued, "no one gets out of this world alive."

Dr. Kline said, "That's a gloomy assessment."

"Mostly it's the here and now. Like I'm almost out of cash. That's just the plain facts. I'm not putting any spin on it," she said. "I had to put four hundred dollars down. Another one hundred fifty for the propane tank. That pretty much cleaned me out."

The rooms in the duplex were cold. It was really a summer house with auxiliary heating. She adjusted the space heater and she lit the gas stove and opened the oven door. The propane scent reminded her of Neptune's Hide-A-Way. She often helped the tenants relight the pilots on their stoves with a foot-long matchstick. The same propane scent permeated the duplex, it was comforting and she breathed it willingly.

The winter after Holly and Jensen were married, Jensen was hired as an intern with the Beef Growers Institute, a national lobbying group. He was assigned to a meatpacking plant in Sioux City. He was sent there to help employees address public relations issues. The nation was becoming anti-beef and it required a grassroots turnaround. He took the job, and Holly drove out to meet him.

She drove straight through and Jensen was there to greet her. He was standing out in the cold, his breath white as phlox. He looked like a real rancher in a new shearling coat. Holly ran out of the car into his open arms. He wrapped her inside his sheepskin jacket, folding the dense blond wool over her head, and she felt all the warmth she would ever feel in his tight hold. It lasted all night and into that first spring.

If she thought of her husband at all, she might as well think of that showy sheepskin coat, its sweet, tallow smell.

She had made one mistake, but the dominoes kept falling in a straight row of incriminating details gathered from her personal history. Dr. Kline took notes on legal pads with pencil-thin green lines. The green lines had bled on the yellow paper; they weren't lines so much as blurs. What did her probation officer write between these blurs? What would happen to these documents? Holly wanted to burn them.

Holly arranged her brush and comb on the knotty-pine bureau upon a yellowed doily. She decided she would soak the dirty lace circle in a bowl of Clorox. The idea of bleaching the doily was oddly reassuring. Perhaps she was regaining her domestic instincts. She purchased a package of potpourri, a jumble of citrus rinds and herbs to boil on the stove. She hoped its lemony scent would overwhelm a familiar undefinable trace of clean musk that lingered on certain hand towels and unisex T-shirts that she had shared with Jensen.

She walked through the little duplex and switched on the lamps. The bedroom had recently been painted with "sand paint" to cover up flaws in the plaster. The surfaces were sharp and gritty. As Holly made her bed, she brushed the back of her wrist against the wall and the blood rose in tiny dots. She licked the small red grid from her skin. She made the bed with the same floral sheets and set the pillows straight. At two A.M. she finally went to bed, pulling the blanket high, until its icy satin binding touched her throat.

She was sinking into dreams when the lights blazed again next door; a platinum square fell across her wall. She pinched her eyes shut but the neighboring light washed through. Holly wondered how much longer until the invalid next door succumbed and his caretaker was released from her duties. Certainly the schedule was difficult for the vigilant soubrette. Holly lifted herself on her elbow to watch the illuminated curtain, the nurse's familiar outline. Earlier that evening, Holly had been impressed by the queer dance, its unflinching charity, which in silhouette had appeared doubly genuine.

Whoever was sick wasn't to be envied, but she felt a wave of jealousy. A personal nurse was a luxury, wasn't it? Then Holly recognized that she didn't wish for comfort but for its opposite, the opportunity to attend to someone, to look after a beloved.

Holly heard the screak of a window sash. A woman, quite older than she had imagined, was leaning far out from the third-floor bedroom, her hand inserted in a tight, white muff. She was shaking the muff loose from her wrist. It was a sock; she stretched its elastic cuff, letting its accordion ripples snap shut. The wind tugged it out of her grasp. She inserted her fist in its mate, then shook it free.

Holly stood up and tugged on her flats. She found her overcoat in the dark kitchen and pulled it around her. She walked outside, across the clamshells. She picked up the socks, which had landed like dog ears on the bare hydrangea. She looked up.

"You want these things?" Holly called up to the woman above.

"Watch out. They're contaminated," Rennie said.

Holly dropped the socks. She imagined the viral contagion that the invalid must be dying from. "Shit. You can't just throw these infected things around."

"We're fighting a war up here," Rennie said. She didn't elaborate.

Holly said, "You're fighting a war?"

"One battle at a time."

"Sorry to hear that." Holly looked up at the woman, who was out of uniform and wearing her nightdress. The fouled socks had repelled her, but Holly lingered below the window. She cherished the moment of drama. "Is your patient very ill? Is it HIV?"

Rennie stared down at her.

"You have a local doctor? I guess you drive into Providence? Does your patient need a specialist? There's a HIV network. It's a hot line. Do you have that 800 number?" Holly asked a string of questions.

Rennie told Willis, "It's our neighbor. She's vaccinated with a phonograph needle."

"Shit. Was I talking too fast? I thought I was showing some concern. Christ."

"Don't worry. The patient is fine. Except for the fleas."

Holly wasn't following the woman's explanation. She watched Rennie's face. Despite her many years, it was the face of a sprite, fully backlit with her silver hair ribboned loosely over her shoulders. Holly shrugged and moved back to her duplex. She waited on the porch until Rennie slammed the window. The morbific socks pulsed in the wind where Holly had dropped them on the garden walk.

Chapter Two

During his recuperation, Willis checked his potency at odd hours, several times a day. He solicited events from his carnal memory, and when that was depleted he left the house. He loitered on the Cliff Walk with a girl from Salve Regina College. The girl was a nursing student, right off of her shift at Château-sur-Mer Retirement Village. She wore a disposable paper cap, a white triangle high as a wedge of angel cake. Willis crushed it in one hand and sailed it into the beach plum bushes. The girl retrieved the hat, creased it flat and plunged it into her coat pocket.

The afternoon was raw. Joggers wore surgeons' masks against the windchill. Oldsters passed through, wrapped in Synchilla mufflers up to their eyewear. Willis steered the student to a private love nook behind a retaining wall, out of the wind. The cliff went straight down to where the sea sudsed the rocks. She came right along with just her fingertips alert in the palm of his hand. She was hypnotized by Willis's looks. Willis was half Cuban and his hair was rich as ink without a touch of sorrel in it. His pale skin and dark Latin crown was the kind of thing that made other men feel challenged. Willis unhooked the leather toggles on her jacket. She wasn't entirely a novice, but her mock complaints increased when he reached under her warm clothing. His right arm was still bandaged in a plaster cast and he rolled its icy surface against her bare skin. He siphoned her breath with harsh, toothy kisses.

The light was going. Loose mare's tails stretched deep across Rhode Island Sound. Newport has its layers of veneer; historic houses were a polish or a bright corrosion along the famous coastline. Most of the old mansions had been acquired by the Preservation Society and tourists came each season to sightsee it into the ground. Native year-rounders were ordinary, with love and trouble at their own level. Two days before, at Newport Hospital, a baby was stillborn. The brain stem was intact, but it didn't have the cortex. Willis felt jittery about it. He knew the baby's mother, Sheila Boyd, a laughing girl whose bright, ebullient nature had proved only to tantalize a mean fate. Of course, it was just luck. Luck was a wild filament, like the jagged arc in a light bulb.

The stillbirth was the town's table talk for longer than necessary, but Willis understood that if you live on an island you're under a microscope. Aquidneck Island was a torn cuff of land with three different bridges threading it to the main coastline. Each span grafted the island to every vein of commerce, healthy or not. There were potato farms and nurseries inland, but its jewel was Newport. A New England seaport puts a spell on its population; the indifferent rolls and shivers of the surf were like the town's collective respirations.

Willis made love to the nurse despite the cold and his waffling symptoms from Rennie's morphine. He waited while she fastened the barrel clasps on her coat and then he walked her into town. She tried to hold his hand and pushed her icy fingers into his vent pocket. Willis saw that the love act had made her clingy and he let her explore the flannel lining of his jacket. The boots he wanted were on sale at one of the plush leather boutiques on Bowen's Wharf and he took her along to get her opinion. He stopped in front of Northern Lights Leather to study the window. It was a pair of golden Luchesse cowboy boots on a Lucite pedestal. "Shit. I'm in love," he told her.

She stared at the boots.

The toes and insteps were embossed with patterns of gorgeous raised nubbins over the tawny hide; the calves had miraculous eagle-wing sewing. Willis imagined wearing the boots, walking into Narragansett Tavern through the stale puddles of Rolling Rock. One of the tap handles leaked, leaving a constant rivulet of beer across the floor. It was bad luck to step over the stream, Willis had to touch it with his shoe on the way in and on the way out too. Willis liked to put out a cigarette wearing good boots, grinding the stiff, triangular sole against the littered tile. He walked the nursing student inside the leather shop and they sat down in the row of seats.

They waited for the salesperson to finish a transaction. Willis told the nurse, "The question is—just what does that sign really mean?"

"That sign there?" she said. "It says SALE."

"What does it mean?" Willis said.

She laughed, two impatient coed snorts. "It means they're going to cost less money."

"But from what height does the price make its descent?"

"Its what?"

"It's all relative," he told her.

She moved across the room to look at a fringed handbag; she fingered the leather strings. "How about Friday night? Doing anything?"

He knew that was coming. He ignored her invitation

and told the salesman, "Ten and a half, maybe eleven."

She stood in front of Willis. "Well, what about Friday?"

Willis said, "That's the end of the week. The end of the week isn't good."

The man came back with the boots. Willis worked his left foot into the high leather cuff, then tugged the other one on with his good hand. He stood up and walked a wide circle around the girl. He stopped before a knee-high mirror and studied his feet.

The girl said, "They're kind of pointy, aren't they?"

"They're good."

"What about your toes?" she said.

"Perfect," Willis told the salesman. "These on sale?"

"Not that exact pair."

"Shit," Willis told the girl. "See what I'm saying. That sign doesn't have the fine print."

"Now wait a minute," the salesman said. "We have these same boots. Smoke-damaged. In our cellar show-room."

"These boots here?"

"Smoke-damaged. Fifty percent off. You rub the smoke off with a chamois."

Willis sat down and removed the expensive boots. He had to retrieve one sock from inside the tight leather toe. He nested the gleaming footwear in a big box and picked up his old boots.

The salesman said, "Hold on, I'm telling you. These smoke-damaged items are a steal. They're the same boots except for a little stink; it works its way out. It was a storage trailer fire. It smoldered for days just like a backyard smoker, but everyone buys these smoke-affected boots. We sold a pair to Kevin McHale. You know McHale? Number 32? See these ones I have on? These were smoke-damaged."

Willis looked at the man's glossy boots. They had square toes with a strap and buckle around the ankle and were not to his liking.

The salesman pointed to a narrow hallway running between stacks of shoe boxes. "Go right through to the back and down those stairs. Jimmy's working down there today."

Willis noted that as soon as he was pegged for the second-class inventory he was put on a first-name basis with the staff.

"I'm not going in the basement," the girl told Willis.

"Why the hell not?" Willis said.

"Maybe it's got rats, right on the harbor like this."

"It's fine," the salesman said. "Go see. Our irregular merchandise is hardly any different from what's up here."

Willis went down the narrow staircase. The old seams in the foundation walls were mortared in odd patches and the light was weak. They walked into a wide, carpeted room. The Salve Regina nurse shuffled close behind him, sinking her finger in the waistband of his jeans. He nudged her loose. The cellar smelled remarkably like the aftermath of a major firefighting event. Boxes of smoke-damaged leather were rank in the moist, sea-level showplace. The odor was both coal tar and pork rinds. He sat down again and waited for the man named Jimmy to come back with the style he wanted. He tried on the smoke-damaged boots. It was the same fit. The heels were high and steady, but the leather was marred with dark pewter whorls. He rubbed the cuff of his jacket over the cloudy toe, but it didn't shine up.

"These are top of the line. Look at that stitching," Jimmy said.

Willis saw that the golden sewing looked muddy in some places. "I just take my chances the smoke comes off?"

"Look. It's your decision. A little squirt of Windex. It cleans right off."

The tinged boots were comfortable. Willis paid half price for the boots and they went up the stairs and out to the street. The girl wanted to set up their next meeting. Her Timex had a digital calendar and she kept turning her wrist to look at the date. "It means something to me," she said.

He told her, "You wear Speedo underpants? Let's slow down a little bit."

"Well?" she said.

"Take it easy. Rome wasn't built in a day."

She sank her fist into his flannel pocket and they walked up Memorial Boulevard.

The girl had become moody. She wasn't having any fun. He walked her down to the water where conservationists, beachcombers, kids getting out of their schoolwork were scrubbing landmark boulders with grease-absorbing towels. A tanker had spilled grade-two heating oil, leaving deposits on First Beach. Volunteers organized into cleanup groups to patrol the affected shoreline. Willis watched Audubon professionals chase black ducks across the flats until the birds spooked and lifted off. These ducks, Willis knew, were black on their own account, but Willis kept out of it. The sea mist rolled in with the odor of a basement furnace, its oily grates and laden filters.

Willis studied the shoreline. On the facing cliff, an off-kilter flagpole fronted the house where he lived with his stepmother. Rennie sometimes ran semiotic greeting cards up the pole, burlap sacks painted with the names of her old associates coming in on a diminishing fleet of stern draggers and side trawlers.

He led the girl away from the beach when there were

only a few people still on the flats scrubbing rocks. The cars on Memorial Boulevard had come to a complete stop. The Salve Regina girl had started to pick a fight with Willis. She stood in the middle of the traffic, tugging Willis by his hair. People looked surprised to see a nursing student in her white tights and translucent nylon uniform beneath her three-quarter coat. Willis had given her the brush-off without much explanation and he was riding out her tantrum. Drivers tried not to gawk at the couple, shifting to look at the endangered beach. Circles of tainted kelp still littered the sand like shiny greased saw wheels.

The girl was jerking his taped wrist and kicking the stiff shank of his new boot. He pulled his arm free, then steadied her face to administer two abrupt kisses, bossy pecks. It looked like a science book display of nurturing dominance in a subset of the primate family. Again, the girl took a shag of his hair. His hair had been cropped short in the Navy but it was growing out in a wild black halo. She ripped a tight clump of it. The roots came out whole, rounded, like tiny white pupae.

He butted her face.

She circled her fingertips over her cheekbone where a little egg was rising. Willis touched her cheek, inspecting her sore spot. He said, "Miss, that's a shiner in the works."

"Willis Pratt, are you serious? A black eye?"

"I regret it," he said.

"Wait a minute. What did you call me? Did you forget my name?"

He said, "I was talking about your eye."

"Fuck that. What's my name?"

"I didn't forget."

"Say it," she said.

"Look. If 'Miss' is too formal for you—" He shoved her

through the traffic and back onto the sidewalk, away from the onlookers. She shrieked and ran ahead of Willis. He was right behind her, stepping on the heels of her cream-colored shoes. When she turned to face him, she was standing in her stocking feet. She was a tiny girl, and in her tights she looked like a pixie who had lost all her magical abilities. She was helpless against her own bad temper until she grabbed a rock from the gutter, a chunk of pink curbstone. She crashed it down on Willis Pratt's arm.

His plaster cast released a small puff of dust.

"Apologize for that," Willis said.

She laughed with pleasure. She jabbed the sharp rock at Willis, weaving her arm back and forth in a cobra's zigzag. Plaster chalk sifted over his jeans. She went for his face, but he lifted his heavy white arm across his eyes. She hammered the cast with metered accuracy until the bone-colored fabric ripped open. The plaster was pulverized, revealing the mesh wrappings, the inner fluff, and a tattered gauze sock.

A swell of white powder drifted in the still air.

She dropped the rock at her feet. Her jaw fell open, then she shut her mouth.

Willis waited for the pain to level off, testing its edge and duration. His arm was blazing with ripped nerves. He recognized a possible setback in his recuperation. Perhaps it was a major setback. His mending fracture felt freshly skewed. Without his trying, a twenty-milligram morphine sulfite suppository surfaced as a vision. Rennie's heavenly wax nugget: one end was tapered, the other end had an indentation for his fingertip. He acknowledged the pharmaceutical ingenuity behind the notch for his index finger.

The girl went back to where her shoes had come off. She toed them over and slipped them on. She went around a parked car and waited on the other side.

He walked over to her. "Settle down," he said.

She didn't say anything. Her lips made a two-inch crease.

"Listen to yourself," he said.

She crossed her arms and lifted her chin, then dropped her face and squinted at him.

"Do you hear what you're saying?" he told her.

"I didn't say shit."

"The language I'm hearing. From a nurse," Willis said. The tremolo in his voice was unrehearsed and added authenticity to his reprisals. The nursing student looked suddenly dazed, like a sparrow after it hits a plate-glass window. She was ashamed of her assault and the wounds she had delivered.

Willis reached into one of the parked cars, touching the radio knobs with his left hand.

"From Pilgrims Landing, it's WPLM. 'Sophisticated Swing.' "

He didn't have a key for the ignition. The radio was dead.

"Musical methadone for your nostalgia addiction," he said. Willis learned every kind of radio patter; he had an automatic memory for whatever came across the air waves. Yet his words were broken off. Pain was causing his lungs to tighten in a mock asthmatic reaction.

"It's me, honey, your dean of déjà vu," he told her. He started to sing. He was singing ragged phrases.

"Make the world go away. Get it off my shoul-ders. Get it OFF MY SHOUL-DERS."

A mist of sweat sparkled along his eyebrows. His face was losing color, chalk tones drifted higher. He looked pale as a china Madonna.

" 'Another Melancholy Midnight' with WPLM," Willis said. His heart wasn't in it exactly and she could tell. She wasn't smart enough to have known it all along. She watched him, but her anger was diminished. She arranged her tangled hair, pulling it free from her jacket hood. This girl had wanted to fight and she handed it right back. Now she was finished for the night. She closed her icy fists and pulled them inside the cuffs of her jacket. "Are you through?" she said.

Two neighborhood women were walking back from the beach cleanup. He would have opened it up to conversation, invited dialogue, but the women ignored him.

Willis called after them, "Hey, do-gooders. Ecology babes—"

The Salve Regina student saw her chance. She trotted off and tagged up with the other women. Together they walked away from Willis.

"Come on, Debbie. Debbie Cole—" he called after the nursing student. The fact that he said the girl's true name forgave something in his behavior, but the Salve Regina student didn't turn around.

"Hey, *girls*," Willis called after them. "*Girls*, wait up. Just a minute—*GIRLS*."

He watched the women until they became blotty in the circles of the halogen streetlamps. The surf at First Beach scrolled across the pebble sheet in rich, percussive phrasings. Willis weaved on his feet, as if the audile suction of the waves was, and had been for years, a great source of fatigue. The blood swam away from his face. Tiny silver smelts thrashed behind his eyes. The pain in his arm had migrated into his balance nerves and he lost his legs.

Chapter Three

Fritz Federico accompanied Willis to the emergency room at Newport Hospital. Fritz was second-generation Portuguese-Italian, but his mother chose Germanic nicknames for her kids. Giovanni Federico became "Fritz."

The physician on duty took one look at the fresh X-rays of Willis's wrist and told a nurse to telephone the hospital's resident orthopedic surgeon. They had to get the specialist out of the swimming pool at the Viking Health Club. Willis had a compound fracture; the earlier break had opened up again and there was a new sawtoothed break two inches higher. The edges of the shattered bones looked feathery against the lighted screen. The nurse injected Willis's arm with Xylocaine. When the arm was numb, the physician touched Willis's wrist with his fingertips and then he used his thumbs, applying pressure, massaging the splintered bones into place. "Feel that?" he asked Willis.

Willis said he couldn't feel it.

"You will later. No question about it."

Willis could have told the doctor that he wasn't interested in these rhetorical questions.

The surgeon spent a long time with Willis. The feathered bones were difficult to realign. A few resistant circles of ink marked Willis's shoulder although the insect bites had faded. The doctor kept quiet. When the arm was set, a nurse in dreadlocks pulled a new white gauze sock up to his elbow. She layered sheets of polyester fluff over his wrist, snipping the roll with a big scissors. She said, "I wondered you didn't have 3M fiberglass. Why you have plaster?"

Willis shrugged.

"Three-M fiberglass much lighter. Three-M comes in all kinds of colors. What's your favorite color?"

"White," Willis said.

She stared carefully at Willis. "Don't play with me," she said. "I'm got these shears. You just feeling mean."

Willis smiled at the nurse.

"Ted Bundy had a nice smile like that. He use his cast to attract girls. I seen his story on *Unsolved Mysteries*."

"I thought that case was closed."

The nurse stood back and crossed her arms. "I'm just saying. It's a mystery what men do."

Willis was grinning. A firm, unflinching crescent. Even a forced smile tugged a muscle in his right cheek, creating an irregular fissure like the hips of an apple. The dimple had always allowed him some slack with figures of author-ity—schoolteachers, dental hygienists, women standing in the express line at the Almacs. Right now he needed a shave. The stubbled pucker in his cheek only accentuated an idea of wayward innocence; it gave him a reckless look. The nurse let it go. She said, "That 3M fiberglass is good. Last fall, we have teen halfbacks come in busted up and we do those arms in their school colors."

Willis nodded at the nurse.

"It was fun-nee. But for you, the doctor wants plaster again. He needs plaster so he can weight it more on the one side. Son, son, *son*, that wrist is pul-verized."

The nurse talked until the arm was packed and

wrapped. The physician smoothed the wet plaster sheets the way he wanted. "This will have to dry some more before you leave the hospital. You don't want to knock it when it's wet," the physician told Willis. Willis agreed to wait a half hour until the plaster was firmed up.

Willis might have shown up at the Navy Hospital, his file was there, but they would have written another psychological report. Willis didn't trust the Navy doctors. When he was in Norfolk, they had prescribed a psychotropic drug. He stopped taking the drug when he started having side effects. He couldn't make enough saliva. He asked Fritz, "If you were a doctor and could make your way, would you go near a Navy base? Would you want to ride some carrier back and forth with a mob of white hats?"

Fritz said, "It wouldn't be my first choice. Maybe a sub."

"Let me inform you. Submarines, you have to hot bunk with who-knows-who. Sleep in shifts. You can't scratch your ass."

Willis smiled again at the nurse; her dreadlocks showed several little colored balls of lint. Maybe she just hadn't looked in the mirror. The nurse offered him a pleated cup with two tabs of Tylenol with codeine. He refused it. He wasn't getting back on that narco merry-go-round. He had business to do and didn't want to feel woozy.

Fritz had the car loaded with three thousand dollars' worth of stolen tools from Metric King. One-hundred-forty-eight-piece Master Sets, metric sockets and wrenches, SuperKrome flare-nut wrenches and metric hex-bit sets, whole trays of crowfoots and wobble extensions. Along with the wrench sets, Fritz had foraged a big item—a Porsche Turnkey Diagnostic System, the whole works: computer, display terminal with keyboard, hard-copy printer with roll out, adapter cables, everything snug in a portable console on casters.

The nurse again showed Willis the pills and rocked on her heels. "It's numb right now, but that pain will come on."

Willis shook his head.

"Suit yourself," the nurse said. "I'm glad I don't baby-sit you." She started to walk away holding the tiny cup.

Willis called her back. "Can you tell me something? About that baby?"

"What baby you mean?"

"My friend Sheila Boyd. Her baby."

"Why you interested in that? That was sent someplace in Dixie. That went to the Research Triangle. A hospital down there was on a list for one of those."

"So what happens now?" Willis said. "They dissect it?"

Fritz said, "Let's get moving. The minute hand—"

The tools were just sitting there in Rennie's car in the hospital parking lot. Fritz had to get rid of everything that night and he was nervous about waiting around at the hospital. "You had to break your wrist tonight. You forgot our appointment," Fritz said. He poked Willis's arm with his pointer to see if it was hardening. Willis's cast wasn't drying fast enough. Willis left the emergency room stall and went into the men's room to heat the cast under the electric blower. Even that didn't dry the cast, so he left the hospital with Fritz Federico when his arm was still doughy.

⦿⦿⦿⦿⦿

Willis had agreed to help Fritz only this once. After his troubles in the Navy, Willis didn't want to be part of any wise schemes. He wanted a regular job. An old friend of

Rennie had lined something up for Willis. Willis had his hackney license and he took a part-time job driving a box trailer for Narragansett WASTEC, collecting fifty-five-gallon barrels of liquid waste from casting companies, enamelers, and other sites in the jewelry industry. With his injured arm, he was hired only as a substitute driver to ride shotgun and fill out the inventory sheets on a clipboard. Willis was paired up with a fellow named Carl Smith and together they collected plating filters, cyanide sludge, nickel sludge, metal hydroxides, and stripping acids. Wastewater with heavy metals. Every WASTEC truck had a wordy statement running the length of the trailer: "Hazardous Waste Repackaged, Transported, Disposed & Manifested."

The waste barrels couldn't go to the Johnston landfill and had to be hauled to a transfer station or to Stablex, where the waste materials were incorporated into concrete slurries. It was harsh work, mostly heavy lifting, which he begged off because of his broken wrist. Instead, he inspected the loads. The barrels weren't always sealed correctly; they had leaky bungholes and sometimes fumes escaped. The best part of the job was riding with Carl Smith, who didn't keep his rule book with him. Carl Smith lived on a disabled trawler, the *Tercel*, which he had purchased for a dollar. The ship wasn't seaworthy but he could keep it moored at Warwick Neck cheaper than paying rent on an apartment. With Carl, everything was a matter of money. One time, Willis went out to the *Tercel* for Brompton cocktails. His party with Carl lasted a whole weekend, but Willis couldn't tell you what happened in between daybreak and nightfall and from dusk to dawn.

"Carl likes those heroin Slurpees? That's a bit hardcore," Fritz said when he heard about it.

"I'll try anything once," Willis said.

"You're not going back for seconds?" Fritz said.

"No. Carl's not my social equal," Willis said.

Fritz said, "The day I punch a clock is the day time stands still."

"There's no easy money, dickhead. Your freelance jobs end up being twice the work. Remember, I got busted with just a carload of Kools," Willis told Fritz.

Fritz said, "That's not too shabby. That was honorable. There's nothing wrong with a carload of Kools. For starters—"

"At WASTEC, I just show up and I'm on the payroll. I don't know what they do with the stuff. It's 'repackaged, transported, disposed, and manifested.' I don't lift a finger."

"Did you look up that word in the dictionary?"

"What word is that?"

" 'Man-infested.' Sounds like some girls got '*man*-infested' in an alley. Doesn't it? It has that porn sound—"

"You like to hear things," Willis said.

"Okay, I like the sound of it."

"Want to know a funny thing?"

"What funny thing?"

"That lettering peels off the truck. It's magnetized. I could steal that word for you if you want."

"You could get me that word off the truck? What would I do with it?"

"That would be your decision. I'm just saying, you think it's such a hot word, you can have it if you want."

Willis had known Fritz since middle school days. They were paired up by the school psychologist to receive counseling when the boys suffered coincidental deaths in their immediate families. The same week that Willis was orphaned, Fritz lost his little brother in a freak accident when a sand dune collapsed. After a nor'easter, there was severe

beach erosion and a section of dunes became unstable.
Signs were posted. The warnings said: LIVE SAND. Fritz was
running the top ridge with his brother when the shelf broke
loose. Fritz tried to dig his brother out, scooping the sand
off, but the hill kept shifting and he wasn't excavating the
exact place. EMS workers had to drag Fritz off the beach,
his fingertips bleeding with raw abrasions. Rescue workers
found six open graves in the dune where Fritz had searched
with his bare hands. These were serious mortal chores left
incomplete. The emergency crew had to bring in a backhoe and grade the dune to find the body.

Willis and Fritz were classmates until Fritz spent his
senior year in the Training School in Cranston, behind an
electric fence, and from there went to New England Technical College for one semester, where he developed a high-
toned engineering vocabulary, just enough to irritate Willis.

The Rhode Island coastline, its unruly surf, was not a
good place to abandon property and Willis decided to sink
Fritz's stolen items in the freshwater marsh near his stepmother's house. Fritz said, "Why can't we leave the items
in the back of Ames Discount with the bales of crushed
boxes?"

Willis said, "Look, you're dying to fit into this mode?
You want to be in business by yourself? Do I have to tell
you? Stolen property can't be left around with our dabs on
it. It has to disappear. Think of it this way. Taking a loss is
preferable to leaving a detail. A detail on the loose can show
up down the line. An unattended fact can wag its tail
months after. We've got the Coast Guard sniffing around
because of the oil spill."

"True," Fritz said.

"Fuck, yes, it's true. They're everywhere. They get a
team effort hard-on with these oil spills."

"Agree. They're forcing us into the interior."

"That's right."

"We'll keep this local, a site-specific event," Fritz said.

"Only ants should crawl on it."

Easton Pond was a big freshwater lagoon behind First Beach, right off Memorial Boulevard. Bailey's Brook fed the pond, and its water level wasn't affected by tides. At its deepest point, it was only fifteen feet down. It was a city reservoir and the water department patrolled the area now and then, but it was a better choice than driving over to the Mount Hope Bridge. Their dump-load was too heavy to lift over the railing. They would have looked conspicuous parking at the crest of the bridge where fishermen staked out some favorite spots between the lantern posts. Even in the middle of the night, no matter what time of day, these single-minded men pulled in scup and hake, bony fish that collect around the legs of bridges.

Willis steered the car into the marsh grass and cut the lights. He worried that it might sink in the muck, so he stopped just four feet shy of the lip. It wasn't close enough to the bank to haul the heavy tools. He tapped the accelerator until the windshield sloped when the front tires touched the mush. It was his stepmother's big sedan. He took it over from Rennie without assuming official ownership.

Fritz said, "Let me just say this, I didn't plan on asking for your help."

"You can't blow the paper off a straw without my assistance."

Fritz scratched his face. Little pimples had surfaced midline on his cheeks and at the corners of his mouth. His rosacea was coming back, a winter rash, and nerves made it worse. Fritz was high-strung and skinny. There wasn't much to him. His physique was slight, legs like window poles. He walked on the balls of his feet, as if at any given moment he might be required to sprint ahead of the group. In cold weather he shivered in lightning-fast tugs and rolls of his shoulders, vibrating like a tuning fork. And always, his face was blank. He never had any expression. He never had anything on his face. Willis envied how that gloom lived *outside* of Fritz instead of in his head. Fritz went right along, wearing it on the outside when Willis had a buildup, a pinging, a roaring noise he couldn't escape.

Willis had seen local Cape Verde women in Newport. If one of these women was widowed, she wore black for months, sometimes years, waving her flag of grief; yet she went about her business, shopping at the Almacs, chatting away at the Norgetown. The only bitterness was in the dark clothing. In the same way, Fritz was safe behind his blank mask. Even eating ice cream Fritz looked bleak, but he also looked peaceful, as if giving in to it was easier than fighting it off; chocolate stained the expressionless corners of his mouth.

"So tell me, how did you pinch this stuff to perfection?" Willis said.

Fritz said, "I drive my sister's car into Metric King. The shop at Two Mile Corner. I was interested in some wipers. Just some wipers."

"Blades or the whole arm?"

"That's what I was going to find out. No one was around but Albert—"

"Which Albert are we talking about?"

"The young guy. *Sweet* Albert. Princess Feet. And guess where he's at. He's in his van behind the place. The windows are misted up."

"Princess Feet has company."

"Magazines. That's my feeling. I've seen some of these gay rags. I saw one called *Inches*."

Willis said, "*Inches?*"

"The official title above the masthead."

"It's to the point."

"Anyway, the garage is empty. Cleared out. I hear a voice. The voice says, Help Yourself. I see the Porsche thing. I tip it into my backseat. The wrenches—in metal drawers and trays. I load them up like egg cartons. Fifteen minutes later my shopping list is complete. I'm across town."

"And where are you now? The minnow piss-hole."

"It got fucked up," Fritz said. "My brother-in-law's snooping around on the carport, writing down serial numbers. Can you believe this? He says he's going to put the squawk on me unless I unload the whole package. It's out the window."

"What about your sister?"

"She's ready to throw me out. I'll be homeless. I'll be on the grass triangle in the center of town, with all those ginks sleeping in their paper bags."

"No man is an island."

"I'm telling you. I can't live outdoors. I can't snooze under Venus and Mars," Fritz said.

"Maybe you can practice," Willis said, "because you're not getting rich this way."

Willis looked back at his friend's face. "What's the matter? You're having that old nightmare?"

"That's right. The same one. I wake up. I'm one of three on a bench at the ACI."

"And why do you think it's always three?"

"Three is a spooky number, isn't it? Shit, I don't know why it's three."

Willis said, "It's like Calvary. When I was in Norfolk, I saw those three crosses. They're everywhere. In a field. In the woods. They surprise you. It's supposed to be Jesus and the two thieves. You think, who in the hell put these crosses out here? It's the nineties. Who went to all the trouble? It's real spooky shit."

"Jesus and the two thieves? Shit, I forgot about them."

"I guess you did. Never mind, we sink the stuff. Splash. We're in rinse water after that."

Fritz got out of the car and went to find the dinghy he'd left in the tall grass earlier that day. He pulled the blunt-nosed wooden pram parallel to the car. It was a tiny, bright yellow boat, a local mascot. The diminutive rowboat was usually moored in a reserved slip in front of The Black Pearl, an upscale restaurant on Bowen's Wharf. Its stern said *Crouton*.

Willis said, "The *Crouton*. Shit, I'm impressed. How did you get it?"

"Like it? I knew you'd like it."

"Really. You thrill me to death. You just walked off with the *Crouton*?"

Fritz said, "You definitely like it?" Fritz rested his head on his shoulders, enjoying it, tasting relief in his friend's approval. "I knew you would like it." He was almost grinning, an intense flat line. "I rowed it out to the other end of Thames Street. It was simple. Preps were watching right out the window, drinking Heinekens. From glasses. I just shoved off."

"With their *Crouton*." Willis liked the story.

The stolen tools were still in trays wrapped in an Indian blanket. The Porsche electronics were in a big console on casters, maybe they could roll it, but the grass was long and thick. Willis started to load the wrenches into the dinghy.

"Point. Boat goes in the water first, don't you think? We launch the boat first?" Federico said.

Willis didn't like to make little mistakes like this and

he had to shift it over to Fritz somehow. He couldn't see how, so he clucked his tongue in random rhythmic phrases. Fritz shoved the pram into the blackness ahead of the car until it lofted on the water and Willis held the stern rail with his good arm. Fritz dragged the weighted Indian blanket over the spartina, raking its silvery stalks. They went back to the car and lifted the console out. The readout panels caught the moonlight in glowing bars. They tipped the heavy machine into the boat and shoved off. Willis lifted a glossy oar and snapped it in the oarlock; its new coat of shellac smelled sweet in the cold air. He shoved the oars to Fritz.

They glided through the darkness, watching the house-lights along the hillside, trying to judge where the center of the pond was by the corresponding landmarks. Fritz rowed out. He started singing "The Wreck of the Edmund Fitzgerald." Willis used his teeth to nip the fingers of his single glove until he had it off. He hit Fritz in the mouth with its heavy leather cuff. "Shut up. Stop dicking around."

Fritz kept singing.

"You idiot. You're a Chinese fire drill, you know that?"

Fritz went ahead with the ballad until Willis was laughing against the heel of his hand. Again he told Fritz, "Shut up, Federico. This isn't *Star Search*. I'm sticking my neck out sitting here."

When they reached the middle of the pond, Willis unwrapped the tools from the Indian blanket. They watched the occasional traffic on Memorial Boulevard in the distance. Willis took a handful of the wrenches and opened his fist under the water. Both men immersed fistfuls of the expensive tools; shiny jaws glittered and were gone. All sizes of SuperKrome sockets like scores of silver knuckles. Universal joints, some flexes. The crowfoots went in, the wobbles. Willis took his time, resting the wrenches on his knees before pitching them in. He recognized a sense of waste. The chrome tools caught the light from a wide girth of stars, bright enough to illuminate the silver bones as they sank beneath the surface. The electronic console was a different matter; they had to tip it over the gunnel and use their weight to counter it, submerge it slowly so it wouldn't splash. The cabinet screaked against the boat, making a minor racket. Cormorants lifted off the bank and circled the pond, their taut canvas wing beats made an upsetting, pre-historic flapping. More birds hooted bloodless tones, then quieted. The cabinet sank under the water.

"Wait a minute," Willis said. "I can still see it." They could find the top plane of the big cabinet, a pale square in the moonlit water. It was only two feet under the surface.

"You know. This is giving me a pain," Willis said.

"Deepest apologies."

"I'll have to tip it over. Give me the oar."

"Let me do it," Fritz told him.

Fritz lowered the oar into the water and tried to shove the cabinet, knock it over. It wasn't coming. Then Willis pulled his new boot off and handed it to Fritz. He peeled off his sock and Fritz pushed it inside the boot. Willis threw his leg over the side of the boat and kicked the machine. The water was icy and he felt the cold climb his leg and tighten like a vise. He leaned farther out of the boat and kicked the heavy machine off a muddy shelf. The cabinet sank away and the rotted muck floated up to the surface; blackened stalks of eelgrass drifted loose.

Fritz rowed the *Crouton* back to where the car was parked and got out of the boat. He tugged the dinghy on shore, through the weeds, with Willis still on the bench. Willis might have stood up and jumped out, to ease the weight, but he didn't. Sometimes their relationship bled further, into an intimacy they couldn't understand or acknowledge, but both men accepted their stations. Fritz pulled the dinghy into the high grass until the tall weeds splashed over its hull.

"Aren't you going to return the boat?" Willis said.

"You're kidding?"

"It's an institution, isn't it? It's the *Crouton*. People will miss it."

Fritz said, "Listen to yourself. You sound like some kind of church boy. Christ. Maybe I'm starting my own institution."

Willis put his boot on and got into the car. He tried the ignition but it wasn't turning over. He tried it a second time, and the engine grabbed; its open throttle growled over the wide surface of the pond. Coming out of the sand road, they peeled onto Eustis Avenue. A police cruiser was parked on the street; its engine was running.

"Watch it. His Kodak might be loaded," Fritz said. Willis slowed his speed, but the cruiser was empty. Willis said the officer was probably in one of the houses getting a handout.

∾∾∾∾∾

Willis switched on the heater to warm his wet pant leg. By this time his cast was firm, but Fritz had left little fingertip notches in the plaster. Willis wanted to find the Salve Regina girl to see if she had cooled off, but he didn't know which dormitory to start at. They drove into town. A few weeks before, the Chamber of Commerce had nailed huge green shamrocks to the elm trees to celebrate Saint Paddy's. No one had collected them. The high beams hit the scalloped foil medallions.

"There are just enough of these party themes, one after the other, to keep me going," Willis told Fritz. He pulled over and got out of the car. He tugged a shamrock loose, panned it under the yellow streetlight, then he walked around and put it on the dash. The decoration was for the Salve Regina nurse. Her farewell clover. He didn't like their violent parting and he wondered if she felt sorry. He'd accept her apology and give her the souvenir. He wasn't sure the shamrock was the right memento.

"I think she's in Watts Sherman House. That big one," Willis said.

Fritz whined, "Maybe she's in Wakehurst or Carey Mansion. Who knows what dorm she's in? She could be in any of those. She could live off-campus. My sister lived off-campus."

Willis told Fritz, "You go inside and tell them to have her come down. I'm waiting."

Fritz said, "Are you asking me to go up there? There might be some nuns inside there. I can't deal with nuns."

"You're a chickenshit."

"Point. A girl going to Catholic nurse school has big ideas. She wants a doctor someday. She doesn't like it when someone like you gives her the heave-ho. It's bad for her self-concept. If she did like it, you would have brought out the fox. Was she fox or bitch?"

Willis picked up the shamrock and fanned his throat. "Actually, we were an equal match, we were on the same card. That's why she bored me, initially. I like to go outside my class." His eyes felt blurry. His pain was surfacing again, making everything jiggly.

"I'll tell you what I think," Fritz said. "A little Salve Regina pussy goes a long way. It lasts a lifetime."

"A lifetime for you isn't the same as for me," Willis said.

Fritz said, "I'll live twice as long as you."

"May you live as *long* as *you want* and *want to* as *long* as you live."

"Where did you hear that one?"

"That's a chestnut. Rennie told me that one."

"Why do you want a nurse anyway? You could stay at home and try that new girl next door."

"Haven't had the pleasure yet. Besides, Rennie says she's a pyro."

"A pyro? Maybe that's your type."

"Christ, this stinks. Does this arm reek?" Willis waved the new cast under Federico's face.

"Smells like you've been hanging Sheetrock, smells like that white mud."

"Where do I drop you off?" Willis couldn't follow the yellow line without feeling it slice through his eyes. "Where do I set you down?"

"No hurry," Fritz said.

"I'm asking, where?"

"Split up now? It's still early. We just started. I thought we were going for a pitcher. I'm thirsty."

"Jesus, you're a long streak of piss. Right here." Willis crushed the brake pedal; the suspension shivered with the hard stop. Fritz got out of the passenger seat and stood beside the car. They were in the middle of nowhere, halfway out on Ten Mile Drive. The surf was tearing into the silence. Other than that, it was the dead of night.

Fritz leaned in the window. "Come on. You don't look so good. I don't care if you can't take it. Who's going to know but me? I've got Darvon at the house," he told Willis. "I've got Empirin—"

"Empirin? Since when do they still sell Empirin? What's the shelf life on Empirin?" Willis moved across the seat, hunched over and vomited. Pain moves all around the body, finally into the gullet, into the acid rising now, into his throat. A fiery gloss of sweat sealed his eyelids shut. He rolled onto his back.

Fritz said, "Okay. So, now what are we doing?"

Willis laid the back of his heavy arm over his eyes.

Fritz said, "All right. If it's nothing to you, I'm driving. Time for the switch. Nothing personal. I'm behind the wheel. As of this minute—" His nerves were showing. He didn't find pleasure in taking charge.

Fritz went around and got behind the wheel. He rode Willis over to Rennie's house on Easton Way. The house looked over the water and the cliff erosion was getting bad enough to give it a tentative appearance. The foundation shelf was beginning to tilt. Fritz pulled slowly up the drive.

"Don't hit the bike," Willis said. Rennie's three-wheeler was parked by the cement walk. The handlebars were threaded with gaudy plastic blossoms. Rennie used the big tricycle to go into town. She put her shopping in its roomy double fender baskets. The shrubbery was over-grown in briery dikes around the first floor and Fritz couldn't see if Rennie Hopkins was still awake. Rennie was often awake at night if she was having pains from her recent operation; some of her intestine had been removed. The surgeons discovered that the cancer had migrated into other organs, so they closed her up, already defeated. They didn't have all of it.

Fritz parked the car beside the tricycle and he took Willis to the door. They had to stoop to get under the trellis, which was growing too low with thorny vines. Rennie met them and Fritz helped her lead Willis inside. The woman's nightgown was too long and she batted its full skirt behind her, one side, then the other. Her billowing nightdress made an immediate impression; it was like the transient appearance of a good fairy. Rennie had seen Willis like this before. She pushed him down in a kitchen chair.

"Not in the mood for this, Rennie," he told her.

"Do not insult the crocodile until you have crossed the river," she told him.

He looked over his shoulder at the double sink, trying to avoid the eye-to-eye with his stepmother.

"Well, what happened?" she asked him.

"He got clobbered," Fritz said.

"Shit," Willis said, his chin resting on his chest.

Fritz helped Rennie walk him upstairs. From the bedroom window they could look across the water to the Cliff Walk. Most of the big houses were dark, except for Ochre Court, one of the big halls at Salve Regina College. Butter-yellow window shades glowed like squares of English toffee. "Willis got into a little trouble tonight," Fritz said.

Rennie said, "I'll tell you what I think, Willis doesn't get into trouble. Trouble gets into him."

"Whatever which way," Fritz said.

"It always happens to his kind. *In love with love.*"

Fritz said, "Point. Myself, I don't think it's worth the personal cost."

"Now, explain this to me. Was Willis using his arm as a club again?"

"Not this time; one of those Salve girls smashed his arm with a rock," Fritz said.

"A Salve girl? Now, that's pathetic." Rennie shook her cloud of hair. "You go through them. From one to another," she told Willis, "like bumper cars."

The men liked the vision. They laughed.

"I speculate she was a little bitch, the fox terrier type," Fritz told Rennie. "Willis tells her to get lost. He tells her she's coed history and she got up on her hind legs—"

Rennie said, "A rule of thumb: treat a tramp like a lady and tease a lady like a tramp."

Fritz said, "Maybe Willis couldn't pinpoint what she was. This girl attacked him. We got the arm reset tonight at the hospital."

Rennie said, "*We* did? We went to Newport Hospital? We have to pay for the emergency room if we go to that private hospital."

"When you break something *you* can go over to the Navy hospital," Willis said.

She wasn't listening to him. "When did this happen?"

"Who keeps track of time," Willis said. He reclined on his bed and crossed his arms over his breastbone, pinching his eyes tight and blinking them open again.

"That's twice it's been reset. What did that last doctor tell you? If you break your arm a third time you'll have a permanent deformity," she told him.

"What do they know?"

"I should think that they know quite a lot. War being their forte, they know about patching people up."

"Why don't you shut up."

"Don't say 'shut up' like that," she said.

"Christ, he's terrible, isn't he?" Fritz told Rennie. Fritz was shaking his head, almost grinning.

Rennie shrugged; she knew it was the pain talking. Rennie was experienced in all levels of late-night misery. Her first two husbands, both fishermen, had been killed at sea.

Her first husband, Bill Hopkins, fished on the crew of the *Teresa Eve*, a sixty-foot eastern-rigged dragger. In 1964 the *Teresa Eve* was lost coming back overloaded from the scallop grounds. The catch was left on deck unshucked instead of being bagged and stowed in the hold. They were loaded up, with an estimated seven hundred bushels, but the captain went back for another tow. Bill Hopkins had survived many storms—he once rode out a seventy-knot whole gale—but that night the weather shifted and they hit what they call "a queer sea." Captain Alberelli was following one mile behind the *Teresa Eve* in the *Karen and Marcy*. He said it was a black night—"real stone black." There wasn't much wind, hardly any wind at all to bring a sea that high. He saw enough freakers that night, he put his crew below. He testified at the Coast Guard hearing that the *Teresa Eve* must have caught one at the quarter. The loose catch would've shifted, and if she had her scupper plates fastened and the scallops clogged up all the cut-outs, the water she took on wasn't freed. From what they could figure out, she went down stern first, she didn't roll. Divers found her sitting upright, gear stowed, pretty as you please, boots lined up, slickers on hooks, paperwork still in its envelope in the wheelhouse. There was a heavy concentration of loose scallops in the immediate area around the wreck, a thick carpet suggesting the weight of the catch was more than substantial.

Whatever happened, happened fast. Captain Alberelli on the *Karen and Marcy* watched her lights go out as if someone had "flipped a switch." Alberelli looked back at his radarscope and the target was missing. When the *Karen and Marcy* steamed over to search, her crew heard voices from the water. They shined lights, but the dark swallowed all but eight foot of their beams. They searched for the location of those cries, but after several passes in the dark, the voices stopped. All six crew were lost.

Some of the bodies were recovered the following winter, pulled in unexpectedly with tows, but Bill Hopkins remained missing.

Five years after that, Rennie's second husband, Sonny Costa, a lobsterman, died in a boiler mishap just four hundred yards off of Point Judith.

Rennie was one of only a few New England women to be awarded the title "Kiss of Death." The title was handed down by tiers of gossip which swelled from village to county, from county to the state lines, then it went state to state. The "Kiss of Death" distinction required at least two husbands dying at sea; one alone didn't earn the dooming label. If a woman lost two or more husbands at sea, she earned the title without question. That was that.

Rennie was known as the "Kiss on Aquidneck Island." When *Good Morning America* broadcast live from Newport, they taped a story on the decline of the New England fishing industry. They heard about Rennie and asked to do a spot with her. They wanted to film Rennie on the widow's walk at the Captain Whitehorne House. A publicist told Rennie that her story was a romantic fable.

"In a coon's ass," Rennie said to the ABC intern. "I never wear it on my sleeve."

She stood over the bed and rubbed the heel of her hand across Willis's sweaty hairline.

He didn't want it. He grabbed her hand and threw it off. "Just shut the door on your way out," Willis told Rennie.

She walked out of the room.

"And you." Willis motioned to Fritz Federico.

Fritz was dismissed; he left the room without any hurt

feelings. Rennie stopped Fritz in the kitchen. "You can have a corn fritter, pan-sized, or your usual. Corn fritter or buttered johnny cake?"

"Either one?" Fritz said.

"Killer, you name it," she said.

"Only two choices tonight?"

"Decide soon or I withdraw my invitation."

Willis leaned back against his pillows. He was used to the weight of his cast, its steady pull. His arm tingled if he didn't feel the weight, so he let his arm drop over the side of the bed. The stretching sensation kindled stabbing needles. These little needles didn't bother him and he was falling asleep. Then he was awake.

He didn't sleep. Before daybreak, Rennie came back into the room. "Here," she told him. "Don't you want these?" The foil card caught the hall light and glittered.

He told her, "No. I don't want it."

"You look horrible," she told him.

"I'm driving a truck today."

She said, "You are not. You can't drive one of those monsters in your condition." She placed the silver row of morphine in an ashtray beside the bed.

"Look," he told her, "a honeymoon habit was all I wanted."

"*There was Morphine Sue and the Poppy Face Kid, climbed up snow ladders and down they skid—*"

"That's nice, Rennie, that's real charming. You can keep your poetry rhymes to yourself."

"I'm not finished. *Let me tell you about Cocaine Lil, she had a cocaine dog and a cocaine cat. They fought all night with a cocaine rat.*"

He turned on his left side and lifted his broken arm so the blood would run out of it and the throbbing would stop. Rennie patted his hip. Her tenderness was firm, no-nonsense; it eased him more than it irritated him. Rennie would have been quite willing to administer the rectal pain-killer if he had allowed her to. Rennie seemed to find her own relief and comfort in these midnight acts of bedside service. Willis brushed her hand from his hip. "Go to bed," he said. She left the room.

Whenever Rennie placed her maternal reins on him, he tossed them loose. That gossamer harness belonged in the hands of a ghost. His real mother was dead and he didn't much like to watch Rennie wrangle with Wydette for the privilege. He wouldn't give up Wydette; he wanted them both. Outside, the light was rising. A yellow warbler started to sing: *sweet, sweet, sweeter-than-sweet.* He listened to its tentative first phrases until the bird was rolling along and Willis was sunk in woolly, dreamless morphine.

Chapter Four

On Saturday afternoon, Holly joined a crew of volunteers working on the oil spill. The Audubon leader instructed her: This creature is salvageable. *This* one is too poisoned to return to the sea. She fingered a coal-black scallop, rubbed it against the heel of her hand, but the grime was clinging to its notched shell. She was making a collection of dirtied sea litter—gluey skate eggs, tar-encrusted moon snails, tainted weed—for a display at the prep school. Her job as a prep cook at Saint George's School included several peripheral duties, one of which was attending to the glass cabinet in the front hall; Holly thought the polluted shellfish and dirty kelp would be a good educational exhibit.

When Holly was finished at First Beach she returned to the duplex to continue unpacking. The refrigerator smelled stale and she washed out the bins, then she unpacked some dishes so she could eat dinner. She had a package of Chinese noodle soup and she tore open the cellophane with her teeth. She broke the noodles over the churning saucepan and stirred the stiff clump. She looked around the kitchen. The cupboards showed circles of fingertip grime around the ceramic knobs. That would be easy to spruce up with a little Spic 'n' Span. The linoleum was pocked where the heavy kitchen table legs had sunk in; around every chrome foot there were several interlocking circles, like the Olympic logo. She blinked in another direction and saw flames rising on her front porch. Tongues of mottled orange and spirals of smoke drifted waist level.

Fire lifted and swerved in the wind. She dropped her mixing spoon and ran over to the screen door. Her porch was burning. She couldn't identify its source. Just then, another swatch of fire floated toward her cottage. Big sheets of fire drifted in the wind and caught on her railing. She went outside and stamped on the burning litter. It was still coming, sheet after sheet. Holly looked across the drive. The woman next door was setting fires. Large square pages floated to Holly's side, flames curling and twisting the edges. Holly recognized the woman from the week before. The woman stood with her hands on her hips, although she didn't have any figure, any hips. A man was standing beside her. The man was a good ten years older than Holly and dressed in a full-length jogging suit like a NASCAR driver. He was folding a big map but the woman jerked it from his hands and tried to light it on fire. He grabbed her wrist and peeled her fingers open. He took a plastic butane from her hand.

He walked over to Holly to make sure the fires were out and he helped her collect the sooty leaves. They were architectural drawings. Floor plans. Holly recognized the demarcations showing the living room, kitchen, dining areas, the tiny crescents drawn with dotted lines to show which way the doors opened. Bathroom fixtures were inked in, square sinks, and the toilets like tiny Bartlett pears.

"I'm sorry," he told her.

"What is this?"

"It's a villa at Château-sur-Mer, but my mother's not ready to go."

"No, I should say she's not," she told him. She could smell his sweat tingeing his synthetic jogging sweater as he stooped over the curls of ash.

He said, "My mother's got cancer. Maybe that explains this kind of behavior, I don't know."

"Your mother doesn't look sick," Holly said.

"Today she's wired. Another day, she's doubled up."

"That's terrible," Holly said, "but aren't there two people over there? A sick fellow and his nurse?"

"That other one, he's a stray. Wait here, I'll clean this up," he told Holly. He walked across the clamshells and into Rennie's house to get some cleaning solvent. He didn't look at his mother, who waited at the top of the stairs. Her hair was in two taut braids the blue-white color of cement block; everything about her looked strong and tricky. She came down the stairs and walked over to Holly, but Holly wasn't sure how to greet her.

"I'm not an arsonist at heart," the woman said. "Some people start fires for less reason than this."

Holly didn't know what to say.

"You moved over here from town?" the woman said.

Holly looked at her and nodded.

"I saw you consorting with the enemy. I'll forgive you. I'll just assume you didn't know what you were doing."

"Excuse me? Those scraps hit my porch. What was I supposed to do?"

"My oldest is putting the screws to me. I almost died last fall. That's what they *think*. He says I should sit at Château-sur-Mer and play Euchre. He says I'm running out of time, but he means I'm running out of money."

"I see," Holly said. She didn't want to hear any more.

"I didn't mean to frighten you. I was making a point—"

"I guess *so*," Holly said. The woman opened her hand. Holly wasn't herself; she stared at the woman's hand. The woman kept her hand open until, at last, Holly accepted it.

"Rennie. Rennie Hopkins," she said, pumping Holly's hand.

The woman was at least sixty-five; she was tiny and hardly a hundred pounds, but Holly felt her grip. It reminded her of those schoolyard games when children hold hands and the leader jerks her fist to make the whole line whip.

"I'm Holly Temple. I work up at Saint George's School. I cook."

"You're renting your place from Nicole Fantasy?"

"Isn't her name Fennessey?"

"Fennessey. Fantasy. Nicole goes around in another dimension."

Holly said, "Oh. I don't know anything about that. I haven't seen her today. I don't know when she gets home."

Rennie lifted the back of her hand to her lips and whispered. "Miss Fantasy—Fennessey to you—comes and goes, depending on her customers."

"Her customers?" Holly was just about to ask Rennie what she meant when another car pulled up the clamshells, going too fast. It was a large, old sedan; its rear end fishtailed as the driver braked hard. The clamshells sailed, hammering the clapboards. The driver stepped out of the car and left the door swinging.

"Where's Munro?" the young man called to Rennie. "Just tell me where and I'm taking care of it. Don't ask me how."

Rennie pointed to her big house and told him, "Make it short and sweet, please. He's giving me the hard sell."

Holly noticed that the young man had a broken arm in a new cast; its glistening length caught the porch light in blinding swipes. Instead of walking over to Rennie's house, he climbed onto Holly's porch and popped into the kitchen. He started rustling through her utility drawers. Using one hand, he jerked the silverware bin open too far and the Oneida stainless clattered to the floor. Holly walked after him. "What are you doing? There must be some mistake, you're in *my* house."

"Just a second," Willis told her.

"What's going on? I'm telling you, this is my place."

Rennie came in. She stopped at the rubberized threshold, letting the storm door slap her hip.

"Who is he?" Holly said.

Rennie said, "This one is Willis. The other one is Munro. Willis is my stepson. Munro is the real McCoy." Rennie was shaking her head in wonder, as if she couldn't make sense of it herself.

"Are you saying you know this person? Well, can you ask him to get out of my house?" Holly said.

"You must have a knife somewhere in here?" Willis said.

"A knife? You want a knife—"

In his haste, Willis upset a cardboard box of skillets. Heavy cast-iron disks clanged like tiny manhole covers; one pan rolled into Holly's ankle and she felt a painful vibration, her funny bone.

He paced another way and kicked something over. It was her plastic sack of stained marine specimens.

"Have you got enough fish heads for supper?" Willis said. His smile threw her off balance.

She grabbed the bag from him and it spilled onto the linoleum in a fetid heap. Tarry scallop shells, skate eggs, black nuggets of moon snails, sand eels with tiny pepper-corn eyes.

"These things are ecological victims for my students. From that oil spill," she told him. She felt her teeth grind-ing, her fillings meshing their silver saddles. She was amazed at his nerve. She was a couple years his senior, but he didn't seem to acknowledge the earned distance of those years.

Willis said, "What kind of exhibit? That's just regular gurry. Fish slop." He was watching her when he turned around and walked into an opened drawer. He banged his wrist and yiped. His eyes were shiny. His face seemed broken into sharp planes under the geometric pattern of his thoughts, or it was from simple pain. His skin was very pale, with a bluish tint like the bone china features of ceramic dolls; his face was hardly a tone deeper than his plastered arm. His arm dangled awkwardly unless he pulled it in and held it against his waist. Once or twice Holly thought she caught him wincing.

"Look, I just need something to chase a vulture," he told Holly. He was eyeing the kitchen clock which was part of the furnishings. The clock was shaped like a coffee per-colator with a lighted glass knob at the top that bubbled in sync with the second hand. Right below the clock there were some kitchen decorations, two oversized wooden utensils like the kind displayed above a salad bar in a steak house. A three-foot wooden salad fork and a matching spoon were bolted to the wall. Willis tried to pry the fork loose. It wasn't coming.

Holly looked over at Rennie Hopkins. "What the hell is he doing? Is he trying to wreck something—"

Munro returned to Holly's porch. He plucked at the knees of his nylon pant legs before he squatted down. He tried to clean the soot from the floorboards with a soapy sponge. He had an open bottle of ammonia. Holly read the bottle label that said WARNING: IRRITANT in bold letters.

She walked onto her porch and told Munro Hopkins, "You don't have to bother with that. I'll take care of it myself."

He didn't look up.

"Really. It's perfectly all right," she told him again. Munro didn't listen to her and he scrubbed the porch floorboards, rubbing the sponge in brisk circles until the foam rose over his hand. Then he saw Willis. Willis came out of the kitchen with half of the giant wooden spoon, leaving its splintered remains still bolted to the wall.

Munro threw the sponge down and walked across the driveway to his car. Willis sailed after him, taking long strides. He tapped Munro with the broken utensil. The spoon was softwood but it made a dull smacking sound when it struck Munro's skull.

Munro reached his car and turned around. "I'm warning you," he told Willis. Then he started to cackle. His laughter had an ominous clarity in the still twilight. It was more than an older sibling's power; it had the villainous tenor of someone on a higher perch. He stopped laughing and told Willis, "Look at yourself. A cripple. Look at that spoon. Where's your Maypo?"

Willis said, "Rennie doesn't want you around here. Don't pull in here again." He gripped the spoon in his left hand and rolled it across his knee, rubbing the denim the way he might clean fish guts from his knives.

Munro leaned back against his car. He crossed his arms, giving it a chilly, patronizing flourish.

Willis told his stepbrother, "Take that retirement crap and cram it up your ass. Maybe this spoon goes in and I dig the shit out with it."

"I'll tell you what. This is a legal matter in which you have no input. Try something like this again and I go into town. I'll let them handle you down there. I can get the correct paperwork for you. I don't need Rennie's signature."

"She lives here with *me*. She *dies* here with me," Willis said.

"Now, that shows a lot of sensitivity. Say it again so she can hear you." Munro sat down in his car and started the ignition. It was a new sport coupe; the engine whirred quietly, like a dishwasher.

Munro leaned out the car window and signaled to Holly. "Ignore him. He's a pest. Thanks for the chat," he said and he steered the tiny sports car over the clamshell driveway.

Willis yelled, "Clear off, horse ass—"

He came back to the women.

He held out the broken spoon to Holly. "I've seen these at Apex. I'll get you another one. I'll install it."

"Install it? You'll screw it on the wall?"

"He can fix it for you," Rennie said, "he's handy with everything." She turned to go back inside her house.

"I'll do whatever you want," Willis told Holly, fingering the spoon. "Maybe I can glue it." He was still concentrating on his stepbrother's car, watching until its diamond-shaped taillights were gone. Then he looked at Holly. "You talked to my brother? What about?"

"I didn't talk about anything." Her denial of it sounded more ridiculous than Willis's accusation.

He stood squared before her. His showy leather boots had thick heels which pitched him to a threatening height above her, and his lean frame looked postmodern, post–punk invasion, all in all like some nihilistic cowboy. She felt him turning it another notch, thumbing the psychological dial. His eyes pinned her. His eyes gave her the impression that they not only saw but *generated* whatever he saw about her. Willis Pratt made her feel nondescript. His skin was pale as milk, like anemic Victorian maidens, but his hair was dark and luscious. Beside him, her own dark hair looked coppery. Then, he was, of course, insane. That was it. Isn't it true that certain madmen had luxurious manes. What about Manson? Madmen glowed.

Then Willis reached into her Toyota, touching the radio knobs.

" 'Sounds in the Night,' with Jack Lazar," Willis said. "WHDH. Ever listen to Jack Lazar?"

"No, never," she said.

"A word of warning: your lonesome minutes make empty hours—"

Holly pivoted on her heel and walked six feet away from him. He kept talking. His voice was rich and smooth, expertly tongue-in-cheek, like a disc jockey who talks over a record. He started to whistle a tune as he prowled around Holly. Willis continued to whistle the song. He slowed it down, held its phrases, until Holly thought she recognized the melody. "I Can't Get Started," a deliberately smoky, yet faithful interpretation. He whistled through his teeth, the haunting, almost atonal sound of men who have learned to whistle in any number of situations, at all hours. Then he was singing the lyrics, *"I've flown around the world in a plane—I've settled revolutions in Spain—I've got a house, a showplace—but I get no place—"*

She turned around to face him.

He shrugged.

He said, " 'The Music of Your Life'—do you ever catch that program? It's one my favorites."

"You're kidding? What about rock 'n' roll?" she asked him.

"What about it?"

He walked a circle around her. "Here's a tip: the half-moon talks half-truths." He looked at her, grinning.

She looked up at the sky. She didn't see any moon. The evening sky was overcast. He's crazy, she was thinking. One of these idiot savants who can memorize radio patter. She thought of the others, Rennie and her older son, they too didn't promise an easy spring. Why they included her in their confrontation, Holly didn't understand. She was just *in the way* of it, like a dog or cat at the center of a family argument, sure to be kicked. After her arrest, she promised herself that she would never again exhibit her personal trials for public scrutiny. If she was a vessel of bad nerves and disappointments, the vessel should never tip. The image of a bed on fire seemed a remote dream, yet it had been a high point for Holly. No other feeling had equaled that triumph.

She watched Willis Pratt brushing up the remaining soot on her front porch. She told him not to bother with it.

"This situation got out of hand while I was away. I wasn't around to look out for her. Rennie's pretty good, she's usually wise to things, but Munro shouldered his way in when she was sick. Now I have to take control."

Holly said, "Well, there sure seems to be a difference of opinion—"

"That's right. There is a basic conflict of opinion."

"What exactly?"

"I'll tell you exactly. My stepbrother thinks he exists. I have news for him. He does not exist."

Holly was convinced of Willis Pratt's conviction to ignore simple irrefutable fact. He twisted the blackened sponge and his cast became cuffed in grey suds. Sometimes his bottom lip betrayed a spasm somewhere else in his body. He handed her the sponge.

"That's not mine," she told him. She wrung it out and handed it back. "That's from *your* house."

Her voice clearly revealed the burden of making his acquaintance. She hated letting on that he was just too much for her. She watched him walk across the driveway. He hadn't even said good night to her. Except for his radio voice, he didn't use any small talk. Perhaps he knew that small talk would have tipped it a new way. She waited on her front porch for a minute, searching the black seascape. When she looked again at the big house, she saw a hall light switch on. It was the stairwell window between the first and second stories; Willis was climbing the steps. Holly waited for him to reach the landing. She was startled to see him searching the window for her, shielding his eyes from the overhead bulb. She turned away and went back inside the duplex.

Chapter Five

Wydette died when Willis was thirteen. Driving home from Horseneck Beach, Willis still wore a white crescent of zinc oxide across the bridge of his nose, imitating the lifeguards. He had spent most of the day with Wydette exploring the salt marsh. Wydette had seen a kingfisher there for the past three seasons. The bird liked to perch on sagging cables along the beach road. The kingfisher had a big scruff of feathers, a beautiful crest like a hatchet, an ivory neck ring, and a strong beak like the blades of Wydette's sewing shears.

Wydette had left Cuba as a young girl. She was naturalized in Florida at the age of eighteen, the same year she was named runner-up to Miss Jacksonville. At the beach, Wydette wore a sarong bathing suit, tropic island style, like the one she had worn in the beauty pageant. The suit left a distinct tan line, straight as a carpenter's level across her cleavage.

Willis's father, Lester, preferred to stay put under an umbrella. He had a Coleman cooler with a six-pack of beer all for himself and a six-pack of White Rock ginger ale for the rebound.

On the drive home from the beach, Lester stopped in

Fall River to buy drinks and sandwiches. Wydette ordered a sausage and pepper grinder and Willis and Lester chose chili dogs with transparent confetti flecks of onion. In the car, his parents started arguing, insulting one another. Wydette told Lester that she wanted to learn how to water-ski. She wasn't really serious and Lester knew she was teasing him. He didn't like her habit of making idle plans just to bargain with him. Lester criticized her, and instead of barking back she giggled with each of his comments about her. She ate her grinder, tugging loose a long strip of green pepper and eating it with her fingers. She encouraged bad table manners and Willis exhaled air through his straw. His iced coffee bubbled over the waxed-paper cup and stained the fabric upholstery. Together, they laughed until his father started swearing and punching the seat between them. Then, with the car going fifty, Lester reached over and took Wydette's throat with one hand. He shook her. The car swerved onto the gravel shoulder and he had to let her go and take the wheel again. He looked better, relieved just to have throttled her once; it was a release, and his anger had crested. But Wydette had swallowed something whole, a wedge of sausage, and she was choking. Willis leaned over the front seat to pound his mother's back. Her eyes looked pinched, then wide with fear. She could not tell him what to do, her voice was on the other side of the obstruction.

Lester pulled the car over to the shoulder and lifted his wife out of the passenger seat. He held her upside down at the waist and drummed her back with the heel of his hand; he bounced her over his bended knee until her dark bangs swept the littered asphalt. Finally, Lester ran out into the moving traffic. He tried to make the cars stop, as if stopping random vehicles could reverse his situation. Speeding cars screeched and sideswiped the inside guardrail. Lester came back to his wife and son. He lifted Wydette upside down once again. She choked to death despite the force of gravity. The force of gravity, that monumental natural law, could not save her, how could Willis? Wydette's face changed, its color deepened, and Willis had to look away.

The winter following Wydette's death, Willis discovered a ship's figurehead from the nineteenth century at the Whaling Museum in New Bedford. The sculpture's origin was a mystery, nor did they know from which ship she was salvaged. The figurehead was known simply as the "White Lady," because she wore a snowy gown under a blue apron. Every Saturday afternoon Willis took the bus to New Bedford and paid student admission to go inside the museum, through the arching whalebones at the entrance, past the harpoons and the baleen corsets. He loitered for an hour near the subject of his erotic nightmares. The "White Lady" looked like Wydette. She was beautiful, an evocative wooden bust of a gargantuan woman. The figure was nine feet tall with full skirt draperies swirling around her legs, a blue bodice, and white diamond-shaped stomacher. She wore a large red stone brooch at her bust, a bracelet and two matching necklaces. Her hair was deep brown, and cascaded down to her waist but was bound at the top with a white crownlike headpiece. Like all classic figureheads, she kept her right hand over her bosom, her left hand down at her side. The sculpture stared over Willis. Her maternal gaze was both tolerant and lovingly chastising. For almost a century her face had watched the rough sea and remained sweetly forgiving. He couldn't take his eyes off her. Although the original paint was checked and alligatored, she had the honeyed skin and dark corona of a familiar beauty.

The figurehead looked like Wydette as Wydette looked at her viewing.

All winter the White Lady was his fixation. He wanted to place the palms of his hands on her rough wood cheeks, and with the raw, sensitive pads of his fingertips feel the weathered grain, the notched recesses of her mysterious eyes, her full lips. He couldn't stand around in the museum very long without imagining knocking the figurehead from its permanent station. He looked so agitated, pacing back and forth, that finally the museum guides escorted him out of the building. When he came back inside, he stole an assortment of souvenirs from the gift shop. Humpback whale stamp pads, ships in tiny thumb-sized bottles. In the end, the museum director had contacted the high school in Newport to discuss Willis's student profile. On the advice of the assistant principal, Willis was refused any further admittance to the museum.

That same winter, Willis's father met Rennie at her souvenir shop on Bowen's Wharf. He was hired to fix a sliding glass door that kept jumping its track, and in just three months he and Willis were living at Easton Way. Lester and Rennie signed marriage papers at the courthouse, but there wasn't a ceremony.

It didn't seem to bother Lester that Rennie's first two husbands had gone down at sea. In fact, Lester had a perverse interest in the deaths of Rennie's two husbands. He had lost his wife for no readable purpose; it was no different from the inexplicable seas and boiler eruptions that took Rennie's husbands.

Willis saw Lester trying to shake his guilt about Wydette. Willis didn't think that his father deserved even a tiny snatch of peace, not even a smidgen, nor a fleck. For months he gave his father the cold shoulder, never letting up. He lost his mother and disowned Lester.

When Willis and his father moved into Rennie's big house above First Beach, Willis took the third-floor bedroom which had its own bath. An old clawfoot tub faced the bathroom window. The bathroom window was actually a full-sized storm door which framed a picture of the cold Atlantic, the rough surf breaking its green shingles on the shore. Rennie had a practical intuition about her new stepson. One night, Willis stood up from the tub, naked and dripping wet; he wanted to exit the tepid bath, exit the humid room. He wanted to go right through that storm door. Bathwater wasn't enough. Soap was no use. Its lather was acrid, like white dung. He wanted the wet sea. He rattled the handle on the storm, but Rennie had nailed the door shut.

He sat down again in the tepid water. His guilt expanded like an apron of fungus; it ringed him with layers of cold truffles. He spent hours. Rennie claimed that it was the best seat in the house, and sometimes Willis had to let her use the tub. Her lavender bath salts scented the hall long after she was finished.

Rennie didn't tolerate Willis's obsessive nature or recognize his sickness. When Willis became agitated, she punched his shoulder and said, "Fiddle-faddle." Such a tenderness in fool words startled Willis. Then, if Willis felt like an argument, Rennie too quickly conceded his point. She liked to derail him. She told him, quite simply, "Touché." She bowed at the waist. She was closing it off before he could build up his case.

Lester's heart attack occurred in the car, during a freak Easter snow squall. Willis and Lester were driving home late from a boat show at the Boston Garden. They were on empty stomachs. Heavy snowflakes fell on the windshield and collected like curls of white butter, mounding up in a solid mass. The wipers were working hard but they couldn't fling the heavy snow. Lester pulled to the side of the road. He waited in the driver's seat.

"What are we doing?" Willis said.

Lester looked at the white windshield as if he saw a face in the storm. He seemed to recognize this face but didn't necessarily wish to greet it.

"Why are we stopping? Here?" Willis said. Lester looked ready to answer Willis, but he cupped his shoulder in the palm of his hand and hunched forward in pain. It must have been a terrible crushing sensation in his chest, but worse than the sensation was the recognition. Lester knew what it meant to him, what it meant to his son.

After it was over, Willis sat next to his father for several minutes. Willis tried to reconstruct events; he thought of the cabin cruisers in the Boston Garden. His father perished at this unexpected place, at an absurd moment, while they were tuned to the "Sports Huddle" on WHDH. For a long time, Willis sat listening to the voice of Eddie Andelman discussing Stanley Cup finalists. At last, Willis went around to the driver's side and he shoved his father's body out from behind the wheel. It was difficult to get him over on the passenger side, he was a big man. He was a dead man. When Willis stepped back into the car, the heavy snow sucked his shoes right off his feet. He explored the icy pedals through his wet socks. Willis thought of Lester joining up with Wydette. It wasn't until then that he started screaming. He yelled to Wydette, "Look out! Look out! Look out!"

He rode along the shoulder, testing the feel of it. He didn't yet have his driver's license. When he stepped on the brake, the car fishtailed on the fresh snow. He worked into the traffic and kept driving until he saw a road sign, a blue square with a large, iridescent *H*. Willis believed that the sign had appeared out of nowhere to help him deliver Lester directly to Hell. Willis followed the blue signs; he recited what Wydette used to say, her polite, hypnotic formula: *H—E—two sticks, H—E—two sticks, H—E—two sticks, H—E—two sticks, H—E—two sticks.*

He kept spelling the word until he steered into the emergency entrance of a hospital in North Attleboro. Attendants took his father from the car. They pulled Willis into the bright reception area where they pressed him down into a wheelchair. He wasn't wearing any shoes. What had happened to his shoes? they asked him. An attendant started to write on a chart. They asked him, "Are you under the influence of alcohol? In the past twenty-four hours, have you inhaled or ingested cocaine? Phencyclidine? Dust? Son, you can tell me, have you been using dust?"

"He looks dusty," another paramedic said.

Dust. He knew what they were talking about. Willis had spent time with Lester at Narragansett Park. Back at the horse barns, they had watched a groom administer tranquilizers to a race horse. The pills were the size of golf balls. Before investing his money, Lester was researching the colt's condition; he was asking about the horse's knee.

Its injured knee was the size of a grapefruit.

The groom joked with Willis. "You have a mortar and pestle at home? Here. Grind one of these and you've got yourself an unbelievable buzz." Then the nurses were shaking him. Willis wasn't answering their questions. He was laughing with tears. The tears felt like hot wax and he wiped them away with the backs of his knuckles.

༄

At Lester's funeral, Willis stood at the crest of a hill in White's Monument Village. He tried to feel hate, but hate was too minimal a feeling, so he tried to feel pity. Nothing came naturally except for feeling *nothing*. *Nothing* had a greater complexity of emotions, its icy touch fell across several categories. When the priest asked for a moment of silence, closing his Bible on its snowy tassel, Willis tried to expectorate, but his saliva was thin and he couldn't expel it. He stood in the cemetery next to the small monument where his mother was buried. He remembered her body in its maple coffin, her slender fingers laddered across her chest, her cheeks colored a horrid peach tone, like the stain on a cigar-store Indian. The funeral home didn't know how to match her rich, honey coloring, her Santiago complexion. Then, his father was going in beside her. The murderer beside his victim.

After the service, Rennie Hopkins waited to walk back to the car with Willis. "This is a sight," she said. She was looking over the chalky rows. Willis recognized that two of her three husbands were sunk in the same graveyard, at opposite corners. Even the first one, Bill Hopkins, had his name on a marker commemorating Aquidneck Islanders LOST AT SEA. Rennie was shaking her head. She told Willis, "Every one of them thinks he'll see me later on, in heaven. What am I going to do with that?"

Willis was startled by her confession.

"When I'm finished, remember, I want my service out at sea. Billy gets first dibs. Those other two—well, their spooks will have to swim out to find me," she told him. Willis didn't like being distracted from the cold and dismal plain of his own poor-me, but Rennie cornered him, and he felt his smile surfacing against his will. He tried to shake her off, but she increased her pace and her footsteps fell in stride with his. She didn't say anything more. They sat down in the car and she drove back to the house. It was a beautiful April morning. Even Rennie, widowed for the third time, was taking greedy, deep breaths of the tingling air. The sea had a rich, floral perfume. Already Rennie was trying to imagine new ways to afford the taxes on their waterfront property. But she wouldn't start thinking about money, yet. The air was sweet with chlorophyll scents. She told Willis, "Smell that? That's the old reliable. That's the plankton blooming."

After Lester's death, Rennie went to Family Court and picked up a preprinted Petition for Adoption. Willis was over twelve years old and could nominate Rennie to be his guardian. She showed Willis the simple form, but he said, "I'm not signing anything."

She looked at him. "Is that so?"

"What is this thing? It looks like a car title. Nobody's going to get a pink slip for me. You can't own me."

"What if it's other way? What if this says *you* own *me*?"

He rubbed the back of his cuff over his lips.

"Who says I want to?"

Rennie told him, "You can sleep on it."

Munro encouraged Rennie to give Willis over to the Department of Children, Youth, and Family Services. "He'll do better in foster care, with two parents. You aren't automatically his provider just because Lester Pratt is dead. You don't have any legal obligation."

Rennie said, "Ebenezer lives!"

After a two-day sulk, Willis signed the petition. She could see his relief when he made his decision. She watched him sign his name next to hers. She was smitten by the bold loops of his double *l* across the paper. He crossed his double *t* like a high hat. Rennie submitted the form to the Clerk of Rhode Island Family Court along with two adoption reports which confirmed basic information, such as their proper names and if the names were to be changed, their places of birth, occupations, schooling, and blood types. The court would process the petition, then send a team from the Family Court Investigative Unit to Easton Way for a "home study." After the home study, it might be a month to six weeks before their hearing was on the docket.

But Munro had set a screwball in motion. He alerted the Family Court Investigative Unit of his contentions regarding the adoption and insisted that he be present when they visited Easton Way. He was told it wasn't his privilege. He wasn't a current resident of the home. Munro told them he had important information about Rennie's incapacity to raise a teenage child. They agreed he could submit his concerns to them in writing.

The day before the home study team was scheduled to visit, Willis and Rennie did a major cleaning job on the house. The kitchen linoleum was warped in the center and curled along the edges. Willis tacked the faded vinyl sheet, but the hump in the middle remained. They put a kitchen chair on it to keep it level. The chair looked ludicrous, alone in the middle of the room, so they moved the table.

Rennie and Willis washed windows using newsprint soaked in white vinegar. Vinegar worked best on the accumulated salt scum. Willis worked on the outside, Rennie stood opposite. The windows were difficult to clean because they had divided panes. They were twelve over twelve, double hung, and the work was tedious. Halfway through, Willis dropped his sour rag and walked down to the beach. When the house couldn't be improved beyond a

certain point, Rennie helped Willis arrange his room so it
looked organized, but "lived in." "We don't want to overdo
it," she told him.

The next morning, Rennie boiled cranberries with
three cups of sugar. She let the pot simmer for hours on the
stove. The tart scent enveloped the house.

Munro arrived first.

"What are you doing here?" Rennie said.

"You know the answer to that."

"I order you to leave."

"I'll wait outside on the steps. That will look great."

Rennie sat down on her kitchen stool. "I'm sort of wild
about this kid, don't you see?"

He looked at his mother. Rennie couldn't tell if her
confession had stung Munro or simply itched him. He told
her, "You might think you like this kid, but you're still in
mourning. Just when *haven't* you been in mourning? Christ.
You don't know what you're doing. This kid isn't going to
bring back any of your husbands. Or get rid of me."

"I don't want to get rid of you, exactly. Is that what you
think? Is this about jealousy or money?"

"Well, you don't have too many resources, do you?"

"Which resources?"

"Don't be poetical."

Rennie said, "I mean, in some cultures, sons are a
prized resource."

He smiled at her. "I can't sell you common sense for a
penny, can I?"

"I've made up my mind."

"Carole and I think this is a mistake."

"Your wife needs something more to do with her time."

Willis walked through the kitchen to the stove. He
stirred the steaming berries, which had dissolved into a

violent red pureed goo. He replaced the spoon on its china caddy. He lifted the pot from the burner by its two metal handles and walked it to Munro. He shifted the hot kettle on the pads of his fingers. "Get out of here now."

Munro backed a few steps away from the bubbling fruit.

Rennie said, "Willis."

Willis kept walking toward Munro.

"Relax, killjoy, I was leaving anyway." Munro pushed out the kitchen door and trotted down the porch steps.

Willis returned the kettle to the stove. He blew the heat off his fingertips. He rinsed them under the tap.

The Family Court Investigative Team arrived and toured the house. The day was clear. A Citgo tanker was moving into the channel. Gulls dipped on the wind like newsprint party hats, and the official mood seemed optimistic. One of the social workers asked Willis questions about the adoption petition to make sure his signature wasn't coerced. He volunteered to show them his handwriting and rolled a ballpoint over the back of an envelope. Of course, she had not asked him if his signature was *forged*, and she explained the difference to him to be sure he understood. Munro had given the court an impression that Willis wanted to be placed in foster care. She said, "You know, some boys go to the Farley School. It has an indoor swimming pool. Or, there's an exam for gifted students. We get them early admission at LaSalle Vocational School."

Willis nodded.

"You know what?" she went on. "Some of these foster families have multiple vehicles. Kids can use these vehicles when they get their license."

Willis shrugged.

They questioned Rennie's intentions, her long-term view. "It's our understanding that you are single, Miss Hopkins?"

"Single? Oh, please," Rennie said. "I'm widowed. Thrice."

"What we mean to say—this is a single-parent household?" the social worker said. "We have to take into consideration the absence of a male role model."

The other social worker said, "Your son, Mr. Hopkins, does he have any interest in Willis?"

Rennie said, "He's not your typical Big Brother."

"Do you see a problem there?"

Rennie agreed it might be a problem.

The social workers left Willis with the impression he had free-agent status. He could decide for himself what he wanted to do. If he didn't like how Rennie fussed over him and was attracted to the anonymity he would gain by entering the social system, they would arrange it for him. He tested Rennie's commitment by running through his options out loud at dinner. He stirred his minestrone until a pasta bow tie surfaced and he collected it in the bowl of his spoon.

"That Farley School sounds good, it has a pool," he told her. "Some foster kids get their own cars."

Rennie shook some vinegar over the sliced tomatoes. "I'm listening," she said. "It's real Academy Award material."

"I'm just telling you what they told me."

Their petition was put on the docket and their hearing scheduled for the end of May. Rennie and Willis stood at the hearing in Newport County Family Court before Judge Yarborough. The warm spring wind was blowing into the room through the floor-length windows and Willis could hear the halyards clanging in Dyer's Boatyard. "We don't have the usual adoption surrender because both parents are dead, is that right?" Rennie nodded. The judge recognized that Rennie was the very Renate Hopkins whose husbands had drowned in separate offshore accidents. He seemed genuinely impressed by her desire to adopt the orphan, yet he couldn't mask his curiosity about the nature of Lester's death.

"Now, Mr. Pratt wasn't fishing out of his home port, was he? His crew was out of New Bedford? Mattapoisett? Was it Galilee?"

"Lester didn't fish," Rennie said. She smiled at the judge.

The judge pushed his papers around on the table in front of him. "Of course, you're right. It says here 'heart attack,' excuse me."

"Excused," she said.

Judge Yarborough turned to Willis. "You attend Rogers High School?"

Willis said he did.

"You like your big place out there on Easton Beach?"

"It's good," Willis said.

"Just good?"

"Sure. I like the beach," Willis said. He didn't like being under the microscope. Rennie didn't think he was thinking about Wydette or Lester, he just wanted to be through with it.

Judge Yarborough asked him if he accepted all the terms of the petition. Willis said, "I do." He was instantly horrified by the familiar idiom. How had he managed to say it? The judge laughed at his alarm.

Afterwards, Rennie took him to the snack counter at the Tennis Hall of Fame and bought him a nine-dollar lobster roll. She told him, "Don't think this is going to be within reach all the time."

He looked across at her. She was some kind of obstacle but he didn't know what kind she was. She was building up before his eyes like one of those mysterious stalagmites he'd read about. She was unfathomable and beautiful and there forever.

He tried to keep some distance from her, and he hated it when Rennie answered his questions before he even had the chance to ask them.

"There's a twenty on the sideboard," she told him.

Were his empty pockets screaming?

He couldn't understand her ready-made loyalty to him. He watched her fold his laundry. She smoothed the sleeves of his shirts, tucked the wayward collars, shook out the pant legs of his jeans, their knees bleached and stringy, as if the empty clothes reeked of a sweet substance.

Rennie knew he was settling down with her when Willis adopted Bill Hopkins. Of all the ghosts he could choose from, Bill Hopkins had the most glamour. Willis latched onto him as his one paternal figure. Rennie had told Willis all about the *Teresa Eve.* Then, Willis went to the lending library at the Seaman's Institute and borrowed the transcript of the Coast Guard hearing. He studied the pages until he knew more than Rennie. The hearing transcript stated: "No attempt is made to fix blame." They could find "no actionable misconduct." "No failure of equipment."

Willis said, "Don't you think any time a ship is lost, the finger points to the skipper?"

"Maybe," Rennie said.

"They questioned the skipper's wife, Dolores. Did you know this Dolores?"

Rennie said, "I knew her. Poor girl. They asked her what the skipper had told her about his plans. What did they think he said to his wife? 'Honey, I'm going to load it up past the rails?' "

Willis said, "Captain Alberelli from New Bedford was

behind Billy in the *Karen and Marcy*. *Little Eden* was to the south a-ways and she steamed in when she heard it on the radio. Then it was a free-for-all, four draggers came over. Let's see, it was the *Josephine G.*, the *Caroline*, the *Viking II.* They helped search through midnight; by then they had the Coast Guard utility boats and their big cutter, *Bittersweet*. There was nothing to be seen. Not a plank. Nothing surfaced. It was just too black. Next day, they had divers from the National Marine Fisheries Service come in to investigate the wreck. She was in a hundred and thirty feet. They took short ten-minute dives because of the depth. What can you find out in ten minutes?"

Rennie said, "Just the worst."

"They call it a 'queer sea,' when it gets like that," Willis said. "Lots of freakers. One right after another."

Rennie saw that Willis thought it was colorful. It was as good as a campfire story. She didn't mind his enthusiasm; it was in homage to Bill Hopkins.

Willis said, "Captain Alberelli tells how the night came on like a 'blotter,' it sucked up any shore lights. They were in a blackout, taking some devastating hits. Waves from nowhere. The *Teresa Eve* was getting the same. The seas were eight to ten feet, but it was a head tide, and the sea was building a good top off of that. They had towed five hundred bushel at least, maybe seven hundred—"

Rennie couldn't keep quiet and said, "That was just too many tons of scallops." She could never erase her picture of those scallops. All colors—iris, cinnabar, agate, rose-pink. Layers of little calcite fans spilled in a wide apron around the hull. A team took Polaroid photographs of the wreck. She was sitting in the middle of their haul, like a house cat on a big calico rug.

"Those screams," Willis said. "The *Karen and Marcy*

steamed in and slowed up, just six knots or so, just to listen. They heard cries—"

"It might have been one voice. Just one."

"They couldn't agree on it. Some of the crew said there was more than one, but then it just stopped."

When Willis enlisted, he had hoped to wrangle some time in Newport. He wrote on his dream sheet that he wanted the Construction Battalion Unit, where he could do his hitch building piers or grouting the swimming pools on base. Instead, he was assigned to a military K-mart in Norfolk. After several months, his petty thefts became sloppy.

Willis was sent to the brig, where he underwent three weeks of psychological review. A psychiatrist said his obsessive-compulsive disorder probably resulted from the violent deaths of both his parents and the fact that Willis had spent the remainder of his youth with a woman known as the "Kiss of Death." The psychiatrist wrote in his report that Willis's childhood "echoed with mortalities and sensational events." Lester's impulsive attack on Wydette was the kernel of his neurosis. That scene on the highway continued to rock Willis with waves of adrenaline, an uncontrollable jolt which jellied his nerves, and he never reached the zenith of his imagination to cap it.

Willis's obsessive thoughts seemed centered around his worry that, like Lester's outburst, his moral fiber might snap at any given moment. His vigilance was ongoing and exhausting. Minor tasks and daily chores seemed landmined. When he cleaned the mess hall floors, sweeping the linoleum in peaceful half-circles, he saw himself charging at a plate-glass window with the broom handle. He walked past the petty officer's desk and saw a coffee cup on the corner of the blotter. Why not flick it off? Of course, the black coffee would arc across the white charts. In a crowded elevator he imagined uttering vulgarities—what if he recited the few most graphic facets of a woman's perplexing sum total? He was in a constant state of anxiety. In order to face each day he had to increase, by a degree, the level of his self-imposed austerity.

Like other new recruits, Willis was assigned to some KP for lengthy stretches. During one assignment, Willis became unnaturally concerned with the meat slicer. He was required to slice ham and other giant logs of processed meats, adjusting the blade so the meat slices were the correct thickness—not too thick, but not so thin that they were hard to peel from the stack. The physical sensation of pushing the slicer handle at the right speed and rhythm, watching the meat shave and drop to the wax paper gave Willis a sick stomach. It had nothing to do with the salty meats, it was something else. He began to guesstimate how many slices he could get. He looked at the big clock on the kitchen wall and he worked against times he set up for himself. The routine became something he fretted about all morning before he got on the job, and the mathematical calculations resonated long after he was through with his shift. If he wasn't satisfied with the count, he shaved the meat extra thin to get the figure he was after. He shaved a water-cured ham in micro-thin slices. The meat fell like bright red feathers, unsuitable for sandwiches, and it had to be scooped up and dropped in a kettle for bean soup. Willis was way ahead with the sandwich meats and they told him not to prepare any more. Willis went against orders and walked into the lockers, finding the pressed turkeys.

The psychiatrist explained to Willis that this exaggerated interest in repetitive routine was physiological. For example, nesting birds repeat the same activity, returning with twigs in a monotonous parade back and forth until the nest is complete; this was a survival technique directed by brain chemicals. For Willis, it might be similar. His agenda of petty larcenies wasn't carried out for financial gain but to conflict directly with an inherent, self-invented peril. His crime sprees put Willis in a position of "false duress," in which he sought outside scrutiny by military and municipal authorities just to override his own nervous agendas and self-appraisals.

Other military staff argued with that assessment. Willis was an operator, they said. He was just another psycho-ceramic con man. "A recruit carries on like this just to go home on disability. These punks are taking up needed space. They're mud on our wheels."

The therapist told Willis that he needed to address the deaths of his parents with a healthy attitude. "Your parents are *safely* dead. They can't harm you now," the therapist reassured Willis.

On the morning of his discharge, Willis discovered that someone had stolen a laminated photograph of Wydette. She was standing in line with other pageant contestants, her satin sash drawn in a taut, evocative diagonal from her left shoulder to her right hip. The snapshot was sealed in a flexible magnetic binding that adhered to metal surfaces. He displayed it on well-lighted bulletin boards beside office notices and movie fliers, attaching it to door frames, pipes, file cases, latrine mirrors. When he couldn't find Wydette's photograph, he spent an extra day on base looking for it. He wasn't getting any cooperation and they told him he had to be off base by eighteen hundred hours. He refused. He popped a petty officer who was trying to get him to relax, forget about his keepsake, opening a two-inch cut across the fellow's eyebrow. Willis was already discharged, banished, and they didn't pursue charges. Instead, the quartermaster assigned a guard to take Willis around on his search until six o'clock. By that time, two teams of men were looking for the laminated picture. After everything that Willis had been through during his months in the service, including his incarceration and piss-poor psychiatric counseling, he couldn't understand the mean prank. Willis looked around the mess at the men he knew by name and all the new recruits that had just come on. One of them had the photograph.

It was dark when the MPs drove him to the gate and let him off with his two canvas duffels and a cardboard box of vile magazines, playing cards, nicotine-stained dominoes, and Wrigley's TenPacks he might have left behind for the others if not for what had happened. He was woozy after having drunk a half-bottle of Maker's Mark all by himself instead of handing it off. He stood at the entrance of the base and looked north. Willis had missed his connections and was expected to walk to the bus terminal or hitch his way. The jeep turned around and drove back onto the base.

The jeep came back.

The driver had been watching Willis in the rearview to see if he was moving off government property as ordered.

Willis was whirling around, his right arm extended. He hit one of the six-foot-high concrete posts at the entrance. He struck the post with the flat side of his forearm, the way a cook lops off the top of a carrot, except that the post wasn't acting like a carrot. Willis dropped to the ground.

The driver flicked the high beams. It looked bad. Willis was down on his side, pivoting off his left hip, writhing in a circle through an inch of slush. He was seriously hurt. The driver put him back in the vehicle and drove him to the hospital.

Willis spent two days in the Navy Hospital having his arm set and reset. He didn't like the sensation of the cast cinching his muscles and he had a panic reaction. A physician's assistant sedated him and strapped him to the hospital bed using plush, quilted belts with Velcro closures. On the third day he was released to Rennie, who had flown down to Virginia to take him home to Newport. The intern gave her a doctor's name at the Navy Hospital in Newport. Willis should get some further evaluation. They gave Willis an embossed insurance card which would be valid at any New England base if further treatment was needed. Rennie pushed the card into her wallet. Willis could see that she didn't accept any advice. "The Navy doesn't know what to do with its resources," she said.

The analgesic pills they offered for his broken wrist didn't work for his pain, but he took them hoping they might untangle the knots he felt behind his eyes. His daily tension was almost audile, like a constant vibration, a humming. He couldn't ignore its pulsing, tinny echo. It was like the threatening din of a distant marching band when it walks in place, honing its crescendo, before turning a corner onto the main avenue.

Holly was lying sideways across her bed, just the balls of her feet on the floor. She heard the surf drag a cloak of pebbles back and forth across the sand, a nauseating suction. She felt the tight bale wire of a hangover slicing into her temple. At shorter and shorter intervals, a bird was making a racket outside. Holly hoped it would find somewhere else.

The night before, Holly had started early at the YMCA. She took an exercise class and finished off in the steam room with the other ladies. She listened to someone's story: a husband had lung trouble from working twenty years in the local yacht-building industry where he sprayed fiberglass without wearing a proper mask. The women commiserated and let their towels drop to their waists. Holly, too, peeled open her soggy towel, letting the hot mist penetrate her skin. She was pink as fruit.

She showered, shaving her legs in the shower stall; she nicked herself and the soap swirled pink as it circled the drain. She toweled off and massaged her legs using a tall squeeze bottle of cheap lotion scented with imitation White Shoulders. She was reeking.

She liked walking Newport's Pineapple Dream section.

A "pineapple dream" was a horrid sweet concoction that packed a wallop. The pineapple was a symbol of the colonial shipping trade, and the local bars invented different versions of the mixed drink. Holly never touched it, but Holly liked visiting at least a few different bars. She went on foot. When she walked into the Old Colony, two or three men noticed she wasn't with Jensen and they called her name. A regular dipso sliced off the last syllable and she didn't want to sit with him. Again and again, he tried to get her attention. "Hey, Hol? Hol? Hol—" Her name, severed like that, made her feel wary. Anywhere else it might have made her feel at home.

Earlier that winter, Holly had fallen for a barfly named Kim. If she couldn't find him in the bars, she walked the sidewalks waiting for him to drive up beside her. His old Pontiac was missing a headlight and she watched the streets for this telltale sign. He edged along the curb, idling the car, before swinging the passenger door open for her. They made love in an old house on Hammond Street where he was keeping house with a few local dropouts. It was a bare mattress. The ticking was stained. He centered her hips over the deep rusty flowers, their broad scalloped petals in perpetual bloom. He fucked her or he fucked her mouth. His cum tasted like the sea and it tasted like nails. After a few months Kim left town.

Last night, Holly went with a fellow who took her to his place in old Navy housing. His wife was out of town. His wife was gone, but her things were strewn around. Before they could make love, Holly had to remove a jeweled sewing box from the center of the double bed. Holly admired the sewing box before putting it on the end table, out of harm's way. The man made love to her; he tucked his forehead against the hollow of her throat and she turned her face away. She studied the diminutive masterpiece, its tiny drawers and glossy shellacked shelves where spools of thread were lined up in colorful gradations, the silver thimbles tilted on tiny wooden dowels.

What was the name of that street? Commodore Perry Boulevard?

Holly heard the storm door rattle. She pushed herself up from the bed. The room spun a half-circle and ratcheted backward until again it was level. She grabbed her robe from the floor. Nicole Fennessey had come over to Holly's side of the duplex, carrying a large square of glass. She said she wanted to fix a broken pane in Holly's bedroom, and she walked right through the house into the back room before Holly had a chance to make the bed or straighten up. Nicole was tall, willowy, with a rope of fine blond hair dangling down her spine. Nicole showed Holly the tiny stencil marks on the glass, the letters "TG" at every corner. Tempered glass. Holly tried to focus on the tiny stamp.

"I don't scrimp on important things," Nicole said. "Now, tell me about this fire you had over here. Rennie said it was a conflagration. If you want to burn trash, we share that barrel out in front—"

"It wasn't my fire," Holly said. Dizzy, she sat down on the bed. "Did Rennie tell you I started that fire?"

Nicole was holding a special cutting blade in one hand and a rubber-tipped hammer in the other. She tapped the rubber hammer against her chin while she was looking at Holly. "I'm sorry I wasn't here, but my job keeps me on call."

"You work at the hospital?"

"I'm a massage therapist at Newport Jai Alai and I have private clients all around town. I'm gone all hours. I can't be here to referee the neighborhood."

"I guess not," Holly said. Holly's lips felt swollen and tingling, like a pincushion.

"At least you can't call me a slumlord. I keep my property in good condition," Nicole told Holly. "But what happened to you? Did I wake you up?"

Holly nodded. Nicole seemed on the defensive and she described her busy schedule to Holly. "Massage therapy is a combination expertise. It's an important alternative. There's the mental-health industry, but they forget about the body. They talk and talk and never lay a finger on the patient. Actually, I'm like a psychiatrist. I'm an educated ear. My job is mostly listening. Even if they don't say anything, you listen to that. The silence. I'm kind of a transcriptionist with my hands."

Holly had been in the house only a few weeks, but she had watched Nicole coming and going at odd hours, her long blond braid swinging like a silk pendulum. Sometimes Holly heard the telephone ring.

She heard it right through the wall.

Within minutes after the first jangle, Nicole left the house, carrying a large flat leather portfolio just like an artist might use to transport drawings. Nicole told Holly that the portfolio was actually a lightweight massage table with collapsible legs and imitation leather veneer.

"I take my table to every job," Nicole said. "Otherwise they think they can get me into their bedrooms where they recline on their Perfect Sleepers. If they try something I fold up the table. I break the legs down, crunch, crunch, crunch. I'm out of there before anything happens. My business is portable. I take my table, my bottle warmer—that's for the Egyptian oil. Ointment goes right in my pocket to keep warm."

"Egyptian oil?"

"Yeah, it's basically just baby oil with some sassafras."

Nicole stood on a chair and tried to remove the top grille from Holly's bedroom window. Nicole was still wearing her nightgown, a satiny sack that outlined her hips and buttocks each time she reached up with her arms. Holly wondered if Nicole was aware of how she looked. Holly remembered what her husband Jensen used to say to her; he often said that she looked "ripe." Then Holly realized that she was always thinking too much about sex. Anything could make her think of sex. She looked away. Even the silver finger loops of a scissors left out on her dresser. Everything in the book had either curves or erect lines. Egyptian oil had an erotic ring.

Nicole asked Holly for a table knife to scrape away the old caulk and Holly handed one up. Nicole maneuvered the little window onto the bed. Holly wanted to ask Nicole if she had a particular mate, or if she was, like Holly, single. Except for the matter of sex, a solitary existence was attractive to Holly after years of being paired up with a heel. Being single might be thought of as a pursuit, not a default. She had read about the success of celibate career professionals in a woman's magazine. Women can become their own erotic guides. The article joked about masturbation in double entendres; the writer invented terrible puns, such as: "In a pinch," women can "singlehandedly—"

What was so newsbreaking about that? Just the other weekend, Holly had masturbated in a dressing room at Sears. She had noticed a middle-aged salesclerk in the appliance department. He had a small mole on the left side of his chin. A beauty mark of some distinction. A tiny maroon button half hidden by salt and pepper stubble. It looked undeniably erotic.

Holly said, "Are you raising those kids alone?"

"Do you see a father figure waltzing around?"

"It must be difficult."

With the window removed, Holly listened to the little bird, its bright program.

Nicole told her, "Don't feel funny about it. It's the American way."

Holly said, "After being married, it's hard to reinvent yourself."

Nicole dropped the hammer to her side and peered at Holly. "You do look a little shaky."

"Shit, does it show?"

Nicole looked at her. "You feel that bad, do you?"

Holly straightened up. "Really, I'm fine. My ex-husband, he's not even stateside, so that's a relief."

Nicole took the rubber hammer, tapped a pane loose from the frame, and collected the broken glass in her palm. Then she measured the windowpane and marked the new piece of glass. She scored the glass with the special knife and tapped it gently with the rubber hammer, making a clean break along the scored edge. When she was finished, she rested the new pane inside the frame and puttied the edges. Holly couldn't help admiring the way Nicole handled a man's job.

"When Rennie was sick last year, I went over to give her foot massages. There's a spot on the instep that corresponds to the bowel, the large intestine, but Rennie didn't want me to do it. She's likes to be self-sufficient, you know."

"Rennie told me that she almost died," Holly said.

"Colon cancer."

"Does she have one of those awful bags?"

"No, it was too late for that. The doctors couldn't remove all the cancer. No sense chopping her up. It would have been closing the barn door after the cow got out."

"What's the prognosis?"

"Of course, it's hopeless, but I bring her raw almonds from The Golden Sheaf."

"That hippie store?"

"Call it what you want. Almonds are supposed to have some healing substance like laetrile. I get a pound for her and she eats them, but I guess she knows it's a shot in the dark."

"She's skinny, but she looks tough."

"Staring death in the face gives Rennie a zing."

"Shit."

Nicole said, "She's not scared. Rennie said at her age she has to keep looking down the well and hollering for the echo."

"It must be a mess with those two brothers—"

"Well, she can't rely on them. If I don't see her one day, I try to go over to make sure, and she's always fine. She's got her clam rake and she's down at low tide poking around, or she's in her shack organizing her ceramic jewelry inventory, carding whatever she has left or separating different sizes of beads into coffee cans. Until she got sick, she had a souvenir shop on Bowen's Wharf. She still has a jewelry kiln in the shack, but she's not producing much. You know, I bet some of the glazes she used were carcinogenic. Some of it had lead, anyway. Lead helps color along, I don't know why."

"She make those earrings you have on?"

Nicole fingered the gaudy plastic baubles clipped to her ears. "No, these are Bakelite. These are collector's items, they're like gold now."

Holly looked at them. "Who would have thought plastic would be something fashion important in the nineties?"

"This was virgin plastic. The very first stab at it."

Holly nodded. The talk of Rennie's cancer had made

Holly think of her father, who had died of cancer just two years earlier. She wasn't speaking to her father prior to his diagnosis and when they connected it was too late.

Their rift occurred when Holly had gone over to her father's place after her mother left him for another man. "How can you let her walk out on you like this?" she had asked him.

"What's the point of making trouble," he said.

"She took all your furniture. You paid for it and she took it." The living room was empty except for a few pieces. Feathery helixes of dust twisted along the baseboards every time the heat came on. "What are you going to do about it?" she said.

Her father sat in the one remaining vinyl recliner the color of Campbell's corn chowder. Holly had always depended on her father to take her mother to task for the wrongs she committed against Holly, which were numerable. Her father's sudden surrender was a personal affront to Holly; she felt he was deserting her.

"Oh, come on," she told him, but she couldn't cheer him. She lost her patience. "*Worm*," she called him. The last word she had ever said to her father—*Worm*.

Holly returned to nurse him when he became sick. But he didn't recognize her. Her imperial regret, worse even than burning Jensen's bed, was the one-syllable word she had flung at her father. After her father's death, the hospice volunteer gave Holly a cardboard circle, a Grief Wheel. Grief has a structure; it has stages, remissions, and surges. The stages were "Shock," "Protest," "Disorganization," "Reorganization," and "Renaissance." Within these stages there were cognitive, affective, and somatic manifestations such as "anger," "accusation," "meaninglessness," "intense anguish," "self-hate," "eating disorders," and even "chest pains." A red plastic arrow selected each stage and offered a list of its corresponding symptoms. Holly didn't imagine Rennie's two sons would find comfort in a Grief Wheel, although she had kept it; it was somewhere in her belongings.

Holly picked up a sliver of glass from her bed linens. How could Nicole come in there and litter her sheets with these shards? She shifted the conversation to Willis Pratt. "I think Rennie's son is crazy," Holly said.

"Which one?"

Holly thought that certainly Nicole would know she was referring to Willis Pratt.

"You mean the banker? He's a vice president in precious metals at Fleet National," Nicole said.

"Precious metals? Really?" Holly imagined the gold ingots and platinum bars like neat foil sticks of unsalted butter.

"Yeah, and he's an expert investor. You know, all those funds and things. He's made himself rich. He's got money to burn. Oops, sorry—"

Holly wasn't too happy with it. "Money to burn" was an everyday figure of speech, wasn't it? If people kept dredging up ancient history, Holly would never get ahead.

"Sorry," Nicole said again, tipping her face at Holly.

"Sure, no problem," Holly said. "What about the younger guy? The one with the broken arm. He came in here and busted up the kitchen decorations."

"Which decorations?"

"The spoon. The spoon is half gone."

"That's part of your damage deposit right there," Nicole said.

Holly couldn't tell if Nicole was joking or not.

"He came in here and broke it off the wall. He's a fried egg."

Nicole shrugged. "He's temperamental, but he's on Rennie's side. Rennie's other son wants to put her away at Château-sur-Mer, and she's not budging. I think he's trying to get something official and put her in there against her will. She can't pay her taxes. That's when the government agrees to step in. Until then, it's a family matter."

"How do they know she's going to die?"

"Sweetheart." Nicole looked at her. "We are all—"

"Shit." Holly didn't like the mannerism.

"Dying at home is the goal."

"In her own bed. I see."

The window was in. Nicole heard her telephone ringing. Her son, Lindy, came over to get his mother. Nicole went back to her side and in five minutes she was dressed in her uniform: mustard-color exercise tights and tunic. She hopped into her car. As Nicole backed out of the driveway, Holly heard a horrible squawk. Holly looked out her window to see that Nicole had stopped the car. Nicole had backed her car over the collie puppy. Holly ran down the porch steps and together they pulled the dog out from under the car. The puppy nipped at Holly; its pain was telling it orders. Its jaws snapped, but its eyes looked at Holly with sorrowful recognition. The dog was badly injured. Nicole stood up and swore. She looked at her wrist, twisted the watch face between her thumb and forefinger.

"Stupid dog. She sleeps under the fucking car. But I guess she's all right," Nicole told Holly.

Holly stood up. "Wait. I don't think it's all right. It looks bad to me," Holly said.

Nicole's two children, Lindy and Sarah, stood behind Holly, Nicole across from them. The dog's jaw dropped open and it began to pant.

"I have my appointment," Nicole said.

"You're going to give a massage? Now?"

"When I get back, I'll take her into Sakonnet Animal Hospital. I think I have a credit there for fifty dollars." She left the dog at Holly's feet. Nicole's children were crying. Nicole got behind the wheel of her salt-encrusted Saab and shoved it into reverse.

Rennie came out of her house and stood on the porch. "It's the pelvis," Rennie told Holly. "I can see from here, it's crushed."

"Jesus Christ, I can't believe she drives off and leaves me here with this dog. Her kids—" Her hangover was holding on. She hadn't eaten breakfast. She should have fixed herself a bull shot just to get going. She had booze in her cupboard, but she didn't have any bouillon cubes.

The two children walked back to their house expecting Holly to terminate her involvement. Lindy put his arm around his little sister's shoulder.

"Wait. Lindy—" Holly called to the boy. "I'll take the dog to the vet." The children turned around to face her. They looked like children in a Walter Keane painting. Their big, oversized eyes stared at her in wary gratitude, their mouths blank.

Rennie was squatting down, palpating the dog's abdomen until it yelped.

"Which vet should I go to?" Holly said.

"I hope you're ready to shell out your own cash."

"Oh, I didn't think of *that*. Don't you think she'll pay for it? It's her children's pet."

"Nicole, pay for it? In a coon's ass." Rennie told Holly that Nicole had a way of assuming that events occurred beyond her perimeter of responsibility. "She picked all my pole beans one time and said that they *told* her to pick them. The beans sent messages to her. She was just giving me a hard time. She stole those beans for dinner. She's a con artist. Then, one time she hung out her clothes right before a nor'easter. Which took a lot of brains. The wind tugged them off the line, they blew all over the place and she wouldn't retrieve them. All over the trees and bushes. Brand-new panties. Left there for days. Willis wasn't going to collect them. So, after a while, I took them for myself. They *asked* me to pick them."

"You took her underwear?"

"Ladies Jockeys. Nice ones."

"Oh, I don't know. You make her sound nasty. Nicole seemed all right this morning. Normal. She fixed my window."

"Did that window need to be fixed?"

"What?"

"Was the window broken?"

"I don't know. I can't remember." Holly started to get angry. Why did this woman want to confuse her?

"If your window was broken, you would have noticed it. It's raw. You would have felt a draft."

"You mean she didn't have to fix my window?"

"She was probably just snooping."

Holly went into her house and came back with a laundry basket. She rolled the dog into the basket and put it in her own car. The children ran for their coats and she settled them in the backseat on opposite sides of their puppy. "Don't put your hands near her face," she warned them. "She's going to snap."

Rennie went into her house and came out wearing her car coat. She sat in the front seat next to Holly. "I'll pay for the dog today, tonight we gang up on Nicole to get the cash."

"What if the dog needs to be put to sleep?" Holly asked.

"We'll see about that."

"We don't have permission from Nicole. The doctor will need the owner's permission, won't he?"

"No one is putting anything to sleep. Watch what you say. The walls have ears."

The dog was euthanized. After the procedure, they brought the dog home in the same laundry basket. The dog's weight felt as if it had doubled when Holly lifted it out of her car. That must be what they call "dead weight," Holly was thinking. Rennie said she would ask Willis to dig a hole. They would bury the puppy and put a marker where the kids could plant something later on, after the last frost. Holly left the dog in the basket on Rennie's porch.

Rennie said, "You like seafood?"

"Excuse me?"

"I'm going down to my cable and pick some mussels for lunch. You want some lunch?"

"You're going where?"

"There's an old mooring cable on the beach. I haven't collected mussels for quite a while; it should be a good harvest. *Fruits de mer.*"

Rennie waited for Holly to decide.

Holly's stomach had calmed down but her headache was holding on. She didn't know if she should chance it, mussels of all things, but she liked Rennie's company. "I guess I do need to get some lunch," Holly said.

The tide was moving in and Rennie gave Holly an extra pair of rubber waders. The ridiculous thigh-high boots must have belonged to Willis and she felt strange wearing his boots into the cold sea. The two women waded along the cable until they were in past their knees in the icy water. Rennie's crop of mussels was clinging in irregular hunks

along the rusted steel braid which stretched in a taut line
from the rocky shore out to the depths somewhere. Rennie
plucked the shellfish free and cut any extra weed from
them before dropping them in her metal scallop basket.

"I can't eat much of these myself," Rennie told Holly.
"My plumbing is on the blink half the time."

"But you look great," Holly said. "No one would ever
assume—"

"That I'm a medical throwaway? Well, it's true. They
can get you to a point and then the ball's back in your own
court."

Rennie's flat assessment of her situation encouraged
Holly's protests, but Rennie was correct. Holly had seen it
happen to her father. She couldn't tell Rennie what to
expect, but she wanted to tell Rennie that her father's soul
wasn't extinguished. His soul was like a great wrought-iron
bell that shook Holly with unbearable vibrations, a relentless ringing imperceptible to others. If she hiked alone on
the beach it was inviting her father's scrutiny. She "took a
walk" with her father every time she went out the door, and
he followed her back inside. Since his death, her private
hours had become strangely "unprivate." She felt her father's presence, not as a spirit or a ghost; it was more like a
wounded "eye" out of nowhere. She wanted to ask Rennie
if she planned to haunt Willis like her own father stalked
her, but of course she couldn't say that. She must have
looked peculiar because Rennie was watching her. Rennie
said, "I sure apologize for the other day. People do crazy
things sometimes."

"That's all right," Holly said.

Rennie said, "Sometimes people go too far."

Holly thought she might be referring to Jensen's bed.
Rennie was dredging it up just to let Holly know it didn't
matter to her if Holly had done such a horrible thing or not.

Holly stood in the clear brine and looked the other woman in the eyes. Holly said, "It must be difficult having two sons who feel so opposite."

"It's like the blue and the grey. Two brothers meet on the battlefield; their mother doesn't know which one will come back to her kitchen hearth. She might have a favorite, you know."

Holly said, "Is Willis your favorite?"

"A mother doesn't admit who it is."

"Is Willis rebel or Union?"

"I don't know yet. How can I know which one is on the losing side until the war is done?"

Rennie shook the basket and looked at their haul. It was about four pounds of huge, silvery-black teardrops. "This is plenty, unless Willis shows up."

Holly looked across the water at the house. The cuffs of the cold rubber waders rose up the insides of her thighs and she didn't want to be in them anymore.

"He used to eat this much by himself, but lately he's fussy. I think he looks skinny, what do you think?"

"How would I know?"

They walked back along the beach. Rennie stooped over something in the sand. A big thirty-pound hunk of seal meat had washed ashore, its gorgeous dappled hide intact.

"Struck by a propeller," Rennie said.

"Maybe it's a shark's leftovers."

"No, I've seen this before. A trawler hit it. Poor thing."

In Rennie's kitchen, they stood at the double sink. Holly trimmed the beards off the mussels with a paring knife and Rennie scrubbed the remaining weed from the shells. Rennie steamed the shellfish and Holly ate half of what was set before her. She was late for her shift at Saint George's where she had to start the dinner.

Chapter Seven

Fritz was working for Gene Showalter in Fall River; he was hired to pick up some containers. He told Willis that for two bills they would drive into the general aviation hanger at Green Airport in Warwick, pick up the what-have-you, and they'd drive it back to Fall River.

Willis told Fritz, "Easton Pond was my last foray under the slimy petticoats of your goons in Newport or Fall River, whoever they are."

"This guy is unique," Fritz said.

"Save the introductions. I don't want to meet your friends of distinction."

Fritz said, "This is all velvet. It's plush."

Willis agreed to go along. He told Fritz, "For one, I can deliver the Salve Regina ball and chain at her sister's." Willis was glad for any excuse to get rid of Debbie Cole, the nursing student. The afternoon on the Cliff Walk was just a prelude. A few days after their initial streetfight, Willis went into Douglas Drugs, where Debbie worked weekends. She was repricing a row of analgesics and he waited around for ten minutes until she was ready. She came right along, without asking questions. It was as if he was picking up a prescription. It took ten minutes to get her outside, twenty more and the whole thing was a complete story with a beginning, a middle, and an end. Willis took her around with him every night, but she was wearing thin. Debbie collected horoscopes, little tubes of paper she purchased at convenience stores. These tiny scrolls irritated Willis when she pulled them open and started reading out loud the daily warnings.

Before meeting Fritz, Willis took Debbie to play pool at Narragansett Tavern. It impressed her when the weekenders ogled at Willis's success despite his injury. He asked her to chalk his cue, which she did with cute ceremony, then he propped the stick against his plaster cuff and sighted. He built up the drama. He poked at the cue ball and it clacked where he'd aimed it. He took all the solids but he had trouble with the eight ball. He scratched. It was anticlimactic and the girl complained. They drank pitchers and came back to her tight coed apartment on Fenner Avenue where they ate tortilla chips in bed. The cornmeal grit was making the bed sandy and the girl peeled off the sheet, shook it on the floor, then tucked it under the mattress again.

When the girl was napping, snoring in little nasal sips, Willis decided he was finished with her. After a long ordeal of sex, his knees fluttered as if a half-dozen moths turned back and forth behind the patella in a strange postcoital metamorphosis. It wasn't the familiar honey-dripping landscape of afterglow, it was something new, an unpleasant haze. For the last few weeks, his routine sex life flickered on and off, depending on his program of morphine. On one level he could complete the task, but an abyss was opening up between his expertise and his ability to engender and employ it. Willis went into the kitchen and sat down at the tiny dinette, tipping the chair back on two chrome legs, thinking it over.

He walked around the apartment looking for a drinking glass that didn't have butts and ashes. A bowl of leftover guacamole was turning brown where it sat at the center of the table. In Norfolk, Willis had watched a triple-X videotape, a pretty nice one until the last thirty seconds. In these last moments, the actress turned her back to the camera, bent over to touch her toes, wrapping the palms of her hands around her Achilles tendons, and there it was: green crud in her slit. Guacamole smeared into the vulva of a porn queen has its lasting effect. She was thumbing her nose at her own public, and Willis took account of it.

Willis refused to eat a tortilla chip slathered with the guacamole paste. When Willis explained the video to Debbie, she listened in disbelief. "You're kidding. That dip has lemon in it. Shit. That lemon would sting, wouldn't it?"

Willis poked around the kitchen, throwing the garbage in a bin. He wrapped the violet-stained avocado skins in a newspaper. It was an old issue of the *Newport Daily News*. He read the brief obituary for his friend's stillborn baby. He thought of Sheila Boyd, the new mother. He wondered why someone's family misfortune became his secret burden. Willis felt its indirect weight upon him. He recognized his panic systems gearing up. His panic moved into place the way harpies collect on the cornerstones of buildings. Like the jagged, winged edges of a puzzle, in an instant the beast was fully assembled. Willis had to concentrate on his breathing. Breathing, without direct monitoring, became the central player in these attacks. To help Willis avoid hyperventilation, a Navy therapist had drawn a diagram for Willis; it was a simple box.

Ascend left side: *inhale*.
Cross over: *hold breath*.

Sink down right side: *exhale*.
Return to the starting point: *hold*.
Repeat.

The inch of print about the baby triggered his symptoms.
He was tipped way over the point of comfort. Regardless of
faith, regardless of good deeds or blind devotion, every
routine minute was a notch on a roulette wheel. Because of
this giant-size wheel, Willis kept honed and wiry; he per-
formed his daily tasks amidst a meteor shower of little
chances and threats.

Willis read the simple text about the baby and tore it
out of the newspaper. He folded the clipping several times,
creasing it with the edge of his cast, until it was a pleated
strip, then he folded it again, making sure he ironed it flat.
He took the tiny accordion of smeared paper into the bathroom and dropped it in the toilet. He let it soak in the bowl.
He waited until the newspaper clipping looked saturated,
almost sinking, then he pressed the chrome handle. It
wouldn't flush. The toilet was sluggish. He jiggled the handle. The clipping swirled open. He fished the clipping out
of the toilet water and carried it, dripping, to the kitchen
sink. He drenched it in Debbie's Cuty Polish Remover and
struck a match. He watched the flame licking the solvent
but the newspaper clipping wasn't igniting. He doused it
again, until the white sink blossomed with fiery dahlias,
foot-high crimson flowers. The porcelain turned black,
scorched and smelly. The scrap was, at last, missing.

He went into the bedroom and crawled into bed beside
Debbie, careful not to wake her. She would want to start
over. He wondered about certain physical repercussions
from his job at Narragansett WASTEC with Carl Smith.
What could happen to him if he was exposed to barrels of

toxic sludge? Earlier that evening, he shot cum on the bedsheet. It looked iridescent, it glowed, an elongated, electric
puddle. Radioactive.

"You're crazy," Debbie had told him. "That's just the
reflection from HoJo's." She rubbed the glimmery stain
with her thumb. A big billboard for Howard Johnson's Motor Lodge was right outside the bedroom window. The
sign's blue-green illumination fell upon the rumpled linens.
Willis wasn't taking any chances. He told her, "Good thing
I pulled out." He wasn't ready to father any deformed
children.

In her sleep, Debbie turned to him. He stood up, gentle
as a cat so he wouldn't wake her. More than ever, he did not
desire the human touch.

An hour later, Willis was driving to the Warwick Airport.
Night work. The Fritz shift. Debbie told Willis, "You'll
end up in a facility. You and Federico," she said. "Is he
selling dope? I'll tell you right now, I'm not standing around
in some needle park—"

Willis concentrated on the freeway traffic, finding the
wind door between two semis. He told her, "Fritz didn't
say what's involved. It's not your business, is it?"

Fritz was waiting in the airport parking lot near a private hangar. A jet was whining on the tarmac, but it wasn't
anything to do with them. Fritz sat down in the front seat
and pushed the girl into the middle. "Word is, we go over
to McCoy."

"McCoy Stadium?"

"That's where we make the pickup."

"I thought it was air freight."

"It came in here today. But this place is thick. We have

to go to McCoy, where it's dead." Willis rolled around the airport circle. Debbie was sitting in between and she started to tell them that she wanted Willis to take her back to Newport. "I'll be good. We can go over to Yesterday's."

"Not tonight," he told her.

"No cover after ten o'clock."

Willis said, "If you don't shut up, I'll drop you off at Carl's. He'll take you onto his boat. Teach you manners."

"No cover at Carl's," Fritz said.

"Oh, shut up," she said.

Willis liked teasing her. He turned off the highway and drove out to Warwick Neck. He parked the sedan right on the water. He pushed Debbie across the seat and Fritz tugged her out of the car. They guided her past the pitch-black berths and nudged her to the edge of a finger pier. "See it out there? The *Tercel*," Willis said.

The disabled dragger was moored two hundred feet away, a fifty-foot hulk, everything dark on it except for a yellow sheen coming from the fo'c's'le porthole. The old fishing boat looked pretty grim; even in the poor light, you could see it wasn't kept up. Pleasure boats in the harbor looked white as shirt collars resting on the water. "I'm going to lend you out to Carl if you don't behave," Willis told her.

He went over to a piling and picked up the air horn left chained there by the dock association. He tooted a few harsh blasts. They watched a figure come out of the hatch. It was Carl Smith. He jumped up on the rail and held on to the antique gallus rigging. He looked ashore.

Fritz said, "I wonder what condition he's in."

"His usual condition."

"Hope he don't fall in."

Carl Smith searched the pier but he didn't recognize what he was seeing.

Debbie broke away and ran back to the car. She got in and slammed the door. She had another thought and reached over to lay her palm on the horn. She kept it there until Willis returned.

Willis and Fritz had their joke. It added a little pepper to the rest of the drive. They came into Pawtucket riding the side streets through residential blocks until they saw the Paw Sox stadium, a huge dark horseshoe rising four stories high over the Portuguese neighborhood.

"Your favorite place," Fritz said, talking for Willis.

"Shit. It's a nice park, isn't it? It's small enough to see the little details."

"We saw Chico Walker come up," Fritz said.

"That's right. And we saw The Bird come down."

"Pathetic."

"He had his glory days, don't forget."

"We all do."

The place was deserted. They drove into the parking lot and steered close to the stands. A forklift with a stack of forty-pound bags of fertilizer was parked against a wall. The season was two weeks away. The high beams illuminated four cardboard cartons lined up on the asphalt, already unloaded. A man saw them drive up and he moved away from the boxes, jogging behind the stadium. In a moment, his headlights whipped across the field as he left the parking lot.

"I think that's the guy who left these off."

"In and out, just like that?"

"On schedule," Fritz said.

"I wonder what's his hurry?"

"Not the best sign."

"I'd say that it's a bad sign."

They got out of the car. Fritz rested his elbow in the palm of his hand and studied the row of boxes.

"What's in here?" Willis said.

"We don't open the crates until we get there."

"We don't verify the merchandise?"

"That's right. We don't."

"Live cargo. Exotics," Willis said.

"Bingo. They ice down these boxes, it puts them to sleep so they don't make a racket."

"I don't like it. I don't like anything live," Willis said.

"Agree," Fritz said. "Maybe it's dead already. I don't hear a sound. Then what? Point. Who gets the blame?"

"Usually it's the last link in the chain."

"Us."

"You."

"Yeah, well." Fritz scratched his forehead with his thumbnail. "You're fucking negative, you know that?"

Willis helped Fritz arrange the cardboard cases in the trunk of the car. As he lifted the boxes the contents shifted in small scratching thumps, but he couldn't tell what it was. There wasn't any smell to it, no growls or hissing. There weren't any air holes.

They drove out of the parking lot and went along the river into East Providence. Willis parked in front of Debbie's sister's house.

"Out."

"Fuck you," she told him. She unsnapped the long leather strap from her pocketbook and she started to slap him. The metal clasp stung the backs of his knuckles where they emerged from his cast.

He was shoving her off of him when Fritz opened the passenger door and grabbed her ankle. She giggled when the other man got involved. She liked everything to be a contest. Fritz started tugging her out of the car; Willis pushed her. She fell onto the cold pavement, still trying to smack Willis with the leather thong. She stood up next to the car. She made a fist and lifted it high. She dropped her fist on the smoked windshield; the heel of her hand was a hard crescent, like a little horseshoe.

A small acoustic thud—a few chunks of frozen popcorn fell onto the seat. The safety glass had burst in a conservative circle, the circumference of a SnoCone. Then, in slow motion, tiny silver cracks traveled across the glass, looping like grapevines until half of the windshield was marred.

Willis kept his voice level, but his jaw was grinding. "This is Rennie's car."

"Well, who do you think I am? A chump?" she said.

"She always has to hit something," Fritz said.

She wrinkled her nose at Fritz and dipped in a little curtsy.

Willis brushed his hand over the windshield, fingering the cracks.

"Excellent. Cunt."

"Go ahead. Get it fixed and I'll smash it again," she said. She straightened her shoulders, surprised at herself. Then she looked very pleased that she could mar a big windshield bare-fisted. Next, she was running across the lawn. Her high heels wobbled on the frozen turf and she fell down. She stood up again, laughing.

Willis chased the girl around to the back of her sister's house. Willis grabbed her around the hips. She was screaming for help in tight, delighted shrieks, but the house was dark. Fritz waited on the sidewalk and toed a flip-top cigarette box with his shoe until he had it in the gutter. In the late winter night, the air was without the din of insects or the brushing notes of foliage, and he could hear the girl's laughter. Fritz didn't want to stand around alone and he followed them behind the house. Willis had his jeans opened and Debbie was beneath him, her white legs scissoring. Willis wasn't serious and the girl was laughing. Her breath bloomed and dissolved, bloomed again in little white trumpets at his shoulder.

"Maybe this is the last time. Just one last time," Willis told her through his teeth as he bit the leather tab of his car keys and rocked her, his keys jangling against his chin.

"Oh, Jesus," Fritz told them. "It's the teddy bears' picnic." He walked back to the car and waited.

In a minute, Willis came around to the front.

"You did her with your keys like that?"

"What?"

"With your keys in your teeth?"

"You wanted to hold my keys for me? Anyway, I didn't do it. Shit, I already did her once tonight. She needs to have more?"

They got back into the car and Willis touched the inside of the squint to see if the silver cracks were palpable. "Does that look like I hit something, a seagull or something?"

"A seagull?"

"Rennie's got insurance on this, if it's an accident. Otherwise, it's going to have to stay. Get used to it, Fritz, it's your side." When he started driving, the whole windshield sparkled and blurred with the oncoming headlights.

ை

In Fall River, they took the cartons into Gene Showalter's place, a big granite triple-decker with gargoyles on the front cornerstones. Griffins resting on their haunches. It was an elaborate mansion, unusual in the dilapidated mill town. The house looked over the mouth of the Taunton River, where it spilled into Mount Hope Bay.

"This son of a bitch has himself a house," Willis told Fritz.

"Wait until you see inside. This is no Mr. Average, he's a collector. He's a hobbyist."

"A hobbyist?"

"He's got antiques and weird gizmos all around the place."

Willis shrugged. "I don't like that airy-fairy decor."

"He's got a braille *Penthouse*," Fritz said.

"No shit? Is this guy blind?"

"No, he just collects one-of-a-kind stuff."

"That sounds right. He found out about you. How did he get the braille *Penthouse*?"

"Paid for it."

"That's usually how."

Willis stacked the cartons on the carpet while Fritz introduced him to Showalter. Willis said that he liked the house and Showalter told him that it was a banker's turn-of-the-century mansion, complete with an English "lift." Showalter led them over to the elevator. Willis looked at the wrought-iron platform, the brass filigree on the metal stall, and its shiny accordion gate.

"It goes all the way to the third floor," Showalter said.

Willis smelled the heavy lubricant used on the cable.

"Want to try it?" the man asked Willis.

Showalter held the pleated gate, letting Willis decide. Fritz might have enjoyed taking a ride, but the man seemed to forget about him. Willis wouldn't step on the platform. When Willis refused, Showalter released the gate and it skated shut.

Showalter took them into a room where a big-screen TV was running without the sound; it was the Celtics loping from one end to another. The team shifted back and forth across the screen. Showalter ignored the picture and offered Fritz a rum and Coke. Willis asked for a straight shot.

"With ice or neat?"

"Ice is fine." Willis didn't like the production. Showalter was making it into something. Willis watched Showalter take a single ice cube in the palm of his hand; he tapped the ice cube with the back of a spoon, one strike and the ice cracked into five sharp pebbles. He threw it in a tumbler and poured a good two fingers of bourbon over it. He swirled the smoky alcohol one time and handed the drink to Willis.

"Now, Fritz tells me you've got some Cuban?" Showalter said.

"Excuse me?"

"You're of Cuban descent."

"My mother was from Santiago."

"It's funny, you look a little wan to be Latin. Maybe your mother was the Ivory Girl? Maybe Snow White?"

"He's fair now," Fritz told Showalter. "In the summer he browns. He's well-done by the Fourth of July."

"Jesus," Willis said. "Where are we going with this?"

Showalter told him to sit down, relax.

Willis and Fritz sat down, together, on a leather sofa. The sofa cushions were gleaming, tight pillows of golden hide, and Willis had to keep his feet squared on the floor to keep from sinking back. He had one of his crazy flashes: his dime-store pocketknife scored the leather couch, a ladder of deep gouges, a cruel diagonal tic-tac-toe. He visualized the *X*'s and *O*'s. He imagined the *O*'s with demonic happy faces.

The room was decorated with artwork and bric-a-brac. Willis studied a skinny metal sculpture on the coffee table.

Showalter said, "That's a Giacometti reproduction."

"Looks like Reddi Kilowatt," Willis said.

They were sitting in a library. The books were arranged in glass display cases. There was something wrong with it. Willis blinked his eyes. It was a library, all right, but the books were all tiny, only two or three inches high. Hundreds of doll-sized volumes, various foreign-language dictionaries and Bibles, some with velveteen or gold leather bindings. Willis squinted at the tiny, pristine rows behind the glass.

Showalter said, "I collect these. Miniature books." He pulled open a glass door; the frame fell from the top and rested against Showalter's collarbone as he reached for a miniature volume. He closed the glass door and turned the key. He placed a book in Willis's hand. *Prescott's Conquest of Peru.*

"Is this the whole book. Every word?"

"Unabridged. It's all there."

Showalter looked at Willis. He looked into Willis's eyes in a way no man had tried. Then he looked away. Showalter gave Willis the feeling that he was being briefed and interviewed at the same time. Willis fingered the tiny book called *Prescott's Conquest of Peru.* He was actually wondering about this fellow Prescott.

"I have an interest in these tiny books, being a printer myself. These are really just printing challenges, that's all. It's a mathematical problem—how to fit the print on the page. These books keep increasing in value. Know why?" Showalter said.

"Why?" Willis said.

"They cost to produce, then they get lost. These are so

small, people can't keep a hold of them. They just disappear."

Willis rested the small volume on the arm of the sofa.

Finally, Showalter wanted to see the boxes. "Let's see what we have. This is going to be something new for us, our golden egg," Showalter said.

Willis didn't like the plural form, but he waited as Showalter took one of the boxes onto his lap.

Fritz said, "I don't know about that golden egg. We haven't heard a peep. If it's worm bait, it was worm bait long before we came into it."

Showalter ripped the staples and plucked open the taut cardboard leaf. There it was. A dozen feathered corpses. Vibrant greens with yellow caps. Amazon parrots, not one left alive. Showalter opened the other cartons. Smaller, fruit-colored birds; some of the carcasses were sizzling red like Corvette interiors. Each small body was motionless. Showalter sighed quietly. Willis admired the professional restraint of the man. He had made a verbal contract and he didn't look disinclined to come through with his payment despite the bad outcome of events. But Willis felt there was something odd about Showalter. His posture and gait suggested that he was fighting an injury. It was subtle, as if his spine was not in correct alignment and even small movements had to be carefully mapped or shooting pains might jar him.

Showalter took a list from his pocket. It was a handwritten invoice for the contents of the boxes. He read the list to Willis and Fritz. "Six double yellowheads. Those are Amazon. Those green ones. Six dead ones.

"One pair electus. That must be those two. One is red, one is green, male and female—they're dimorphic. Those right there. They would have got me around two grand.

The grey ones are Congos, a breeder pair. These smaller ones are conures—"

Willis looked at the birds and shrugged in one or two sympathetic body gestures. "Too bad it went bust," Willis said. "Some air holes might have helped."

"Air holes are a giveaway. Besides, they don't need much air," Showalter said.

Willis nudged Fritz. Fritz was sipping his drink, tonguing an ice cube.

Fritz had told Willis that Showalter ran a printing business, one of those InstyPrint franchises, but he was into different illegitimate ventures, and Willis wondered which business was the actual sideline. The mini-books, the parrots? Something brought in the money because Showalter was dressed in expensive trousers and a beautiful jacket. His shoes weren't broken in, they still had creamy soles with the clean black stencil mark at the arch on the new leather, as if the shoes had not yet met the street outside.

Willis stood up after taking the booze. Willis knew that he should never turn down a drink, but he shouldn't accept another one or hang around.

"You fellows have another stop after this?" Showalter said.

"That's right." Willis plucked his car key from his tight pocket and sawed the key against the denim, waiting for Fritz.

Showalter said, "Before you leave, I'd like to show you something. Have you seen my workshop?"

Of course, Willis had not seen this fellow's workshop, not recently nor in some distant past life. Willis didn't like the affectation.

Showalter was walking to the elevator. It wasn't an actual limp, exactly, but there was something artificial in his gait. Willis didn't see what else he could do and he followed the man into the elevator. They waited for Fritz to step into the cage, then Showalter pressed a lever. The open compartment sank away, falling from street level into a momentary black abyss.

Then the bulb flickered and the cage halted. They were in the cellar. Showalter shoved the accordion gate open and walked a few steps to touch a light switch.

Fritz and Willis walked off the elevator and followed Showalter into a large carpeted room. The room had a plush sectional sofa, an overstuffed horseshoe, and behind that there were two lines of folding chairs. The rows of chairs faced an eight-foot movie screen; its smooth, metallic coating glistened under the fluorescents. At the opposite end there was a banquet table set up with a large projector and stacks of materials.

Fritz said, "He's got his-self a little theater."

"Indeed I do," Showalter said.

"A movie theater?" Willis said.

"This is a slide projector, specifically," Showalter said.

"Filmstrips?" Willis said. "Shit, I haven't seen a filmstrip since Bible school."

Showalter laughed. His chuckle had a natural timbre that made Willis wobble between opposing waves of acute hostility and helpless contrition. It all looked fishy. It was some kind of operation, and Willis understood he was being indoctrinated whether he liked it or not.

"Not movies. This is stereographic equipment. It's a whole different story," Showalter said.

Willis saw that the projector was too large and intricate to be an ordinary family model. Next to the table with the projection equipment, there were shelves of inventory. Showalter showed Willis the slide mounts and matching cardboard mailers, a box of cheap plastic lorgnettes with plastic sleeves, stacks of anaglyphic postcards with corresponding colored lenses—left eye red, right eye green. There was a big spool of bubble wrap, padded envelopes, blisters of mailing labels and RUSH stickers. A rubber stamp with the words HAND CANCEL.

Showalter touched the projector and Willis heard the fan start; a cone of uninterrupted light hit the empty screen across the room.

"Here's a pair for you. And for you." Showalter offered Fritz a pair of ordinary-looking eyeglasses and he gave some eyewear to Willis. Willis took the eyeglasses from Showalter. He was borderline edgy.

"Put your glasses on," Fritz told Willis.

Willis notched his pair over his ears and peered over the lenses at his friend. Fritz looked sheepish. He was in on it, somehow, but Willis couldn't guess the angle. The sooner he cooperated with his friend the sooner he would be out on the sidewalk in the open air. "These glasses are polarized," Fritz told him.

Willis said, "Is that right? What does that mean exactly?"

Showalter pulled open a drawer and found his own set of glasses, nice ones with tortoiseshell frames. He picked up a handheld control cable and pushed the button. In one and the same instant the button cut the overhead lights and a slide appeared on the screen at the other end of the room.

It was Venice.

A bridge arched over a murky canal and a gondola floated beneath it. The scene was garishly three-dimensional. The bridge stuck out. The gondola stuck out. The gondolier's pole poked out of the landscape. Each element of the photograph was suspended in its frozen solitude, separate from the rest of the whole. The three-dimensional scene did not look more natural or realistic than an ordinary photograph, it looked fractured, the buildings and structures revealed in painful gradations. The one attraction might be the feeling that you could reach right in and take the pole from the gondolier.

The cartridge flipped and the next slide was the New York skyline. The World Trade Center's twin towers jumped up; the Chrysler Building, the Empire State; each fought for dominance in a field of aggressive granite shoots.

Willis wanted to say, "What's the point?" but he let Fritz talk. Fritz praised the 3-D scenery in the pictures, the face-to-face feeling it gave him. It was a studied pitch.

Showalter flipped the slides, showing them scenes from an "American Almanac of Stereographic Wonders."

The Grand Canyon.

The natural bridges of the southwest desert.

The Hudson River. The breathtaking ledges of the Palisades.

A ruby-throated hummingbird probing a blossom, its thin black tongue like a waxed shoelace.

Next, a naked woman was crouched in a bathtub. The steaming bathwater was pink; a bright spaghetti rope of blood curled beneath the faucet.

Her wrists were slashed. She had carved into herself right there on screen. Willis recognized the shot. It was Georgina Spelvin in the opening suicide scene of the classic porn film *The Devil in Miss Jones*.

"Shit," Fritz said, "doesn't it look real? She just pops out at you."

Showalter said, "That was directed by Gerard Damiano. He was a realist. Look at this shot. You almost feel sorry for her."

Fritz agreed and poked Willis.

Showalter said, "It's just a souvenir, really. A stereo-scope from pornography's Golden Age. Just for fun."

Willis stared at the 3-D slide of the actress taking her life, her pale opened wrists, her shaved pudendum. The shot triggered a vivid memory of the twenty-year-old film, which Willis had found to be a relatively sad feature.

Showalter was saying, "Look how it spirals below the surface of the bathwater, like real blood. That's salad oil with a squirt of dye."

"Shit," Willis said.

"Wait, we're just thumbing through these; these aren't that interesting yet." Showalter flipped the slides until he found one he liked. It was, without question, a hard-core panorama. The phallus was shooting. In the three-dimensional photograph, the pearly elongated puddle of semen was sailing right at you like a Frisbee.

Fritz was giggling in a jangle of wounded nerves and excitement. Fritz didn't want to disappoint either associate.

Showalter was laughing along with Fritz in that strange, wholesome tone. "Anything look familiar?" Showalter asked Willis.

Willis didn't know what Showalter was driving at.

"Look familiar?" Showalter said again,

"Maybe in a broad sense," Willis said.

"Recognize anything?" Showalter asked again.

Fritz was squirming. Fritz said, "How would *he* recognize it?"

"Don't you see what we have here? A new wrinkle on the industry. Stereographic pornography. Stereoscopes are for connoisseurs. It's a bonanza with a diverse clientele. Eggheads love the scientific aspects. The gay client appreciates the artistic opticals. Our future is with the gay viewer.

Throughout art history, in every medium, the homosexual society is at the cutting edge, they support every wave. In many cases, they are the wave, the first pulse in theater, art, and fashion. Now Fritz is helping me out." Showalter blinked at Willis's old friend.

Willis looked hard at Fritz, as if he couldn't remember his features. "You're doing what?"

"For the money." Fritz talked to the rug.

Showalter said, "Fritz is kind of scrawny as a model— give him a glass of tomato juice, he looks like a thermometer. We're relying on his dominant factor."

"His dominant factor?" Willis said.

"His outstanding feature."

"What is it you're telling me?" Willis said.

"His principal asset."

"I see. I see what you have here. You're running a business right out of your basement?"

"That's correct, and Fritz is working with me. We're shooting some stereoscopes. Pornscopes. Fritz makes cash as a model. Now, you wouldn't be interested in that?"

Willis wanted the story from Fritz. Fritz was tongue-tied.

Showalter flipped the slides forward until one fell onto the screen. It was Fritz eating a spoonful of gelatinous red goo from a can of One Pie cherry filling. His penis was erect.

Willis couldn't look at it for very long. He said, "Who buys this stuff?"

"Not sickos," Fritz told Willis. "They're Einsteins. College grads."

Showalter said, "I market the entertainment, but I want to start moving the technology. The technology is where the money is going to be. People can't walk into K-mart and compare prices."

"I guess not," Willis said.

"Kodak isn't mass producing these items. A lot of these cameras are antique; they're homemade gems, worth thousands. Then you've got a nice mail-order selection, all kinds of affordable stereoscopic camera equipment and accessories—my idea is to mix in the pornscopes, maybe some sex toys—"

"You're an antiques dealer or a smut king?" Willis tossed his polarized glasses on the table.

Showalter flicked on the overhead light. "It's simple manufacturing and sales. You could learn from me, you haven't met your potential."

"My potential? What do you know about my potential?" Willis said.

Showalter told him, "I have an eye for material."

"Put your eyes back in," Willis said.

"Take a minute to listen to my ideas," Showalter said.

"Where's the exit from here? Where's the bulkhead?"

"I'll take you upstairs, but wait a second. I want you to take a minute. Think about it."

Willis was walking ahead.

They boarded the elevator and found opposite corners.

Fritz told Willis, "He wants us for a fag scene. Us together. I said we won't do it."

Willis stared at Fritz as the elevator strained. They hit the first floor and the accordion gate popped open.

Willis shouldered his way off the platform, but Showalter kept stride. He was reciting studio fees, adding them up to attract Willis. Showalter wasn't getting through to Willis and switched his approach. "I'm also looking for drivers plain and simple. I'm having trouble with distribution. The mail is tricky. I had someone over here asking me questions about my mail-order business. I have some front material, Audubon subjects, birds and insects. I showed that inventory. Flowers, 3-D rhododendron—it packs a wallop. All that Sierra Club material. Just the same, they're sniffing. I might have to deliver merchandise by courier. You interested?"

"Four Eyes Smut Will Travel?" Willis said.

Showalter smiled. "That's deliciously tasteless, but we need something incognito," Showalter said. "If not you, someone can make a little money. Moonlighting is lucrative these days. Have you got a steady day job?"

"WASTEC."

"But you haven't driven a trailer for a week."

Willis said, "What is this? You have a telescope or something? You can watch Cranston from here?"

"It is my understanding that you don't have a steady job."

Willis stopped in his tracks. He turned around to look at the man's face to see just what he was implying.

"Jobs are hard to come by," Showalter said with a stainless voice, not empathy, not ridicule. Showalter walked them over to where they had left the dead birds in their cardboard boxes. Fritz accepted his two hundred dollars and started to peel some bills for Willis, but Willis shoved it away. They turned to leave.

Showalter stopped them. He paid Fritz another fifty to dispose of the birds' remains, but he was talking to Willis. Willis seemed to attract his attention more than Fritz could. Showalter told Willis, "Get rid of these in Rhode Island, not in the commonwealth. Rhode Island keeps its eyes closed tighter."

"Sure," Willis told him, but he didn't exhibit any further commitment.

Showalter said, "I'm going to try another source. He guarantees live delivery. Of course you pay more for guaranteed wildlife. Tonight was one thing. I took a chance—"

Willis was outside before Showalter finished.

Showalter was saying, "Maybe the next time we'll do better. You know, these birds can be trained to talk—"

Willis was already pacing down the sidewalk. He drove the car away. "You should find a better crowd," Willis told Fritz.

"What crowd? You're my crowd."

"This Showalter gink. Show-me-yours. Show-you-mine."

"Just call him Gene. Gene Showalter," Fritz said.

"*Mr.* Show-me-yours."

Fritz said, "Point. Here's two hundred. New bills, I've got paper cuts."

"Two hundred isn't shit." Willis drove to a rural area in Warren where he knew about an old landfill that had been officially closed down. The property was permanently sealed off with a big gate made from mortared telephone poles to keep dump trucks from unloading, but Willis and Fritz were able to walk right in through a pedestrian opening in the fence. The dump was used as a shooting range and they walked across a carpet of shotgun shells and low dunes of tiny lead pellets like black fish eggs. Willis shouldered a carton of exotic death, but he couldn't handle any more with his bad arm and Fritz took the others.

Willis pictured the weekend sportsmen nailing several rounds into the feathered corpses. It didn't feel right. Willis found an empty barrel behind a stack of rusty corrugated roofing material. Willis dropped the box of birds off his shoulder right into the empty barrel. Fritz stacked his boxes on top of that. Willis wanted to have a last look at the birds. He took one of the birds from the top carton and held it for Fritz. Fritz had a Penlite and he scrawled the tiny wafer of light over the dead animal. It was one of the yellow-fronted Amazons. Willis pushed his index finger through the bird's soft breast feathers; the iridescent sheen of the lime-colored down had an intensity of color Willis couldn't disconnect from. He ruffled the feathers under his thumb, exposing variegated chartreuse swatches. He stretched a wing open, counting its serrated coverts. The bird's flight feathers were deeper green. He let the wing fold back. The bird's face was startling. Across its yellow crown and hooked bill was a convincing, placid wisdom.

Willis smoothed the bird with the palm of his hand. The bird's eyes were clear amber, like drops of caramelized sugar.

It was almost dawn when Willis left Fritz and drove home to Rennie's house. The house was getting overgrown with vines and needed a pressure-cleaning job, but Willis liked the buildup of woody fingers. He went upstairs to his room and fell back on the bed. The quilt was fresh, Rennie must have washed it and hung it out on the T-bars. He could smell the salty beach air which had a positive affect on the polyester filling. Rennie knew he would end up just where he was, no matter how complicated his nights. He was thinking of Fritz, how Fritz couldn't manage his greed. He could hear the wind tugging through the screens, which always sounded good against the background surf. He was surprised to hear Rennie's footsteps coming onto the porch. He recognized the way she stamped three times, her slight weight shifting from one foot to the other, getting the sand off. She must have been down on the beach or out in the detached garage where she kept extra cooking pots that wouldn't fit in the cupboards. Maybe she had fired up the kiln, but Rennie had stopped making jewelry when she ran out of powder glazes, and she didn't want to restock.

She must have seen the car parked in front, the silvery zigzag on the windshield. He listened to her arrange canned goods in the lazy Susan; he knew the way she liked the soup stacked, consommé in front. He was drifting in and out of sleep, listening to the sea roll and flatten down the slope of the dune. Again, he was alert. For Willis, the first stretch of sleep was always bracketed by fears. Was it rest after work, or the difficult work of finding rest? The preparatory stillness before unforeseeable events. The calm before or the calm after?

He fumbled through the top drawer of his night table and found the card of drugs. He removed the foil and plowed it in. Willis felt one moment of regret. His regret made him angry, but he didn't blame Rennie for sharing her morphine. She gave him the little boxes with the belief that it was a legitimate prescription from an authorized chemist. They might have been sweet orange tablets of St. Joseph's baby aspirin. Maybe she was shutting her eyes to it because she was dying and wanted his company in her scary routines. Rennie didn't seem to know that he was in over his head. She had enough to contend with directing her own decline.

He listened to the house noises, the heating pipes knocking, room to room. He felt suddenly at ease, the way people feel immediately better when placed in oxygen tents and they don't have to concentrate on the pull of their lungs. Then he smelled yeast rolls, the first wave of scent from the preheated oven, a flood of cinnamon rising through the warped floorboards.

☙

In his altered sleep the birds awakened. Their beaded eyes tightened and expanded in an intelligent perusal. They flapped their bright magenta wings, fanned their crests. They perched on the piebald doors of the car and flew inside the windows, lined up along the dash like bowling trophies. The birds stared at Willis. Screeched. The sound they emitted was both wild and familiar, a fiery squawk without accusation or insult, like the sound of someone stepping on a house cat. Just an announcement. A presence. Here I am.

Chapter Eight

It was afternoon when Willis came downstairs. Rennie was sitting in the old captain's chair; its arms were polished by her sweater sleeves. The chair's uncomfortable spindles looked like fossilized bones Willis had seen in a *National Geographic*. The hard chair had always been Rennie's spot. Willis had replaced the Fresnel lens in its usual place on the narrow sill beneath the fanlight. The sun burst through the glass throwing distorted shamrocks across the walls. Willis stooped and gave Rennie a kiss, holding his cast against his waist to keep it from bumping her.

"How much longer do you need that?" Rennie said.

"Four weeks."

"It's filthy, maybe we can use some kitchen wax on it. Simonize it. I have a bottle in the cupboard."

He took a homemade sweet roll from the Spode plate, letting its heavenly weight register in his hand. The pastry was laden with egg and ripped apart in long feathers of yellow cake. It was something he could eat without sitting down at the table. She often offered him these portable servings, letting him stand at the window, or pace around, ruffling through papers and magazines, as if he was looking for his own belongings and couldn't find anything familiar.

She gave him a mug of tea and dropped a spoon in it to pull the heat off. Willis looked down at a bowl of kidneys soaking in milk. The deep umber knots glistened like fart opals in the white broth. She told him she was making a stew, the milk absorbs any uric acid left in the meat.

Rennie knew that Willis felt uncomfortable when she planned the meals ahead of time. Stew required a commitment from him to show up. He was telling her, "I might not make it."

"Your way with words," Rennie said, "it's always refreshing. Let's not cringe at routine pleasantries—"

"Shit. Didn't I say good morning? I swear I said it."

"I'm not keeping track. How's the car? How is it running for you?"

"You saw it? The crack in the windshield?"

"Can't miss it."

"I got behind a gravel truck spilling asphalt mix. I'll get it fixed next week. Maybe you've got the insurance for something like that, a gravel truck—"

"Windshields are tricky when you live by the seaside. *We* say it's a gravel truck, but they say that since we park it on the water, it's sand blowing on a daily basis, making little pocks and ruining the glass. They'll fight it."

"This is a regular smashed windshield, Rennie, they won't try to prove it was blowing sand."

"It's Amica. They're testy. *You* call and tell them that story." Rennie walked over to the sideboard and penned something in a little notebook.

"Is that a shopping list?" Willis asked.

She shut the little notebook and dropped the pen on its cover.

Rennie said, "Do you want kale soup? I've still got winter kale in the garden. It's tough. It's holding on."

"Look. Stop the production."

"It's good to have you back from Norfolk. How long have you been back? Two, three months? First month doesn't count. You weren't exactly clean and sober. You still using my stash? Do I have to go to CVS and get more?"

"Well, shouldn't you have it on hand? I mean, in case you need it yourself?"

"I'll get refills. Maybe you can do some work around here—"

"Sure I will. Exactly what?"

"We could do some reshingling," she said. She didn't sound serious.

"Sure. I'll get some cedar shingles. Next week."

"It's Munro," Rennie told him. "He's getting counsel. He's not going to let us stop his plans—"

"He was lucky I didn't kill him. I told you, don't worry about him."

"He says I can't take care of the house anymore. There's a problem with cash flow."

Willis said, "The house looks fine. There's nothing wrong with it, is there?"

"Nothing. Nothing essentially wrong with it." Rennie took a butter knife from a drawer, but Willis shook his head about the butter. From habit, she rubbed her thumb over the blade before she put it back. It was good to feel the dull blade of a knife when it was supposed to be dull.

"The house needs paint," Willis said, stuffing a pillow of cake into his mouth. "It's those vines. They have little sucker feet and they eat right through the trim on the window frames. I can pull them down and get a pressure cleaning kit at the Rent-All."

"The greenery has nothing to do with it. Maybe it's the only thing holding the house up. It's me. *I* should have the sucker feet." She wasn't laughing. "Munro wants me to have a condo at Château-sur-Mer. His treat."

"Tell him to go fuck himself."

"We can't afford this house unless he chips in. It's blackmail. He won't let us stay here."

"How much has that drone been giving you?"

"Just about everything."

Willis stopped chewing. He went over to the sink and spit out his mouthful of fluffy cake so he could talk. "What? You never said he was paying that much. He's been paying everything?"

"Everything."

"He pays my way? I'm going to throw up."

"Don't eat so fast."

"Don't joke. Are you saying we have money problems? Am I blind or something?"

"It didn't make any difference until now. Now he wants to make decisions." She hid her hands behind her apron as she talked.

"I didn't think it was about money. I thought it was about philosophy."

"We have plenty of that. We've got loads of philosophy." Willis looked stunned. Rennie rummaged through some drawers while he found his legs. She said, "I've been getting dunned by Marcy Oil. Narragansett Electric. Even Ma Bell has her knickers in a twist. My household budget is hanging by a thread."

"But you have the house. It's waterfront property."

"Water, water everywhere and not a drop to drink."

Willis walked into the next room and through to the front parlor, then he turned around and came back.

Rennie said, "Munro says he's not going ahead with the property taxes. It's blackmail. He wants me to sell the place. Century 21 was over here but I chased them out."

"Taxes? How much?"

"Next year I get Social Security and that would almost cover the taxes on this house, but then he'd freeze me out some other way. He won't pay my grocery bills at Almacs. He wants me on the inside looking out."

Willis said, "It's not going to happen. Not a chance." He marched through the room thinking how to back it up.

Rennie said, "Château-sur-Mer is supposed to be better than those motel-style nursing homes. What's the difference? Once you admit defeat, you might as well live over a grate on the sidewalk. Château-sur-Mer is where the upper crust crumbles."

"It's for millionaires. We aren't millionaires," Willis said, but he waited for her to confirm his assumption.

"Not exactly."

"That's the place next to Salve Regina, right? That big setup on the Cliff Walk? I know someone who works in there. A candy striper or something—"

"You mean that little nurse? That's what I'm saying. Candy stripers are for hospitals. I'm not going back to a hospital. The brochure says it's '*resort* retirement.' The last resort.

"First, they put you in something called a 'villa,' then they cut you back to an apartment if for some reason you can't walk across the lawn to the dining hall. Too many cricks or tummy troubles and it's into the infirmary you go. Where it comes on a tray. The last thing, it's a tube through your nose. The shortcut, you don't have to chew it. You know—"

"Come on." Willis didn't want her to continue, but she was building momentum.

"It's the Last Supper every night. Enter at this *villa* level, then its downhill all the way. It's the last stop. Everybody off the train. They don't even try to pretend."

"Munro's crazy. That's years from now. What are you? Fifty? Sixty? You aren't ready for all of that."

She looked at him; she was touched that he tried to deny her failing health. He didn't really want to know her age. He had never really figured her in chronologically; she was a constant, her age didn't matter. He could have told her Wydette's age, down to the minute. Wydette would have been fifty. Willis remembered Wydette's theoretical age, year by year, because she never reached it. Wydette never fulfilled the obligation of those years. Where was Wydette when Willis was sick with throbbing pains and Rennie washed the ochre vomit stains from his sheets and towels? Who took care of him now? Rennie even sliced his meat. He couldn't handle a knife with his broken arm. She carved the meat, giving extra attention to how she arranged the rare slices across his plate, creating an attractive fan, rose-colored fingers of beef. He was a grown man, but a broken arm made him like a child again. He could hardly zip his pants. He left the brass rivet unbuttoned unless he asked her to do it.

The house belonged to Rennie, but none of her three husbands had left her enough money to keep it up. For years Rennie made souvenir jewelry, lighthouse pins, sand-dollar earrings, lobster-claw and sailboat charms which she had sold from her "eight-month" shop. Sometimes, Rennie went to the flea markets where she displayed her old clothes, her extra teacups, which brought good prices, but she didn't have the energy anymore. She could have un-loaded Wydette's things, which Lester had tried to salvage. Wydette's shoes were still lined up in the attic along with her stirrup stretch pants folded and sealed in white Jordan Marsh boxes. In a small envelope, Rennie discovered the calcified stub of Willis's umbilical clamp which Wydette had saved. Willis had seemed disappointed when he examined the tiny relic. He told Rennie that he had always expected the cord to look like the frayed painter on a rowboat.

Willis had the kitchen faucet disassembled. The chrome escutcheon, the tiny O-ring, the packing washer, and stem sleeve were lined up on the counter. He needed a seat wrench, and he went through the kitchen closet until he found what he wanted.

"It's a tiny leak," Rennie said. "I can live with it."

"You shouldn't have a hot-water leak," he told her. "The furnace kicks on."

She sat down at the kitchen table and watched him. She couldn't remember just how much water had been dripping. She figured Willis was making a point. He would take care of the house until the bitter end.

It was the first time she noticed his boots. She examined the marled, smoke-damaged leather. He hadn't mentioned where he found these secondhand boots, so she kept quiet. Perhaps he had arrived at those boots through private circumstances.

Willis replaced the faucet and tightened the retainer nut with a cloth-covered pliers. With his left hand he threaded the tiny screen onto the spout. He reached under the sink to turn on the connection. He pulled the tap open and the water convulsed twice, then flattened into a steady line. He twisted the handle shut. The spout bled a few drops. Then it was dry.

Chapter Nine

Between the two houses, there was an oil drum for burning trash. Nicole and Rennie shared it. Holly saw Willis Pratt at the edge of the cliff standing over the trash barrel. Standing beside Willis was another young man; a lean and nervous type was shivering, sinking up and down, as Willis lit matches and tossed them into the drum. Willis lowered something into the fire. He stepped back. He looked up at the sky. His face showed a strange, undefinable disturbance. Willis reached into the rusty barrel to strike additional matches out of the wind. Cooking grease sputtered where it was heavy on the paper sacks. He had the fire going and he added some dirty swatches from the rag box. He lifted another heavy bag of kitchen scraps and put it on. He moved back and threw the remaining pack of restaurant matches into the barrel.

Holly came out of her house. She skirted the stranger and ran up to Willis. She looked inside the barrel. A small, compact mound prickled with sparks. She knew it was the puppy. "What are you doing—" she hollered. She rose up on her toes to get a better look, but the smoke lifted in a heavy screen and she couldn't see through it. "You can't burn that dog out here where the children might see it."

She was standing in the smoke; she moved to the other side of the barrel, but the wind shifted again. Her stomach was clenching and she felt her saliva increasing.

Willis looked at her. He scratched the tip of his nose with the white cuff of his cast. He looked like he was trying to understand Holly's non sequiturs. She could see him *pretending* to make the leaps.

"This is sick!" she said.

He looked at the fire.

"Put that out. Put that fire out right now."

He turned to face her square. His eyes looked wide, then they grew distant. He said, "That dog? That dog is around the house. I dug a hole. You can have your bow-wow funeral when the kids come home from school."

"Are you saying you made a grave?"

"Over there—see that hole?" He shoved his arm in the direction of the little grave.

Holly saw the trench in the sandy yard. "Oh," Holly said. "I see it." Her eyes were swimming, her confusion and shame washing higher. She looked at the fire again.

Willis told Fritz, "This is Holly Temple."

Fritz said, "A Christmas baby?"

"Close enough," she said. Her face was stinging.

"This here," Fritz said, "is Rennie's garbage. Just the ordinary."

"I thought I saw that puppy go in," she said.

"You wear contacts, Miss Temple?" Fritz said.

"Shit," Holly said.

"You wear glasses, Miss Temple? How's your prescription? EyeWorld can grind some new lenses in an hour."

Holly said, "Will you cut out the 'Miss Temple' routine."

"Excuse me. Miss *Holy* Temple."

"I was waiting for that," she said.

Willis let Fritz have his say.

Holly didn't wear glasses. She marched back into her house and slammed the door. She shut the window, which was opened a crack. Already her rooms smelled of smoke, like a landfill incinerator—burned grapefruit rinds and pork-chop bones. She felt incredibly stupid. Then she realized she couldn't hang her wash. How could she hang her wash if people were burning their garbage on the only sunny day? She allowed herself to feel this new insult; she was happy to shift it over.

In five minutes she came back outdoors and got into her car. Willis was still there with the skinny outsider. Willis was standing in the trench he had made for the dog. It came up to his shins right below his knees. He stood there, keeping a silent, horrible posture. She didn't acknowledge the little grave he had made and she looked away. He was crazy. Of course, he was crazy. She tossed her hair away from her face and squinted in her rearview to back down the driveway.

Holly couldn't think about it now; she and Robin had to cook for a hundred and fifty. There were big sheets of stuffed peppers to bake, and they could be tricky. The peppers along the outside edges of the wide pans always blackened while the middle ones were too soggy. The kids hated stuffed peppers anyway. The students would eat stuffed peppers or they would starve. She received her paycheck either way.

Until the summer season started at Neptune's, Holly was pleased to work with Robin in the big kitchen at Saint George's. She knotted the cord of her full-length rubberized apron which fell to her shins. The front bib stopped at her collarbone. It didn't matter how she looked underneath. The peppers were roasting and she liked the sweet tinge it gave to the chalky hallways. In this manner, she reached out beyond her tiny station, and the kitchen assumed power over the academic workings of the place.

The kitchen had modern equipment, but she liked best the grey marble slabs where she could slap bread dough and tug it back under the heel of her hand. The big stainless sinks had tall gooseneck faucets, and she filled ten-gallon speckled kettles until they were almost too heavy to lift over to the big double range, where eight burners could go at once.

It was institutional fare, but sometimes Robin made it interesting. Robin liked making soups. Clear soups. Root soups. Bean soups with smoked hocks. On the spur of the moment, Robin whipped fresh cream by hand, in a huge bowl set in a trough of ice. After the main course was finished, she walked out into the dining hall with the giant bowl in the crook of her arm and she dolloped satiny clouds of topping onto individual servings of sweet berries as students and faculty sat mesmerized. For this, Robin was loved.

Holly envied Robin's friendly relationships. Most of Neptune's tenants never even saw Holly. Except for a few repeat families, no one remembered her. They moved into the shacks long after Holly was finished setting up. She left a number-ten envelope for tips, resting it against the bureau mirror, but only about a third of the guests remembered to leave a gratuity. If a family was late at checkout and Holly stood around waiting for them with her trolley of sheets and towels, her industrial spray gun of Windex hung on her apron, they might notice her and say hello. Maids are not supposed to chat it up. But Robin had open lines of communication. She made molded candies in the shape of the school mascot and sold them at soccer games. At the holidays, Robin made giant Yule logs decorated with chocolate bark shavings and meringue mushrooms. These logs were placed at the center of every table, and students slapped each other's hands to keep the centerpiece whole until the final course was over. Then, like savages, the students sawed their knives through the sugared crust and fought over the dense chocolate wheels. They told their parents about Robin and she received lavish Christmas presents from the contrite mothers who boarded their children.

Following Robin's example, Holly shaved the rind of lemons, little hysterical twists of yellow with which she decorated the heavy slices of sauerbraten. She made gingered apples for the pork roast or dyed turnip roses whenever the dinner looked too bland or gloomy. She learned from Robin that basic nourishment must be embellished with excitements.

Elliot Tompkins, a don and biology teacher at Saint George's, was also a trustee at the nearby Norman Bird Sanctuary and he often stepped into the kitchen to use the refrigerator for a jar of barnacles or some specimen from the marsh needing a cool temperature. He wanted the toaster oven to incubate woodcock eggs, but it didn't always work out; its thermostat wasn't precise. He came in to see what Holly was preparing that night. After he sniffed the steaming platters, making acid Mimi Sheraton comments, he turned around at the door and recited the same daily remark to show his solidarity with the kitchen staff. "To serve them all my days—" he announced with bittersweet refreshment. He liked making a pun while referring to the famous saga about an English public school instructor. He identified with the British and had adopted their courtesies and mannerisms.

Robin timed her butterknot rolls to come out when the peppers were ready. Next, she placed her fruit jumbles in the warming oven to take the chill off the refrigerated tart shells. Holly and Robin worked well together and everything was ready when they heard the students filing in, the chairs grinding backward over the oak planks, the silverware clanging as the students unfurled their napkins with abandon and some of the utensils landed on the floor.

Student servers came into the kitchen to collect trays, the pitchers of milk and ice water, and ceramic bowls of chunky butter pats. The self-important prefects came next to retrieve their tables' vitamin supplements and the various medications, which were kept in the refrigerator. When the meal was in progress, Holly started scouring the roasters and kettles. She kept her industrial-grade rubber gloves on a hook in the pantry, the same gloves she'd seen fishermen use to scale fish or shuck oysters. Holly snipped a Brillo pad in half and she started to soak the broilers in scalding water. She used the edge of a spatula to loosen the caramelized sugar scrim from a big twelve-inch pie plate.

Holly was drying a colander when Willis Pratt walked into the kitchen. He startled Holly and the colander slipped out of her hands. When she picked it up she saw its aluminum mesh was dented. She stared at the gash in the colander's silver hip. Willis leaned against the heavy butcher-block table, which stood on four girthy legs in the middle of the floor. He fingered the marred surface of golden wood and looked at Holly.

"What do you want?" she asked him. She tucked the colander on a rack above the sink. She kept working, stowing utensils and scraping her fingernail against an adhering particle of onion. She was unwilling to face him. She lifted a heavy trash bag by its corners until the plastic film stretched under the weight, then she cinched the bag shut, tying its four corners.

"When are you finished here? Maybe we can talk," he said.

"Still have the dishes. They go in the machine, but it gets loaded twice. Two cycles. The tables aren't even cleared yet."

"I'm having trouble with your assumption about that dog," Willis said. "It's bothering me." He paced around slowly. He picked up a long starched towel and he tucked it around his hips expertly, the way a waiter knows how to make an apron from a table napkin. He picked up a dishrag and wrung it out in one hand over the sink. He started to circle the rag over the countertops. When he stopped scouring, she picked up the rag and tucked it in a hamper.

"That dog? Oh, forget it. I overreacted." She started spraying the sink.

"I have a problem with these violent ideas. These visions. Now you're telling me I was trying to burn a dog—"

"My mistake. Really. I apologize."

"Once something gets in my head, I might as well have done it."

"You're kidding. You might have set that dog on fire?"

"Not until *you* put it in my mind. That's what I'm saying."

"I said I was sorry."

He looked away from her and she was overtaken by his honesty. Yet, when he turned to watch her again, he looked fine. She thought that this was some kind of a line he was giving her. It might be that easy for him sometimes, telling a girl his troubles, but she wasn't going along with it.

She told him, "Did you ever try a psychiatrist?"

A student walked through with a tray of condiments. Holly took it from the boy and shoved the tray into the big double-sided refrigerator.

Holly was ready to show Willis out, but she had trouble looking him in the eye. She saw his slender figure, the *form* of him, leaning against the big appliances. She started to sway, imperceptibly, in a tide of anger. Then, when he looked at her directly, she felt light-headed, insubstantial, as if he might blow her around the room like a piece of fluff.

"I can't talk now," she said. She looked at his face. His skin was tight over his sharp features, like the porcelain gloss on exquisite figurines. His military haircut had grown out several inches to a modest length, a circle of unmanageable silk tassels. In the harsh kitchen light his tight pupils looked glossy and hot, wet black snips inside washed violet spheres. She was upset about the way he had tucked the towel around his waist, his aggressive, take-control-of-the-room act when he rinsed the dishrag under the tap. She stared at the white towel, which rose over his groin, and remembered to lift her eyes to his face. Such a fair complexion coupled with his immediate jaded aura was startling. "You'll have to leave," she told him.

Willis stepped up to the counter where Holly had begun spooning tapioca pudding into individual servings. He lifted a glass dish in the palm of his hand; the pearly mound trembled and shook.

He carved into it with a teaspoon.

He ate a mouthful.

She watched him swallow; his Adam's apple triggered. She felt a delicious icy wave roll up her spine. She wondered if he knew what he was doing or if, in fact, Willis was innocent of the tremendous impulse she was feeling. She heard the students in the dining hall scratching silverware against their stoneware plates, a ceramic crescendo.

He might have seen that her resolve was melting away. He looked at her again, with complete familiarity. He looked at her the way a mechanic sees a big table of parts he has just disassembled, deciding *if* and *when* to put them back together.

"Well, good night," Holly told him in a firm voice. The sound of her own voice embarrassed her and she brushed her apron with the heels of her hands and backed away. She turned and hurried into the crowded dining hall, where she knew he wouldn't follow. After she pushed through the swinging door, she turned around and looked back through its porthole. Willis had strolled out the back door. He had permitted the neighborhood tom to wriggle past him. The lean cat leapt to the countertop and started to lick a greasy serving spoon. Holly came back into the kitchen and clapped her hands beside the stray. It didn't jump down from the sink. Again she clapped her hands. She couldn't scare it. She lifted the cat into her arms, cradled its haunches and rode her chin across the notched tips of its ears.

Chapter Ten

Holly and Rennie directed the children in the burial of their dog. They prepared a small ceremony; it was like Brownie theater. Holly burned a candle, cupping the flame with her hand, but there was a strong southeast wind and the candle kept blowing out. Rennie had several yellowed holy cards from various wakes in a dresser drawer and she divided up the cards between Lindy and Sarah.

The children sifted through the cards, distracted by the dramatic portraits of the saints. Holly told Rennie, "That's a nice idea. It keeps their minds off the matter at hand."

"Their minds will come back to it," Rennie said.

"Well, it helps for now, anyway."

Lindy fanned his cards before Rennie.

"Wait a minute. Give me that one. He's my patron saint." She took the card from the boy and put it in her pocket.

Holly arranged the dog in the shallow trench and smoothed her hand down its dull fur. Lindy placed seven dog biscuits, the remainder of the box, beside the puppy's muzzle. Holly waited for the boy to tap the crumbs from the box, then she spooned the earth with the trowel until the puppy was covered. When the children went off, she tamped the grave with the flat edge of a garden hoe until the soil was packed down tight, but she could still feel the hump of its carcass beneath the topsoil.

It was dusk when Willis came over to the duplex. The water had warmed up during the day, just enough to grow a hairy vapor across the surface of Easton Pond at sundown. Holly stood beside him on the porch and they looked at the reservoir. Willis said he was sorry he had disturbed her at her job. He asked her to come out. Holly put on her sweater-jacket and pushed the cuffs past her wrists. Willis put Holly in the car. She stared out the shattered windshield as if it was nothing. He appreciated her restraint. Willis drove with one hand on the wheel, his broken arm rested in his lap. The plan was simple. They were taking a drive.

She sat tentatively on the bench seat beside Willis, her hands on either side of her hips. Why did her hips feel suddenly fragile, like two flared, bone-china saucers that might easily be smashed? The alternative might be just as bad, they might be put on a shelf.

Willis drove into a new housing development, several identical Cape Cod–style houses nestled against a sloping field above Narragansett Bay. He pulled around a cul-de-sac and stopped the car, letting its rough idle shake until the gear shifted another fraction. "See that house?"

"That one?"

"That's right. She's in there."

"Who's in there?"

"The mother of that baby. Sheila Boyd from my high school."

Holly fingered the collar of her jacket. "The mother of what baby?"

"Sheila's baby was born dead." Willis stared at the pastel front door of the little Cape. "She's a really nice person. One of these people you just can't see getting knocked around. I should stop in and say something."

"What could you say?"

"Shit. Anything. You know, whatever you say to someone who's been through it."

"Yeah," Holly said, "then what?" She saw Willis was having trouble communicating; his obsession was all over him. It was like a net. Holly could see him snagged inside it, but he couldn't see through it. His stillness was unnerving. She didn't know the next step.

"I'd like to go ring that doorbell. You know, go in there and tell her my condolences."

"Sure, I'll wait here," Holly told him.

"Can't."

"Well, of course you *can't.*" Holly flip-flopped. "You can't just go in there like a family member. Why don't you just let it alone. I'm not making a criticism, but maybe you shouldn't dwell on these tragedies. My father's dead. Once they're dead, they're dead."

Willis said, "I try to imagine them. I don't mind trying. I like to give it the benefit of the doubt."

"Are you talking about ghosts?"

"The human spirit," he said.

"Maybe you could think about it once a day. Like when you pray," Holly said.

"I don't pray. Not since I was a kid. Do you pray?"

"Shit." They turned their heads and looked out opposite windows. "No, I don't take time to pray. Maybe we should start up again."

Holly used to go along with her father to the Presbyterian church at Four Corners. The minister used those four corners in his sermons each Sunday, inventing antithetical metaphors, such as the corners of guilt and innocence; wrong and right; faith and despair.

The Sunday light clothed everything, streets and sidewalks in bleached muslin. She sat in a polished pew beside her father. The gleaming rows smelled like Murphy's Oil Soap until her sinuses felt raw. Her father watched ahead, listening to the sermon, ready to follow the broader guidelines. Her father might be stinging from his losses at Lincoln Park dog track. Sunday mornings, Holly listened as her father shaved and dressed for church. If he mimicked the track announcer's voice, his ascending singsong as he sights the mechanical rabbit and calls the start, "AND HERE COMES YANK-EE—" he had had a lucky night.

Willis steered the car away from Sheila Boyd's Cape-style house. He wanted to show Holly another place. A graveyard by the sea. The misty twilight was perfect and eerie; it almost necessitated a cemetery visit. He drove along the salt marsh and rocky meadows of Second Beach and onto Indian Avenue. He pulled over at a forlorn place, a few empty acres called White's Monument Village, and turned off the ignition. They got out of the car and started to walk.

Willis led Holly to a divided area in the park. Holly saw a stone monument that supported a large bronze scroll. The scroll had the word BABYLAND on it. Willis fingered the bizarre compound word. He said, "These little squirts didn't know what hit them." The scroll was a smarmy salutation welcoming children to their new home:

I saw a ship a-sailing, a-sailing out to sea,
and oh, but it was laden, with children good to see.
Strong arms that held the sails tight,
Red cheeks that laughed at cold,
And every child upon it was worth his weight in gold.

"That's sick," Holly said.

"That poem comes from the Gorham Monument Catalogue. Gorham is like Hallmark or American Greetings for the burial industry. This poem isn't unique. There's nine hundred of these Babyland scrolls in cemeteries all over the United States. Think of it."

"How do you know that?"

"Fritz used to work here cutting grass. The grounds-keeper was a chatterbox."

"I guess it's a lonely job," Holly said, "tending graves. I bet it makes somebody want to yack."

Holly didn't like the poem. How could children be given such a short straw. She didn't like the sentiment that a child was only worth its weight in gold. Willis walked ahead of Holly to a fresh excavation. The earth was carefully removed. All four incredibly short sides were expertly smoothed. It looked square as a lunch pail sunk in the velvet lawn. The grave did not yet have a marker.

"This one's for Sheila's baby," he said, "when it gets back from the Research Triangle."

"When it gets back from where?"

"When the medical students are through gawking at it."

"How do you know whose grave this is?"

"A hunch. It's too small for me. So I know it's not mine." He looked at her. "Shit. It's about the size of a breadbox," Willis said.

"Out of the *oven* and into the *breadbox*," Holly said.

He didn't like the joke. The baby cemetery was more than he could handle; for Willis an acre of tiny, doll-size skeletons was plenty enough reason for a man to slit his own throat.

"I'm not fucking you in a cemetery," she told him.

He turned to face her and shrugged.

"Is this your idea of romance? Making love in baby graveyards? That kind of thing went out with the beatnik generation."

He walked ahead, taking long strides. He went over a knoll before Holly could catch up. He was thinking of his mother's grave in detached ruminations. Had the little chunk of sausage that had choked Wydette been buried with her remains? What happens to the undigested stomach contents, the velvety gruel left inside the bowel? All of it was part of the same soup, stirred by the worms.

Holly caught up to him and they stood together looking at the chalky grid, intensified in the twilight. Willis steered her over to his parents' simple monuments. Both stones were engraved only with the surname Pratt. Lester was on the left, Wydette was on the right. In a few more years, no one would remember whose side was which. Willis had always thought that there was some sort of deception being practiced. The anonymity of the family name seemed crude.

"Do you always bring girls to meet your folks like this?"

He was surprised by her words and laughed. His laughter was exciting to Holly, it exposed him. Real laughter erupts from a man's soft interior, and she was pleased to feel its luxurious notes dissolving in the air around her. She tried another quip, but it wasn't successful; he was on guard after the first time.

Holly said, "Ever been to Neptune's?"

"That string of summer shacks?"

"My home away from home," she told him.

Willis took her over there. He told her, "I always liked the place. You can see it from across the cove. These shacks are white, all right, like a row of teeth."

"It's nice, isn't it? Yachtzies can see it offshore. They

sail into the Ida Lewis Yacht Club to rent moorings and ask about this place. They can see these shacks all the way out in the sound." She made Willis park the car and she walked him down the string of shacks, telling him their distinctions and peculiarities. Each cottage was boarded up; Holly had to paint the interior with words. She even tried to describe the shelf paper in the cupboards. The wallpaper. The matching curtains. Everything was cabbage roses. "I start changeovers again in about a month."

"What exactly happens at these changeovers?" he said.

"I work my ass off. People start coming and going. I tell you, it's a view of the world. People check in and they check out. You get a picture of someone. After one week of vacation, some fellows look good, they're satisfied. Other ones look worse for it, like they can't accept the fact that life is ninety-five percent hard work at a regular job and only one week off. I watch it all. They party it up, get some big lobsters. Did you know everyone puts his lobster down on the linoleum before they shove 'em in the pot? I think that's a scream. They have a feast, then they sink into gloom. It's a whole spectrum of feelings."

"What about these hooks?" Willis said. He pointed to the empty hooks over the front doors of the cottages.

"These hooks are for the flower signs. You know, 'Lupine,' 'Myrtle—' " She recited the names of the flowers. The bare hooks over every door gave Willis an uncomfortable feeling. It was the same feeling he got when he saw blank granite monuments displayed on the front lawn of the stonecutter's shop. Holly told him that the signs were removed and stored until the summer season so the wind couldn't lift off the lettering. "The wind out here," she said, "is like a chisel."

Willis put his arms around her waist and leaned into her

on the doorstep of one cottage. "Which one is this?" he said.

"Clematis," she said. It had an anatomical sound, which she hadn't yet noticed after all her years there, not until that moment.

He tugged her and rattled the door handle. He moved his hips against her, as if he was climbing through her. He shook the door. He was playacting, but she knew he wanted in.

"Locked," she said.

"You don't have privileges?"

"No. But I have my other keys with me."

"What keys?"

"My old apartment. The place with the sinkhole. You hear about it?"

Willis said, "Everyone in town knows the place. It's a regular attraction."

"Want a closer look?" She might have been talking about the sinkhole or something else. He studied her face.

Willis admitted that he was curious.

They rode into town and parked on Spring Street. Spring Street was dead. In the twilight hours, the world resumes its clarity, everything is arrested. Night falls over the town the way a drop of water pins a flea with its minute surface tension. Willis knew that a flea could survive until the water evaporated; but he often didn't think he would emerge intact from any given night. He looked up. A pink moon was eroding, cherry of morphine. When he had these thoughts, his eyes started to hurt, his sinuses stabbing. He rubbed his knuckles across the bridge of his nose to soothe the pinging. Holly watched his moods shift. His modulations of feeling were disturbing, yet she disliked men who never washed over a certain level.

They walked around the sinkhole, skirting the flat chunks of broken asphalt. Her apartment house was still condemned, but she saw construction had started. The joists had been shimmed and the foundation was partially filled in with gravel and chalky-blue hardener. The front door of the building was left wide open. She ignored the NO TRESPASSING signs and took Willis inside the building, as if nothing had ever happened to suggest that the building might, at any minute, give way to its years. Willis followed her up the stairs. The hall was dark. The electricity was shut off.

Once inside the apartment, she found the drawer with the hurricane candles. Together they tapered the wicks and lit them with kitchen matches. Willis arranged the candles along the kitchen windowsill, letting the wax drip on the ledge before grinding the stems into the hot puddle. She sat down at the dinette set, which was coated with concrete dust from weeks of jackhammering in the street outside. Willis sat across from her and pushed the heel of his hand through the powder, reaching for her. The candlelight stuttered in the draft, one waffling gold zone.

The building's decay seemed a strange catalyst. It was a phantom dwelling; the sinkhole's gaping pit attained the dreamy character of a castle's moat. They didn't have to remember the exterior world, their lives already in progress; their irrefutable pasts seemed, suddenly, open-ended.

They moved to the sofa. He was careful not to rest his plastered arm against her bare skin, until at last she asked to feel its chilly swipe. He tugged it gently over her hips and guided it along her mound of Venus. She pinched her legs closed upon it. She released her hold and they laughed. She shivered with temperature shifts; pleasure surges ricocheted through her erogenous landmarks in one cluster response. Her sharp inhalations couldn't keep up. Willis liked hearing her shaky respirations, which vacillated with his touch, as if he manipulated a magic throttle.

Willis rolled onto her. His skin was flushed where the candles threw their light. The hair at his temple smelled like hard-milled lavender soap, like old-fashioned boxed soaps sold in department stores.

He was holding back. "Wait a minute. Are you all right?"

She told him yes.

"I don't know," he said.

"I'm fine," she told him.

"Are you sure? Some girls are just like Chia Pets. Next day, they've sprouted."

She wondered what he was talking about. "Bean sprouts?"

"Just think a minute. Think of Sheila's baby."

Holly couldn't imagine it.

Then he started again, his reserve was crumbling. In his mind, he said Holly's name. Her name was an illumination, her name flared like smudge pots along a remote runway. Again he held up. Now it was his romantic notions which dizzied him with their complexity, or it was morphine which almost stole his erection. Holly seemed to recognize that he had moved ahead of sex, and she told him to concentrate on one thing. One thing.

He fucked her and let his mind rest.

In a moment, Willis jumped up. The window was blazing. Candle wax had puddled and ignited the jacquard curtains; even the window sash was catching, its old linseed paint snapping. The flames rose up both sides and across the top valance.

He went to the sink and turned open the tap. The water was off. Holly took her sweater and hit the flames with its little cuff, but it only fanned the blaze. In the dark, the golden frame was hypnotizing, and Holly stopped her efforts to stand beside Willis and watch. The fire threw a sheet of light across their bodies and they looked back and forth at one another with only a slight veil of modesty.

At last, Willis picked up a kitchen mat and rubbed it over the window frame, clockwise, as if he were dusting the furniture. The thick rug robbed the flames of oxygen and the window grew dark. The scorched wood released its immediate scent.

"Shit, that took off fast," Willis said. "This old paint—"

"You weren't there yet," she said. She pulled his hand to her bare waist, but he had lifted his jeans from the floor and was tugging them over his legs.

"Come on," she said.

Willis said, "Not here."

She tugged his sooty fingers.

"Jesus, girl." He peeled her hand off his wrist. "I'm sure someone saw that fire in the window. It was the fucking Fourth of July. They're dialing 911."

He drove her back to the duplex. He parked the car in his usual spot against the side of Rennie's house and he walked Holly over to her porch. Willis stopped dead in his tracks. He was eyeing something.

Some nights, a family of skunks congregated at the porch steps and Holly had to pick her way carefully. She looked for the skunks. She didn't see anything.

"What is it?" she said.

Willis rubbed the heel of his hand against the white clapboards. Then Holly saw the writing. Someone had spray-painted the side of her house. The metallic paint swirled in two-foot-high script.

Two silver words: "Size Queen."

The eerie pronouncement was repeated five times across the width of the house. Each letter *S* was meticulous, like a dollar sign. The sizeable *Q* had a slight flourish, its silver tail curled once around like a piglet's.

She pushed past Willis and went inside her house. He came after her and waited for her to scrub the palm of her hand over her face at the kitchen tap. The smell of burning wax clung to her. "Who would do that?" she asked. "Would Fritz do that? Is Fritz jealous?"

"Fritz would never do that."

"Are you sure?"

"He wouldn't do it. Fritz is an extension of me—"

"God, that's weird. That's what I mean. That's sick," she said.

"You're not listening. Fritz doesn't destroy property."

"And I do? I destroy property, right? Fuck you."

"Not what I'm saying."

"Well—"

"Your old man? Mr. Softee."

"I told you, it's *Carvel*. Not Mr. Softee. And Jensen's in India. He's on the other side of the world," she said.

"How do you know? How do you know what side of the world he's on now? You can't be sure. Where is that fuck-head? At this very minute?"

The idea disturbed Holly and she let Willis walk her into the bedroom and tip her onto the bed. He unfastened her layers of clothing. He promised that he would paint the clapboards. "At daybreak."

"Before people can see it," she said.

"Rennie's got a gallon of white-white in the shack. I'll roll it on thick as you want. I'll roll it until you tell me to stop—"

She was going along with him. He was making her laugh. He was saying the words out loud. The two silver words. He whispered the words against her ear.

"It's true," she said. "It's true, it's true, it's true."

Chapter Eleven

Rennie asked Holly to go with her to visit Château-sur-Mer. Holly had the afternoon free until four o'clock when she had to report to work. She had not seen Willis for a full week. After Willis had painted the side of her house, he disappeared, as if he, too, was shamed by the vandal's assumption. Holly wanted to show him that in the full sunlight the silver lettering bled through the layer of new paint. Holly agreed to accompany Rennie to the retirement community where they would meet Munro and have lunch. Lunch was a sales campaign and Rennie said that she didn't trust that all the meals would be as good.

Rennie told Holly, "Munro thinks I haven't paid attention to him. If I go there to look it over, I can make an educated decision against it. It looks better on paper if you log in the research and catalogue your protests. I will have made a legitimate survey of the place."

"They might make you sign something."

"I have to play their game."

"But once you're a player—"

"I'm a rat running through a maze, but I'm not coming out where they want me to come out."

Holly said, "Right, we'll go into the forest but we'll drop bread crumbs."

Holly saw she wasn't helping. Rennie was a nervous wreck. She walked across to Holly's place two times as she was dressing. "Should I wear my good clothes? Good clothes will prove I can still take care of myself, but I don't want to get gussied up. I don't want to be another satin doll at the doll museum. On the other hand, if I look drab, Munro will say that I'm losing interest in life, like someone who never gets out of her housedress."

Holly went next door and helped Rennie choose a nice wool jersey dress. She poked through Rennie's jewelry tray and found a necklace and brooch to soften the neckline. Rennie, still in her slip, sat on the edge of her bed. She let herself fall back on the mattress, her hands at her sides. "I can't stand charades," she said.

Holly said, "Just be yourself."

Rennie said, "You know that saying 'What doesn't kill me makes me stronger'?"

"I guess so."

"Well, that used to be true for me. I took my knocks. I developed a thick skin, but too much is too much," Rennie said.

Holly couldn't keep a serene distance; she fell back on the bed beside the older woman. Together they stared at the ceiling. Holly followed the crown molding as it turned the corner. Her fingers slid over the quilt and she squeezed Rennie's hand. Holly thought that Rennie's decision to visit the retirement center might indicate a little change of heart. Rennie didn't have the stamina she had appeared to have that first night when she burned up the floor plans. There were occasional days when Holly didn't see Rennie around the house at all, she must have been in her bed. Rennie seemed aware of the fact that she *looked* sick and tried to erase the notion with a fancy swear about the weather or a lighthearted spray of ridicule against Munro.

Rennie said, "I guess they're ready to ladle it out over there, we better be first in line. First served, first to finish, first excused."

"It's good to be on time where you're getting a tooth pulled. No sense postponing it," Holly told her.

Rennie finished dressing. Holly saw a little book on Rennie's night table. It was an old autograph book with a suede cover. Holly flipped it open and read some handwriting in a scratchy fountain pen. "Open the Gate! Open the Gate! Here comes Rennie, the Grad-u-ate." The fountain-pen ink was faded to a pale violet. She turned another page. "Do not throw rock at mouse and break precious vase."

Holly kept reading with fascination. She found a sing-song stanza excerpted from a poem:

> *Love seeketh not itself to please,*
> *Nor for itself hath any care,*
> *But for another gives its ease,*
> *And builds a Heaven in Hell's despair.*
> *So sung a little Clod of Clay*
> *Trodden with the cattle's feet—*

Rennie saw what Holly was reading and she snatched the little book out of her hand. "Do you mind? Don't you think I've got a secret or two?"

"Sure," Holly said. "Sorry." Holly recognized what Rennie was doing with that little book. She was just trying to hold on to everything. Just hold on to the threads.

On the drive over to Château-sur-Mer, Holly mentioned to Rennie that she had not seen Willis's car. Was it in the shop?

Rennie said, "Since when are you interested in cars?"

Holly said, "Shit."

"Willis has been doing a full shift at WASTEC. He's spending nights out on the *Tercel* with Carl Smith. Then, there's Debbie. Debbie takes up a lot of his time." Rennie wrinkled her nose; she kept her eyebrows arched, her cheeks puffed out, waiting for Holly to suffer a fit of pique. "Well?"

"Well, what?" Holly said. She wasn't going to take the bait.

"As if he needs *three* mothers," Rennie said.

"Which three mothers?"

"Me, Wydette, and, if the shoe fits—"

"Ready for lunch?" Holly changed the subject.

"If it's lobster Newburg, watch out. The cream sauce in these places is like library paste. It coats your throat for a week. Lobster should be served whole with all its whiskers."

"It won't be Newburg, will it?" Holly said, relieved the conversation had turned.

The driveway into Château-sur-Mer was neatly landscaped, the sidewalks edged meticulously in the precise way private mental hospitals keep their emerald lawns perfected, but there was always someone crying in a corner, someone sitting alone on a glider wringing her hands.

They met Munro at the sales office at Château-sur-Mer. He stood in a large foyer at the entrance to the main wing of the old mansion. The door was framed by full-length stained glass panels and the light streamed in, washing fruity colors over Munro's pinstripe suit. Munro was very solicitous of Holly, taking her coat off, supporting her sleeve as she withdrew her arm. He let her elbow ride over the tips of his fingers as he tugged her sleeve. He apologized to Holly for the recent behavior of his stepbrother. "He makes himself a pest, but don't worry. He's harmless."

Rennie said, "When that cast comes off—"

"He'll never have full use of that arm," Munro said. He turned to Holly. "I broke my collarbone when I was a kid. Fell off the monkey bars. I still have a knot right here." He tapped his finger against his lapel. Holly noticed his pinkie finger. A thick gold band set with a flat diamond the circumference of a thumbtack. She saw his expensive clothes; his suit wasn't off the rack. He looked ready to operate in some cutthroat executive exchange.

Inside the lavish administration building, there were several large urns of long-stemmed roses. The double-headed roses were oversized and dewy. Holly never saw so many roses. It was like the dressing room of a diva on opening night. Munro plucked two roses from the arrangement and offered one to his mother; he turned and gave the other rose to Holly, first passing the bud beneath her nostrils. He commanded her to inhale its fragrance. Holly sniffed the rose obediently before she could stop herself. Munro was patronizing her, plain and simple, but she couldn't ward it off. He was one step ahead of her, enjoying it.

A receptionist in a tight lavender sweater-dress announced their arrival. Holly watched Munro follow the woman's curves in a quick appraisal. The assistant director stood up from a deep mahogany table to greet them. "Dick Snyder," he said. It had a slimy ring. He shook Holly's hand, mistaking her for Rennie's daughter.

"Oh, I'm not her daughter," Holly said.

"You're not the daughter?" Dick Snyder said. He squinted at Holly for a fraction of a second, as if to rethread a needle.

After that, he made efforts to address her in conversation although he had dismissed her importance. He concentrated on Rennie and her son, seating them in mauve leather chairs at the giant table. The conference table reminded Holly of the time she sat down with her lawyer to fill out the divorce papers. These glossy table leaves in lawyers' offices never saw food, but Holly visualized a large family at the archetypal dinner table, its initial presentation, several course additions, up until some unexpected debacle.

Snyder began with a few simple statements that he believed would assure anyone. "Château-sur-Mer is a member of the American Association of Homes for the Aging—"

Rennie said. "What kind of membership is that? Does that rank up there with my Sierra Club?"

Snyder wasn't disturbed by her remark. "Well, let's see what you think. We'll look at the pictures. Pictures are worth a thousand words, isn't that the saying?"

Rennie said, "That's one we haven't heard before." She rolled her eyes.

He lifted a large, embossed photograph album from a stack. He opened the book to a full-color aerial photograph of the retirement complex. He started at the top of each laminated page and pushed his index finger down the margin, directing their attention to every detail. He discussed the heated swimming pool, pointing to the chrome ladders; he told them about the clubhouse with two separate lounges, game rooms, exercise rooms with treadmills and Stairmasters. The pavilion, the sunken theater, the library rooms with overstuffed chairs and hassocks so residents could elevate their feet while reading. "For important circulation," he said.

"Library circulation?" Rennie said.

Snyder lifted his face and grinned in her direction.

"Remember that for your next customer," Rennie told him.

The outdoor recreational facilities included tennis courts, grass and clay. Two boccie courts. Horseshoe courts.

Croquet court. "Croquet is getting to be a favorite, we might expand it to the side lawn—"

"What about shuffleboard?" Rennie asked.

He looked at her, trying to gauge her level of resentment. She might have had a serious interest in shuffleboard, but he already knew she was getting prickly.

Rennie stared down at the plastic-coated pages.

Holly understood the sales pitch. It was the same when you went to buy a car, the salesmen relied on the literature. Even preachers who know the word of the Lord, backward and forward, carry their leather-bound copies. If it's in writing, it increases in dimension.

Rennie's grand Victorian manse, with its rusty shutter hooks and peeling paint, made these new apartment interiors look as slick and unbelievable as the glossy perfume ads in fashion magazines. Snyder said, "Of course we offer Handymaid Services, Mini Bus Transportation, full parking. We have recreational-vehicle parking. Do you own a recreational vehicle? Many of our residents have travel homes—"

Munro said, "No, she doesn't travel that much. Not anymore."

Rennie nodded in agreement. "I really don't go an inch."

Snyder described every room in detail, ending his presentation with a description of the bathroom. "Tubs have grab bars. Shower stall has nonslip waffle texture. Towel bars with heat switch—"

Holly said, "Heated towels? Shit. Just like Leona."

The salesman was startled but he maintained his evenness.

Munro heard Holly's remark and he crossed his arms, tucking the palms of his hands under the armpits of his jacket as if he might have wanted to strike her. Snyder speeded up the presentation and showed them an entire book devoted to Château-sur-Mer's medical facilities. He called it "Guaranteed Life Care." It meant, quite simply, that there was always a bed reserved in the infirmary for each resident. "These are luxury quarters," he told them. "In health or sickness, luxury is a constant."

"I've got my living will. I won't need these fancy digs." Rennie announced.

Snyder nodded. "It's good to have a living will, Miss Hopkins, but sometimes people change their minds at the last minute. They want to keep going."

Rennie looked out the window at the fog coming in off the water, long, thick tails of it like polyester filling.

Holly picked up one of the application sheets from the table. It was a medical questionnaire of some kind. She began to read it halfway down the page.

D.   MOTOR CONTROL:
___ Dresses self: ___ Minimal assistance;
     ___ Total assistance
___ Feeds self: ___ Minimal assistance;
     ___ Total assistance

E.   CONTINENCE   Urinary: ___ Yes   ___ No
                  Fecal: ___ Yes   ___ No
     COMMENTS:

F.   MENTAL STATUS:
___ Oriented, alert
___ Confused, depressed
___ Suspicious, combative
___ Other

G.   LOCOMOTION:
___ Ambulant   ___ Semi-ambulant   ___ Cane
___ Walker   ___ Wheelchair   ___ Bedfast

Rennie saw the questionnaire too. "The end of the line for the Little Red Trolley," she said to Holly.

Munro collected the sheet of paper from Holly's hand and brushed her wrist back into her lap. He squeezed her hand, keeping it in her lap. "Behave yourself," he told her.

The tour included a visit to an occupied apartment. Snyder explained that the gentleman who lived in the unit received a decrease in his monthly maintenance fee by agreeing to show his apartment. His unit had a spectacular view, dead square at the elbow of the Cliff Walk, right above the historic old Tea House Pagoda perched on a ledge of rock. If it wasn't for this selling point, Snyder might not have bothered with the bristly resident who followed them from room to room. "Closet space galore," Snyder said.

"Can anyone reach the top shelf? Want to try it? Who wants to volunteer?" the stranger said.

"Waste disposal and trash compactor. Built in," Dick Snyder said.

"I need a compactor for my S.S. Pierce sardine tin. I don't have the strength to crush it. Christ."

Rennie started to laugh at the man's bitter remarks.

"Everyone has full cable hookup."

"*I* should be Ted Turner," the man said, with great theater, as if he had recited the remark in the same way, every day, for months. "We were born too soon, weren't we?" he said to Rennie. "Before fiber optics. Before satellites." This, too, was well rehearsed.

"What did you do for a living?" Rennie asked him.

"I ran a little paper mill over in Westerly. The paper went to Connecticut Valley Envelope Company, exclusively. They produce window envelopes for banks, other banking supplies."

"My son is in the banking business, he probably uses those window envelopes, don't you, Munro?"

"No. That would be regular bank operations. My department does not use window envelopes."

"He's got watermarks on his stationery. A big shot," Rennie said about Munro.

"You're telling me," the man said. He stepped up closer to Rennie. He looked at her. "Just who am I talking to?" he said to her. "Do you mind if I take a closer look?"

Rennie was trying to gauge the absurd question.

The man went over to a desk drawer and took out a magnifying glass, a large blurry lens with a long SureGrip handle. It was the kind of tool poor-sighted individuals might use to read the *New York Times* or the *Wall Street Journal.* The man waved the glass up and down Rennie, then kept it six inches from her face. He squinted through its warped circle. He saw her.

"You're an attractive woman."

"Listen to this," Rennie said.

"I'm not a pushover. I'm particular," he told her. "Your eyes are nice."

"In a coon's ass," Rennie said. "Did you have cataract surgery? Did they leave the stitches in too long?"

The group laughed in nervousness, a simultaneous release of disguised emotions, almost like something in an Up with People grande finale. It was all that was necessary and they left the man's apartment to go inspect the dining hall.

Once or twice, Holly noticed the way Rennie studied a detail, as if she was really looking through a window into another life. More than usual, Rennie appeared physically frail. Her ankle wobbled on the uneven pavers and she didn't recover her balance as quickly as she might have. The next moment she was trying to prove her pep, stooping to pick up a pine cone and sailing the sticky pod at a catbird perched along the second-floor eaves. Holly was surprised to see the eccentric man at his window. He was pantomiming a scene, jerking an invisible rope around his neck, as if struggling with a noose. Snyder guided Rennie ahead. Holly kept watching. It was a disturbing sight because the man didn't stop when they acknowledged him. He wasn't interested in the audience reaction. He stood at his window and jerked the invisible rope; his tongue protruded, waggled for air.

They stopped inside the building that housed the formal dining rooms. They waited before a velveteen signboard that listed the luncheon entrees.

"It's all so programmed." Rennie turned to Munro. "I don't always eat at the same hour. I don't rise and shine *with the crowd*."

"Someday you will appreciate that, you'll be grateful for a schedule," Munro told her.

"You're stampeding me," Rennie said.

Snyder was becoming impatient. He didn't see a sale looming on the horizon any longer and he excused himself when someone called him away.

Munro turned to Holly. "Could I see you for a minute?"

He walked into the empty dining room and turned around to see if Holly was coming in there.

"What does he want?" Holly asked Rennie.

"He just wants to complain about me to someone. Go ahead."

Rennie sat down in a wing chair and Holly went into the dining room. Munro pulled her wrist until she was out of view of his mother. They walked behind a big table already set with a new white cloth, flatware, and bowls of low-fat imitation butter pats. "I thought you were going to help me," he said.

"I never said I was helping you—"

"Do you have any common sense? She's a sick woman."

Holly picked up a gleaming silver-plate salt shaker and turned it over. The white grains started to sift onto the white tablecloth. She pulled it up and unscrewed its cap. Again, she poured it out. The salt spilled, an instant gritty mound. She lifted the pepper shaker. Munro grabbed her wrist.

"You're just what I thought. A nut case. Listen to me. My wife doesn't want her living with us. You understand? I'm between a rock and a hard place."

Holly didn't believe that Munro was worried about his wife; he looked like someone who knew how to juggle women. Perhaps he had a wife *and* a lover and he didn't also need his mother. She was having these skimming thoughts and before she knew it, he was cupping the ends of her shoulder-length hair. He was crushing her hair in his hands.

"Mercy," he said. "Just give us a little mercy."

Who was he talking for? He might have meant, give a mother and her son some help, but Munro had edged closer in a sudden wave of heat that made her spring backward, out of his way.

"What are you trying here?" she said.

"Tell me if you aren't interested."

"What?"

"Don't rush. Just tell me if I'm wrong. I've seen you—"

He meant that he had seen her, a woman alone in her spare arrangements. Maybe he knew about Willis. She studied his fingers for any trace of the silver spray paint. His fingers were clean and pink. He watched her carefully. Perhaps he was thinking she was pathetic and just a bit of trouble to get around.

"You're just as crazy as your brother," she said, testing

it out. She hated herself for her sudden ridicule of Willis.

Munro took her elbow and walked her out to where Rennie was sitting. Residents were beginning to show up for lunch, and Rennie was watching the parade of strangers. Most of the crowd looked vigorous and at ease. Then a row of oldsters arrived in wheelchairs. Two stooped ladies hobbled through the lobby with aluminum walkers.

"We have to skip lunch," Holly said. "I feel sick."

Rennie brightened. "You probably caught something here. These places are hotbeds for germs."

Holly pulled Rennie out of the dining room. Dick Snyder was missing from sight and he didn't try to retrieve them. Munro stood on the sidewalk and watched as Holly put Rennie in the car.

"It was very educational," Rennie told her son. "It was good hands-on experience." Rennie adjusted the sun visor and leaned back in the seat.

Munro ignored his mother and told Holly, directly, that he appreciated her help. He would be in *touch*. He was smiling at her, but she didn't let on that she felt his threat.

Holly drove back to the house. She stopped on the road and reached into her mailbox. She found an airmail letter from Jensen. She tore the frail tissue envelope while the car idled. Inside the envelope was a tiny bean with an ivory stopper. She tugged it open expecting the usual elephant carvings, but the tiny ivory shavings were startling. The glistening flecks of tusk were perfectly carved phalluses. Miniature bones with swollen heads. "That lewd creep," she said.

Rennie pressed her fingertip against Holly's palm to lift one of the carvings up to her eye. "Cobra," Rennie said.

"You mean these are snakes? Are you sure?" Maybe Rennie was correct. Whatever it was, Jensen was continuing his harangue from abroad. The flecks of horn were difficult to collect and return to the little bean. Rennie watched as Holly pulled her fingertip across the tiny opening until each flake was deposited. Then Holly walked Rennie up the steep porch stairs. She waited for Rennie to rest and catch her breath before she put her key in the door. Rennie weaved slightly, like someone three sheets to the wind, but she was just exhausted. Holly told her, "Maybe you should eat something. It's two o'clock."

"Too tired to eat."

"I'll put the tea kettle on anyway." She walked over to Rennie's big white stove and turned the knob. Nothing happened.

"Matches are in the can," Rennie told her.

Holly struck a match and dabbed it at the black circle until the gas ignited one side, then it traveled around, making a complete halo of blue flame. "I have to be at work in an hour. It's my turn to do Pizza Night."

"It's your turn? Well, go ahead. Go home. You need to retrieve your wits for something like that. Pizza Night."

Rennie sat down in her chair. She was staring at the afternoon sunshine coming in the fanlight, her eyes losing focus. She wasn't falling asleep; she seemed to be studying an internal thread that Holly couldn't gauge.

Holly gave Rennie a mug of tea and a bottle of pickled herring. Rennie couldn't twist the rusted cap. Holly tried it. Then Holly found a bottle of Scotch in the pantry and poured one golden inch into a juice glass for herself. "Want some of this?" she asked Rennie. Rennie declined.

"Have some herring," Rennie said.

Holly sat down across from Rennie and used a fork to stab the contents of the bottle. Together, they ate the cold, winey fish from scalloped Spode saucers.

Chapter Twelve

The same morning Rennie toured Château-sur-Mer, Willis went into Fall River a second time with Fritz. Fritz was supposed to pick up a fax machine at Circuit City and deliver it to Showalter's InstyPrint franchise. It was a regular courier job, but Showalter asked to see Willis. "It's some kind of power meeting," Fritz said. "You don't have to show up."

"I'll hear it," Willis said. "Just don't forget me."

"I'm back in ten minutes, okay? I'll turn around and deadhead right back here to get you."

"Don't speed. Don't get stopped in this town. They red tape every moving violation. It's Mayberry, New England."

"I know that," Fritz said.

Willis felt a little tingle in the soles of his feet coming into Fall River. It was the town in which Wydette had choked to death and he often went the long way around to miss that stretch of Route 24 coming into the city. His breathing was halting in frozen drifts. They drove past the old knitting mills, big empty textile factories where every sweater he had worn in childhood had been purchased discounted.

Fritz let Willis off at Showalter's house and he took Rennie's car to deliver the fax machine at the franchise. Showalter met Willis at the door and cupped Willis's elbow, leading him across the foyer. The hand on his elbow felt spidery, a slight yet perceptible clawing. He shrugged his arm loose.

"*You* are the missing piece of my puzzle," Showalter told him.

"How is that?"

"You're a capable person. You're switched on."

"Is that right?" Willis said. "Are we talking about parrots again or that four-eyes operation?"

"You're no nonsense. Just what I want."

Willis waited until Showalter was finished dishing out the applesauce.

Showalter sat down at a long desk. The wide desktop had buttery leather veneer embossed with straight lines of glittery gold fleurs-de-lis. There was nothing on the desk. It looked big as a double bed.

"Let's go back to these stereoscopes."

"Let's go back?"

"It turns out Federico looks a little scrawny. Fritz should try to bulk up. After his principal asset, he's a little too skinny for someone's normal taste—"

"I'm not interested in that line of work." Willis stood up.

"That's fine, that's fine. Don't get me wrong. I've got something else for you. Some exotics sitting in Fairfield."

"Connecticut? All the way down there?"

"Just a couple hours from here, really. You'll take my vehicle."

"What's wrong with my car?"

"These are big containers. The birds are sizable. The world's largest—"

"Ostrich?"

Showalter's eyes pinched shut then popped opened again; his face softened, as if he was suddenly reminded of a realm of innocence he had lost sight of. He told Willis, "Not ostrich. These are parrots. A proven pair. Together they're worth more than twenty-four thousand. Hyacinth macaws. Incredible blue, like lapis."

Willis knew about lapis. Rennie had used lapis when she made jewelry. She had turned out a lot of souvenir junk, but once in a while she made something on order, something special with semiprecious stones.

"Okay. Let's say I hire you to get the birds extracted and delivered to an address in Jamaica Plain?"

"Extracted? What do you mean, extracted?"

"My ex-wife has the pair. She was in on this in the beginning, now she's sold her half back to me."

"She sold it back, so what's the problem?"

"Let me say it this way. *She* is sometimes a problem."

"Just one thing. Are these her birds?"

"They are no longer her property."

"If they aren't hers, why does she have a hold of them?"

"You can ask her that question yourself. Want to try it?"

"I will for four hundred."

"Three."

"Shit, you're going to chizz me for one bill? Four is my payout. I take even numbers."

Showalter lifted the pleated shade until the afternoon light fell in a sheet across the room. "How are you with women?" Showalter said.

Willis thought it was a loaded question. It was pointing at him.

"Are you good with women?" Showalter asked again.

Willis tried to deflect it, but he didn't know how, so he ended up saying just about anything. "I get along."

"Is that right?"

"You asked me."

"Do you talk your way, or fuck your way?"

Willis looked at Showalter. Was it a matter of personal curiosity or just business? "I can do both at the same time while drinking a glass of water," Willis said.

Showalter looked tickled.

Willis didn't actually wish to amuse this fellow.

"Cash up front," Willis said.

"I don't think so."

"How do I know you won't walk the check?"

"Is *trust* such a dirty word?" Showalter said.

Willis didn't visualize four hundred dollars. He wouldn't subject himself to these cockeyed moments with Showalter unless he imagined a big deal. He saw a cornucopia of brilliant Amazons and maybe some four-eyed photography to cash in. Enough for Rennie's deathbed cookie jar. Only some big cash could get rid of Munro. Maybe with twenty grand Munro could be banished from Easton Way. Willis stood up to leave.

Showalter placed the heel of his hand on Willis, right at the small of his back. It couldn't be confused for anything but what it was. He told Willis, "I don't like to hear no." He grinned at Willis as if he had wheels turning.

The doorbell chimed and Fritz had walked inside. Fritz tagged up with the conversation. "I guess No is No."

Showalter told Fritz, "You should be downstairs in the studio."

"I should be downstairs? Right now?" Fritz said.

"That's right."

Fritz shrugged and looked at Willis. Fritz followed Showalter into the elevator. Willis didn't like seeing Fritz hijacked and he walked after his friend, into the open cage.

He shifted his legs. He felt the elevator rock side to side, an unsteady pendulum.

When the elevator stopped, they were greeted by a young model, a girl around seventeen or eighteen. The girl had a hard look despite her young age. Her bleached hair was perfectly trimmed in a nice bowl cut, revealing her pale throat and the ashy nape of her neck. She was wearing swimwear from the 1950s, a two-piece sailor suit with a short pleated skirt.

"These the guys?" she said.

"We're in negotiations," Showalter said.

"In what?" she said.

"Shut up," he told her. "Give us a second."

"Who's she?" Willis said.

"That's Miss Ingersoll."

"Ingersoll? Sounds like something you put on an itch. Ingersoll. Sounds like an analgesic ointment."

"For a hemorrhoid flare-up," Fritz said.

Miss Ingersoll didn't seem jostled by Willis's attack on her name. Showalter went over to a table and he jimmied a magazine from a tall stack. He handed the magazine to Willis. "Read this one-page summary. It will only take a minute of your time. It tells you all about the 3-D industry. It's got the specifications. All you need is one camera and a slide bar, or you can use two cameras set up just a little bit apart. All an audience needs is a handheld viewer, or if you want to project slides, like we have here, you have to have a silver lenticular screen and some polarized glasses. Not too big an initial investment. This tells you how easy. It has some nice stories about the history. Did you know that the movie star Harold Lloyd was into it?"

"Harold Lloyd?"

"He took shots of Marilyn Monroe and Bogart, Dick

Powell. He's got one of Roy Rogers and Trigger. Real as life."

Fritz said, "Was Trigger live or stuffed?"

"What are you asking me?" Showalter said.

"Was Trigger live? Because you can't tell in a still photograph if the horse is stuffed or not."

Willis took the magazine and leafed through it. It was a mail-order catalogue. He picked up another magazine from the table called *Infrared Nudes in 3-D*.

"Is this why you're here?" Willis said to the girl. "You want to be an infrared nude?"

"What's it to you?"

"Nothing to me," Willis said.

"So why did you ask me? You don't like looking at 3-D hot pix?"

"Never tried it."

"It makes people dizzy. It's not for pussies."

Willis said, "The mouth on you."

"I've never had any complaints."

"Really? No one offered his advice until now? Shit, can I submit a clue?" Willis said. "You look like you need a lesson."

"A riding lesson," Fritz said.

"Ever have a saddle sore?" Willis said, testing her resilience.

She whispered to him, "You think I like to hang with Showalter? He has a tube up his prick so piss can flow. He has to fill up his piss bag. It's taped to his ankle. He has to pull out the tube to have a fuck."

Willis looked back at the little chorine with a wave of queasy fascination. He didn't know whether to believe her.

She registered his disbelief. "I'm telling the truth. I've seen everything now," she said. "Just about everything."

Showalter was moving around the room setting things up. The slight hobble in his gait might have been explained. Showalter was trying to make the studio set look like a boardwalk. He had a blue sheet suspended from the ceiling, the Atlantic shore, and some big cardboard cutouts of Atlantic City and Merv Griffin's gambling resort. The cutouts were promo items he picked up from somewhere. He was draping the blue fabric the way he wanted, so the swirls in the material didn't overtake the foreground subjects. He left the room for a minute and went to a freezer in a corner of the cellar. He came back with a cherry Popsicle and handed it to Miss Ingersoll.

She peeled the wrapper off the treat and waited in front of the camera. "Go ahead," she said. "Let's start. I'm only eating just one of these Popsicles. These bother my fillings."

Willis told Fritz, "I'm saying my goodbyes, are you ready?"

Fritz looked back at the girl. He shrugged.

She saw there was going to be another delay and she went to sit in an office chair, slapping her knees open and closed in noisy swipes. Her Popsicle had started to sweat, but she didn't suck it.

"We can't do the shot," Fritz told her.

"What's this now?" the girl said. "I've been waiting here for an hour."

"There's been a mix-up," Fritz announced to the room.

Showalter wasn't listening to Fritz. "This is not a mix-up," Showalter said. "It's a red-letter day. You'll leave here with a wad of cash. Call it what you want. Afternoon delight. It's a natural exploration—"

Willis turned around, bumping into a coffee table. A stack of CDs clattered over. He was leaving the room.

"Hold on, beautiful," Showalter said with a great deal of style. His words sparkled.

Willis said, "Hey, dreamboat, why don't you accept the facts? I'm not changing my socks." Willis looked back at the man.

Showalter was holding a gun on Willis.

Willis didn't expect to see a gun.

Showalter looked refreshed by the little wave of peril he had released upon the room.

Willis pulled himself together and faced off with the man. He watched the oversized pistol, its muzzle, a small dark circle attractive as a keyhole.

"Federico," Showalter said. "You're the dresser."

Fritz said, "I'm the what? The dresser? Shit, I didn't sign on for this. I don't think so—"

"Shut up. Walk over there and unbutton your friend. Nice and easy. We don't want to pinch anything."

Fritz didn't move.

Willis started to walk toward Showalter.

Showalter said, "Now just wait there, Willis. Think. I'm making a formal invitation—"

Willis kept coming.

"Freeze," Showalter said. He laughed. A patient, schoolmaster chuckle.

Willis looked at the man holding the gun. He was sizing him up one final time; it wasn't an easy appraisal. Willis was making hairline adjustments in his calculations when the gun went off.

Willis hollered. Showalter shrieked with amusement. Miss Ingersoll sat where she was, cupping one hand under her dripping Popsicle. Willis rubbed his waist where a paintball had exploded in a messy red circle, his abdominal muscles stinging. The gelatinous red dye felt greasy in the palm of his hand. He rubbed his hand on his jeans.

Willis went after Showalter and knocked him against the table. A stack of mailing labels fanned across the floor. Willis took the paintball gun from Showalter's hand.

"I can't believe it," he told Fritz, "this double-breasted scumbag paintballed me." He pulled the gun up to his face to read the grip. "With a Splatmaster." Willis aimed the gun at the end of the room and pulled the trigger three times. The paint cartridges hit the silver screen and burst into bloody chrysanthemums.

Showalter groaned about the cost of his equipment.

"Tough shit," Willis told him. Willis tossed the gun on the table and whacked Showalter halfheartedly with his cast.

Fritz called out, "Don't use your sore arm—"

"Use the other arm," Miss Ingersoll instructed.

He had the popular vote. Willis switched arms and struck Showalter again with the side of his fist. He stood back. "You marked me." Willis started laughing.

The others took their cue. Their laughter came in peaks and valleys, a sinister choir of edgy, mistrusting relief. Showalter tried to laugh loudest, over their trio, until Willis pushed him away and the older man fell to his knees and curled into the duck-and-cover position.

The girl followed Fritz and Willis into the elevator. They rode upstairs. Willis felt his pulse grinding into his fingertips. His broken wrist was throbbing. Miss Ingersoll sat down on the big leather sofa and dialed a telephone number. No one exchanged pleasantries. They heard the elevator cable whine and the cage sank. He didn't want another round with Showalter so Willis took Fritz out to the street.

Fritz stepped onto the rocker plate of the InstyPrint Econoline and slid behind the wheel. Willis got in beside him and unfolded a piece of paper with the address in

Fairfield. Fritz followed the urban streets and rolled it onto the freeway.

The truck was stenciled all over, front and back, with the InstyPrint logo and local telephone numbers. Willis sat in the passenger seat thumbing through a booklet of business-card samples he had found on the seat. He told Fritz, "Maybe you can duck out of the porn biz, my friend."

"Give me a break."

"Federico, I hardly knew ye."

"Green, green is my valley."

"You're set for life as long as it rises."

"Look, this was brainy stuff. It was 3-D. Like he said, they shoot it twice. They move the camera on a slide bar. They get two exposures sixty-five millimeters apart. It's all scientific. Showalter's got state-of-the-art equipment. That paint gun, that's one of those survival-game weapons. Looked pretty real."

"It was real, all right. It was a real mess. Are you happy with yourself?"

"Shit. The hours are good."

"What about Miss Ingersoll. What is she like?"

"She would have been good. We'll never know."

"Tell me, you could do it in front of the camera, come home, and still look it in the eye?" Willis had a straight face.

"Money makes it numb and happy."

"Tell the truth. You don't mind that guy?"

Fritz told him, "Gene is all right. He's not mental or anything. Some of these porn kings are criminal. Like last week, we saw a film where they had this big roll of fly-paper."

"Excuse me?"

"You heard me. That stuff could rip your skin off. That

stuff could tear the lace curtain right off its rod. It was some
kind of torture textile. They had these boys right on a big
sheet of it."

"You're kidding? Flypaper?"

"There are some weird people on the planet," Fritz
said, calming down.

"Showalter wanted you to recline naked on a sheet of
flypaper?"

"Never. I'm telling you, Gene isn't so bad. Only once,
he had a piece of rawhide. A long stick of rawhide like you
would feed to a dog. Rawhide has flex, it snaps. Gene
started smacking my ass. He wanted my ass to look bright
and rosy."

"Shit. Well, did it get rosy?"

Fritz braked hard for a car that was just creeping. They
were going fifty and the truck skated in tight swerves side
to side until they twirled a half donut on the gravel shoulder. Fritz pushed it back into gear and merged again with
the traffic. He didn't miss a beat.

Willis took another breath. He said, "You're crazy to
model in the first place. Next it might be that noose business. You've heard of that?"

"I've heard of it."

"What if they forget to loosen the rope in time. That
could step right over the line into manslaughter. That
would be a nice snapshot."

"You don't have to tell me. It's in the papers. Their
shorts around their ankles."

"How about this idea? We collect these birds and see
what we can do with them."

"Interesting revision," Fritz told Willis.

"Why should we be the middleman?"

"We don't have to negotiate with Fall River?"

"Every time we go in there it's *Let's Make a Deal*. Curtain number one, curtain number two. Fuck that."

"All right. We'll face that bridge another time."

"Look, you aren't listening. We burned that bridge. Fritz? It's torched, you get it?"

∽⊗∽⊗∽

"What happened to you?" the woman asked Willis. One side of his shirt was blood red where the stain had expanded above his breast pocket.

"Your ex shot me with one of his expensive squirt guns."

"An accident?" she said.

"He sighted the shot."

"From him, that's a compliment," she said.

"I figured it was," he told her.

She was dressed in white leather jeans, like a go-go ghost from *Shindig*. She showed them through the first floor of her big half-furnished ranch and into a chilly pool house in the back. Vapor lifted from the heated lanes, giving the space a forlorn mist.

"I keep them out here by the pool. Maybe you could just drown them."

Willis studied the large cage. It was empty except for a huge whiskey barrel.

"That's their next box," she told him. Her words alarmed the occupants and one bird emerged from the barrel. The bird faced Willis, a creature so vibrant and showy it couldn't possibly exist outside of dreams. A dazzling blue parrot, over three feet in length. Its ultramarine feathers were the intense color of bridesmaid chiffon; its long azure tail extended below its perch like crisp first-place ribbons. Willis had never seen anything like it. The bird's feathers were not an earthly tone, and when the second bird emerged from the barrel, the blue aura was multiplied, creating a small expanse of heaven.

But when Willis reached into the cage to transfer the birds to a carton, one of the macaws bit his hand. The bite drew blood.

"Shit. It's wild. Showalter didn't say these were carnivorous."

Fritz looked at Willis's hand. In the fleshy web between his thumb and forefinger there was a peculiar incomplete triangle, a beak imprint, bleeding. Willis sucked the wound clean.

"She has three hundred pounds of biting pressure per square inch," the woman said.

Willis looked at the woman.

"That's more than I have," she said. She grinned at Willis.

He smiled in return, his dimple fat as a rosehip.

Willis could see that the divorcée might be walking some kind of high wire between the past and present. She left the room and came back with a plate of tuna salad sandwiches. "My guests didn't show up," she said. "There's a ton of these."

Fritz looked at the plate and chose a fat square.

Willis declined, rubbing the blood from his lips with the cuff of his jacket. He picked up a plush velour towel from a pool chair and wrapped it around his right hand. Then he put his plastered arm into the cage and started batting the birds with his cast until one of them was subdued and he pulled it through the door and slammed it into a box. He went after the mean one three times again. The macaw pecked at his plaster cast, leaving powdery gouges. Willis decided it wasn't worth it.

"Don't give up," she said.

Willis reached into the cage again.

Fritz said, "I don't know, sweetheart. That one there is like a lobster."

"Don't call me that," Willis said.

"What?"

"Don't call me sweetheart." Willis pulled his arm out of the cage and let his eyes rest on Fritz until Fritz acknowledged his warning. He walked around the cage in a mock contest with the parrot. It turned to face him at every corner.

"If you don't take it, I'll have to shoot it," the woman said.

The longer they waited there, the more this woman was leaking out her feelings.

She told Willis, "You're taking her mate, you know. Maybe she'll die of heartbreak."

"Can that happen to it? Heartbreak?"

"It never happened to you?" she said.

Willis couldn't help smiling at her tough remark. He said, "So, I have the male here, and the *mean* one is the female?

"That's right."

"Yeah, that sounds natural."

"The female is worth more because she's the egg layer, but either way, you lose half what they're worth when you break the pair—"

An alarm system suddenly erupted with a brutally loud horn. Willis stood up. He looked around the room.

"Is that your security system? Sounds like a steamship."

"It's the wind. The wind has been triggering it. They put sensors on the panes. The glass vibrates in the wind and sets it off. It's nobody. It's like a joke. They're supposed to come out and fix it today. We had an appointment before lunch."

Willis understood the plate of sandwiches. They were for the electricians. He went over to the woman and picked up the platter. He lifted a fluffy taupe-colored square and he pressed it into his mouth with the heel of his hand. He chewed it. It had a rich, cold taste.

The woman's eyes opened wide, but they adjusted. She let one side of her mouth curl higher than the other side.

They left Fairfield with the single macaw. Willis was driving the truck, testing its acceleration. "Not bad for such a boxy shape," he said. He was feeling better heading east again. He started singing. Rosemary Clooney's moment in the sun. *"Come on to my house—my house—I'll give you my wage and a bird in a cage—"*

Fritz went in the back of the truck and cut a hole in the carton with his knife. He peered at the bird. "It looks freaked," Fritz said.

"Of course it's freaked. Anything this fucking beautiful is doomed. To begin with, it's on the wrong continent. It's in exactly the *wrong world*. How would that feel to you?"

"That would be a bad feeling."

"What turn of luck do you think it's having?"

They drove into Fall River to pick up Rennie's car. Willis called Showalter from a pay phone two blocks away from his house.

"I've got one bird, singular," Willis told Showalter.

"I know. She called me to say you couldn't manage the other bird."

"That other one wasn't user-friendly," Willis said.

Showalter said, "And how about her? How was she acting?"

Willis said, "She was perfectly reasonable."

"Reasonable? By whose definition?" Showalter said.

"You had to be there," Willis said. "Listen. I'm making a change in plans. I'll let you know exactly what I need when I figure it out." He hung up the phone.

Willis waited for Fritz to start the sedan. Fritz pulled away from the curb and Willis tailgated in the InstyPrint truck. He lay on the horn as they rolled past Showalter's big place. They rode hopscotch all the way back to Newport. When they arrived at Easton Way, Rennie had not yet returned from Château-sur-Mer. Willis lifted the weathered two-by-four that sashed the double doors of Rennie's shack. He parked the InstyPrint truck inside the tight interior. He took the carton with the macaw over to Holly's porch, and when she didn't answer the door, he got her key from Nicole's pegboard and walked right inside.

Chapter Thirteen

Holly rinsed the fishy saucers and left them on the drain board. She helped Rennie upstairs. Rennie said she wanted a nap, but Holly recognized the symptoms of a physical collapse. Rennie got into her bed and tried to cross her arms, but her arms were too weak and they fell to her sides. Holly tucked her in and placed a glass of water on the end table. Plain tap water didn't seem like enough. Holly wondered if she should get Rennie some Gatorade. Gatorade had electrolytes. What exactly these electrolytes did, Holly didn't understand, but Rennie seemed like a candidate. Finally, she left Rennie and walked over to the duplex. Willis was waiting on the porch.

"Where have you been all week?" she said.

He told her, "Lost without you."

He had said the right thing, but she pretended to ignore it. She asked him again, "What have you been up to?" Willis was much taller than she was, she had to lift her face.

She liked the sensation.

A few weeks earlier, she wouldn't have liked it at all.

She checked her accelerating thoughts. After one week, her desire was distilled into a toxic elixir. She felt its poison inebriation. She didn't like his brush-off for a week; she had even begun to think it was for the best, it was a stay of execution, but maybe something important had happened. She was ready to hear it.

Willis looked overly alert. He was smiling, then he relaxed his mouth. He smiled again. It was something ridiculous. He looked like a child elected by his ball team to report a broken window. "God. What is it?" she asked him.

"I need to ask you a favor," he said.

"What kind of favor?" She watched his smile crimp at the corners and diminish, until his lips were flat, and she sensed that whatever he was asking, it wasn't something insignificant. They stood inches apart. His jeans were smeared with something, maybe it was brake fluid. She noticed that the color of his eyes, this close, had the intensity of lilacs. She shouldered past Willis and walked into her kitchen.

She pulled her coat off and turned around.

It was perched on the back of a dinette chair, facing her, the ruffled blue pneuma of a South American god. A huge parrot with gentian feathers. The bird trembled. It paced back and forth on her kitchen chair, its great claws working to keep it balanced on the narrow perch. Its face had gaudy yellow eye rings, circles of naked skin around deep black pupils. There was another naked strip outlining its lower mandible, a bright lemon clown-smile painted on. Its huge beak was grinding; it bit the cushioned back of the chair, tearing a hole in the vinyl cover. The bird eyed Holly and shivered as if its nerves were shattered.

"My god," she said. "What in the world—"

"It's a macaw. It's the biggest breed. A hyacinth."

"A hyacinth macaw? It's unbelievable."

"Can you keep it for me?" Willis said. "Just for a day or two?" Willis knocked his forearm against the bird's breast until it climbed onto his cast. "I can't keep it in Rennie's house while they're looking for it."

"Don't tell me. It's stolen?"

"I *rescued* this bird."

"It's a hot bird?"

"Look, do you need a Beltone? I said I rescued it."

"I don't know anything about parrots. I can't keep this bird here. He'll wreck stuff. Look at that chair."

"I'm finding a cage. Fritz is on it right now. A bird like this needs a big cage, so it might take us a little time."

"Someone needs a cage," she told Willis.

"You really feel that way?" He looked at her. "I'm fucking crushed."

She didn't answer him. He seemed to know that her feelings were running amok. Holly looked at the bird on Willis's arm. The bird had stopped shivering. It moved onto Willis's shoulder, biting the collar of his thermal undershirt, its strong beak puncturing the binding. Willis freed his shirt and shifted the bird back onto the chair. It walked back and forth on the chair, then halted beside Holly. It turned its face sideways and stared at Holly with one eye. The macaw seemed to recognize that it was central in their negotiations. In turn, Holly peered at the bird; the macaw jerked its head up and down in mock regurgitation. It enjoyed claiming the center of attention.

Willis said, "It's hand-fed and really tame. Its flight feathers are clipped so it can't really fly. It's worth about thirteen grand at least. It has a mate, together they're worth twice that much. Breeder pairs get a price."

"It has a mate?" Holly was stalled on that information.

"I'm in the driver's seat. This fellow Showalter has the female down in Connecticut. He's going to ride over here and ask me about the male."

"You were supposed to deliver this male bird? Where? To a pet store?"

"I think it eats sunflower seeds." He was trying to maintain a counterfeit level of expertise to enlist her to his side, but he didn't have his information.

Holly looked at the two of them. Gorgeous primitives, feathered or not. "You don't even know what it eats? You take a pet without knowing the first thing—"

"This is not a pet. This is a magnificent animal."

"No kidding."

"I'm going to sell it—"

"Not from here," she said.

"Rennie needs cash."

"Does Rennie know about this bird?"

"Maybe it's not for sale. Maybe I've fallen for it."

The bird voided a milky circle on the floor. Holly would have to find newspapers. Holly thought of Elliot Tompkins, the don at Saint George's who was a trustee of the Norman Bird Sanctuary. He might tell her what to do about a giant macaw. The bird was tearing plastic strips from the chair and flinging them in all directions, then plucking loose the polyester batting from the chair cushion. It wasn't an attempt at nesting but a studious deconstruction of the very thing it rested on. It didn't seem to recognize that if it chewed through its perch it might fall straight to the floor.

Holly's stomach muscles were hurting. Maybe it was the herring she had eaten at Rennie's, but she knew it was Willis. When he stood near her, within a few inches, she felt her abdominal wall ache; her pelvic sling became suddenly tensed and heated. She recognized every sign of it. Then the bird emitted its first shriek; it was celebratory, pleasurably abrupt, wild. It stood on one foot and stretched open its huge wing, a glorious fan of serrated cobalt.

Holly sat down at the kitchen table. She watched the parrot pace until it stopped to preen, drawing its hooked beak down an individual feather. She opened the vegetable bin in her refrigerator and found a wizened ear of sweet corn. Willis broke it in half and offered it to the parrot. The bird stood on one foot and held the cob in the other claw. He plucked the kernels, sending most of it around the room. Then Willis brought the bird into the bathroom where it could be confined. Holly lowered the shower-curtain rod so it could have a perch, but the bird was too heavy and the rod collapsed.

Willis was reciting suggestions. He seemed comfortable giving her orders. The shower curtain was wet and difficult to reorganize on its pole. Willis gave her minimal assistance; then, he lifted the rod off her shoulders and jammed it back tight. He went into the kitchen and carried the marred chair into the bathroom. Willis transferred the bird to the back of the chair, where it clutched the messy vinyl backing. Holly closed the bathroom door.

"What if I need to use the toilet?" she said.

"I don't think it will bite your ass, if that's what you mean. Just watch your fingers."

"I'm not going in there."

"You'll burst."

She looked at him hard. She took a dish towel from a door knob and folded it square. "I'm late for work," she said. "I have to thaw the pizza dough. I'm behind sched-ule." She left the house. As she backed her Toyota down the drive, she saw Willis through the window at her kitchen sink. The lights were burning. It was a strange sensation to leave someone in the duplex when usually it was empty.

⊙⊙⊙⊙⊙

After finishing her shift at Saint George's, she drove over to Warwick Mall. She looked through racks of bathing suits at Jordan Marsh. After that, she pushed a cart through the twenty-four-hour Star Market. She waited as long as she could and finally she came back to her house. Willis had departed, but when she looked into the bathroom she saw that the bird was sleeping perched on one foot, its beak tucked behind a velvety blue wing. She took her toothpaste and brushed her teeth in the kitchen. When she wanted to use the toilet, she turned sideways on the seat and sat with her back to the parrot. She feared it might bite her and she watched over her shoulder. The bird opened its eye, its amber pupil dilated and contracted, but it didn't unfold from its tucked position.

In the morning, Holly leaned into the kitchen counter in her rayon bathrobe and pecked at the push buttons on the telephone, trying the number she wanted. She dialed the number four times; each time, her fingers brushed the wrong zones of the keypad. She forced herself to slow down and at last she rang through to Elliot Tompkins at Norman Bird Sanctuary, where he worked part-time.

Elliot said, "No kidding, a hyacinth macaw? Shit, that's a rare treasure. That bird is protected by the Washington Convention. I can't believe you have it. We'd love to see it here as a guest exhibit—"

"That's not what I mean. Maybe you can just tell me how to take care of it. It's in my bathroom. It's eating plastic—"

"They'll chew anything. You need a big cage or a standing perch. Where did you get it? Is it stolen or something?" He was teasing her.

"It's been going without food—"

"Look, I'll keep it at my house. I've got an empty flight and we can stick him in there until you find a good cage. I'll put you in touch with the Bay State Cage Bird Society. A bird club. They're having an avian yard sale. There might be some cages available. You might find what you need."

The idea of such an organized event made her stomach clench. Who kept parrots? Fat men with eye patches, Hell's Angels on Harleys. It was the Long John Silver motif; little old ladies preferred finches and budgies. Willis didn't fit either profile. "Didn't you just say you might take it for me?"

"Is this a stolen parrot, Holly? Don't bullshit me—"

She told him that it was a rescued bird.

"Since when is that Pratt kid with Animal Rescue?"

Holly was surprised that he understood.

Elliot agreed to come and get it off her hands.

When she placed the receiver back, Willis was at the door with a bucket of peanuts and sunflower seeds. He waltzed right through the kitchen and into the bathroom. He took time to notice that she wasn't even dressed, her delicate robe was a thin rosy flow from her hips to her ankles. When she moved, the fairy cloth seemed to whisper little remarks and she pulled the cord tighter. "What are you staring at?" she said.

"Well. It's all right there, isn't it?"

Willis brought the bird into the kitchen. It flapped its huge wings, revealing an open window on each side where its flight feathers had been trimmed. Willis placed the bird on a heavy wooden curtain dowel. He spilled the seed mix across the window sash and the bird started to eat.

Fritz came up the driveway in Rennie's car. He knocked on the door frame and came into the kitchen. He said, "No luck finding a cage. Everything at Pet Doctor was teeny-tiny. For itsy-bitsy canaries." Holly introduced herself again. In turn, Fritz told her his full name, with his saint's name thrown in. "Giovanni Francis Xavier Federico."

"That's your confirmation name?" She smiled. She couldn't tell what she felt about him. He seemed pleasant enough, but he didn't smile. He looked her way with a complicated empty expression. This empty expression seemed like simplicity itself, but then she noticed a grim tightness in his jaw as if his teeth were wired.

Fritz had something in his coat. He said to Willis, "Feel this."

"What are you saying?"

"Here, pinch it."

"Pinch it?"

"Right here. I'm serious."

Willis tapped the small bulge in Fritz's jacket. "What've you got?"

Fritz lifted his lapel and tugged something free from his coat. It was alive. A little teacup Chihuahua, not much bigger than a rat, but its eyes were marble-sized. The eyes were the biggest thing on it. Fritz put it on the floor.

"What is that, a flea?" Willis said.

"Man's best friend."

Willis toed the dog until it flopped over, barking in short irate squeaks.

"I couldn't resist," Fritz said.

Willis said. "How much did it put you back?"

"Two-fifty."

"When I'm trying to get a lump of cash? You sink our capital into something like that?"

"Want it?" Fritz said. "I mean it. For you. Here, take it. I want you to have it."

Holly said, "No dogs."

"What does she mean, 'no dogs'? Who is she talking to?"

Willis said, "Take it easy."

Fritz told Holly, "Point. This is a pedigree canine. It isn't just a dog."

Willis took the puppy and circled it against his cheek and over his forehead like a chamois. "It's nice, Fritz. Really nice. But we have a serious financial investment with this bird, and since Holly is helping out, let's not push it."

Fritz pressed the puppy into his coat again and waited for Willis to tell him the plan.

Willis said, "This is what we do. We wait and see." He was grinning, as if he had eaten the pie off a windowsill. The planning stages were his best moments, when reasonable dreams promised reasonable rewards.

"Is he kidding?" Holly said.

Fritz said, "He's saying, wait and see. Isn't that what you're telling us?"

Willis said, "Shit, do you need an ear wax removal system? We sit."

"Good enough for me." Fritz crossed his wrists behind his head.

Willis looked between the two of them. "Showalter will dictate our move. He'll come looking for his truck, number one."

"You have this fellow's truck?" Holly said.

"In Rennie's shack. I plan to sell it back to the company. Then he'll have to purchase the bird, give me a cash advance on it."

"A kind of pressure switch," Fritz said. "That's plush."

Holly said, "You're kidding. Isn't that like extortion?"

"Listen to her. Miss Kojak," Fritz said.

"Don't mind him," Willis said.

"Well?" Holly said. "Explain the difference."

"I'm not too worried about Showalter. He's over a barrel."

"He's put his own dick out," Fritz said.

They were teasing her.

Holly said, "I can't wait for this to happen. This plan you're talking about. I want the bird out of here. I have a friend at the Norman Bird Sanctuary who said he will take the parrot. He's an expert aviculturist—"

Willis said, "That would be good except this bird is my big cash item, I'm not lending it out."

"Look, this isn't a parrot hotel," she said.

"Why not? What else has it got going for it?" Willis said.

She turned around to look at him square. She smoothed her robe. She tugged it closed.

"It's not a love shack or anything, is it?" Fritz said.

Holly looked at him, surprised.

"A love shack?" Fritz said again. "It's not earning what it could." His voice exhibited a clarity he hadn't revealed in the last five minutes.

Willis was feeding the macaw a peanut and didn't object to what Fritz was saying. They were implying something, but what? Could they actually be suggesting that she was down at the heel and moving toward a lower social status? Moving at any noticeable velocity? Holly went to the sink and filled the kettle. She felt her underarms glowing with heat; the rayon robe was sticking to the small of her back. "You're very funny," she told Fritz.

"Wait and see," Fritz said.

Holly made a large pot of tea and set it down on the kitchen table. She watched Willis pour two cupfuls of sugar in the pot and stir it around with the measuring cup. It was an odd mannerism; he stirred with the Pyrex cup like a cook on a wagon train. How could anyone like something so sweet? It belied a childlike trait and she was searching for anything to round out the picture, to take the hard edges off. Because, when the two men were together like that, Willis was knocked down a level, into ordinary punkdom. She studied Willis to pinpoint his redeeming features. His eyelashes were dense and long enough to leave spider-leg shadows on his cheekbones from the overhead fluorescent. She gave him the benefit of the doubt. But she didn't think she wanted to entertain Fritz Federico much longer; his peculiar mannerisms, his flat speech and spooky loyalty to Willis upset her.

The Chihuahua's homely face emerged from within Fritz's coat. It kept licking its leather button nose, its flat tongue curled over like a wet ribbon of chewing gum. Once and again, Holly looked at the percolator clock on the kitchen wall, its orange bubble blinking *two seconds, two seconds*.

Holly took a frying pan from the cupboard and whacked it on the burner. She twisted the knob on. She decided to make eggs for Willis and Fritz. She would fix them something to eat, and they could be on their way with that blue dinosaur. The bird was making a mess hulling the peanuts, tossing its head as it ground the nuts in its beak, ingesting only a fraction of what it pulverized.

Willis sounded very pleased about her breakfast invitation. "That's perfect. We eat. Then we all go over to your bird guy. Maybe he has a cage."

She opened her refrigerator. She didn't have eggs after all. Willis told her he would get them from Rennie. Holly walked outside with the men. Fritz put the dog on the ground where it released a tiny golden puddle. "You better invite Rennie," she told Willis. Willis went into his house. Fritz went over to the car to get a ceramic dish he had bought for the puppy. The dish said "Doggie" in calligraphic letters. Fritz handed it to Holly so she could read it back to him. Holly thought the bowl was much too large for the Chihuahua. "He can swim in it," she told Fritz. He didn't like her criticism. She turned another way to look across the cove. The expanse of green water seemed to oxygenate her vision; the retina screen was soothed and she could return her gaze to Fritz. She looked Fritz straight in the eye as she handed the heavy dish back to him. His empty face was getting the best of her. Then, Willis came down the steps with a carton of eggs. "Rennie's sick this morning," he told Holly. "She's in bed."

"She's in her bed?"

"It's a bad day for her," Willis said. "I hate it when she doesn't get up. It looks bad if Munro comes over."

Holly told Willis, "I'll make her some toast."

"Look, don't go over there. It's a strain."

"No it isn't. It's no trouble."

"I'm telling you. For Rennie, it's a strain. She's not up to company."

After everything, Holly didn't like being identified as an outsider. She started walking over to Rennie's house. Willis came after her.

"I'm going to see if she wants something," Holly said.

"You're on private property," Willis said. It was a stupid remark. He looked at her and shrugged. He wasn't smiling and he wasn't frowning.

Rennie was in her bedroom sitting up in bed. Her hairbrush was balanced across her knees.

"I can't even drag it through," Rennie said.

"Feeling worse today?"

"Just a little weak. That hairbrush is like an anvil."

Holly picked up the hairbrush and lightly brushed Rennie's hair at her temple. "Feel weak as a kitten?"

"Weak as a mouse. That's a degree worse. After mouse, what comes next?"

"I don't know."

"Weak as a fly. Then what?"

Holly imagined a string of diminutive creatures and insect life, but she didn't extend the list any further. Rennie's skin looked odd, the dull ochre tone of a gum eraser. Holly knew this change of color might indicate involvement of the liver. Holly brushed Rennie's hair until she grabbed Holly's wrist and took the hairbrush out of her hand. "I won't have any hair left," she said.

Holly thought she understood the mood swings of the dying. But Rennie was staring at her in such a bold perusal, she wasn't sure if she knew.

Willis asked Rennie if she wanted any medications from the closet. Rennie refused. She laughed. "You're asking *me*? That's a switcheroo," she told Willis.

He didn't like her teasing and he ducked out of the room. Rennie's laughter took a toll and she leaned back on the pillows to rest. She looked at Holly. "What's happening over there in your place?"

Holly didn't know what to say. Perhaps the parrot was meant to be a secret. Willis came back through the room with a new box of Coffee Nips and the *Newport Daily News*. He put the offerings in Rennie's lap.

Rennie told him, "A bowl for the candy would be nice."

Willis left and came back with a milk glass dish. He emptied the Coffee Nips in that.

"That's better. I'm sick, but I'm still following Emily

Post. Now, tell me. What are you up to, you and your play group?"

Willis didn't answer.

"Yes, tell us. What exactly are you doing?" Holly said.

Willis looked at Holly. He didn't like a gang-up like that. He smiled at her, but he was angry. He started to sing "Delilah," an old hit by Tom Jones. He sang the first verse. He paused. He sang the refrain. Willis knew the second verse.

"Unreal." Holly crossed her arms and waited while Willis repeated the refrain. His voice ascended above the muffled pumping of the waves, the terns' triple screaks, the tinny knocks of sheet-metal hammers coming from a storm-gutter renovation two houses over.

"He has a nice voice, doesn't he?" Rennie said to Holly. "He takes good care of it. He gargles with whitewash."

Holly grumbled her affirmation, but Rennie was too tired to elaborate on the joke, her eyes fluttering trying to stay open.

Rennie said, "Munro wants to know what that truck is doing in the shack. That InstyPrint truck? In our shack."

"Munro has been here?"

"Last night."

"Where was I?"

Rennie said, "If you don't know where you were, how would I know?"

"I was looking for *her*," Willis said. He glowered at Holly. "Where were you?"

"Are you asking me?" Holly snapped. "I was at the mall. I live my own life, you know."

"Well, when you decide who's living what life, and where, send me a postcard." Rennie turned on her side.

They left her alone to rest and went down the stairs. When Rennie heard the kitchen storm snap back, she picked up her book, found a blank page, and wrote a note to herself: "One time around went our gallant ship, two times around went she; three times around spun our gallant ship, and sank to the bottom of the sea."

࿔࿔࿔࿔࿔

Fritz was down on the beach with the Chihuahua. Holly could see a little speck racing in circles near the foamy edge. The dog would be washed away if Fritz didn't look out. Holly walked into her house after Willis. She had left the frying pan on the burner; it was red hot. She smelled the harsh fumes from the new Teflon coating. She went over to the stove and lifted the pan off the blazing circle. The intensity of the chemical smoke was making her cough. The fumes burned her eyes.

Willis saw it first.

The parrot was on the floor, under the kitchen table. It didn't look good. It looked dead. It was asphyxiated. The chemical from the nonstick coating had poisoned the air and the parrot must have succumbed in a matter of a few minutes. Willis took the bird outside and tried to revive it. He held it upside down by its feet and shook it like an umbrella; its wings flapped open and closed artificially. Its round eyes were shiny and blank. It was finished.

Few words were exchanged. Fritz came inside and learned what had happened. "I guess no one wants to have eggs?" Fritz said.

Holly handed Fritz two raw eggs, folding his knuckles over them. "Okay, Ichabod. You make yourself some eggs," she said. "Any style."

"I think I just will," Fritz said.

Holly went into the bathroom and locked the door. Willis took the bird into Rennie's shack. He opened the door of the jewelry kiln and crammed the animal's body inside, creasing its stiff unruly tail. He could have plucked a long blue feather, but he decided he didn't want it. He suddenly recognized its particular shade of blue. It was like the voluminous whorls of petrified fabric on the antique figurehead, the "White Lady." He shut the door of the kiln and set the dial.

He went back to Holly's. She was frying an egg sandwich for Fritz, working the spatula under its golden crust. Fritz was holding a stiff one-hundred-dollar bill, teasing the puppy. The little dog was invigorated by the game, its tiny jaws snapped at the currency. The game annoyed Willis and he grabbed the bill away from Fritz. He brought it up to his face and studied the blue and red flecks, thin crescents sharp as dolls' eyelashes embedded in the creamy paper.

They were eating their eggs without a lot of gab when someone knocked on the door. It was Elliot Tompkins from the Norman Bird Sanctuary.

Holly explained to Elliot that the bird wasn't their problem any longer. They had found a new home for the macaw.

Fritz was enjoying his breakfast, slapping a hunk of butter on his plate and dabbing the end of his fried-egg sandwich against the blob. "Willis found a home for it. A nice hot, dry climate."

Willis stared at Fritz.

Elliot Tompkins put a book on the table. *The Parrot in Health and Illness*, a large volume, fully illustrated. Elliot said, "Holly, I thought this would be a help, but I guess it's too late."

Willis tore a bite from a heel of buttered bread and lifted the heavy text. The book opened to a central page. A photograph showed a parrot nipping a fishing sinker. The caption under the picture said, "Lead Poisoning." Elliot Tompkins wasn't pleased to leave the book in Willis's hands and he took it back.

"Maybe I'll look at that some other time," Willis said. He stood up and shook Elliot's hand.

Chapter Fourteen

Holly was sitting upstairs with Rennie. Willis's dominoes were spread across the quilt. Rennie was teaching her the game. When it was Holly's turn to shuffle the ivory pieces, Rennie recited, "Shake 'em, Jane, my fingers are in pain." If it had been Willis sitting opposite, she would have said, "Shake 'em, Jake, my fingers ache." Holly wasn't allowed to take her turn until she repeated the correct refrain. The extra pieces were left in a pile called the "boneyard." Every time Holly believed she understood the rules, Rennie invented additional restrictions. "That's double sixes. You can't put that there."

"You did last time," Holly said.

"Maybe I did. Whose draw is it?" It wasn't malicious, perhaps Rennie couldn't remember the game. Even so, the ladder of "bones" grew across the covers in hazardous angles until they spilled onto the floor.

Holly looked out the window and noticed two men prowling the edge of the cliff, lighting smokes. Then, the tiny Chihuahua scrambled across the driveway. Nicole's kids were running up and down after it. The Chihuahua galloped back the other way until Lindy scooped it up and handed the dog to his little sister. The children tugged the dog back and forth between them.

The last time she had seen Willis, he was in Rennie's shack painting the InstyPrint truck with a straw broom and a gallon of K-mart Rustbuster. Fritz knew someone in New Jersey who might want to buy the truck off them. Willis didn't want to drive two hundred miles with InstyPrint writing all over them. Holly had watched the men sweep the broom over the new van, the dead black paint dripped unpredictably; it had the consistency of pudding that wasn't set.

Rennie came over to see what Holly was looking at. The hem of her nightgown dragged in a soft crescent, dusting the old oak planks. She paired up with Holly and watched the intruders. "Are those men with you?" Rennie asked Holly.

"With me? Of course not."

"Those surveyors are on private property."

"Is that what they are? Surveyors?"

"They've got a tripod set up. They must be making a survey. Did Munro give them permission to pace out this plat?"

"Is that what they're doing?" Holly said.

"Century 21," Rennie said.

"You mean those real estate professionals?" Holly said.

One of the men in question walked up the middle of the driveway in long strides and wrote something down on a clipboard. Next, he pushed a wheel gauge across the lip of the cliff.

Rennie teetered by the window in her harlequin satin bed jacket; the clownish jacket over her skinny frame made her look like a Mardi Gras puppet.

"They can survey all they want but I'm not selling," she said.

"Of course not," Holly said.

"They think they have the authority. We'll see. In shallow waters, shrimps make fools of dragons," Rennie said.

Holly nudged her back to bed.

"A person is sick upstairs and they're disturbing her rest. Go tell them that," Rennie said.

The phone started ringing.

Holly went to the hall table and picked up the receiver. Showalter wanted to know about Willis.

"Willis is driving today," she said.

"WASTEC doesn't have him. Who's he driving for?"

Holly said, "Shit, I don't know. In any case, I'll tell Willis you called."

Showalter said, "Willis is making life harder on himself. Plain English. Tell Willis that there is a late charge on my vehicle. A severe penalty if it comes back after hours. You tell him that. Number two: the animal needs proper attention. Do you think that's happening? It's getting proper attention?"

Holly said, "What animal?"

Holly noticed a sudden change in the telephone reception, a hollow echo. Rennie had picked up the other line in the bedroom. Holly heard Rennie say, "My son Willis is a free agent. If you contract with him, you have to pay whatever he wants and accept his terms."

Showalter kept quiet.

"You should be ashamed of yourself trying to strong-arm this girl." Rennie put herself firmly in the ointment, whether he liked it or not.

Then Rennie started coughing. She bent over and hacked and hacked into the hem of her bed jacket. Holly replaced the hall telephone in its cradle and went over to Rennie. She patted her between the shoulder blades.

One of the surveyors had come onto the porch. Holly heard him knocking. Rennie said, "Bring him in. Let's hear it."

Holly helped Rennie downstairs. She noticed Rennie's whole posture had changed, crumpled. She walked without lifting her feet. Her nightdress swallowed her up. Her gown might have been perfect if Rennie could stand straight and throw her shoulders back.

The workman stood on the rush mat and waited for Holly to answer the door.

Holly invited him into the foyer. "Are you from Century 21?"

The man laughed. "No. We're Invisible Fence."

Holly looked outside the door and saw the man's partner working in the yard. He was planting vinyl flags on wire stems around the perimeter of the property. A score of flags in a straight line to the edge of the cliff. Holly wondered what kind of surveyors would place tiny flags in the dirt like that.

"Invisible Fence? What's that?" she said.

"We fit your dog with an electronic collar. It can't move beyond those flags without getting zapped. You have a dog problem here?"

"Fritz has a dog."

"The name on our work order says Federico?"

"That's right. His sister won't let him keep the dog at her house."

"We're finishing up. We need a signature."

Rennie came over. "Explain yourself," Rennie told the man. "Who do you represent? Did my son commission you to harass me?"

"Your son?"

"Aren't you from Château-sur-Mer?" She tugged the man's cuff and pulled him into the parlor. The Fresnel lens showered lemon-lime twists and slices all over him.

The man said, "I think we're on different tracks here."

Rennie turned to Holly. "Is Munro out there in the car?"

Holly said with some finality, "Rennie, this isn't anything to do with Munro." Either Rennie had turned a corner and had lost her coherence or she was putting on an act.

She turned to Holly and changed the subject. "Where's that little pea? The one we got in the mail? I want that pea. It's driving me crazy."

"It is? Rennie, you never said you wanted that thing. You really want that pea?" Holly tried to calculate Rennie's actual level of dementia. She looked at the contractor and looked away.

The man went to the door.

Holly told him that Fritz would sign his paper. Fritz was in the shack. She turned around to see Rennie climbing back upstairs, taking the bannister in both hands, tugging herself up the incline, one riser at a time. Holly asked her if she wanted to call a doctor about her relapse.

"The doctor reports to Munro," Rennie said.

"We can get a different doctor if you need something."

"*If I need something,* she says."

Rennie's irony was stinging. Holly followed Rennie upstairs, thinking it was unfair when Rennie talked like this. Her own father, as he faced death, would never have been so acid—if he could have talked in his last days—but Rennie was smiling at her now. She was sitting in bed, writing in her doomsday book. Something in huge indigo letters.

Chapter Fifteen

Paint fumes had collected in the tiny garage and the men were feeling sick. Holly opened the plank doors and braced them with old cement blocks to ventilate the shack. "You idiots," she said. They dropped their arms and watched her until she was finished scolding. Willis told her to stand in the doorway to keep a lookout.

"Is Showalter coming over here? He says you make life difficult for everyone," Holly complained to Willis.

"Forget him," Willis said. But Willis wasn't sure if Munro had squawked to the police about the truck. Munro might keep it to himself for a while and use it as an ace later on. Willis understood how a snitch might savor his opportunities.

Fritz was watching the puppy learn the limits of its environment. Once or twice, they heard it yip if it edged over the Invisible Fence. It fell back on its haunches and tipped its head sideways as if it was examining its situation. Nicole's children looked forlorn until Fritz explained that the row of flags didn't prevent them from playing with the dog as long as it stayed in its ghost corral.

"It's not going to learn if they keep lifting it out." Willis told Fritz. "You throw your money around, you know that?"

Holly watched them work on the truck. The InstyPrint lettering kept floating up. Random words reappeared through the dark coat. The truck looked like a Magic 8 Ball where psychic warnings surface.

"This doesn't cut it," Willis said. He backed up and crossed his arms. He didn't seem very concerned. He wasn't really interested in disguising the truck or driving the truck to New Jersey. Holly saw that Willis liked marking the van the way dogs kick dust to cover their waste. He was happy just to defile it.

"Point," Fritz said. "It's black, isn't it? We leave here at dark. It will blend right in with the night. Shit, this is a fucking night-mobile if I ever saw one."

Willis said, "Let me ask you. Who's on the highway at night? Swarms of cruisers. Our two taillights all by their lonesome look sweet as cherry Life Savers. The paint won't even be dry on this thing."

"The wind will dry it."

"I say we wait another day and apply a second coat."

Fritz agreed to postpone the trip.

"You know what we have? We have an Insty *hearse*."

Fritz was laughing with the same recognition. Fritz was right there, at the same mental spot. Willis sometimes wondered how they arrived there together like that.

Holly didn't join in. "I don't see what's so comical. Let's see how you two pull it off before you laugh it up. Get rid of the thing, then you can try out for *Late Night*."

Willis and Fritz had never been successful with any scheme. Despite their brotherhood, or whatever it was that gave them a boost of telepathy and kept them united, they had never once turned a profit.

At sixteen, they had tried to sabotage a rubber-duck race, a fund-raising event for a capital campaign at Newport

Hospital. The hospital sold rubber ducks representing chances on a sports car. The race was held at the Newport Country Club. A lively freshwater stream threaded the golf course through dense pitch pine and beach plum. Willis thought he and Fritz could sneak into the underbrush, hide out, and defraud the hospital.

They waited in the undergrowth before dawn. A cold dungeon t'ick moved in from Brenton Point; the fog coiled their hair and water dripped down their cheeks. At daybreak the greenskeepers rode machines over the course, vacuuming up the condensation from the short grass. One of the workers started whacking the thicket with an iron. He sliced the golf club through the branches over their heads with little regard for the sports equipment until Willis and Fritz emerged and he chased them off the golf course.

While the men painted, Holly discovered boxes of shiny beads and enamel buttons, plastic rosettes and hollow beans, white discs with rolling black poppyseed pupils, a thousand tiny doll's eyes. Rennie's jewelry supplies, beside the doomed truck, added to the desolate feel of the shack. It was like a Warehouse of the Damned. Holly's mother had saved old buttons like these in a glass jar. Each button was singular, unique, lost from its set. They were saved in hopes of one day matching up with their likeness, their own kind. Other than the small, white, interchangeable shirt buttons, most were never claimed. They were artifacts. Every artifact represented a specific family member, and all of these members, like the buttons, were estranged from the rest.

She stacked the boxes against the garage wall and went outside. She leaned against the door and listened to the men bicker over the gallon of paint. She slid down the side of the plank door and rested on her heels. She saw someone coming up the driveway.

She recognized him immediately, it was her ex-husband, Jensen.

Jensen was wearing his shearling coat. After all these years, he had dug it out of the closet. He was wearing the coat to motivate Holly, she knew he didn't wear it for his health.

"Shit," she told Willis. "Look who it is. It's that no-neck back from Kanpur." She was trying to make light of it, but her nerves were jittering. She wanted Willis to come out there and take stock of it.

Willis walked out of the shack to take a look.

Jensen called to Holly, "Hello, you." He walked right over to their circle and slapped his two hands down on Holly's shoulders. He kissed her forehead. "Missed you a little bit," he told her. His shearling coat looked small on him. He might have gained some bulk since they were first married.

Jensen said, "Jesus, I heard about what happened to our old apartment. That sinkhole. Weird—"

She looked at him. She imagined that he was insinuating something.

"Well, Holly. I'm glad you found yourself a new place." He didn't look impressed.

"Where's Sarojini?" Holly said.

"Setting up."

"Where would that be?" She hoped it was off the island.

No such luck.

Jensen said, "We've got a nice spot on Catherine Street. Sycamore House. It's kind of an investment property."

"What about your Carvel franchise?"

"I'm still there for now, but I'm not staying there forever."

"You finally got tired of dishing up soft serve? You bought that big place? That mansion they turned into apartments? She give you Indian money for that?'' Holly said.

Willis said, "I know that place. That's a busy chicken ranch. Vaseline on every doorknob."

Jensen said, "It was in the wrong hands. We're renovating. We're gutting it."

Holly winced. The term was common construction jargon, but when Jensen said "gutting," he seemed to enjoy the double consonants.

"Why aren't you at your Swami ice cream shop?" Willis said.

Jensen turned around to face Willis. "Who's asking me questions?"

"This is my neighbor." She kept his name to herself. "And, that's Fritz." She pointed to Fritz who looked pretty awful, like a Hollywood punk. He was wearing a new pair of skintight jeans, like he had just robbed them off the rack. "You can memorize their pretty faces and clear off."

She walked back inside the shack and Jensen followed her in there. He started telling her that he had come to a realization. He said he realized that a girl didn't burn up a bed without there being a trace of feeling left in her heart. He told her that he had come to appreciate that, and he wanted to tell her she wasn't alone. "I've got a speck of emotion for you too, girl. I guess it clings for a while."

"Sorry to hear that. It can cling to the bitter end," she said, "but I don't feel anything."

He picked up her hand and rubbed his knuckles over it. He dropped it again.

"What the fuck do you want? You want something, I know it," Holly told him.

"Thing is. I heard Neptune's for sale. I might want to buy it. I wanted to be the one to tell you. You wouldn't want to hear that news from a stranger."

Holly looked at Jensen. She knew that he wasn't telling

her the truth. She knew when Jensen was lying, his lips looked tight, as if a smile was fighting at the corners.

"Salvatore hasn't said a word about this to me. I say you're full of bullshit." Yet she felt her heart pounding. Her summer job was the glue on her calendar; the other months tore away in the wind. Holly figured that Jensen was alarmed to see Willis and had come up with something to get her in a lather, something to provoke her. Holly said, "I say the day you buy Neptune's, I go down on the beach and part the sea."

"You can still have your job. We'll keep you on." Jensen pressed his thumb against the glossy truck. It left a little print on the wet finish, intricate as a scarab.

"I'm through listening to this," she started talking so she couldn't hear him. "We open up in three weeks. Salvatore gave me my keys yesterday. Double sets. We're ordering two hundred new towels, waffle-weave, all sizes. He's putting in a washer so we can do our own sheets instead of sending them on the truck. He didn't mention anything about selling the place to you. That's a nice fantasy you're having."

Jensen said, "Will you calm down? You're shrieking. You should have your tonsils out, you know that?"

"Are you finished?" she said.

"Holly, I'm just saying I'm going to be your boss." His smile was running high from one end to the other.

"Fuck off, Jensen."

Jensen was looking back and forth between Holly and the two men holding the wet brooms. "What have you got here, a chop shop?"

Jensen took a hold of Holly's elbow and he tried to steer her outside. He had a funny gloss over his eyes, as if he had just peeled onions.

Jensen told her, "Let's take a little drive together. Old time's sake. Let's ride over to Neptune's—"

"Get serious," she told him. "You're not getting any." She might have been speaking for herself or for Sarojini. Her tone suggested a universal consensus.

Willis didn't like what he thought was happening and he shoved Jensen out of the shack. Fritz pulled the old cedar plank doors shut and Holly tucked the board into the wooden rests. Jensen knew he was banished and he bowed at the waist, sweeping his arm through the air. He turned and started walking away.

Holly yelled, "Don't call me, I'll call you." It was a babyish thing to say, and she enjoyed saying it.

Her ex-husband turned around to face her, shrugged, then kept walking away. She watched him get into an expensive new car fully financed by his Indian connection. He cranked the sun roof a notch to entice the fickle spring sunshine.

"I guess he's not through with you," Willis told Holly.

"Please don't say that. He gives me the creeps."

"No question about it. He left that calligraphy," Willis said.

"What calligraphy?" Fritz said, letting the garage door swing open again.

"Nothing," Holly said. She didn't want to talk about it. She thought Fritz had a funny look. He was almost smiling. As much as she knew about Fritz, she wasn't sure if it was Jensen who wrote those two silver words.

Fritz dribbled mineral solvent onto Willis's hands as he rubbed a rag over his knuckles, then Fritz took the rag and Willis splashed the solvent onto Fritz. Except for the harsh fumes of the petroleum distillate, it looked like a loving anointment of some kind. Afterward, their hands looked clean, but Willis's cast was spattered, a loose spray of black paint like watermelon seeds.

Chapter Sixteen

If she sat on the radiator by the window, Rennie could see the channel off Brenton Point. She folded a velour towel over the uncomfortable plumbing ribs and she had a warm, pleasant seat from which to look out. She removed a pair of German binoculars from a leather case. She lifted them in one hand to watch, but she was having trouble squinting through the lenses. The magnifications were off. She turned the focus one way and turned it back; she found something. A dragger was steaming in, just west of Elbow Ledge. She saw its doors hanging, stowed on the gallus. The bridle and towing warps were winched tight on the net reel, still puddling underneath. She was steaming into State Pier Number Nine, or into Parascondola's, where lumpers swarmed on board to sort and offload the catch for the processors. Rennie thought of Bill Hopkins on the *Teresa Eve* coming back loaded to the rails with nary any freeboard left, her skipper a fool for money. She looked back at the water and followed the dragger stem to stern to see if she could identify its skipper or any of its crew. There was one man working on deck, cutting through a fouled piece of net and laying it in strips. Two crew stood outside the pilot-house, gripping mugs of coffee or maybe it was Cup-a-

Soup. Sonny Costa had changed to soup when too much dragger coffee had his stomach acting up. Then Sonny quit taking instant soup on board because the MSG made his fingertips tingle. After all his caution over what he fixed himself in the galley, she blew right out of the water.

Rennie was surprised to discover that she couldn't tell if the boat she watched was coming in or going out. She rubbed her thumbs into her eyes and watched again. The boat seemed to waver, drifting above, then below the horizon line. Her eyes were acting funny. When Rennie used to watch a boat come in, she could almost always identify its crew, and she could see it in their faces if the trip had been worth it or not.

She pressed the glasses against her eyes until the bridge of her nose started to ache. The boat started to hopscotch across the water. She didn't know if she was losing her mind or just losing her vision. She shuffled back to her bed across the room, hardly making headway. She shoved one foot ahead of the other, afraid to lift her feet from the floor. Normal ambulation had become precarious. The floor shifted like a porch glider. She got back into bed and pulled the sheet over her knees. Rennie started to recognize that the transition wasn't going to be an easy thing, after all.

At one o'clock, Willis brought her a bowl of cream of chicken soup with a dollop of sherry. She was grateful for the mild chicken scent, which transformed the room. He sat beside her and made sure she swallowed it all. Willis looked splattered with tar and she asked him if he'd been riding the roller again, or did they have him raking.

"Rennie, I don't have that job anymore. Remember? I'm driving at WASTEC now."

"You're not tarring roads?"

"A long time ago. I didn't much like it."

"That's right. Tar has a bad smell." She seemed to be thinking hard. Perhaps she was imagining the acrid scent of tar when she sat up straight in bed and projectile-vomited. Her chicken soup laced with sherry shot across the covers. Willis stood up and looked at what had happened. It was one of the first times anything like this had occurred in his presence and it took him a minute to act. Rennie flopped back against the pillow and groaned. Willis collected her feather comforter where the vomit had pooled. He took the quilt into the bathroom and put it in the bathtub. He didn't know if he should wash it or if it should be saved for the dry cleaner. He made a final decision and ran the shower over it, then he shook it out and took it to the hall window. He pushed it through the window and shut the sash on its tail. It luffed on the wind like a huge, swollen sail. He went back into the bathroom and moistened a washcloth and took it back to Rennie. She was lying on her side, her knees drawn up, her arms around her ankles. He touched the washcloth to either side of her mouth. She had vomited with such force, her lips weren't even soiled.

"I'm having a little bit of pain," she told him.

"I'll get a doctor for you. Who do you want me to call? Do you want to go the hospital?"

"None of the above," she said.

"What doctor do you want?"

"Ask me tomorrow. Maybe that suicide doctor."

Willis said, "Rennie, please don't joke."

"That suicide doctor? I think he's a scream."

"How about your morphine?"

"Now, tell me, if I'm pudding from the waist up for very long, who's going to watch this place?"

"What needs watching?"

Rennie sighed and pulled herself up on her elbow. "Do me a favor. Pick up my binocs and see what's out there. I think it was the *Christy and Roland*. She's worse for wear, but I was glad to see her. Look about two o'clock, west of Elbow."

Willis went to the window and twisted the binoculars. He told her, "Flat calm. Flat as a plate. Everyone's out. Lots of privateers seeing what they can do. Must be mackerel, slews of tinkers this time of year."

"The *Christy and Roland*?"

"She's gone in," Willis told her. He knew that the *Christy and Roland* hadn't been launched for at least five seasons or more.

Rennie said, "That was my hunch. She was going in." She dropped back against the pillow.

The room smelled unpleasant and Willis lifted the window and propped a book under the sash.

"Hey, that's my book. You'll break its spine," Rennie told him.

"Are you reading this book? Who's going to read it?"

"Don't be so rude," she said.

"Well, I'm not going to read it," he said. His feelings were jangled. He felt his eyes burn. He cupped his hands over the bridge of his nose and secretly dabbed his eyes. He looked back at her, over his glistening fingertips.

"Give me that book. I'm writing in it."

He lifted the window sash and picked up the book. He thought she was teasing him, but when he opened the tissue paper pages he saw her large, looping script. He read a few lines:

> *We don't drink and we don't chew,*
> *and we don't go with boys who do.*

> *If you don't like my apples,*
> *then don't shake my tree;*
> *I'm not after your boyfriend,*
> *he's after me.*

"What is this? Limericks?"

"A little bit of everything. It's my high school auto-graph book. I've been revising it."

He flipped the pages. The passages were in various different inks and were signed by strangers.

> *When in a far and distant land*
> *and you see the writing of my hand*
> *but my face you cannot see*
> *so dear, think of me.*
> *—Goldie*

He turned another page. He recognized Rennie's script, a lopsided stanza, scrolling at a thirty-degree angle across the discolored paper.

> *They went to sea in a Sieve, they did,*
> *in a Sieve they went to sea:*
> *In spite of all their friends could say,*
> *on a winter's morn, on a stormy day—*

Willis said, "I remember that one."

"The Jumblies," she said.

"This is your autograph book from high school?"

"It had lots of room, so I've been writing in it. These words have been coming into my head from everywhere. If I don't write them, they get louder and louder."

He looked hard at her. "You hear voices?"

"I think it's my own voice, but it starts up whether I know it or not. Maybe I'm thinking out loud."

"That's right. That's good. If you think of something, put it in here." He handed her the autograph book.

"It's really nothing," she said, "some poems and nursery lyrics, but I was thinking it will need a title when I'm finished."

Willis told her she should try to invent one. "How about this for the title: *Today Is the First Day of the Rest of Your Life.*"

Rennie blinked, shocked by his ability to ignore available evidence. "I don't know. Maybe it should just stand on its own."

"There you go," he said.

She could see the pain she was causing him. He massaged his chin with the heel of his hand to erase some trembling nerves. Rennie realized that she had never seen Willis cry. Not one tear. Not even for Wydette. She felt moved by his blurry eyes, but like one of the two women before King Solomon, she didn't want his tears even if they belonged to her.

Willis stayed near Rennie for the rest of the day and he didn't invite Holly to come over. When Holly called him on the telephone he agreed to see her for only a half-hour. She watched him come out of the house, kicking the crushed shell ahead of his feet as he came across to the duplex. He lay down next to Holly in Holly's bed, but he didn't remove his boots.

She couldn't hide her disappointment. "You're a pill tonight," she told him.

"Swallow me."

"You're poison," she said.

"Take a sip."

She thought it was love talk, but it wasn't.

He was lying on his back with his arms crossed behind his head. He didn't look happy. She tried to nibble his throat, but he pushed her chin away. Sometimes Willis seemed to invite sex and a second later not want it. Holly recognized his darty eyes and sheepish face; it was the morphine. Sex was a thinning penumbra around his busy world of fighting off pain. A little pleasure with Holly wasn't worth scrimping on his medication. If his arm didn't ache his head was always full of horrors. Holly wondered about morphine; where did it get its name? It sounded like a chorus girl—Doreen, Nadine, Morphine. The drug heroin, too—why the homonym for the female protagonist? These feminine names alone made Holly jealous when Willis had to choose between her and Miss Emma, which was, of course, morphine's little nickname.

She didn't force the issue; she knew Willis was worried about Rennie. After a few minutes, he walked back to the other house. Holly let him brood on his own. If Rennie was beginning the dying process, who was she to jump in? She told him, "If you need me."

When Willis was gone, she got out of bed and wrapped the blanket around herself. She went out to the front room and turned on the portable television. She watched the Weather Channel. They predicted a nor'easter coming through in the next day or two. She listened to the Weather Channel until they gave the automated offshore buoy reports for Hudson Canyon, Cashe's Ledge, and George's Bank. She didn't want to hear about the weather out in the middle of the ocean, it gave her a queasy feeling to imagine the seas building. She flipped the channel and found "The Movie Loft." A picture was just starting. The familiar RKO radio tower twirled slowly at the crest of the globe; its signal flashed tiny lightning bolts. It didn't matter which film came after, Holly loved that radio tower. Its dramatic perch at the top of a desolate world seemed eerie and thrilling at the start of every RKO picture.

She thought she heard Willis return, but it wasn't anybody. Five minutes passed and she heard it again. Footsteps on the front porch, the hollow thud of someone walking over the planking. She felt her scalp tighten; the roots of her hair ached where the follicles contracted. Someone was moving around outside the duplex. She telephoned over to Willis's house. He didn't pick up. She dialed again. The same hollow jangle. She turned on all the lights and went back to her bedroom. She couldn't tell if it was more than one person, but she heard the clamshells chatter under a sneaky procession. She didn't know why Willis didn't answer the phone, maybe the ringer was turned off for Rennie's sake. She would ask about it in the morning. She listened for footsteps but the wind had picked up, sucking the screens and whistling around the corner eaves. Perhaps the noises she had heard had not been real. Holly hated how fear was sometimes manifested in a presence: a shrub's dark profile, footfalls audible in the rain, shadows shifting across the windows like someone's loose jacket and slacks.

Chapter Seventeen

Saturday morning, Holly was reheating a pan of coffee. There was a tall ship out on the water. She watched its white sails stiffen like a bullet bra, the wind corseted in its tight sheets and rigging. She recognized the ship. It was the *Eagle*, a Coast Guard training vessel from New London, but that knowledge stole its romance only slightly. It was heading back before the squall. She sat at the kitchen table and rested her coffee mug. She was surprised to see a tiny book centered on the built-in lazy Susan. Where the book had come from, she didn't have a clue. She picked up the miniature book and read the title, *The Red Pony*. She thumbed its pages; the print was almost too small to read, but she found a highlighted passage. Bright yellow ink exaggerated the miniature text, but she couldn't decipher it. She went into the next room to find her sewing box. She used the dime-size magnifying disc on a needle-threader and she read the highlighted passage. It was a place in the book where a ranch hand cuts an airhole in a horse's throat. She felt a sudden chill roll across her shoulders and down the small of her back. Who had underlined this graphic paragraph and placed the book on her table? She remembered that she had wiped the lazy Susan clean with a dishrag just the night before.

She walked into the front room where the little TV rested on a straight-back chair. She pulled the knob and waited for the picture. It was *Sunrise Semester*. A car drove into the lane. Holly saw it was Munro Hopkins driving a Vista Cruiser station wagon. A woman sat in the seat beside him. Holly thought she must be Munro's wife. It must be her Vista Cruiser that Munro was driving. Holly watched them get out of the car and take a moment to look out at the sea. They stared at First Beach for a minute, but it didn't seem to transport them as it always did Holly. They turned around and started walking into Rennie's place. Munro's wife was attractive; she had a perfect frost, her blond strands expertly integrated with chestnut waves. A frost such as that took a lot of time and effort at the beauty salon; they have to tug individual clumps of hair through a tin-foil colander.

Holly pulled on her jeans in such a hurry, her toenail snagged the tight cuff and she felt it split away from the cuticle. She sat down on the bed and looked at the tiny edge of blood framing her big toenail. It wasn't serious and she limped to the closet to find her shoes. Holly wanted to meet Munro's wife. She might be a key, she might be the seed of good or evil that inspired her husband's quest to remove Rennie from her Land's End refuge.

Dressed in her sweatshirt and jeans, Holly walked right into Rennie's kitchen. She acted as if she was there out of habit; she belonged there. She heard Munro's wife calling instructions from upstairs. Munro was in the front parlor dialing the telephone.

Holly feigned a businesslike importance and started emptying dishes from the kitchen drainer, trying to hear what Munro was saying.

"—probably in the next half-hour. That's terrific. We appreciate it," Munro spoke into the telephone.

Holly went over to stand beside Munro. "You're taking Rennie to Château-sur-Mer?"

"Carole and I think it's best."

"Where's Willis?"

Munro sliced his fountain pen through the air in an emphatic Z. The swooping Z translated into: Who knows? Who cares? He returned to his telephone conversation.

"Willis!" Holly called through the house. Perhaps he was sleeping, but she knew he wasn't around.

Munro was finished on the telephone.

"You haven't seen Willis?" Holly said.

"He's probably down at the Needle Exchange. Never mind about him."

Holly ran up the staircase and found Rennie sitting up in bed, her legs dangling over the side. Carole was trying to tug a sweater onto Rennie's arm. Rennie resisted or she was just too weak to assist, and the woman was finding it hard to dress such a floppy doll. "Give me a hand, will you?" Carole asked Holly.

"Rennie, you don't have to leave this house," Holly said.

"Who do you think you are?" Carole said.

"Have you got the legal papers to haul her off like this?"

The woman ignored Holly and finished buttoning Rennie's sweater although one arm still dangled.

Rennie's eyes looked blank. She was drugged into a stupor.

Holly said, "What did you do to her?"

"That's what we're concerned about. She's self-medicated, who knows how many of these things she's been using."

Holly saw the milk glass candy bowl on Rennie's bedside table. The bowl held several opened cards of morphine suppositories along with her Coffee Nips and lemon balls. Next to the bowl, a pyramid of wrappers, twists of colored foil ripped in half, resembled exotic fishing lures.

"She might be trying to kill herself with these," Carole said.

Holly looked at Rennie's face. Rennie returned the look. Or did she? There wasn't a twinkle coming or going.

Holly kneeled beside the bed and took Rennie's hands. Her hands were warm. Holly gently pinched Rennie's cheeks; her face seemed slightly puffy. "Are you okay, Rennie? Are you all right?"

Rennie mumbled a sentence, but it didn't sound right. It sounded like the five vowels in a creaky sequence, "A, E, I, O, U."

"Rennie, it's me."

Carole said, "Maybe the cancer's hit her brain."

"Shit," Holly said. She didn't like Carole's indifferent tone.

"Or, maybe she's just doped up. Like that Willis. She's high," Carole said.

Rennie shifted her posture when she heard about Willis. She brightened, perhaps at the sound of his name. Rennie told Carole, "High as a churchmouse in the communion cup."

Carole was alarmed to hear Rennie's voice, but Holly sat down beside Rennie and fingered the collar on her nightgown. She squeezed her shoulder.

Carole told Holly, "Don't squeeze her so hard."

Rennie said, "Who says so?"

"Well, dear, your bones are brittle, aren't they?" Carole fingered the foil wrappers and let them sift onto the floor.

Rennie said, "*Every kiss and every hug—seem to act like a drug—*"

Holly recognized the song.

Then Rennie started coughing. Her lungs sounded soggy as a sponge.

Munro's wife whispered, in her own defense, "It *does* get into the brain. It metastasizes. It hits the brain."

"Will you shut up," Holly told Carole. But it was upsetting to see Rennie come back alive and talking. It might have been easier if she had remained cocooned in her unconscious symptoms. Holly saw that Rennie's sheets were stained with bile-colored circles. Her gastrointestinal condition had worsened; all her systems were failing.

Munro was waiting in the doorway. He talked to his mother, but she responded with the same indecipherable and blowzy "A, E, I, O, U." Rennie decided for herself when she wanted to make the effort or not.

Rennie was going to be removed, no matter what. Holly decided to help them take Rennie to the car outside. Munro lifted Rennie from the bed. Holly arranged her gown.

Munro told Holly, "Look, we can handle it. Is that all right with you?"

Rennie had only one arm inserted in her sweater and Holly folded the loose half over Rennie's shoulder, tucking it in. The innocent gesture was almost an enshrouding, and it so disturbed Holly that she pulled the sweater sleeve off, letting it trail. She opened the storm door for Munro and he carefully chose his footing going down the front porch steps. At the car, Holly didn't know what else she could do. She kissed Rennie's cheek and Munro tucked his mother into the backseat. His wife sat in the backseat with Rennie to keep her propped up.

"Wait," Rennie said with some difficulty. "I would like the Fresnel."

"What is she saying?" Munro said.

"The Fresnel lens," Holly told him, "from the lighthouse. I'll get it." She started up the porch steps.

Munro called after her. "Don't bother. She can't take that thing over there. Where are they going to put it?" Munro drove the car away. Holly watched the silver cloud of Rennie's wild unbraided hair in the rear window of the car.

Holly dialed Narragansett WASTEC, but she knew Willis wouldn't have left Rennie at a crucial time like this. He was probably down at the Almacs buying soda crackers or something that would rest easily on Rennie's stomach. Willis had told Holly that it was awful to watch Rennie suffer a full round of vomiting after he had just made an offering of cream of chicken soup.

Holly went next door to alert Nicole. The children answered the bell. Fritz's Chihuahua puppy was asleep inside a boot beside the door. She looked twice at the boot, the little dog curled inside its leather cuff. It was the kind of thing she might see on a picture calendar.

Nicole looked at Holly. "Don't worry, Willis will get her out of that place."

"Can he do that?"

"I bet he can with a lot of fanfare."

Nicole left the room to take a shower and get her day going. Then the phone was ringing. Holly picked it up. A man wanted an appointment for a massage.

Holly said, "Nicole can't make it. She's got her afternoon lined up." She hung up the telephone.

She went over to her side of the duplex. She sat at the table and fingered the tiny book. Its mystery added a discomfiting flavor to everything else that was happening. Holly started to find the percussive sound of the clamshell driveway increasingly unnerving. Living in a place surrounded by calcified chips and shards, Holly couldn't ignore the traffic outside her windows. The prowlers and intruders began to stack up in an audible progression. Again a car drove up. It *sounded* like Rennie's car, the same wheel-base churning the crushed shells. When Holly walked outside, she saw a police vehicle lined up beside the duplex. An officer got out from behind the wheel.

She was surprised to see the police officer. In her nervousness, she stole a glance at the morning vista, a green sea with doily-white chop from the approaching storm; the tall ship was a speck on the horizon. She greeted the uniformed man. The officer shaded his eyes with the palm of his hand. His leather jacket and accessories squeaked as he adjusted his position before her. He was squinting. Holly moved a quarter-turn so the man wouldn't have to look directly into the hard, white eastern light when he spoke to her.

"Are you Holly Temple?"

"I was yesterday."

"Well, that's real good." The officer wasn't any too thrilled. He pulled a tiny notebook from his back pocket and flipped the pages until he found what he wanted.

Holly waited.

"Miss Temple, you need to speak to Detective Downey. That will be downtown. I can drive you over right now, or you can follow me in your own car."

"I need to follow you? To the police station?" Holly felt her stomach wall rise snugly into her diaphragm.

"They want to see you at the station. You know where that is? It's right on Broadway and Collins—"

"I think I know."

"We're right across the street from the Store 24."

"Across from the Store 24? That place with the quart-size coffees?"

"Yeah, that's where we get it. We just about keep that place in business, I guess," he said.

Holly couldn't wait any longer. She said, "What is this all about?"

"I'm not at liberty to discuss it with you," the officer said.

"Oh, give me a break. Are you kidding? Don't you have to explain why you're standing here on my porch—"

"At this point in time, we are just asking you to come downtown. They can't hold you longer than two hours."

"Two hours?"

"Two hours without a warrant, that's the law. We'll drive you back here. Or, you can follow me in your own car. Is that your Toyota?"

There were plenty of reasons she might be questioned. She was still on probation for a recent conviction of malicious burning. Perhaps her name was already on a list of possible suspects for whatever action had happened around town. Then, the truth was, she was standing there with full knowledge of stolen property. Some of that booty had been alive one minute and dead the next. Irretrievable goods worth several thousand dollars. Just one hundred feet from where she was standing, a stolen vehicle was concealed, a truck which she had helped vandalize with a Polish paintbrush.

Holly chewed her lip. She faced the officer and felt her secret whip its tail. She was a fraction away from blurting out all the facts with complete annotations. She realized she shouldn't bite her lip in front of the officer, it would make her look fishy.

"I don't like what you're saying," she said.

"You don't have to love it," he said.

Holly crossed her arms and adjusted her weight on one leg, so her hip protruded at a slight, defiant angle.

"Miss Temple. You were a tenant at 67 Spring Street? You had an apartment there until the sinkhole?"

"That's right. Number six."

"That whole place went up yesterday."

"It went up?"

"Systematically torched." The officer looked past Holly to give her a minute to think, but his head was tilted, as if he was listening for termites in the door frame. "They want some information from you. Either you come with me or they'll have to get you there with a lot of music."

She didn't like hearing his slang. "What does it have to do with me?"

He looked at her. "I can tell you this much. They've established reasonable grounds. They're just waiting on the affidavit and arrest warrant to come back."

Holly looked out at the water. She couldn't see anything. Her eyes felt like duds, solid glass spheres. Of course, it was a mistake, but the mistake blazed before them like an irrefutable vision. A burning bush. A visit from the Virgin.

The officer told her, "They have reasonable grounds to charge you. A witness has you *at the scene.* If I was you, Miss Temple, I'd come right now. It shows some good faith— that would help you later on."

She remembered the first time Willis fucked her—his hair brushed her cheek, its scent of milled lavender soap, and then the bright red fire from the linseed paint tore across the windowsill. She almost said to the officer, "Look here, we put that fire out," but she stopped herself. That happened weeks ago.

The officer said, "You've had an impromptu visit with the Fire Marshal before, isn't that right?"

The officer couldn't erase his easy smile. She had been arrested for setting fire to her husband's bed. Her probation officer, Dr. Kline, had said it was like shooting a horse while she was still mounted.

"Are you telling me that my old apartment house burned down?" she finally said, as if she had just adjusted the reception on her set.

"You can take your own car," he told her, "or come with me."

Suddenly, she wasn't sure if she could perform simple physical tasks such as depressing the clutch or moving the stick shift through its temperamental H-pattern.

Holly got into the police car. She sat in front with the officer. She settled back in the upholstered seat and stared out the windshield of the cruiser. The officer rolled it around and headed out the drive. Holly's big toe started throbbing where the nail was ripped. The pain was remote but insistent. Its small, self-contained protests opened a switch track. Tears started to roll down her cheeks in un-stoppable glassy strings.

Munro had come back to the house and was standing on the porch with two bright leather valises. He saw Holly sitting in the cruiser. He looked at her and smiled; his smile wasn't in the least ironic. It was as if he had known, all along, that Holly would end up riding out of that driveway on her way to the slammer.

Chapter Eighteen

Munro was in the front parlor when Willis entered with his grocery bags from Almacs. He dropped the bags to the floor. Some tiny cans of Ensure rolled in all directions. A quart jar had smashed, leaking Tropicana juice. Munro didn't look up from his work, thumbing through Rennie's insurance papers. A single cup of tea was balanced on the bamboo table. This one serving, still steaming, appeared to have usurped all of Willis's domestic privileges. Willis turned on his heel and went upstairs to Rennie's bedroom. He returned to the parlor and stood there facing his step-brother.

"Look who's here. Roar of the jungle," Munro said. He swiped his hand through the air in a limp-wristed lion's paw. "What'd I tell you? Rennie's safe and sound in a nice place. Away from this opium den. Just how long have you been getting high with Rennie's prescription medication?"

"Fuck you, Munro."

"Are you in pain now?" Munro said. "Did you run out of Bangkok Ex-Lax?"

"She won't get the bed warm. I'm going over there."

"Hold on a minute. First, maybe you should find your girlfriend. She's been kidnapped."

"How's that?"

"Some fancy dude drove her out of here. Nice car. Holly didn't look too happy about it. She was a regular Tiny Tears."

Willis's afternoon itinerary was beginning to look unmanageable. He had to spring Rennie and find Holly, as if to reclaim the two women he needed to travel between opposite cusps of the quarter moon. Willis was certain that Munro had described Jensen when he said that a flashy car had pulled away with Holly.

Willis drove over to Sycamore House and parked in the tenant lot. Some girls were sitting on the verandah wearing their silky business-wear, even in the spring chill. The cigarette smoke was making a screen. He asked them about their new landlord. The girls didn't know where he was. They were told to smoke outside while welders used a torch. Construction had started at the back of the house; a demolition trailer was parked under the eaves. A chute was running from a second-story window into the open bin. Big sheets of rotten tar paper littered the yard. Willis called up to a worker, "Seen your boss?"

"He's at the Carvel," the man called down before shooting an asphalt shingle past Willis.

Willis was getting back in the car when Sarojini walked out. She was wearing a sari. The thin gauze dress was expertly tucked around her slender figure like a length of sunlit cloud.

"What do you want?" Sarojini said.

Willis said, "Is Jensen at his store? Did he have Holly along?"

"I think you make a mistake."

"Yeah, well."

"My husband is at the ice cream counters."

Willis noticed she had an extra *s* there. Ice cream counters. That tipped her hand. She was a certified foreigner.

Willis parked the car right across three vertical spaces, paying no mind to customer conveniences, and walked into the Carvel franchise. He stood behind a line of customers. Nurses from Newport Hospital were on break, dressed in white nylon slacks, still carrying instant electronic thermometers tucked into their waistbands. He wondered just what temperature he was; he felt hot as a desert. He waited at the end of the line behind someone's pilled nylon hospital coat while a teenage soda jerk filled a plastic boat with a fat coil of soft ice cream. He recognized the black nurse who had worked on his arm. She recognized him. "It's Ted Bundy," she said. She was grinning with a shelf of white teeth. "Ted Bundy with his decoy arm."

"That's right," he said, enjoying her familiar, wide smirk. "What's my temp?"

She eyed him. He was making a friendly request. She lifted her thermometer and fished around in her pocket. She found what she wanted and tucked a sterile plastic sleeve over the wand. She inserted it in Willis's mouth. He waited a few seconds. The thermometer beeped. She removed it from under his tongue. "Ninety-nine point two," she told him. "That's normal."

"Normal? I felt hot."

"We all do ev'ry once in a while. It don't mean we're sick." She was gleaming.

He looked through a window and saw Jensen was in a back room. Willis pushed through the swinging door. The room was just about a freezer and Willis watched his breath shoot over his collar. Jensen was standing over a stainless steel table with sixteen little ice cream cakes resting on paper lace doilies. Jensen was decorating the cakes with a bag of frosting, wrapping the bag around his wrist and squeezing it out a silver nozzle.

"I'm looking for Holly."

Jensen said, "Look downtown. Mod Squad paid her a little visit, is what I heard."

"Excuse me?"

"She talked to me this morning. She's at the station doing some elegant shit-stirring. That's all I know."

Willis went around the table to get eye-to-eye. Jensen's breath feathered through his mustache and disappeared. "What are you trying to tell me," Willis said, "Holly was picked up?"

"The house on Spring Street burned down. They're asking her all about it since she's made herself a local celebrity. This is a small town. They'll carve it on her gravestone. 'Close Cover Before Striking.' "

"Vincent Silva's place burned down? When was this?"

"Other night."

Willis said, "She was over there with me, that's a couple weeks ago. That couldn't of done it."

"Maybe she went back there all by her lonesome."

"Why would she do that?"

"She's a sick girl," Jensen said. "*Love*sick. For me and everyone else."

Willis looked at the man holding the bag of icing.

Jensen said, "Like I said, she called me here."

"Maybe she tried me first."

"That's right. You weren't answering. She was ripped about that. They told her if she's charged and they have to hold her, bail will be set at around thirty thousand. She only needs ten percent of that to come home. That'd be three thousand, she says. She asks me, do I have it? Three thousand? She's asking *me*. Sure sounds guilty."

Willis circled the table with the rows of little cakes. He

collected them one by one in his hands until he had a frozen stack of eight. He dropped them to the floor and put his boot down on the airy tower. The ice cream rose up over the ankle leather. Willis walked outside leaving a few slick footprints.

Jensen watched him go. He called after Willis, "Shit, man. I understand, believe me—"

Willis went to a pay phone and called the Newport Police Station. He asked an officer, "Is Holly Temple over there? When can I get her? How long is that? When is she finished?" None of the answers were answers.

He drove home. Nicole was standing in the driveway when he got out of the car. Nicole pushed Willis's hair from his collar and rubbed his shoulder, pinching the deltoid between her fingers. "Shit, that's rock hard. That's from tension. Want a massage for that?"

"Christ," he said. She didn't stop pinching the muscle.

He removed her hand from under his tangled hair.

"Hey, what if I go sit with Rennie for a while?" Nicole said.

"You'll go sit with her?"

"I'll watch her until you show up."

"Never mind. I'm going over there myself."

Nicole said, "They've probably got tight security at that place. Did you think of that? Security?"

"Shit. We all want security. Everyone wants it. You know how to get it?"

"How?" She waited to hear a bleak speck of his wisdom.

"Only one way. We get cozy in our dirt blanket."

Nicole tugged her blond tassel around her waist and twirled the tip like a rabbit's foot. "Willis, you need a dose of sunshine. Maybe some bee pollen. You need dandelion salad," she told him.

He shrugged his shoulders and walked into his house.

He telephoned Fritz. Fritz's sister was reluctant to wake him. "You don't know how Fritz acts when he's half-asleep."

"Asleep at noon? Try some cold water," Willis told her.

"You come over here and throw cold water on him."

"Beth, it's an emergency."

"So call 911. Why you calling me?" The woman was teasing now and she told Willis to hold on.

He heard the sound of her shoes tapping across the linoleum. In a minute, he heard the same tapping coming back the other way. "Fritz says he's coming over there. He says he heard about the fire."

"He knows about that fire? Ask him where did he learn it?"

"Willis, I'm not standing here for your back-and-forth. Okay?"

"I'm sorry, Beth. You're great."

"I just put up with it," she said.

Willis hung up the telephone. He was feeling his stomach walls clanging and he remembered that he hadn't eaten any breakfast, or much of anything for twenty-four hours. He didn't want any food. Munro's teacup was still where Munro had left it on the bamboo table. He thought of Rennie in Château-sur-Mer. Rennie would have to wait still another while. He'd get her home.

He didn't want to think Holly had anything to do with the Spring Street place. He didn't know much about her family history, but he believed he had researched the rivers of her interior, he had drilled down into the water table and it was clear. Holly liked her domestic chores at Saint George's, and she loved cleaning those flower shacks at Neptune's. There was something simple about the attention she afforded it. She was an innocent victim, unless victims can't be considered free of blame. Maybe innocence in and of itself was a weakness, a selfish trait. The facts would emerge just as worms rise to the surface in the rain. He didn't lose faith in Holly.

But if the police were going to hold her, he had to find cash to get her out of hock. He figured he would hit Showalter for the cash. It was going to require a bit of bartering. The magnificent parrot was a pile of ashes, its carcass consumed except for the tough knob of the wishbone and the silvery tungsten breeder's ring from its foot. Willis had the InstyPrint truck; at least he had a *version* of it. Maybe that would be something to trade for cash.

Willis telephoned Showalter. Willis said, "I'm asking three grand or thereabouts for the truck."

"Three for the macaw?

"Forget the macaw, I'm talking about your truck."

"I don't want the truck," Showalter told Willis.

"You don't want your truck?"

"No."

"I'm not following you."

"I've got that truck reported stolen. It's been written up. I don't actually desire it back in my possession."

"You reported it? What if I just deliver that truck, drop it off right there in front of your place. That would invalidate the paperwork, wouldn't it?

"Go ahead, deliver my truck. I'm not paying cash for it."

"Let's talk about it," Willis said. Willis remembered what Showalter had asked him—"Do you talk your way or fuck your way?"

Showalter said he was willing to discuss the bird, he wasn't interested in the truck. "I hope that bird is in good condition. If it's unhappy it might featherpick till it's denuded. Is it chewing its feathers?"

"Chewing its feathers? No, it's not doing that," Willis said.

"That's good." Showalter told Willis to come up to Fall River at three o'clock, after the Miniature Book Society was finished with their buffet luncheon.

Willis said, "I'm on my own timetable."

Showalter liked the desperate tone in Willis's voice. He told Willis, "I have to see how you get out of this. This will be good. Tonight I won't need to get over to Blockbuster Video."

∽∾∽∾∽∾∽∾∽∾∽∾∽∾∽∾∽∾∽

Chapter Nineteen

∽∾∽∾∽∾∽∾∽∾∽∾∽∾∽∾∽

Rennie surfaced from her last morphine supplement and noticed that her room in the Life Care Infirmary was decorated with a nautical theme. Sea charts hung on the opposite wall; she couldn't read the soundings from where she was, but in the immediate corner beside her bed, an ocean topography map showed the Grand Banks, seamounts, and abyssal plains of the western Atlantic. She curled on her side and studied the map of the ocean floor and found it more than a bit comforting. She recognized the landmarks—Hudson Canyon, Kelvin Seamounts, and Flemish Cap—all the sobering checkpoints of the deepest unreachable canyons. She thought of Bill Hopkins sifting down that deep to where there wasn't a fairy's hair nor a filament of natural light.

A nurse came over and lifted her wrist. The nurse looked at her watch. Rennie was roused by the girl's cold fingertips and she adjusted her eyes at the intrusion. The room wasn't decorated as she had thought; it wasn't decorated at all. She searched the peach-colored walls for the picture of the ocean floor. It wasn't in its frame. She felt the nurse tugging the damp sheet out from under her hips.

"Did I wet?" Rennie said.

"Just a little," the nurse said.

"We can't have that," Rennie told the nurse. "What time is visiting hour? Make sure I'm dry for that." The congestion in Rennie's lungs made it difficult for her to talk. She tried to clear her throat, but her cough reflex didn't respond. She couldn't expectorate a drop.

The nurse explained that there was no visiting hour per se.

"None, 'per se'? Well, any minute, then," Rennie croaked through a congestive veil, "my son will arrive."

The nurse turned a crank for an outside awning. The heavy green fabric lifted away.

"More," Rennie said. "I can't see the water."

The nurse told her that the water was on the other side of the building.

"Are you sure that's not the water out there? I don't have my cheaters," Rennie said, her voice gurgling. "I thought I saw a Coast Guard dory go out from Castle Hill. It's not a good sight to see. The crew in their storm skins. It could be the *Christy and Roland* in trouble."

The nurse said, "That over there?" The nurse looked out the window, searching the tended lawns. "That's just the sky."

After a few minutes, a doctor came into the room and listened to Rennie's breathing with a stethoscope. He tugged the stethoscope out of his ears and shoved the rubber tubing into his breast pocket. He palpated Rennie's stomach and under her rib cage where the liver was distended with knotty masses. Next, he pressed his fingertip up and down Rennie's forearm, watching the indentations and wells it left in her bloated muscle. She was swelling up like a ripe papaya. The nurse wheeled a tray of instruments wrapped in sterile towels and parked it beside the bed. The doctor unfolded a towel and found what he wanted. He inserted a long needle into Rennie's thorax to tap fluid from her lungs. He attached the needle to a tube that led to a plastic bag fastened beneath the bed. Immediately, rosy fluid started to dribble. "This will make a little difference for you," he said.

"I'm waterlogged?"

"So to speak, yes."

"That happens to the ancient fleet, doesn't it?" Rennie said.

The doctor agreed. He didn't waste reassurances. Rennie rubbed her nose with the back of her hand. She was distressed by the smell of urine on her fingers. She had been pinching her wet bedsheet. The mild trace of urine acted like smelling salts, and Rennie suddenly recognized what was happening: her body was shutting down all of its mechanical stations—diesel, Heister, VHF. Then she sank away from the certainty of her recognition. She fell into a half-sleep that was not restful sleep. Such a half-sleep only nourished the transformation that was occurring.

Chapter Twenty

Fritz had the Chihuahua puppy on his lap, its tiny claws scratched white lines across his Levis. He wasn't pleased with the plan Willis told him. They were giving the dog away. "I paid for that Invisible Fence and now I ain't got a dog."

"Get yourself a new one."

"I like this one."

"Look. This is something I have to do."

"Shit, Willis, stop trying to save the world."

"Fuck you."

"You're going crazy," Fritz said.

"For you it was a short journey, a shortcut. A hop, skip, and a jump."

Willis steered into the cul-de-sac where his high school classmate Sheila lived. He parked the car in her driveway. Every window shade was drawn, as if they expected an air raid. The shrouded windows made a strong image; it was the last little bit of inspiration Willis needed in order to take the dog away from Fritz, tugging it back and forth for a moment of grief until Fritz let go. Willis walked up the path. He waited at the pastel front door and sneaked a look through the sidelight. Sheila came down the hallway and opened the door.

"Willis Pratt? Hey, I haven't seen you for years. What happened to your arm?" She tapped his cast with her tapered fingernail.

She was dressed in blue jeans and a ruby-red sweater. She had hunks of cotton between her toes where she'd been painting her toenails.

She looked on the way to recovery.

"Sheila. I was sorry."

"Yes. Everybody's been so nice."

"You haven't had a funeral yet."

"No, we haven't got him back from North Carolina."

"That medical school still has your baby?"

"What's the hurry, anyway," she said.

Willis saw her point.

"This puppy wants a home," he told her.

"You're kidding? You bringing me that dog?"

"It's pedigree."

"Yeah, but I don't know."

"It's tiny. Won't eat you out of the house like those Labrador retrievers."

"I can't have a dog."

"Please take it. Take it. From me. Please, Sheila." Willis looked at the young mother. She was a mother, once and again, despite the premature outcome. This realization humbled him even further. He kept his eyes on her.

She seemed to recognize his immensity of feeling, even if she didn't understand its nature. He was making amends for private reasons, who was she to prohibit him from trying?

He shoved the dog to her. She took it from him.

"It doesn't weigh anything. Like a toy," she said, twisting it around until she was face-to-face with its squished mug.

"Yeah, but it's got its own power pack."

"You really giving this thing to me?"

Willis started to walk away before she handed it back. He wanted her to take it from him, his kernel of misery. Maybe that little four-legged thing could disperse it evenly between them. He sat down in the car and shoved it in reverse.

Sheila followed him down the flagstone path and waved goodbye. She rested the dog on the walk and it sniffed the air, then it nipped the lacquered cotton puffs between her toes. She controlled it with the heel of her foot. The dog rolled over.

"Look at that," Willis told Fritz. "Isn't that good? Love at first sight."

The elm-lined street didn't have a single parking spot. Showalter's mini-book swap 'n' sell luncheon was going full tilt; some members had drifted onto the side porch and Willis surveyed the pointy-head, teensy-print population as he rolled the car along, looking for a space. They parked two blocks up the street and walked back to the front stoop. Fritz touched a lighted finger-pad that fired a jangle of chimes. No one came to answer the door. They walked into the house and joined the hustle-bustle around the buffet table. Willis saw the blond chorine, Miss Ingersoll. She looked back at him and wrinkled her nose like a coked-up Doris Day. He was surprised to see a man wearing a collar scooping ham salad onto a plate. Next to the priest, a sister was twisting a carrot stick in a bowl of sour-cream dip. Willis couldn't take his eyes off members of the clergy when they were engaged in ordinary domestic routine: buttering rolls and smearing mustard on corned beef. He didn't like thinking of all that food masticated and digested, going in and coming out of God's holy servants, same as it did everyone.

"I didn't think priests would go for these tiny books," Willis told Fritz.

"There's a hundred midget bibles in Showalter's bookcase. Tiny psalms. They can fit the Ten Commandments on a page the size of your fingernail."

"Is that a fact? The Ten Commandments on your fingernail," Willis sounded it out. He was looking for Showalter. Showalter saw him from across the room and signaled to Willis to pick up a plate. Willis took a china plate and stabbed at a slice of smoked turkey. He was suddenly overtaken by hunger or hunger's remembered role, and the table of food was too much to resist. He filled his plate with meats and macaroni salad, fruit ambrosia, little wheels of pumpernickel bread. Fritz followed after him, scooping a hunk of rice pudding onto the rim of his laden plate. The pudding jiggled onto the floor. Fritz took another hunk of pudding.

Willis stood against the wall and forked the food into his mouth. People came in and out of the room, making agreeable conversation. Willis nodded to strangers who tried to edge past him, directing their polite apologies so he would let them through to graze the huge table. He flattened his back against the wall when a man told him, "Can I squeeze in?"

"No problem," he said. The man wedged himself beside Willis, and they ate standing elbow to elbow. The stranger balanced his heavy plate on the palm of his hand. He noticed Willis's cast and said, "Can I help you?"

Willis wondered what this fellow wanted to do, spoon feed him? Play airplane? Willis declined any help. He pinched the gold edge of his huge dinner plate in his bandaged hand and levered it with acute accuracy. He shoveled the remaining food into his mouth. He rested the empty plate on the mantel beside another Reddi Kilowatt sculpture. The stranger shared his appreciation for the artwork and looked at Willis.

"Yeah, that's a masterpiece," Willis said. He rubbed his hands on his jeans.

He walked over to Showalter who was flipping through a tiny volume while a priest waited, grinning.

"This is the one," Showalter was saying, "that started it all."

The priest said, "My collection has room for that one if you ever want to part with it."

"I don't believe I could ever let it go, even for an old friend."

Willis interrupted, "Thanks for the food, but I'm on a tight schedule."

"You can wait a while."

"We need to talk. We need to have our powwow."

"It takes two to have a powwow, and I'm in the middle of my luncheon."

"We talk now, or I give the padre the *Deep Throat* slide show," Willis said.

The priest straightened up when he heard Willis. Showalter didn't show alarm. He scolded Willis for intruding, as if it was a matter of upbringing. Showalter said, "Another magnetic performance, Willis."

"I thought so."

"Just watch your mouth. This is Father McDermott, one of my preferred customers."

"No shit?" Willis said. "He partakes of *Infrared Nudes*?"

The priest smiled. Willis couldn't guess what was behind it.

"Excuse me, John," Showalter called the priest by his

given name and wheeled around to face Willis. "In my office."

"Which office? The bat cave?"

"No, my office." Showalter led the way to a room on the first floor. Willis recognized the huge leather desk he had seen once before.

Fritz followed Willis and they stood two abreast to face Showalter. Willis looked focused on a goal, and Showalter sat heavily in his leather chair to hear it.

Willis said, "I need three thousand for the truck, whether you want it returned or not."

"What about the bird?"

"I fell in love with it. I'm keeping it for myself."

Showalter said, "I knew it. You let it escape, you let the fucking thing ride off with the gulls?"

Willis pulled his pocket inside out. He found the solid breeder's band that had been on the macaw's foot and dropped it on the center of the desk. Showalter picked it up and examined the little ring.

"Worse than I thought," Showalter said.

"Yes, and it will get worse." Willis pocketed the band and sat down on the edge of the desk.

Fritz took a seat and lit a cigarette. He put the cigarette down in an ashtray. The ashtray held some loose rubber bands and the acrid scent of burning latex drifted up.

Willis told Showalter, "I'm saying I need cash, maybe we can work something up."

Showalter watched Willis with interest, trying to read his face. Willis had a new expression; it showed a hair of experimental tolerance for Showalter, and Showalter was enthused by it.

"Okay. Beautiful. Let's say we make arrangements, what's your idea?" Showalter's face was suddenly flushed.

Willis said, "Today's the day. Time to take a giant step

outside your closet." He smiled at the man. "That's all you really want out of life, isn't it?"

"And you want to sell it."

"For three thousand dollars."

Showalter stood up. He towered above Willis, who lounged on the desktop. Showalter grabbed Willis by his inky forelock, tugged his head back and lowered his face to just an inch above Willis's. He twisted the taut curl of hair another notch and centered his lips over Willis's startled cameo. Willis shoved him off.

Fritz yelled to Willis in his childlike Italian, *"Inna la ponza! Inna la ponza!"* In the stomach!

Willis didn't bother to strike Showalter.

He rolled an oyster around in his mouth and spat it on the plush rug.

He could almost taste Showalter's cologne, an expensive lemony scent.

Fritz was heated up. "You don't kiss this man," Fritz said. Willis studied his friend and couldn't come to a ready conclusion. He turned again to Showalter.

"The fact is," Willis said, "I need the money. You can buy it from me."

"Who says I will?"

"Oh, you will.

"Not this very minute."

"I need the money now. Three whole ones or thereabouts."

"I've got the house full of people."

"Maybe they can call it a day. Give the creaky collars a doggie bag."

"I might be interested in what you're saying, but I want a real series. You have to agree to let me shoot you in a couple scenes?"

"More paintball?"

Showalter laughed in the lowest octave. A rich basso profundo that unnerved Willis. He told Willis, "You're too good to be true, you know that? Don't worry. Beautiful. For you, just the ordinary will be top of line. Whatever we want."

Whatever *we* want. There it was again, that plural pronoun. Willis had no intention of meeting his end of it.

"Tell him, it's not so bad with your eyes closed, is it, Fritz?" Showalter said. "Fritz can never keep his eyes open."

Fritz was sitting behind the big glossy desk, resting his head against his forearm. He looked morally sick by their discussion of a merger.

"Cash up front," Willis said.

"I don't think so," Showalter said.

Willis said, "Money on the table." Willis didn't recognize the sound of his own voice; his terse clichés, *cash up front, money on the table*, were rolling ahead of him as his scheme fell apart.

"It's Saturday. I can't do my banking. Vault is closed, so to speak," Showalter said.

Willis moved to the window. It had started to rain, glassy pipettes struck the pane and burst into wet shatters. He turned around. "You say you don't have it?"

"Not today."

"Well, that's a bitch." Willis sat down against the radiator. The radiator was hot and he stood up.

Showalter told him that they could have their appointment the next day. It was business, after all, and spontaneity wasn't always a plus in these matters. Willis wasn't listening. He signaled Fritz and they walked out of the office and through pods of the religious and the geeky. Priests, sisters, teensy book designers and dealers, a man dressed in a tartan, Miss Ingersoll, who was cupping a dish of olive pits in the palm of her hand. They found the street. Willis walked into the rain. Its lines felt sharp against his face, it rinsed him of Showalter's plush interior rooms.

"Holly might spend her first night in jail." Willis was genuinely disturbed by the idea of it.

"Everybody has to," Fritz said.

Chapter Twenty-one

Holly's buttocks felt numb from sitting so long in a hard plastic banana chair at the Newport Police Station. She answered questions from Detective Downey and a rotating entourage. Her probation officer, Dr. Kline, was taking notes. Holly watched her write down her statements, but she wondered how they were paraphrased.

Detective Downey said, "How many candles are we talking about?"

"I don't know," she said. "Maybe six."

"Those Hanukkah ones, or what?"

Holly said, "Hurricane candles. What's the difference? Wax is wax. They sell them at Marine Specialties."

The detective was concerned with every specific. She told him she had witnessed two small fires—Jensen's bed and the momentary blaze that scorched the window. Each was a tiny golden seed and never a torrid harvest. She would have liked to watch both fires bloom beyond their initial stages into total fruition but she didn't say so.

An hour into it, Detective Downey told her she might need to arrange bail. Holly wanted to make a phone call. They told her she could make as many phone calls as she wanted. She couldn't get Willis. Holly tried Robin. The line kept ringing. She called Jensen at Carvel. She started crying. A detective handed her a quart-size coffee with double sugars from Store 24. She took a gulp and regained her composure. She hung up on Jensen.

She had started by telling them about her personal life in order to buffer what she couldn't reveal about the stolen parrot and the truck. She told the detective how many times she had made love to Willis Pratt; it wasn't an impressive number of times. Detective Downey didn't question her about drugs and she didn't have to betray the embarrassing details about Willis and Miss Emma's backdoor visits. Still, Detective Downey gave her the impression he was waiting for a detail that would clinch his suspicions. He lifted his eyebrows when she described her first time with Willis—missionary position. Telling it made her feel cheap. It wasn't any of his business, but she told him every detail of their first night together: their visits to Sheila Boyd's Cape-style house, to Babyland and Neptune's. She told Detective Downey that they ended up in her old apartment on impulse. They had a little fire from candle wax. It wasn't a copycat fire, as the police were suggesting. Willis put the fire out.

The detective remained skeptical and she started to doubt herself. For the past hour she had suffered from an audiotape loop in her head, a schoolyard chant and childhood admonition: *Liar, liar, pants on fire!* The more questions she answered, the faster and faster the rhyme came. She hesitated, then she told them about driving home and finding the two silver words.

" 'Size queen'?"

"That's right," she said.

"Size queen." The detective was interested. His interest made his eyes look swimmy. He seemed less curious about the vandalism to her duplex and more interested in the realm of desire that the words described.

"You know what they say," Detective Downey told her, "it's not the meat, it's the motion."

"Well, that's a golden oldie," she said. Holly guessed he had an itsy wiener of his own.

"It's not the meat. It's the motion," he told her again, as if he really needed to convince her.

"Oh, yeah? How would you know?" She had lost her temper. "Right about now I'm thinking of calling a lawyer. This is starting to smell like that Clarence Thomas thing."

The detective didn't have a point of reference. He wrote the name on his notes, then crossed it off when he finally remembered. For the fourth time, the detective asked her to describe the morning she had set fire to her husband's bed. The questions seemed to shift from one alleged crime to the other. Yes, she had started that earlier fire in Jensen's apartment.

That's the one they wanted to hear about.

When she started her narration, the circle of officers leaned back, ready to enjoy the familiar details she offered. Smiles wormed over their faces. Detective Downey asked her if she wanted to burn other items belonging to her lovers. Did she want to burn clothing? *Playboy* magazines? Did she ever want to set fire to an automobile or any other high-ticket item?

Holly clamped her mouth shut. Yes. She saw them all: Detective Downey in his cheap wool suit, stretched at the knees and elbows, baggy as a camel, the officers in dark blue uniforms, her probation officer in Liz Claiborne separates from a Cranston discount outlet. Holly imagined all of them turned to char, like the creosote victims of Pompeii, entombed figures standing around the stationhouse holding quart-size coffees.

Chapter Twenty-two

The nor'easter was churning inland; dense veils of moisture advanced on the horizon like heavy green army blankets moving across on a clothesline pulley. When Willis drove into Easton Way, Holly ran out to greet him. He crammed the brake. Fritz banged into the dash. Willis turned to his friend. "Shit. You okay? I'm sorry."

Fritz rubbed his shoulder where it had slammed the dashboard. Holly yanked the door open and wriggled into Willis's arms.

Willis said, "They let you go?"

"For now."

"You're off the hook?"

"I don't know. Those assholes. I'm suing for harassment. They had me there for three hours. That extra hour will cost them."

"They didn't bring charges?"

"Of course they couldn't bring charges. I didn't start that fire." She glared at Willis, then melted against him again.

He patted her. "Shit, I thought you were in a big mix-up."

"Turns out, it was a heat gun. Painters were stripping the clapboards with a heat gun and that old linseed paint caught. It smoldered until long after quitting time."

"A heat gun?"

"You know, an acetylene torch. So what do they do? They bring me in. For a chat. They can't forget about me. I'm getting a lawyer."

Fritz pushed her shoulder. "Did you know Willis almost took a blind date with an eye doctor to buy your walking papers?"

Holly said, "Excuse me?" She put her face in front of Fritz. "I'm out of there without papers, aren't I? So, what's it to you?"

"You just aren't worth all this trouble," Fritz said.

"Shut up," Willis told Fritz. "It's not anybody's fault." He smiled back and forth, trying to lasso them in. "I couldn't have done it with Showalter anyway."

"That's right, the trouser snake is hibernating," Fritz said.

Holly said, "Willis, what if I was in jail and needed that cash? You wouldn't do it with that guy? Even for me?"

Willis looked between Fritz and Holly, stunned by their duet. He had not seen it coming. He walked into the house. His skin was flushed. It prickled in inextinguishable blotches. It was his junkie itch. Next, his headache drilled his forehead like a nailgun. He had a long evening ahead, getting Rennie wouldn't be a walk in the park.

He went upstairs to his bedroom but his drugs were missing. He had finally depleted his supply. He went into the bathroom. His spine felt cold and achy. He found a tower of little color-coded boxes behind the old beach towels in the linen closet. Rennie had made a run to the CVS two weeks prior to her weak spell. Green boxes were twenty milligrams. Willis felt immediately grateful for Rennie's foresight. Each individual box had foil cards with twelve suppositories. He made a quick addition in his head, but the math seemed too difficult in his frazzled condition. He tried again. He made an exact calculation. Two hundred and forty footballs.

He took a carton and peeled off its cellophane seal like a shoelace of red licorice. He inserted a deuce. Two was maintenance, three still took him off. He didn't want to cloud up when he had serious planning to do. On the other hand, he was shaky and wired; he figured he might as well tuck a third.

Holly came up to him as he was buttoning his pants with one hand. She grabbed the waistband of his jeans and pressed the rivet through its hole. She kissed his lips, which tasted slightly salty.

"Cold cuts," he told her.

"Cold cuts?"

"I went through a chow line at the mini-book society."

Holly tried to follow him. "Mini-book? Hey, do you know anything about some little books? I found one of those little books this morning on my kitchen table. Did you put it there?"

Willis was walking down the stairs.

"Well, did you put it there? Willis, I'm asking a question—did you put it there?"

Fritz was at the landing. "If you can't tell where he puts it, you're in trouble, girl."

"I wasn't talking to you," she told him.

Willis was in the parlor. Munro's teacup was still where it was.

A piece of Fleet Bank stationery was secured to the sideboard. It was a letter from Munro scratched out in black ballpoint.

WILLIS—

OUR MOTHER IS VERY SICK. DON'T DISTURB HER FINAL DAYS ON EARTH. I'VE CHECKED THE PLATES ON THAT

TRUCK. IT'S STOLEN. YOU KNOW THAT. I KNOW THAT.
NEXT TIME, BETTER GET MAACO.

Willis held the sheet of paper by one corner and walked
into the kitchen. "Look at this," he mocked. "I'm scared."

Holly had a circle of linguica sausage frying. Its spicy
scent overtook the empty house. It didn't feel right to have
Holly at the stove instead of Rennie and he tried not to let
it bother him.

"I'm not hungry for that tube steak," he told her. "We
ate a lot of free food an hour ago."

"You can't eat this?"

"Can't," he told her."

"Oh, nice."

"You have it," he told her.

Holly looked at the fat rope of sausage in the black
cast-iron pan. She hated to ask Fritz, but she turned around.
"Ichabod, do you want some of this?"

"No sale," Fritz said.

Holly stabbed the meat with a fork and took it over to
the enamel waste can. She pressed the lever with her toe
and dropped the greasy coil in the garbage.

Willis said, "Okay, this is what we do. I go over to Château-
sur-Mer and get Rennie checked out nice and easy, just
like she's leaving Motel Six. We might even steal a couple
towels."

"What do I do?" Fritz said.

"Wait, I'm telling you. First, before I get my girl, we
drive the truck over to Easton Pond and roll it in."

Fritz wedged his fingertips in his tight jean pockets.
"What is this now?"

"You know where we ditched those Metric King surprises? We drive the truck into Easton Pond same way."

"Excuse me?"

"Just drive it in as far as you can, it will fall off that shelf, I think."

"You're crazy."

"We'll wipe it down with Amour All, get our dabs off the upholstery."

"I'd rather drive it over to my sister's, keep it on her carport. That's as crazy as I get."

"Listen, Munro is sitting back, licking his lips. I can't live with that."

Fritz said, "Try to live with it."

"Can't."

"We steal it. We paint it. We sink it? That's enough to fill up the whole blotter."

Holly said, "He's right. These last days are crazy. I can see the police log tomorrow morning. The whole left-hand column dedicated to us."

Fritz turned around to Willis. "I guess I have to tell you. Gene didn't report the truck. He never called it in."

Willis said, "It's not stolen? Munro thinks different."

"Munro's a bull artist."

"Are you saying Showalter's letting you off?"

Holly ran the tap and took a drink of water.

Willis tried to sort it out. How many charades were happening at once?

Holly said, "Well, they're still eyeballing *me*."

Fritz said, "You love it."

Holly said, "Dr. Kline says they have to come up with a probable-cause hearing or drop the whole thing. They know it was a heat gun, but they love the story about me and Jensen. They're sickos!"

Fritz eyed her. His look implied that maybe it *was* her, maybe *she* had some of her pages stuck together.

"What are you staring at, Ichabod?" she said.

"Excuse me, Miss *Ho*-ly Temple," Fritz said.

Willis ignored it. "I don't want the truck here. When Rennie gets back, everything has to be square."

"Square? Everything's warped," Holly said.

"Man himself invented the wheel," Fritz said.

Willis pulled the palm of his hand down his face. He said, "Look, we weight the van, and it will roll right into the drink. It can stay there a few days until someone decides to find it. By then, Rennie's in heaven."

They looked at Willis.

"Shit. I know it's happening. She's suffering. I don't have any control over it. It's her jumping-off point that has to be secured." Willis was already walking out the door. The rain was running through its list of options: a coy smattering, then a mist, then an impatient torrent, then again, a mist. The wind was roaring northeast and the halyard on the flagpole was pinging. He went into the shack and lifted Rennie's old kiln with a great bit of difficulty. He immediately dropped it, jumping back so it wouldn't get his boot. Fritz helped him lift the heavy stone-lined oven and they shoved it into the truck. Willis didn't think that the kiln alone was going to do it. He went into the house and dialed Carl Smith. Willis reached Carl on his rusty tub, the *Tercel*.

Willis said, "You know those barrels sitting out back at the Cranston Warehouse? The ones from Balfour? Those ones we stabilized with that concrete slurry mix? I need a couple of those."

"Those are regulated."

"Shit, those've been sitting there forgot-about for weeks."

"You need them? For what?"

"Just do."

"It's Saturday. Now, why do I want to come off my boat and go to work?"

"I have to have a couple of those barrels, tonight," Willis said directly.

"Need paperwork for that. You have your paperwork?"

"I have it."

"What paperwork exactly?"

"The long green kind," Willis said. "Winter kale." Willis enjoyed bringing Rennie's soup into it.

Carl Smith was chuckling. "That sounds right. Just why in the hell you want those barrels?"

"I need them over here. For a demonstration."

"That's a rope of sand," Carl told him.

"All right, you think of something on your own."

"Kale rhymes with jail," Carl said. He clucked his tongue. "I'll haul them for a buck and a half. Why not make that two bucks and some of those little footballs. I guess you have extra of those?"

Willis wrote three figures on a pad by the phone and showed it to Fritz. Fritz nodded that he had that much cash.

Willis confirmed the damage and concluded the ritual with Carl. Carl clicked off.

Fritz was staring at Willis, impressed. They walked outside and took the car to Easton Pond. They drove over the grasses a couple times, back and forth, to test the surface and squash the weeds down a little so they could roll the truck through at twenty miles an hour; that was their plan. What they couldn't achieve by their wits and know-how they could achieve with a little acceleration. A flat speed of twenty or twenty-five miles an hour.

The little pram was still hidden behind the weeds, but

Willis noticed some fishing gear and crumpled juice packs in the bow. "You been fishing?" he asked Fritz.

Fritz shook his head.

"Kiddies found the *Crouton*."

Fritz said, "Shit. This is my boat. This isn't a childcraft moppet liner." He crouched over the dinghy and collected the sticky juice containers, tossing them over his shoulder.

While the men were gone, Holly went back into the kitchen and pressed the lever on the waste can with her toe. She lifted the sausage out. She slapped it on a plate and sliced the meat into individual bites, bright greasy pennies which she ate with her fingers.

The light was going. The wind was stirring the empty branches until the treetops rolled in tight circles like wire whisks. Carl Smith steered into the drive in his pickup truck. Willis had expected to see the big Narragansett WASTEC trailer, but of course this was a private job, something between him and Carl Smith. They discussed business sitting side by side in the pickup cab. Willis gave him the cash and a twist-tie bag of Rennie's morphine. Fritz lurked around in the driveway, looking jealous of their height over him. They brought him inside the cab to share a toot of crack. Fritz accepted, rubbing Carl's lip prints from the stem before he took his turn.

Then Carl backed his truck into the doorway of the shack and used his block and tackle to lower the concrete barrels into the back of the InstyPrint van. When the first concrete cylinder went in, the van sank on its haunches and didn't bounce back; the second slurry was a greater insult. The tailgate sagged and wobbled on its suspension until it steadied above the floor's surface by only a few inches.

Carl Smith was shaking his head and laughing at the InstyPrint truck. "Looks like a tar baby," he said.

"That's what it is," Willis said. "Our very own tar baby."

Carl wanted to use the telephone and Willis said go ahead. He saw Carl was already organizing something else. When he was gone, Fritz complained. "Shit, that guy likes chasing the dragon. He's a cry for help."

"Carl's Carl," Willis said.

"He should dial 1-800-COCAINE."

"Shit."

"You know, 1-800-ALCOHOL. 1-800-COCAINE. 1-800-WHATEVER. He's a cry for help if I ever saw it."

At dark, Holly drove ahead of the men in the sedan and parked on Eustis Avenue, where she unfolded a paper napkin of linguica and continued to eat the delicious garlicky wheels of meat.

Fritz climbed into the van beside Willis and Willis backed the truck out of the shack. Willis worried that the tires might blow from the weight.

Fritz said, "The rims will hold. It's just a half-mile to the pond. That is, unless you want to change your mind."

Willis was feeling pretty positive about this end of the operation. There was no question that the truck was going to sink, they just had to get enough momentum to roll it past the shelf and into the deep. He looked at the gas gauge. The needle touched the red zone. "Shit, we're on fumes," he said.

"That's enough, isn't it?"

The windshield wipers couldn't keep up with the rain and Willis was straining to see, but he felt fine. He felt that rare sensation after finalizing a homemade scheme; they were at the crest of it, and from there it was all downhill.

Willis told Fritz, "I'll drop you with Holly. Wait in the car. No reason for both of us taking the bumps."

"Point. I'm already sitting here. I'm riding with you," Fritz said.

"I'm saying. Get out of the truck."

Fritz stared at Willis. "I'm not sitting with her."

"Shit. This is what it is. I'm going to come in fast from Memorial Boulevard. That's a sharp turn. We'll ride over the weeds, and gun it when we hit the bank. We need a bit of speed to blow it off the shelf. We'll have plenty of time to climb out. Crack your window."

Fritz unrolled his window so the water could wash in fast. The heavy slurries would pull the pond in without any help from them.

The radio was playing Stevie Wonder. "Yester-*me*. Yester-*you*. Yester-*day*." They rode up and down Memorial Boulevard waiting for a window in the traffic. Behind the rain, oncoming headlights throbbed with oversized bulbs. The job would take all of one minute once the boulevard was clear, but the cars kept coming. Willis wondered about the gas. "Yester-*me*. Yester-*you*. Yester-*day*." Finally, the road was empty and Willis steered off the shoulder and into the marsh grass; he accelerated over the humps of weeds. The radio was blaring and Fritz was hooting, "It's the blind leading the blind—" Their wild laughter ascended as Willis steered the truck straight into the reservoir.

When the front wheels touched the bank, Willis crammed the gas pedal for a surge. The truck shot forward but never went airborne as Willis had hoped; it careened into the pond at an abrupt angle. Its nose plowed the watery wall. The truck tipped and went face first; the concrete barrels shifted and crashed into the bucket seat where Fritz sat.

The bucket tore off its rivets and pinned Fritz against the dash.

Willis saw the headlights illuminating the green murk as the water washed in over the doors, the wet night sluicing in both sides. The heavy nose of the truck continued sinking as the tail end rose up. Fritz was taking the weight of the concrete slurries and he screamed for Willis until his lungs couldn't draw any breath.

Willis tried to push his friend loose from behind the barrels of blended cyanide and concrete. Fritz was pinned against the glove box. The barrels worked closer each time the truck was jostled by the changing water level.

Never before had Willis confronted a greater physical force than this. Not lightning nor hurricane, nothing like this dumb monster—weight. Perhaps it was the icy water; Willis felt paralyzed. He watched the scene unfold. He recognized a familiar sensation, the passive burden of the witness, that grim eternal duty, so difficult to shirk. Then Willis pulled himself out the window. He swam around to the other side. His cast drank up the pond water and a few bubbles escaped. He tugged open the passenger door. The cab was filling up and Fritz was burbling, then jerking his head back in panic. Willis could hear the radio speakers still grinding out the Stevie Wonder classic; its cockeyed refrain warbled through the cushion of water. By some weird fortune, the cab light had not yet shorted and Willis saw, in full detail, how his friend was crushed against the dashboard. The water was up to his collar. Fritz eyed Willis, following Willis with a helpless attention. It was the patient eye of a manatee or dolphin behind an aquarium window. It was as if Fritz accepted that they were in separate worlds, their fortunes on opposite sides.

Then Fritz's eyes started to flutter. Willis talked to Fritz. "Federico," he shouted. "Federico, look at me. Look at me. Stop dicking around—"

Fritz's face turned pale and shocky. It went blank. His friend's lost face triggered a final commitment from Willis. He swam away from the truck and stumbled up the bank. He looked for the *Crouton*, but it wasn't where he thought. He thrashed the weeds, twisting at the waist, swiping his arms left and right through the silver grass until he found the dinghy. He seized the glossy oar from where Fritz had stowed it neatly under the bench; the oar felt like a toothpick. He waded back to the truck and tried to pry the barrels apart using as much leverage as he could get with the oar. He felt the cement cylinders shift a little, not enough to make a difference. The oar snapped. Willis took a breath and sank underwater. He leaned against the door jamb and kicked the barrel with his legs. His strength was cut in half in the heavy water; it was like kicking through a chain-mail curtain. He surfaced again and stood on the rocker panel of the sinking truck. He kept his hand under Fritz's chin, keeping Fritz's face steadied above an almost imperceptible swirling which signaled that the truck might still be settling.

He couldn't tell if Fritz was breathing. Willis pressed his face to Fritz and tried to detect his struggle for oxygen. Fritz wasn't relying any longer on an exchange of air. Willis made a production trying to administer mouth-to-mouth. His busy efforts seemed to awaken Fritz. Fritz came back and forth from that other territory. Back and forth from the *almost dead* to the *almost living*.

Holly had seen what happened and had run up to a house to call Rescue. She came back to the car and stayed clear of the spectacle when the grassy bank lit up with floodlights and the optical tingle of emergency flashers. Men in slickers swarmed over the bank. Willis sat in the weeds, shell-shocked. Someone wrapped a white blanket across his shoulders. In minutes, a team freed Fritz using a winch harness and boom on an Exxon tow truck. They brought Fritz on shore and stabilized his spine in a neck brace, then transferred him to a stretcher. Willis weaved back and forth beside his friend. He lifted Fritz's hand, but the paramedics made Willis drop it. Holding Fritz's hand could jar the spinal column. Willis was reluctant to obey the icy instruction to let go, as if his bond with Fritz might be irreparably severed.

The emergency workers predicted that it wasn't as bad as it looked. Fritz might have a crushed sternum. One lung was collapsed, but Fritz wasn't going to die. Willis wanted to go along with Fritz to Newport Hospital, but the questions started coming at him.

He faced the uniforms and snapped into a different role. He said that he didn't know anything about the truck; he was driving by in his own vehicle when he saw the accident happen. He saw the driver was in trouble and he had tried to assist. He cooperated with the officers and walked over to Rennie's sedan in order to fish out his license and registration. When he reached the car, Willis got into the driver's seat and started the engine. He cut away before the police had decided whether they were supposed to go after him.

Holly had watched the exchange from the levee knoll above the reservoir, and she started walking off in the dark. Willis circled around and saw her figure flare up in his headlights. It was Holly's distinctive gait—half child-like, half feral. He pulled the car over and she sat down in the seat beside him. "You're getting good at this," he told her.

"Fight or flight," she said. "There's only those two options."

The storm was coming in. A raw, relentless blow which might have encouraged some people to dip into their kindling bucket and "make a fire," and have a cozy situation. When they came back to the house, Holly flicked on the kitchen light to find that a leak had pooled rainwater on the linoleum.

Willis said, "When it's coming at an angle, the rain creeps under the bald spots in the shingles." Holly found the mop while Willis went upstairs to get his dry clothes. He was shivering as he talked to her, but she couldn't tell if it was the cold or a complete nervous exhaustion.

"You need to get in the bath," she told him.

"No time. They'll be over here as soon as they scratch their heads for a while."

"Take a hot shower at least."

"I'll do that when I've got her home."

Holly had forgotten. She had forgot about Rennie.

Holly didn't think she could survive another reckless hour added to that day. She snapped at Willis, "Do you think I can do another thing tonight?" She couldn't give a fiber more of herself to any cause or stray kitten. Then she saw she was being selfish. "Maybe you should get Rennie tomorrow, after some rest."

"There's no rest period. There's no time-out in hell," he told her.

She was tired of his same morbific tune and she didn't want to humor it. She climbed the stairs behind him. "You'll need your wits to take her out of there. Look at you. You look like a drowned rat. You look," she waited to find the courage, "like a white punk on dope."

He turned around on the stairs and offered her a tight

smile; his cold lips were blue like the silvery skin on Italian plums.

"Look at yourself!" she scolded him. He looked so pathetic, she changed her tune. "You're going to freeze to death in those wet jeans."

"I need to call the hospital about Fritz," he said.

"I'll call while you fix yourself a bath."

Holly talked to someone at Newport Hospital who wouldn't release information. "Why not?" Holly said into the telephone. "What if I'm his sister?"

Holly dialed again and talked directly to the nursing station in Emergency. The nurse reassured her that no one who had been admitted that night was in a mortally serious condition.

Willis was sitting in the claw-foot tub in the third-floor bathroom. Holly leaned over him and swished the hot water back and forth with a facecloth. "Shit, Willis, this is *too* hot, you don't even know it. You're schmecked!" She twisted the cold-water tap and added more water. She went into his bedroom and came back with the radio. She hadn't heard too much singing from Willis lately. Singing phrases from old songs was a stress-relieving mechanism for Willis, but she hadn't heard a peep from him. He was losing any tiny bit of charm he might have once possessed. She told him, "Sing that Bobby Darin thing."

"Which one?"

She was holding the radio, looking for an outlet. "You know, the one I like." She started to sing it. Her voice was wan and fetching. *"There's a rainbow 'round my shoulder, and it fits me like a glove. There's a rainbow 'round my shoulder—"* She looked at him. Her eyes were rainy. "That one."

"Christ," Willis said. He didn't start singing. "Don't

drop that thing in here," Willis told her, eyeing the dangling cord.

"You want music don't you?"

She rotated the dial. It was set on the weather band, receiving NOAA Weather Radio, which announced the strength of the storm. The gale wasn't as severe as the "Storm of the Century," but they were calling it its little sister. The storm was mostly in the form of sleet and rain, but the sleet clattered like tacks across the gables as if a team of roofers were driving nails.

Willis couldn't separate the image of Noah, the ark builder, from NOAA, the acronym for the National Oceanic and Atmospheric Administration. He had always found the similarity reassuring when he listened to the weather reports with Rennie.

That night, a dragger was late coming into the State Pier. The *Glamor Girl* with four crew aboard was caught in rough seas.

"Rennie wouldn't like to hear that," Holly said.

"She wouldn't like to hear it, but she'd glue her ear on it," Willis said. "She'd listen all night."

Willis spent many storms sitting beside Rennie at the kitchen table as she tracked the movement of a particular squall and any member of the fleet that might be caught offshore. She'd get out her Loran-C chart for George's Bank and Nantucket Shoals and look for herself. If there hadn't been an actual distress signal, she'd mark where they sent their last VHF radio, their LORAN numbers with their line of position, and from the last LOP intersect she'd estimate where the trouble might have happened.

The *Glamor Girl* was steaming back from Cultivator Shoals. Willis wondered if maybe their LORAN antenna had snapped in the gale or spray had shorted the console. With zero visibility and no LORAN, a ship can be turned around. Perhaps they decided to run ahead of the storm and had moved out of range and couldn't use their VHF. If the missing ship was disabled somewhere within the Boston Harbor traffic lanes or local safety fairways, another trawler might happen on them. Most likely they were steaming out to avoid the swells, that's what everyone always hoped.

Holly and Willis listened to the weather statement until it finished its tape loop and repeated the same information. "Storm Warning in effect. Seas building fifteen to twenty-five feet. Northeast wind fifty knots with gusts. Water temperature thirty-six degrees."

Holly punched the radio band to FM. It was "Eric in the Evening." Again, Willis had missed its signature theme, which was all he ever wanted to hear, but Willis told her to keep it on the next song, an astonishingly mournful flügelhorn doing the mellow lines of "Make Someone Happy."

Holly kneeled on the tile and leaned her elbows on the graceful ivory lip of the old tub. She rested her head against her arms. Willis sat forward to kiss her. His lips invited her and they kissed long and sorrowfully.

They sat like that until the water was tepid and Willis looked pink and sleepy. He stood up dripping and Holly handed him a towel. He scrubbed it over his legs and arms just as they heard a racket at the front door. A couple of voices rolled off terse salutations, official jargon of some kind, and the door burst open.

"The police—" Willis said.

Suddenly, glass was crashing. The Fresnel lens must have been jostled from its perch in the parlor. The hull of glass hit the floor and shattered. After that surprise, Holly and Willis were astonished to hear a quite perplexing and unprofessional peal of laughter. It was Munro.

Willis whisked into his bedroom and grabbed his wet

jeans. "I have to get out of here, now. Can you handle this?"

Holly looked at him and tipped her face up and down in a terrified affirmative. He yanked bureau drawers open looking for a sweatshirt. Holly handed up a dirty sweater from the floor. He pulled on his soggy boots as the visitors started up the stairwell.

They went back into the bathroom and locked the door. "Shit. Do you have keys?" he whispered.

"Keys?" She had her complete set of rings for the summer cottages, that was all.

"The freaking car keys are downstairs—"

"Mine too," she said.

"Well, that's perfect. He looked around the bathroom. "Listen, pretend you're in the bath," Willis whispered. "Then meet us at Neptune's later on."

"Neptune's? You're going to Neptune's?"

"It's changeover Saturday. Isn't that it? Changeover Saturday?" Willis said.

His connection thrilled her.

Willis was sifting through the linen shelf, throwing the towels on the floor. "Where's the cube?" he said. "Jesus Christ. That Carl Smith. He's pinched it all."

"You're kidding? Carl took your dope?"

He was weaving on his feet, having a difficult moment assimilating the bad news.

At the same time, the visitors were attempting to lift the bathroom door off its hinges.

Willis went to the other end of the bathroom and started tugging the storm door. What had always served as a budget picture window was again revealing its lifelong potential as an emergency exit. He jerked the handle. He forced it, tearing it loose from its rusty tacks. The wind whipped the thin Plexiglas panel wide open. He looked into the black rain. Below him, at the rear of the house, there was nothing but puny treetops, two peaked maples and a sweep of wind-torn olive shrubs. In the driveway, it was Munro's Vista Cruiser.

It was Munro bringing in the second-shift constables like he had promised. Willis heard them outside the bathroom door, fussing with the antique lock.

Willis looked back at Holly, he was grinning madly.

"You can't jump from this high—" she told him.

Willis leaned out the mystical opening in the wall. The rain churned in a glassy horizontal weft. He reached for the silver fabric, as if seizing a curtain tassel. He sailed from the third floor. Willis fell clean of the building. He landed on the olive bushes, which tossed him again, then rolled him off awkwardly, like from a circus net. Holly leaned out the open door and saw that Willis was running off favoring his leg, but he was all right. He was already pedaling Rennie's three-wheeler around the back of the duplex, skirting the vinyl flags of the Invisible Fence. Holly recognized the Vista Cruiser in the driveway as she tugged the storm door shut.

She didn't much feel like facing Munro.

She tore her clothing free and stepped into the chalky water. She was lathering soap when Munro and Dr. Kline walked in. She covered her nipples with her soapy forearm. Holly couldn't believe it. Dr. Kline said, "Holly. We're here to make a drug intervention. Do you understand? Where is he?"

"You're doing what?"

"An intervention." Dr. Kline handed her a towel.

"I see. You have a fancy word for bossing people around," Holly said.

When Holly was dressed, she sat down at Rennie's kitchen table, Munro and Dr. Kline across from her. "No, I haven't seen Willis all afternoon. I was at the station with you, Dr. Kline," she said with a little vinegar. "Remember?"

"Come on, Holly."

"I was with *you* and that *detective* and *everyone else*. Why are you pinging me about Willis? I don't manage Willis."

Holly told them she wasn't going to be pleasant about it any longer, she was writing everything down, making a list for her lawyer.

"When did you get yourself a lawyer?" Munro said.

"Well, shit. Today's Saturday, you know."

Dr. Kline said, "Holly, you have every right to be upset."

"No shit."

"Pretty upset, huh?" Dr. Kline said.

"What do you think?" Holly said. She crossed her arms and leaned back in her chair.

Dr. Kline said, "You were doing fine until you came over here and met this fellow Willis Pratt. I don't think you understand the dynamics. There's a lot happening here. Was that a stolen truck? Was that hazardous waste he dumped in that reservoir—"

"Excuse me?" Holly said. She bit her little fingernail. She had no idea that Easton Pond, that grubby algae hole, was the city reservoir. She didn't think twice about the barrels Willis had used to weight the InstyPrint truck. Now the world of events was rotating on a greased axis. She felt a little confused, but she shoved the cuffs of her sleeves over her wrists and knitted her fingers together on the tabletop. She regained her composure. "I don't follow you. How is that germane to my situation?"

Holly's tone surprised Dr. Kline, and her penciled eyebrows lifted and froze in a thin double arch, like a seagull
silhouetted against an horizon. She told Holly, "What about
checking into the Stopover Shelter for a few days?"

"You're kidding. The Stopover Shelter? The SOS
house downtown?"

"It might be a safety measure for you until this resolves
itself."

"I'm not going to that flophouse for battered women.
You want me to go in there with all those sad stories? Do I
look battered?"

"Sometimes our bruises are on the inside."

"Oh, Christ."

Munro said, "I warned her about Willis."

"Who gives you the right to warn me? What are you
doing here anyway in Carole's Vista Cruiser?" Holly hissed
the four syllables, *Vis-ta Cruis-er*, showing her disdain for its
undeniable suburban resonance. "Where's your sports car,
that red one?"

"The wagon is the family car. This weekend I'm involved in family business. I guess you're family now."

She wondered what claim to her he was making. "Are
you through yet?" she said to Dr. Kline. "I don't have to sit
here all night?"

"Did I get my message across?"

Holly told Dr. Kline that she understood. She was supposed to steer clear of Willis Pratt.

Munro added, "Honey, you're linked to a stolen truck,
toxic waste, and maybe or maybe not that big old fire in
town. I'd say you better cherish your days on the street."
He was trying to rattle her but she wasn't whimpering yet.
He reached under the table and pinched her knee. He kept
his hand cupped on her knee. She felt its heat through the

denim. She suddenly realized that her delinquent behavior might be a turn-on to Munro. He might wait there forever, with his hand on her, until she agreed to do a little horizontal dancing. She pried his fingers off her leg and stood up. She took the broom from the kitchen closet and went into the parlor. She swept the broken Fresnel lens into the dustpan. The glass brushing against the thin tin plate made quite a racket. The gorgeous glass was scattered everywhere in tiny chlorophyll chunks and flowerets.

Chapter Twenty-three

Willis pedaled the oversized tricycle along the Cliff
Walk. He was pumping hard. He reached through Rennie's
plastic flowers and grabbed the handlebars dead center to
get the greatest traction. He remembered the line from a
pop song: "You say plastic flowers never die, but I say
plastic flowers never live—"

He was bleeding from a cut over his eye where a branch
had gouged his forehead in the fall. The storm was throwing everything at him; tags of yellow sea foam like rancid
shaving cream clung to the high rocks and sometimes lifted
up and caught him. The winding path along the granite
cliffs was mostly unlit, and he rolled through the dark from
rote memory, past the historic houses whose names he
knew by heart, Hopedene, Seaward, past Forty Steps. He
veered too near the perilous edge only once or twice,
enough to shock him from his drug daze, which kept him
moving numbly against the wall of rain. The sound of the
sea was assaultive and wearying as he steered the bike
toward Château-sur-Mer. He began to understand that he
wasn't taking his stepmother anywhere without finding a
proper vehicle. He knew it was a shot in hell, but Willis
thought that he might find Debbie at Salve Regina College
and she could arrange to get him a loaner.

The campus was two doors down from Rennie's new home in the Château-sur-Mer Life Care infirmary. Willis could get Rennie over to the college and put her into a borrowed car. He looked for Debbie in the college snack bar. He strolled through the blazing laundry room where girls were sitting astride the Whirlpool washers reading swollen coin-op copies of Stephen King. He finally found Debbie in the library, where she was staring at a five-pound volume of *Gray's Anatomy*. She wasn't alarmed to see him. She was glad to be distracted. Willis saw the pages spread open to a detailed diagram of the peritoneum.

"Look who it is. Mister Wonderful," she said.

He stopped in front of her and smiled his invaluable smile.

"What are you doing here? This isn't a 4-F Club meeting."

"Don't you mean 4-*H*?" he said.

"No. I mean what I said, 4-F. Find 'em, feel 'em, fuck 'em, and forget 'em."

"That's nice. Sass and more sass." He was puffing from the bike ride.

She looked at him hard. His pants were soaking wet and sliding off his hips. He didn't have the time to grab some underwear, which might have helped to keep them up. His cast was sodden, like a swollen loaf of rising bread dough. His hands and face were red as beets from the cold, crashing rain. She looked at the spongy cuff of his cast where his sore red fingers protruded.

"God," she said, after she completed a nurse-style up-and-down.

"You know what, Debbie? I need a favor."

"I guess you do. Have you looked at yourself?"

"I need a car for a half hour."

"A car for a half hour? *I* should get you a car?"

"Okay, okay," he told her. "Look, our trouble is ancient history, right? I never said sorry. I'm saying it now."

That's all she seemed to want to hear. She was satisfied.

Willis leaned against the institutional library furniture as if he couldn't stand up without it. His pupils were tiny as specks from his fading dose of morphine and she couldn't tell what he was seeing through those tiny pins when he looked at her. She didn't like the feeling.

"I saw your mother in the infirmary. On second shift, I go around and do the blood pressures. I'm really sorry, Willis."

"That's where I'm heading now. Want to help me out, or not?" he told her.

"Maybe I can get a car," she said.

"That's beautiful," he told her, "that's my girl."

Some of the other students had started to take notice. Willis was making a puddle from his saturated clothing. Debbie leaned over and kissed him. She must have been wild about him for one little duration of time, and her tenderness was genuine. She straightened up and walked him past the girls who were ogling him. He was amazed that she had any regard for that short-lived spell that had come and gone between them. She stood outside the building with Willis. The violent rain was knifing through the streetlights like drawers of shiny flatware spilling from the sky.

"Can you bring a car here, say, in a half hour?" he asked her.

"There's nowhere to park tonight. Look at this, it's packed. It's a concert. Chamber music at The Breakers mansion. A big deal."

"Hell, just double-park it somewhere right here," he told her.

She agreed to do it. Then she warned him, "They have at least three toughs on duty at Château-sur-Mer. They carry aerosol deterrents."

"They don't wear a gun?"

"Look, these aerosol deterrents are nasty. That's oleoresin pepper gas. That stuff can stop a grizzly. You better watch yourself."

Chapter Twenty-four

Willis got back on the bike and rolled past the last mansion before Château-sur-Mer. Debbie was right, a big gala was happening at The Breakers. Floodlights were cranked up illuminating the flashing rain. Newport elite were filing inside, everyone wearing black tie underneath their raingear. The weather must have shattered people's expectations for glam photos; the society page was a washout. Willis pedaled through; the tricycle spokes twirled wheels of rainwater on either side of him. Willis sighted drifts of women on the marble steps, their hems skimming the puddles. The ladies lifted their long skirts in a collective perpetual-motion curtsy. When the steps were empty, workers passed brooms along the underside of the canvas awning to keep the water from welling. The water slid off in sheets.

Water, water everywhere.

He rode the bike past the rococo pile-up and onto the quiet grounds of Château-sur-Mer. He located Rennie's Life Care wing, but he couldn't find the entrance to the building. He walked around the ground floor, peering inside the windows wherever he could. He saw a grey head, another grey head. A bald dome. He recognized the eerie blue light and looked inside to see quite a sizable TV room.

He found a door and walked into the building. He asked a woman resident to direct him to the Life Care unit. She looked back at him, baffled. After a moment, he realized it wasn't his question that had puzzled her. She was lost in a labyrinthine brainteaser of her own.

He didn't wait and walked down a long hallway. His wet boots squished on the polished tile. He knew his boots were ruined, and it cut him down some. The battered, swollen footwear was a peculiar, subliminal threat to his well-being.

Willis searched the doorway of each room and saw whatever it was his fortune to see: a man hunched in a chair, a woman attached to a dialysis machine, another had a tiny television on an expanding arm positioned two inches from her face, her nose against the screen. His heart was in his throat. Only now could he actually picture Rennie in this forbidding place.

He turned a corner and reached a nursing station. It looked odd to Willis, the lamps were too soft. The illumination came from indirect sources. It looked like mood lighting. Silk flowers were abundant in muted vases. He knew he had reached the right location: the hushed interiors of the dying.

Rennie was at the end of the hall. She was propped up; a green tank of oxygen stood on casters next to the bed. Her skin was an alarming, deep ochre. She pulled the nostril clip tubing from her face and let him kiss her. She had an IV drip of some kind, the needle inserted and taped to the back of her hand right above the knuckles. She was woozy but awake. She looked him over.

"Oh, mercy, what happened to you?" she said. Her voice was tight.

"Today was hell. If I ran it down for you, you'd shit." He looked her in the eye.

"I bet it would make a good movie. You were born for it. A spaghetti Western."

Willis was glad to see her teasing him. He laughed at her joke and then he suffered a sudden round of startling, convulsive shivers, as if he'd been holding them off until then.

"You're catching pneumonia," she said. "Get under the covers." She motioned to the empty bed next to her own. He climbed into the tall bed and pulled the blankets to his chin. He was trembling from an unfamiliar cold. The cold seemed generated from within, as if a transfusion of icy blood was circulating through him, tip to toe, and all his intestines churning a frozen gruel. He shivered violently. "Look at us," he said, his teeth chattering.

She studied him as if she relished every speck of what she saw, despite his bedraggled condition.

Willis fell back on his bed, the room started to revolve slowly the way the Tilt-O-Whirl wrenched into gear at Rocky Point Park. He knew he should be getting on with it, but his limbs felt loosely sewn to his torso. He had a strange sensation, as if his trunk was stuffed with powdered glass. He felt like a cloth doll, his muscles had diminished into a granulated essence. Most of all, he felt the sensation of lying abreast of Rennie, both of them aiming in the same direction, into the wind of oblivion.

Rennie tried to rouse him. "Are you flying or dying?" she said. "Who's baby-sitting who?"

He leaned up on his elbow. He shook his head like a dog with a gnat in its ear. He felt everything sifting. "Shit. Wait. I'm getting you out of here. Hold on a minute."

A nurse came into the room. "What have we got here?" Her voice was amicable.

"My son. Caught in the rain."

"Your son? Hey, I thought you had only one son."

"Two," Rennie said. She tried to clear her throat to explain, but she couldn't get her breath behind her words. Her trachea rattled and sputtered.

Willis sat up on the edge of the bed.

The nurse looked back and forth between them. "So this is your other son? Well, you've got the *same eyes*," the nurse said.

"I hope he sees a different picture than I do." Rennie croaked the difficult multiword sentence, leaving wide spaces.

"Now, Miss Hopkins. I don't want to hear you give up," the nurse said as she walked out of the room.

Willis sensed that the nurse was going to announce him to the world. He wiped his face with the palm of his hand and lowered himself off the thousand-dollar bed. He told Rennie, "It's raining out there, so you're going to get wet."

Rennie was grinning through her plastic mustache.

Willis said, "Can you breathe without this?"

She nodded.

"Are you sure? You better be sure." He unthreaded the oxygen leader from where it was hooked around her ears and lifted it over her head. He yanked the IV needle from the back of her hand, the tube came free, but its needle stayed inserted in the vein where it was taped. He left it in for now. He took Rennie in his arms and collected her blanket, but the blanket was too clumsy and he let it drop.

"Don't forget my book," she said.

He saw the tiny suede square on the table arm and he stuffed it in his back pocket. Two women appeared at the door to block his exit. He shifted Rennie in his arms so her feet wouldn't knock the door frame and he kept walking. He made his apologies to the stunned medics. They followed their training—or they had an instinct—and didn't try to stop him. He saw a row of motorized carts, Little Rascals there for the taking, but he decided against swiping one. He marched down the hall through the ambient lighting. He navigated the double swinging doors, kicking each panel wide and rotating through, Rennie in his arms, in a smooth, choreographed moment as steady and fluid as Balanchine.

Rennie hardly weighed anything, but it was awkward walking in the dark, over the slippery manicured lawns. He searched through the impenetrable curtain of rain for the bike, but someone had moved it. He decided to go on foot the half-mile to the college, where he hoped Debbie had cribbed a car.

At first, Rennie tried to hold on, looping her arms around his neck, but it was too much effort for her and she let her arms fall. He stumbled through thick clumps of clover and fell to his knees, but he didn't release his cargo. Rennie bossed him, "One foot in front of the other."

Willis was parallel the great sloping lawns of The Breakers mansion when the security personnel came up behind him. They scrolled a floodlight against his back. His alarming shadow rose up in front of him. He saw an exaggerated image with extra appendages. A towering man-insect. A stiltlike human form carrying its broken human likeness. Willis looked over his shoulder once. Two men were riding an electric cart. Willis didn't stop walking. The driver came alongside Willis and told him to release the patient.

Willis began to trot along the Cliff Walk. The men were cautious and tracked Willis at his own jogging pace. The next thing, Willis darted off the path, tumbled over a low fence of privet and beach roses. He was running across The

Breakers' wide lawn. Rennie's nightgown snagged the rose thorns and he jerked it loose. The men couldn't drive the cart after him; they wheeled around, heading for the mansion's street entrance.

Even in the rain, Willis could hear the musical switchbacks of a piano sonata. He climbed the marble steps that led to the first-floor terrace. Beyond the wide terrace he saw the crowded hall, rows of perfectly coiffed heads; a woman wore a heavy necklace like a diamond-studded garden claw across her daring neckline. All the men wore monkey suits. The sea of faces was tilted at an angle, chins set, eyes peeled on the stage, where a page turner and a pianist worked together. Willis listened to the Steinway throbbing above the percussive rain. He found a side entrance to the building and brushed by a startled female usher who stood at the final row of velvet chairs.

Willis had walked into the Great Hall, the central ballroom of the famous turn-of-the-century mansion. The large room was dominated by a sweeping double staircase, Palladian colonnades, and chandeliers the size of inverted treetop canopies. It was two stories high with a fantastic trompe l'oeil ceiling of blue sky and cotton wool clouds.

Everyone in the audience displayed their commitment to social elegance and avoided craning their necks around at the sudden intrusion. Willis saw an empty chair and plopped down, twisting Rennie face front. He looked at the ceiling mural, its fantastic blue heaven. The fair weather up there seemed like an ingenious invention to counter the usual Newport scud. He threw his head back to admire it; his profile was startlingly pale, his skin white as an ice sculpture. Yet he looked resolved, peaceful beneath that one-hundred-year-old sky.

Rennie was half-conscious and she complained when

he shifted her weight to his other knee. She settled against his shoulder. People could no longer help themselves and started to twist around in their chairs to stare at him. He picked up a program from the empty seat beside his own. He began to read the list of "Twenty-four Preludes, Op. 28, by Frédéric François Chopin."

C MAJOR—AGITATO

A MINOR—LENTO

G MAJOR—VIVACE

E MINOR—LARGO

Then Rennie started coughing.

Ushers appeared and stalked the rows. Willis was pulled to his feet by two alarmingly beefy young men hired for that specific purpose. Willis reorganized Rennie in his arms and walked with the young ushers to the street door. There he saw the Château-sur-Mer security officers in a line, their aerosol deterrents strapped prominently to their belts. Willis turned around again and ran across the oriental rugs, tripping on unpredictable humps. He carried Rennie to the opposite end of the huge mansion. The music stopped abruptly, the pianist put her hands in her lap and stared across the hall. Voices surged in a roar of indignation. People shouted after Willis as if Willis had burgled their personal possessions, as if these recreational minutes were priceless. Willis exited through the French doors on the north side, which had been left ajar so that the big fireplace in the Great Hall could have better draw.

Pounding down the slope, his trunk tumbled ahead of his legs and he fell. Rennie spilled out of his arms. He picked her up, collecting her skewed limbs and arranging her nightgown. He didn't think he could carry her for very much longer. He ran as far as he could before coming upon a chain-link fence at the perimeter of the property. It almost took the heart out of him. He trotted its length until he found a gap where a twenty-foot privet hedge merged with a galvanized metal fence pole.

The security men were in the street around him and he tucked behind a car. The electric cart purred up and down the length of the block. Willis crouched behind the fender of a luxury automobile. He waited. The hem of Rennie's nightgown swirled open in a puddle. When the cart moved one street over, he inched his way back to the library at Salve Regina College. Debbie was waiting in a Ford Taurus. She had taken the time to adjust the climate control and the car's interior was steaming.

He huddled Rennie into the backseat and pushed her over on the upholstery. He sank below the window ledge so he wouldn't be seen. "Drive!" he told Debbie.

"Who are you shouting at! Shit. You want to go to your house?"

"No," he said, "not the house." He couldn't take Rennie home again. He was taking her to a "transfer station." He imagined all the soulless places where the dead are temporarily deposited. The refrigerated morgues, the unsuspecting Dumpsters, the countryside crematoriums like the one at White's Monument Village. Who manufactures these secret kilns? He was seized by a cold hysteria. His lungs ached after his physical exertion. A wild loneliness stirred through his chest cavity, all the pink airways and tender alveoli caught in a speechless throbbing.

Chapter Twenty-five

Holly looked down the row of cottages at Neptune's Hide-A-Way. Choosing the right one for Rennie was almost too great a responsibility for her. She decided on Verbena, the second to the last shack. Two of its windows had been left unboarded and she knew Rennie would be grateful for the natural light. Holly had turned on the circuit breaker in the office, and she was relieved to see the light come on when she walked into the cottage and flicked the wall switch. She had more difficulty figuring out the right connection to get cold water in the shack; she had to tighten all the bleeders before she opened the shut-off valve and the water whined into the pipes. Even with most of the windows boarded up, the gusts of wind stirred through, fingering the curtain hems. The gas stove was the only source of heat and she lit the oven.

She was in the shack for only ten minutes when she smelled something funny drifting up from the stove. A nest of mice had ignited on the broiler pan where they had organized their winter home. She found a potholder and took the pan with the burning nest outside where she rinsed it in the rain. The charred rodent-stench remained, and she left the pan on the stoop.

She didn't let the incident upset her and she prepared the cottage for Willis and Rennie. She studied the shelves along one wall of the kitchen—the reassuring cabbage roses on the shelf paper, roses the size of soup plates. She ran her hand over the roses, then went about making up a bed for Rennie.

She heard a car turn in the drive. She saw a strange girl was driving. Willis was in the backseat. The girl helped Willis lift Rennie out of the car; Rennie looked like a scarecrow. Her head fell back on the crook of Willis's arm, her white hair looked wet and ropy. Holly met them at the door of the cottage.

"Welcome to Verbena," she said, her pride was showing. She loved these shacks and couldn't hide it. She looked back and forth between Rennie and the interesting stranger, but Rennie caught her attention. Rennie looked half alive in Willis's arms. Her other half looked irretrievably gone. Willis didn't look much better.

"This is Debbie," Willis said.

"Oh, sure. Debbie." Holly recognized the name and nodded at the young girl. Debbie was the love interest who had come and gone before her.

Willis arranged Rennie's weight in his arms. He was looking for a place to put her down. Holly shook off her jealous twinge and led Willis into the little bedroom where she had made the bed and left the blanket turned down. The sheets were icy.

"Wait," Holly said. "Someone should warm up the bed."

Willis was soaking wet.

The two women looked at each other.

"Let's both of us do it," Holly said.

Debbie looked startled at the strange request. "Well, I guess it's all right."

Debbie and Holly got under the covers. They each felt shy and kept apart; then they saw that their reserve wasn't going to warm the sheets, so they scissored their arms and legs as if they were making snow angels. Holly felt the cold sheets respond to their exercise with each swipe. They started to giggle.

Willis lost patience.

"Just a few more minutes to heat this up," Holly said. Once and again, her ankle brushed Debbie's and they both recoiled from the contact. They pedaled their legs under the covers and again collided.

Willis sat down in a chair, Rennie on his knee. "This is ridiculous," he said. "We have to get a heater in here."

Holly said, "I saw an electric heater at Nicole's. I can go get it."

Willis said, "I bet it's swarming at the house. I bet they're calling this a kidnap. You're in it now and can't go back there."

Debbie said, "I'll drive over and get the heater. No one knows me there."

"That's right, no one knows her," Holly said. Five minutes ago she didn't know this girl Debbie, either.

Debbie went to get the heater. Willis tucked Rennie into the warmed bed. "I wish I had some dry clothes for myself," he said. "You didn't think of that, did you? Some clothes for me?" he asked Holly.

"No. I didn't remember," she said. She was disappointed that she hadn't foreseen the need.

"Here," she said. "Give me what you have on. I can dry them near the stove while you wear that extra blanket."

She draped his jeans over a kitchen chair near the oven door. The storm was wailing through the cottage, the wind lifted the furry bon-bon trim on the curtains.

Willis sat next to Rennie, watching her, but he didn't

know what to look for. It was the end, he knew that. Yet how long did the *end* go on—days or hours? He thought of the figure of speech "the beginning of the end," which implied that there might also be a *middle*, and then an *end*, to the end. Exactly where was Rennie on that map?

He tried to talk to Rennie and get her to answer but she couldn't say anything except the furry vowel sounds which started to sound familiar to Willis. He tapped her shoulder just to get her to say them, the sound of her slurred speech was in itself reassuring to him.

Debbie never came back with the heater. After an hour, Holly gave Willis his clothes, which were warmed through if not completely dry. They decided to go to sleep on either side of Rennie. They hoped it would happen in a dream while they flanked her. They were in bed for only a moment before they felt the wet sheets and recognized the slight ammonia scent.

"Jesus," Willis said.

"She'll be cold lying like that," Holly said.

Willis stood up and took Rennie from the bed so Holly could change the sheets. She had her key to the linen chest in the office and she brought an armful of bedding back to the shack. She put a towel under Rennie's buttocks and sawed it gently between her legs like a diaper. She tucked her into the new linens; her limbs were so stiff it was like arranging arrows in a quiver. Holly remembered what she was told when her father was dying: death comes soon after the first signs of incontinence. It was an upsetting idea, that everyone's last days would bring back these childlike humiliations.

Sometime during the night, the electricity failed and they were left in the dark. Holly didn't get the lanterns from the office since it would be dawn in an hour. They got a little bit of sleep back and forth. Willis was coughing, which woke everyone up. Then, the storm itself deprived them of rest. It rattled and roared over the shack like a string of cars on a roller-coaster circuit.

In the morning, Holly made coffee on the gas range. Despite the circumstances, she enjoyed testing her occupancy in the cottage. She had never "lived" in one. She reached for kitchen utensils; the little copper measuring spoon for the coffee was in the divided drawer where she had placed it at the end of last season. Everything was arranged where she had left it when she closed up in the fall. For the last several days, Holly had had little control over events and she relished the organized bins of silverware, the stout towers of dinner plates, the nesting cereal bowls.

She scoured the three-piece drip coffeepot and the brewing coffee smelled rich and winy on the cold air. The storm had passed through, leaving the air cleansed and ionized. The cottage was remarkably bright from its two available windows. The remaining windows revealed only the stained particleboard shutters. She gave Willis a cup of coffee and a mug of weak tea for Rennie.

"Why can't she have coffee? How is coffee going to kill her?" Willis said. "At this point." His angry sarcasm betrayed his nervous mood. He no longer had his morning drugs to go with his coffee. "You have to go over to the CVS," he told her, "for Rennie's script."

"I thought it was Douglas Drugs."

"Doug Drug or CVS. She's got two sheets."

"I can't go anywhere right now," Holly said, waiting to see what he would say.

Willis fed Rennie the weak tea with a tablespoon. She was groaning and shifting under the covers. She lifted herself on her elbow to ask Willis, "Where's my autograph book?"

"Hold on. I'll get it," he told her. He found the book on the floor.

Holly didn't want to hear any more from it and she walked up to the office. She called Nancy Brookens, a nurse at the Aquidneck Island Hospice. Nancy Brookens had helped supervise Holly's father's last weeks. Nancy agreed to come over to check on Rennie sometime later that night. Holly didn't explain to the nurse that everything was to be kept a secret, but hospice volunteers are discreet to begin with. Of course she would have to explain to Willis why she had invited a stranger.

When Holly came back to the shack, Willis was pacing around the kitchen in moderate distress. He slammed the kitchen cupboards open and shut as if he was disgusted he didn't find morphine in the sugar bowl with the yellow Domino packets.

"Someone's coming over here to see Rennie. She's a nurse from the hospice service."

"We don't need a nurse."

Willis stopped in his tracks as if he recognized his own row of symptoms lining up before him.

"Are you all right?" Holly said.

"You have two eyes," he said. "Scroll."

She touched his face with the back of her knuckles. One side of his face felt flushed, the other cheek was clammy. He threw her hand off.

Willis instructed her, "Go to the telephone. Get Nicole to bring the heater over here and tell her to see if she can get over to Douglas Drugs." He rubbed his hand over his mouth furiously, as if he couldn't get rid of cat fur. "Shit. Just tell her about it, Holly."

"Maybe this is a good time to get clean, did you ever think of that?"

He ignored her words and walked back into the other room and sat beside Rennie.

"The *Glamor Girl* is still *missing*," he told Rennie in a loud voice. "You hear me? Calming seas now," Willis said, "so it looks *unpromising*. She was lost in the gale, I guess. Rennie, are you hearing me?" His voice was too big for the little shack. Holly watched him yelling to Rennie. He was losing his temper, then he took a breath and started over. He was trying to spark a knee-jerk response from Rennie. Any other time, Rennie would have snapped awake like a fox terrier.

Rennie's eyes looked ahead, blinking every few seconds, but the eyelid didn't wash away her dull expression. She was breathing very fast, in short little sips that hardly lifted her breast. Rennie wasn't asleep or awake. She seemed to be in a pre-death holding area where her mind was free of all external stimuli; even the voice of her beloved stepson was banished from that tarmac.

Holly came over and lifted her wrist, but she didn't really know how to read Rennie's pulse. She felt a tiny puttering, but it could have been her own pulse she was feeling in her fingertips.

"This is awful to watch." Willis rubbed the back of his hand over his nostrils, sniffing.

"Maybe she doesn't feel anything," Holly said.

A car drove into Neptune's circle. It was Nicole and the kids. Nicole walked into the shack with a small electric heater. "Someone named Debbie came over last night. She said you need this heater—"

Willis pulled Nicole inside the door. "Look, can you get over to Douglas Drug for a script?" Willis asked. He recited the prescription number.

Holly took Willis's hand off Nicole's wrist. She took the heater from Nicole and plugged it into the wall, but the electricity was still out. "Do you have power back at the duplex?" Holly asked Nicole.

"Yeah, we've got it."

"You do? I better check the circuit breaker."

Willis again turned to Nicole. He repeated the prescription number.

"Write it down," Nicole told him.

Willis tugged the kitchen drawers looking for a pencil.

Lindy and his little sister walked up to Willis and asked about the puppy. He looked down at the children. He was sorry he hadn't thought about them. Yet he didn't regret his gift to Sheila.

Willis asked Nicole, "Another thing. Can you call the hospital and find out about Fritz?"

Nicole nodded. For Fritz, she displayed a murky apathy. "What about the dog?" Nicole said. "These kids are pitiful."

Willis gave Nicole a piece of paper with the information she needed for the drugstore. "When can you get over there?" he asked her. He was ashamed of his helplessness and changed the subject. "I guess Easton Way is quiet?"

"Last night there was a whole posse. Two different black-and-whites idling for an hour. The air pollution. Your brother was there this morning for a while. Do they know you're here?"

Willis said, "They're not looking for us. Munro knows where we're at. He knows his mother's dying and he's letting me do the dirty work without him. Then he'll charge into it." He took her elbow. "Nicole, get us some refills—"

Holly told Nicole, "Forget about getting the dope. This is an *opportunity* for Willis. Since he's stuck here anyway—"

"Here at the detox ranch?" Willis said.

"Why not?" she said. "You could try it."

"It's a little more than an ice cream habit, Holly, or maybe you haven't noticed."

"Oh, I've noticed," she told him. Her tone implied a lot—she had suffered, she had gone without.

He looked back at her. His eyes were wide and black, like rabbit holes.

It was the first time she had seen him so frightened. Both Nicole and Holly studied him.

"What are you two staring at? Let's invite all the neighbors," Willis said.

Holly told Nicole to get the prescription.

He waited for Nicole to return. His face showed a gloss of sweat, which he wiped away but it came right back.

"What's happening now?" Holly said, seeing a shift.

"Fuck, I don't know. Feels awful, feels like the flu."

He started bouncing a ball, an old pinkie he found on the bookshelf. The rubber was so dry and decomposed that every time the ball hit the floor it sent a cloud of pink dust into the air. He bounced the ball until Holly grabbed it. He sat down again near Rennie, shivering from evaporating sweat.

Nicole came up the drive and Willis went out to her car. She handed him a narrow white bag with a pharmacy sticker on the outside. "We can sign for this one more time and that's it," she told him. "What are you going to do then?"

He went inside the cottage and into the bathroom. His nerves had shattered the minute Nicole arrived and he no longer had to wait. He unwrapped the suppositories and started whistling Roland Kirk's "Serenade to a Cuckoo," something tongue-in-cheek, ridiculously lively. Yet it didn't sound right. It had a bitter, off-key error somewhere in its refrain. Holly couldn't tell if Willis was doing it wrong on purpose.

She went up to the bathroom door, but she respected his privacy and didn't turn the knob. "Christ, Willis, will you stop it. Stop whistling that song," she whispered through the hinges.

Chapter Twenty-six

Rennie was listening to Willis talk about the *Glamor Girl* but she couldn't rally enough strength to surface from the half-sleep which she was starting to prefer over her fits and starts of alertness.

She thought she saw it again: Bill Hopkins' whiskery frontage after five days out on the Bank.

Perhaps it was just subliminal suggestion with Willis going on and on about that other dragger, but Bill Hopkins was pestering Rennie like an impatient suitor waiting for her to pack a picnic basket and come ahead with him. Rennie felt the sweet, separate world she was entering, bordered from the ordinary human world by a clear, gelatinous membrane. She took little notice of current events taking place outside her envelope. She was cocooned in a dissolving egg, in the soothing albumin syrup of recollected love.

Once Rennie rose up on her elbow entirely alert. She told Willis, "There isn't too much that can scare Bill Hopkins."

Willis leaned over Rennie to hear her breathless attempt to speak.

"He's scared of just one thing."

"What's that?" Willis said.

"Cables. Oh, Bill has a terrible fear of cables. He saw a bad accident, a man lost his eye working the hydraulic winch."

"That's ugly." Willis commiserated. He was excited to hear her voice after so long a silence.

"Cables always make him nervous, and there he is working the tows, every time out. Cables. It's an unnatural fear. No, that's unfair—*any* fear is natural, I guess." She flopped back and shut her papery eyelids. Willis was stunned by the spontaneous oratory.

Holly's mouth was wide open, she felt her tongue drying. She told Willis, "Nancy Brookens says they start seeing their dead; their loved ones start coming closer."

"Jesus Christ," Willis said.

"No, really, they start reaching out from both directions."

Willis was alarmed by the idea of it. Bill Hopkins hovering somewhere in the shack. Willis had often imagined Bill Hopkins' plight out on the ocean. How long did he last before he drowned or the cold got him? Did Bill Hopkins have any premonition of his fate when he worked the Hathaway winch and emptied tons of shellfish on deck, then set the rakes back out? With each tow, the rakes pulled in glistening slag heaps of variegated shell, until the mountain rose high as the rails.

When the *Teresa Eve* turned back for another tow, her crew knew it was greedy fishing. When at last she was steaming in, her diesel at full throat, just past Pollock's Rip, the sea was too rough to shuck and bag the catch. Those days they would head into the harbor and do their shucking in lee before off-loading it. That night when they started home, the combers were tight, one after another. The crew stood outside the wheelhouse tipping back D.W. Dante, the on-board brand for the last many years. Everyone had two or three hits from the bottle, enough to warm up. There wasn't room to spread out after dredging almost seven hundred bushels of scallops. The weather was peculiar—black and airless on top, but the sea was running eight to ten feet, with oddball crests. They were out there in weird waters, in the lunatic fringe. The weight of their haul pulled the water up over the freeboard and she rode the chop like a gravy ladle; the sea dipped juices into the bowl. Freakers curled over the rails. Giant combers hit the quarter and shifted the tons of scallops. The next wave crested and rolled in behind her; its black wall plowed over the stern like a garage door slamming, crushing them under. The men were pitched abreast of her as she sank; the whole treasure spilled back. Thousands of notched mollusks twirled loose like Liberty dollars.

Chapter Twenty-seven

The whole day passed. Holly kept looking for any traffic, but Neptune's was a ghost town. No one showed up. Rennie's condition seemed worse.

Willis told Holly, "It's good to talk to her even if she can't hear me."

"Read that book to her," Holly said.

Willis started thumbing through Rennie's tiny suede autograph book. He read some stanzas out loud to Holly, fragments of poems and other oddities.

"The cut worm forgives the plow." They looked at one another and shrugged.

"All wholesome food is caught without a net or trap." Willis said, "I wonder what Bill Hopkins would say about that."

"Think in the morning. Act in the noon. Eat in the evening. Sleep in the night."

"That's just common sense," Holly said. "These must be wise sayings from the Bible or something?"

"Sounds like fortune cookies from Wall of China Take-Out. Look at this." Willis showed Holly the page.

> *Renate*
> *Regatta*
> *Ricotta*

"That's funny. She's playing with her name."

"It's in here in lots of different handwriting."

Holly said, "Her classmates called her these nicknames in her school days. They wrote it in her book and signed their signatures, see?"

"Renate, Regatta," Willis tried it. "Ricotta. That's cheese. I bet she didn't like being called cheese."

"But regatta means a boat race, doesn't it?" Holly said.

"Well, that's okay, then." He kept thumbing through the little book, as if it might explain not only Rennie, but where he himself fit in. He found the nonsense rhyme he had known all along:

> *They went to sea in a Sieve, they did,*
> *In a Sieve they went to sea:*
> *In spite of all their friends could say,*
> *On a winter's morn, on a stormy day,*
> *In a Sieve they went to sea!*
>
> *The water it soon came in, it did,*
> *The water it soon came in—*

Willis stared at the page, letting the poem echo in his head. He saw himself. He saw Fritz. Holly too.

Holly looked over his shoulder and recited the next one.

> *Rennie is the name*
> *single is your station*
> *Lucky is the man*
> *who makes the alteration*
> *—Your sister-graduate,*
> *Margaret Casey*

Willis threw the little book on the table. He was thinking, That's what it comes to. A small, cracked cowhide book of rhymes.

ᕤ

Nancy Brookens arrived at dusk. She looked back and forth between Rennie and Willis and learned the situation. She asked Willis how much morphine he was using for maintenance.

He told her.

"That's a lot." It was a professional assessment not a moral one. "Do you want your drugs more than your freedom from drugs?" she asked him.

It sounded like a rhetorical question, one of those public-service announcements on late-night television. Holly remembered an ad where they cracked an egg on a red-hot skillet. Nancy Brookens said, "This isn't a good time to tackle it, but there's never a good time. You'll have to decide." She patted his shoulder and Holly watched him stiffen.

The nurse went to Rennie's bedside and took Rennie's vital signs. She removed the little needle still taped to Rennie's hand; a tiny drop of deep blood bloomed where the needle had been jerked loose. Nancy Brookens wiped it away with a tissue.

"An IV might keep her around a few more days, you don't want a drip?"

Holly said, "I don't think so. Do we?"

"No," Willis said.

"That's fine," the nurse said in approval. "She's okay, she has her *surround*, that's all she needs.

"Her what?"

"Her *care-giver surround*, you and Willis. It's better than a drip." She wrapped Rennie's arm in a cuff and took her pressure. Rennie's blood pressure was perilously low and her heart rate was up. "Her heart's making a last ditch effort against the poison tide."

"Poison tide?" Holly asked. Nancy Brookens explained that Rennie was suffering from severe sepsis resulting from the advanced destruction of organ tissues. "There's a lot of dead cell material circulating." It was this final toxic assault that would bring on death.

Nancy Brookens recognized Holly's bewildered expression and she put her hands on Holly's shoulders and sat her down in a kitchen chair. "You are carrying a bit too much for one person."

"Thank God you're here."

"I can't stay long, then what? Look at yourself. You aren't even aware of how this affects *you*."

Holly followed Nancy Brookens' eyes. She was staring at Holly's crotch, where a cloud of bright blood had bloomed below the zipper of her jeans.

"Shit." Holly sat down at the table with a burst of hurt laughter.

"See what I'm saying? You even forgot your time of the month. The first rule is: treat yourself like a queen or you can't nurture your family members."

Holly almost said, "These are not my family members. Remember? *My* father died two years ago, right after I called him 'Worm.' " Nancy Brookens probably wouldn't remember that particular detail, although Holly had confessed her story to the nurse when it had happened. How could Nancy Brookens keep track of everyone's expired kin?

When Nancy stood up to leave, Holly accepted a tampon from her personal wallet, and the little basket of goodies from the hospice organization. Homemade brownies wrapped in tinfoil for the family members on vigil. Cans of strawberry Ensure for the patient. Aloe-vera hand lotion and a hairbrush with silky soft bristles, like the kind sold in baby layettes. Nancy Brookens handed her a new Grief Wheel in its cellophane sleeve.

"I have one of these Grief Wheels already."

"Oh, it's been revised since then."

"It's been revised?" Holly was incredulous. "How can they do that? I followed it to the letter the last time. Why did they have to change it?"

"Progress." She handed Holly a hygiene aid in a plastic wrapper. It was a small, pink sphere, a serrated sponge on a lollipop stick. "You can brush her teeth with this," Nancy Brookens said.

Holly recognized the unforgettable totem. She had used the same cellulose lolly to scrub her father's gums with tender attention to the empty plateau where his bridge-work had been removed.

"Watch your boyfriend, if he's upset he might go overboard on his dosage. He needs to get into a program. I'm going to assign a bereavement coordinator for you and Willis, is that okay?"

"A what?"

"Aquidneck Hospice is offering you a bereavement coordinator to help during the next few weeks. It's a wonderful service. I'll put you on the calendar when I get back to the office."

"I didn't have a bereavement coordinator when my father passed away."

Holly thought, I had to coordinate my own bereavement.

"This is something new," Nancy Brookens said.

Holly watched the nurse drive away. She kept looking out the window, long enough for a seagull to land on the driveway right in front of the cottage. The gull had a trash fish. The fish was still slapping its tail as the bird began its feast; first it pecked out the soft bleb of the eye and from there it could tear the meat. She remembered the hunk of seal hide that had washed ashore, its gorgeous dapples.

Willis was curled up on the single bed in the corner, exhausted. Holly was impressed by the effort he was making for Rennie. All that night, Holly listened to the tandem struggles of Willis and Rennie. Rennie's breathing was getting more and more erratic; sometimes she awoke from her dead zone unable to inhale, her lungs were full. Holly propped her up. Her breathing sounded rough, like someone sawing through a plank. Willis was using the morphine to get through it, and still he shivered violently or threw his shirt off in a wave of heat. For a period, in the early morning, they all slept.

At noon the following day, Rennie lifted up in her bed. She whispered Willis's name. He went over to her and squeezed her hand. She told him, "Walk around the house. Look at the shingles. See what needs doing. Get the right count. Buy white cedar not red."

"Sure, I will," he said. "I told you I would."

She patted his knuckles.

He didn't like her coming back and forth; when she talked sense and referred to their family house, his ordeal was worse. It was painful to lose her when she was still handing him orders.

Holly's boss, Joseph Salvatore, arrived at the door. His eyes looked dark and switchy, his whole face showed the concern and discomfort of someone forced to use his authority. "You can't be here," he told Holly. She walked outside with him. He shook his head in two gentle movements, suggesting that he didn't hold it against her but he believed she should know better. "This friend of yours in there—well, Munro Hopkins tells me he is in trouble."

"Did that busybody call you?"

"He knows you work for me. This isn't good for my business."

"I know it looks bad," she told him, "but his mother is dying. She's almost passed on, can't we wait?"

He told her, "Please, sweetheart, take them somewhere else."

She lifted her chin to hide her hurt feelings. She didn't understand why her old friend couldn't see them through. She walked with her boss back to the office. She telephoned Jensen. He told her they could come over to Sycamore House if they didn't mind the confusion and temporary furnishings. He and Sarojini were starting interior renovations and half the house was a shambles. He would rent them a room.

She thanked Jensen, ashamed of the relief which washed through her, head to foot, and over the wire. She hated to be indebted to her ex-husband and give Jensen the feel of it. When she told Willis where they were going, he stood up and told her, "Rennie's not spending her last moments at that chicken ranch with your old Butane flame."

"Well, we can't stay here."

Holly walked over to Rennie's bed and picked up her hand. "Rennie? We have to play musical chairs again— Rennie?"

Rennie didn't display a fleck of comprehension.

Willis walked over. "Holly's not in charge. We don't break camp, we're not going anywhere."

Rennie stared at the boarded window across the room.

Holly leaned over the pillow. Rennie's eyes were wide open in an entirely different way, her pupils dime-size and flattened. Her mouth was slightly parted as if releasing a small puff of air, as if her last breath might have been a soap bubble with a pithy caption, but her last word was what? They hadn't paid attention.

"Willis," Holly whispered. "This is it."

Holly realized that "This is it" was something pregnant women said when they suffered their first contractions. They had not heard a peep from Rennie, no death rattle, no final round of coughing. Rennie had slipped free without an addendum of wasteful emotion. Willis kneeled beside his stepmother. He lifted her hand. He leaned over her body and rested his forehead against Rennie's. His tangled bangs swept her face. His goodbye to her could not have been more straight forward than that, face-to-face, brow-to-brow, an exchange of some wordless essence. It was as if a pneumatic substance lingered in the air until Willis reabsorbed it.

The two of them, faces joined, reminded Holly of those "kissing fish." Holly was surprised to find herself thinking of such an oddball thing, "kissing fish," fish who drift for hours eye-to-eye, in love or aggression, she couldn't recall which.

Willis shifted and sat up. He watched the body for a long time. Holly sat next to him. She was aware of Joseph Salvatore walking back and forth in front of the cottage, waiting for them to leave, yet he was showing some consideration about it. She went outside and told him the news. They would be getting out of the shack. He looked immediately relieved and he asked her to forgive him. It was a simple matter of protecting the business. "Holly. What are you going to do?" he said. "You shouldn't get yourself in these situations, with the wrong people."

"Give us a little more time," she said.

Chapter Twenty-eight

Willis washed Rennie's face and hands with the moistened corner of a towel. Touching a lifeless face was an awakening. Life, its miracle element, was never clearly realized or taken into account until it was evacuated. Her flesh in its dull, impersonal frailty seemed almost an intrusion to his communion with Rennie's disencumbered spirit.

"She needs some decent clothes," he said.

Holly saw Rennie's stained nightdress. "What funeral home are you using?"

Willis looked at her. His teeth were clacking in a new bout of convulsive arctic sensations. "I'm not using a mortuary. Christ, Holly, I'm taking her out myself."

"Out where?"

"Out there," he said.

She remembered the water the way it had looked when she stood outside with her boss. A tipping disc of shivering light, still quite aggravated from the passing storm. "You're not kidding, are you?"

"How long have you known me? When did I kid around?"

"Just a couple times, I guess. I sure loved it."

She had made him smile despite the circumstances, despite their proximity to an actual corpse.

He told her, "Maybe you won't like me when I'm a straight arrow. When I'm the real me. 'Just a-hunk a-hunk of burning love.' What then?" He looked at her.

She liked it when they were two minds with one thought.

They left Rennie alone in the cottage. Holly drove the Toyota to Easton Pond. Willis went into the weeds and came back dragging the *Crouton*. The dinghy was snagged and Holly got out of the car to help him.

"It has only one oar," she told him.

"I know that," he said.

They put the little boat on the roof of the Toyota and Willis tied it down with bungee cord.

Willis said, "Drive on over to the house. Rennie has an oar in the garage."

"You think we should go to the house?"

"If they haven't fussed with us yet, they aren't planning an ambush."

Holly obeyed his instructions. She parked at the duplex and Willis walked over to the tiny garage. She left the Toyota idling, even if it was a giveaway. She almost wanted someone to stop her. She didn't want Willis taking that tiny boat out on the water, with a corpse.

She had no trouble getting inside the house, the door was unlocked. The last of the rainwater was still pooled on the vinyl flooring in the kitchen. Holly saw how it caught the western sunlight streaming in the fanlight. It was funny how refracted light could affect her—best of all, the Fresnel. Holly liked the fact that boats far out on the water saw the same lighthouse beacon she could watch from the safety of her kitchen. One metronomic measure of white light repeated for the lost, the same deaf swirl for those at shore.

Holly went through Rennie's closet, sliding the hangers

across and tugging the dresses off their dancing wire shoulders. She had been thinking of the temperature outside when she remembered that it didn't matter to Rennie, the dress could be thin and flouncy, she wasn't going to feel the bitter cold.

She picked out a floral midlength gown, something summery in a fine, silky fabric. She put the dress in an Almacs bag and went down to the car. She stopped at the mailbox and collected some letters before driving Willis and the *Crouton* back to Neptune's.

There was a letter from Norfolk. Willis tore the letter down one side and blew into the envelope. He inserted his finger and pulled out the photograph of Wydette. A note told Willis that the picture had been found behind a box spring when a new recruit was setting up his bunk. Someone had been nice enough to send it on. Willis looked at the photograph of his young mother, younger than he was at that very minute. It didn't have the force it once had. He flicked it onto the dashboard and Holly retrieved it. She looked at the exotic face. It was Willis through and through—ethereal, erotic, peppery.

Willis unloaded the boat from the roof of the car while Holly went into the shack with the dress. Holly didn't wait for help and when Willis came in, Rennie was ready. The dress looked good; it had a high neckline with a ruffle collar. Willis stared at Rennie in her funeral outfit.

Willis told Holly, "That's Wydette's dress."

"Are you sure? It was in Rennie's closet."

"That's not Rennie's dress."

"Well, what's the difference?"

"I can't bury her in that. Wydette's dress," he said. He looked utterly confused, as if he couldn't make a moral decision about it. He sat down holding his stomach.

She went over to him and tried to embrace him but he

was too hunched over. Tears were streaming down his face, and she couldn't tell the nature of those tears. It might have been acute intestinal cramps. She didn't want to say the wrong thing to comfort him.

"Rennie looks okay, though, doesn't she?" Holly said.

He looked down at the body in the gauzy dress. "What the hell," he said. He shrugged. Holly admired his sudden show of strength.

"Wait a minute," he told Holly. "Do you want that ring?"

"Her wedding band?"

"It's her first one. She always wore it. What good is it now?"

"That little ring?"

"Well it's not exactly an anniversary diamond."

He tried to twist the gold band from Rennie's wedding finger. It wouldn't come off.

His small use of force was upsetting to them both.

"I can't take Rennie's wedding ring," Holly told him sternly.

"That's good, because she doesn't want you to have it. I guess she belongs to Bill Hopkins after all these years. Maybe just her little finger belongs to me."

He walked into the bathroom and closed the door. He opened the taps. The pipes screeched.

Willis wanted to row out two miles, as far as the channel, and release Rennie's body. "I can't have her drifting into First Beach again," he said as he showed Holly the Sears tire chains he had brought from the garage. He coiled them on the kitchen linoleum at Neptune's. The ugly automotive accessories gave Holly an uncomfortable feeling.

"You're putting those things on her?"

"What am I going to do?" he said. "I have to."

"I think you can throw ashes in the water, but don't you have to get a permit, don't you have to be a certain number of miles out at sea to release a corpse?"

"Well, I'm not going very far in that six-foot Winterport. It's still choppy."

"What about your friend, Carl Smith. Doesn't he have a boat? Maybe he can take you out."

Willis said, "The *Tercel*? Fuck, she's razor blades. Her engine's fouled. That boat doesn't run, all she does is float. Even that's a temporary condition."

"He must have a dinghy to get out to his boat, maybe it's better than the *Crouton*."

"Look, two things. He's way over at Warwick Neck, and two, he's a fucking scoundrel. Rennie wouldn't want him at her bon voyage. We're going in the *Crouton*, is that all right with you? You don't have to come along."

Holly didn't think Willis could row all that way with his bad arm. She thought about love, its many tests. So far, she had failed each one. Her father had died before she could straighten things out. Her marriage to Jensen erupted in a humiliating local scandal. If she helped her lover bury his mother at sea, what couldn't she conquer after that?

Chapter Twenty-nine

Rennie was in Wydette's beautiful dress, but the tire chains were wound around her hips and her body was folded awkwardly so it would fit on the floor of the pram. Willis had wrapped her in Fritz's Indian blanket. With the blanket Willis could reel her out slowly, with a little courtesy.

At full dark, First Beach was empty and they waded into the icy surf on either side of the dinghy. They angled past the breaking waves and pushed off. Holly sat on the forward bench, Willis sat between the oarlocks. The oars were different sizes and Willis had to compensate; his strokes were irregular and the boat wasn't pulling as fresh as he wanted. Their weight was slowing them down. He thought about the Sears chains twisted around Rennie's waist. It was a gruesome sight. They couldn't even talk about it. Willis had brought a light, but they didn't need it. The moon put a sheen on the water. Willis watched the texture of their wake across the stern, shiny black whorls stirred out.

"They went to sea in a Sieve, they did. They went to sea in a Sieve. The water it soon came in, it did." Willis recited the poem in his head; its metered form helped him roll the oars.

"Open the Gate, Open the Gate, Here comes Rennie,

the Grad-u-ate." Already the rowing was tough; his sore arm throbbed and died out, throbbed and died out.

Willis had studied his opportunities according to the tide chart and they had headed out exactly at the ebb. He rowed straight out parallel the Cliff Walk. They saw the mansions from a new perspective, their interior rooms were dark behind brilliant façades. Each house was lit with strategically placed floodlights, strings of lamps across the lawns, beams honed on gargoyles perched across the eaves. This fierce, external illumination when the cavernous homes remained empty seemed eerie to Holly. Empty hulks. Salve Regina College was the exception, its windows clotted with yellow honey. When they rowed past Château-sur-Mer, with its dim, violet panes and oversized awnings, half country club, half mortuary, Holly thought of the man with the invisible noose and wondered if he could see them from his prime vantage point.

Willis rowed for an hour. The sea wasn't calm. It made no alterations to advance their progress. Its indifferent silver sheet stretched wide in all directions and was the most sobering aspect of their journey. An occasional swell tipped the *Crouton* into a valley and drew them up again. Holly's face was a terrified mask.

Willis saw her fear and he started to sing "Volare." It was the reliable melody but he had changed the lyrics. He was singing, *"Ren-a-te, oh, oh. Ri-cot-ta, oh, oh, oh, oh. Your love has given me wings—"*

Holly giggled in tight, painful drifts that hurt her frozen diaphragm. Despite the difficult sea, Willis's voice sounded clear and strong even as the hull was smacked by stiff swells, one after another. Then the lip of a wave shot up vertically, sucking the bow up and over, pitching Holly against Willis. Holly screamed. She grabbed the oars from Willis. He took the oars back. He told her to take it easy.

He knew what he was doing. He worked at the lopsided oars and tacked against the waves so they wouldn't have another surprise such as that one. He rowed past Gull Rock, trying to get as far as Haycock Ledge. He heard the bell at Brenton Reef and he knew he was clear of the cove and in the open channel. He rested the oars when the lights on shore lost their singularity and flattened into a golden line. Then he rowed a tight circle and tucked the oars down below the gunnels.

Willis stood up. "Okay," he said. "Here it is," he announced. He was telling Rennie.

Holly lifted her face to him. "Are you sure you want to do this?"

He stood, straddling Rennie's corpse. He kept his balance—she didn't know how—the boat was shifting sideways. He wrenched the hem of the Indian blanket, with gentle adjustments, until Rennie's body rolled free from its shroud. She went in feet first. In another second, the water closed over her face like black saran.

Willis watched Rennie vanish. He wasn't just setting her loose, he was returning her. Rennie and the sea were one and the same, one seamless element, souls of the same fabric.

Holly said, "Willis, look over there—"

The body had surfaced on the other side of the dinghy. Her face lifted in the swell, matching the oval husk of moon riding the same water. Her face drifted a few inches beneath the surface. Willis rowed parallel. The Sears chains must have slipped free from her hips. The current pulled hard but didn't swallow.

Holly wondered if Rennie's septicemia had made her oddly buoyant. For several minutes Willis steered the dinghy alongside her body, following her out with the tide. The wide black mattress lofted the tiny figure until it was almost vertically astride it. Her white hair fanned across the water. Wydette's gauzy dress billowed around her waist like the pulsing veils of a hydra.

Willis was beside himself. He wondered if he should haul Rennie's corpse on board again, yet he couldn't bear to think of putting her in the ground at White's Monument Village with Lester and Sheila Boyd's infant. Then, as quickly as she sank the first time, Rennie disappeared again. Willis rowed in a circle searching the black water. He turned on his light and panned it back and forth over the frothy chop.

Holly had the palms of her hands flattened against her face. She couldn't bear to witness the next frightening panel in that mural. But Rennie's corpse didn't reappear on the surface.

"I think she's all right," Willis said.

"Are you sure, Willis?" Holly kept her hands over her eyes. Her voice shook with fear-induced hiccups. They were so far out in the water, she wasn't sure she would see her familiar surroundings again—her duplex, the percolator clock, the knotty-pine dresser, her hand mirror where she left it, its ghostly circle splashed upon the ceiling.

"She's safe," Willis said, "she's with the Jumblies."

Holly reached out to touch his arm. She kept her hand on his shoulder as he rolled the oars. His arm felt strange, it was vibrating. She watched him closely. His posture became inexplicably rigid. He dropped the oars. He was having some kind of attack, a slow convulsion, a dreamy disintegration. He tipped forward into her arms.

She held his suffering weight, trying to decide what to do, when a floodlight advanced, a brilliant skewer through the dark, illuminating their dinghy.

A Coast Guard utility boat had been waiting, blacked out. It awakened with untangled precision; its engine kicked in and its running lights flickered wide open. Holly

remembered their Latin motto: *Semper paratus.* Always
ready. A loudspeaker crackled with an officer's firm, in-
structive narrative. "Good evening, *Crouton,* come aside."

Holly sat in the little boat feeling the waves shift the
hull.

Of course, they weren't going to come to her, she should
go to them, but she couldn't shift Willis from her arms to
pick up the oars.

The loudspeaker crackled again, "Identify your captain, *Crouton.*"

The officer's words were strange yet comforting formal-
ities, and in ready submission, Holly shouted their names.
"Captain Willis Pratt," she hollered. It sounded ridiculous.
She wondered if the Coast Guard officer was serious; it
might be yet another formula of ridicule exercised by this
particular branch of the authorities. The officer told her to
wait where she was. She obeyed the officer's directives and
stowed the oars.

A diver had lowered himself into the water to retrieve
the waiflike corpse, wherever it was. Another diver came
over to Holly and towed the dinghy to the ship by its frayed
painter. Then the divers turned on underwater lamps and
kicked off. Their rubber frog-feet slapped the surface and
disappeared.

Willis regained a little ground and started to protest.
"Grave robbers!" he shrieked at them. The divers surfaced
thirty yards out and sank again to continue searching. The
divers came up once and again, their rubber skullcaps
gleaming under the moon. They weren't having any immediate luck. Holly and Willis were ordered on board the
sparkling white utility boat. Willis fell to the deck and
rested on his knees. They tugged his wrists behind his back
and bound them with plastic drawstring handcuffs.

Holly couldn't get her legs back after almost two hours

in the *Crouton*. She stumbled across the glistening deck into a huddle with the authorities. She was so relieved to be rescued, she found pleasure in their uniforms, in the hash marks on their sleeves, in every sign of conformity to military routine. They didn't cuff her and let her hug herself and shiver. The divers climbed back up the ladder, admitting defeat. They would search again at daylight. The body was free to drift into Rhode Island Sound, and from there maybe anywhere. Holly told Willis that Rennie was loose, but he had collapsed. She screamed at the officers to remove the handcuffs, couldn't they see he was sick.

It was apparent that Willis was very ill. An officer snipped the handcuffs and put Willis on a stretcher. They pulled the blanket high and folded the hem at his chin. His wet jeans bled through the fabric.

An officer asked Holly, "Can you tell us the order of events this evening?"

"The order of events?"

"Can you tell us what drugs are involved?"

Holly said, "I guess he might have something in his system." She kneeled beside Willis and plucked his hand from under the sheet.

Other young recruits lined up to peer over the stretcher in a polite queue, perhaps according to their rank. Holly couldn't believe their attention to protocol.

She yelled at the men, "Christ, can't you get someone on deck to help him." Willis had passed out. Under the bright floods, his smooth profile looked pale and cold as limestone with a charcoal smear across his jaw where his whiskers were concentrated. Holly understood he was taking an illicit turn at rest. It was a violent sunken dream from which he would have to surface. She hated to revive him. Then she shook him.

Chapter Thirty

The next morning, Holly sat in the duplex with Nicole's copy of the *Newport Daily News*. The paper was too heavily inked and the headline throbbed: COUPLE DUMPS BODY FROM ROWBOAT NEAR BRENTON POINT . . . LOCAL WOMAN IDENTIFIED . . . COOKS AT PREP SCHOOL. After her notoriety as a suspect for arson, the story didn't alarm her. How many times would her life be put on display? She wondered if all the harassment she had endured might have to do with the fact that she lived on an island—everything was blown out of proportion. Anywhere else, her small, irrelevant crimes would surely be ignored by the busy mainland, the sane interior.

The Coast Guard released Willis to the Newport police. From there, Willis was admitted to the state detox unit at Roger Williams Hospital in Cranston. He spent the night in a lighted room, where aides could watch him. He turned his face into the rubber pillow to avoid the glare. All night, he saw the final transposed image of Rennie and Wydette, one immutable seraph, her floral dress pulsing in the waves.

The next morning, two aides brought him into an office and sat him in a chair across from a counselor. He cooperated and answered as many questions as he could find corresponding thoughts or associations for, and when Willis was satisfied with his interview he closed it off. He told the drug counselor, "That's a wrap. Mission accomplished. Touchdown." He rolled off the chair and limped back to his bed. All his joints were aching, even the balls of his feet were throbbing.

When Munro learned that Willis had been taken from the Newport County Jail to the state detox hospital, he placed phone calls all morning. Munro's attorney successfully made arrangements to have Willis transferred into a substance-abuse program at the swank private hospital Edgehill Newport. The county agreed to the alteration of locale, but it depended upon Willis. If Willis didn't accept Munro's generosity, he'd have to remain in the Cranston facility, where there was often a distinct, razor-sharp urine smell in the stairwells and landings.

Munro went over to Cranston to insist that Willis agree to the transfer. Munro told him, "Look, little brother, I'll pony up the costs, and you can stay on the island. Where you belong."

It was the first time Munro had ever implied that Willis had any place or station in this world.

"Sure," Willis said. "That'll be fine." From the moment Rennie drifted away, Willis had lost his bite, but he had regained his equilibrium. Other than a plague of vacillating cold-turkey symptoms, he felt calm. It didn't matter if Munro wanted the upper hand, and said, "Look here, little brother." Willis was Teflon. Munro's burden was lighter now that his mother was taken care of. Rennie was "safely dead." It means different things to different people, Willis thought.

Willis faced two charges; the first one reflected his violation of the Federal EPA Ocean Dumping Act, a provision of the Clean Water Act. Munro's attorney was informed that the charge would most likely be dismissed due to the sensitive nature of the case and the actual low-risk effects resultant of the crime. People buried loved ones at sea several times a year despite the Clean Water Act, and the EPA took a humanitarian stance. The second charge was "larceny of an item worth more than two hundred fifty dollars." Willis had been charged with the theft of the *Crouton*, not Fritz. The restaurant's management wasn't willing to drop charges. They claimed to have lost revenues during the period their mascot was missing.

Munro told Willis that Showalter had repoed his totaled truck without raising an eyebrow. Munro chuckled and told Willis, "Showalter visits Fritz in the hospital, mornings and evenings. It's all in the family."

Willis nodded at this news. He tried to remember any early mannerisms or clues that could have revealed a love connection in Fall River. He thought of the chewed InstyPrint pencil Fritz wore tucked behind his ear all winter, the Burberry scarf Fritz appeared in one day, as if he'd collected it from a bus seat. The cashmere muffler was so out of place on him, it had to be from a wardrobe in someone's lovesick dream.

When Willis completed the detox program in the upscale hospital, he'd be released on his own recognizance to await his EPA hearing and his court date for larceny of the *Crouton*.

Holly went back and forth between Willis's glamorous setting on Ocean Avenue and Newport Hospital, where yellowed linoleum tiles were glued waist level along the hallways. Fritz was recuperating from a cracked sternum, broken ribs, a collapsed lung, and general malnutrition. His poor diet was a side effect of Fritz's nervous condition and had nothing to do with his accident. Fritz pushed down the scooped collar of his cotton johnnie and showed Holly where doctors had wired his breastbone together.

"They used staples?" she said.

Fritz told her, "This isn't fingertip embroidery."

Holly sat beside Fritz, the TV buzzing at the end of the bed. It was a singles game show. Fritz had a perverse hunger for these blind-date panel discussions.

She looked at Fritz. His skinny shape looked worse in the hospital bed, like a hat tree under the sheet. The thin thermal hospital blanket didn't look warm enough, his knobby knees erupted through the fuzzy crossweave layer.

Showalter appeared at the door with a box of doughnuts from Store 24. Fritz introduced Holly.

Showalter lifted Fritz's pillow from behind his head and wedged it back straight. Then Showalter folded back the lid of the doughnut box and she and Fritz marveled at the pastry selection. They shared the greasy wheels of sugared dough, and waited for the TV show's conclusion.

Chapter Thirty-one

Willis stood on an extension ladder, starting at the
third-floor gable with the Rent-All pressure cleaning gun.
The tool had a stiff recoil and five weeks ago he would have
been too gooned to hold on to it. He swiped at the bees,
hating to dislodge the ancient wisteria vines that were in
full flower, but the house wanted restoration. It screamed
for it. He hoped to paint the Victorian to the specifications
of the Newport Historical Society. They gave him a chart of
authentic nineteenth-century colors for the clapboards and
another chart for the contrasting trim. He wanted the new
paint to match the first coat put on at the turn of the century
when the house went up.

Munro had decided to rent the house during the tourist
season. Summer rentals paid for themselves. He wouldn't
have to let go of the waterfront property. Munro told Willis
he could add a kitchenette upstairs and close off the third
floor for Holly and himself. Winters, they could have the
run of the whole house. Munro wasn't concerned about
Willis's court appearance scheduled for the end of August.
People were sympathetic to the story of a local cancer victim and her loving son who only needed to borrow a rowboat for the evening. The whole town looked forward to the

proceedings. Already the *Newport Daily News* had run two feature stories; one of the headings read: RESTAURANT MAS-COT DOUBLES AS FUNERAL BARGE, and public opinion remained on Willis's side of it.

Willis was gaining some color working out in the sun. His cast was finally removed, the chalky husk sawed up the middle. A fluffy down was growing back on his bare arm where the hair had been rubbed off.

Earlier that week, Willis had called the Coast Guard to ask about finding another Fresnel lens. They invited him to come over to the station at Castle Hill, where they had a mint specimen displayed on a pedestal. The lens was a peculiar notched barrel the size of a watercooler. Willis fingered its cool planes. A recruit told him that these antique Fresnels were getting few and far between. Willis might be able to find one, but he should get working on it right away.

When Willis was finished cleaning the gables and blasting the gritty asphalt buildup from the gutters, he went over to Neptune's to find Holly. The flower cottages were full up and families had their bathing suits drying on the clotheslines. He walked past the tiny kitchens and smelled fresh flounder frying. Willis thought he could identify every fish—whiting, salmon, bluefish, scrod, tongues and cheeks.

He found Holly working in the Zinnia cottage. She was annoyed because children had placed a collection of starfish in the freezer. Sand had frozen into the icy scrim and she had to defrost it.

Holly promised Willis that she would give him the grand tour on changeover Saturdays that she had refused to give to Jensen. Early that morning he had worked her across the soiled linens in the sunny bedroom of the Lupine shack. Outside the window, climbing roses were flexing on the trellis; the surf sorted lace garters across the tan shore. It was a beautiful morning. The world, all its larger schemes, interfaced his secret pleasures. Willis said, "What is that? That smell on you?"

Holly's skin had a strange, sweet odor like floor polish. He kissed her shriveled fingertips, pale as button mushrooms from the mop bucket. "Now you're going to get it," he told her. She fingered the folds of the bedroom curtains luffing over the headboard—the bright pink labium of the cabbage roses, an obsession worth sharing.

Willis looked forward to learning the interior of every one of those shacks: Primrose, Dahlia, Cosmos, Myrtle, and on and on until the summer ended.

That evening at Easton Way, Holly and Willis walked down to the breakwater with Rennie's wire scallop basket. Willis wanted to collect periwinkles from the rocks. It took scores of the tiny snails to fill a dinner plate and they were there for an hour, pinching the slimy boot of each tiny creature until it released its grip. "We have to eat these with a bent pin," he told her.

"You're kidding," she said. "Sounds like a lot of effort."

"You decide if it's worth it."

Willis took her back to the house and he told Holly how to steam the periwinkles with garlic and white wine. The kitchen smelled fragrant with chablis and spice and the rich steam from the tiny mollusks. Holly had retrieved the saltshaker house from Jensen and she set it on Rennie's pedestal table. Willis didn't like the tiny replica with its caked nozzles, so she removed it. She would put it at Neptune's, where she could enjoy it.

With two full plates, they sat down across from one another. Willis removed a new safety pin from its white card. The pin had a bright yellow cap like the kind used for baby diapers. He bent the pin straight and handed it to Holly.

About the Author

Maria Flook has published two collections of poetry. Her first novel, *Family Night*, was a finalist for the PEN/Ernest Hemingway Award. She teaches writing and lives in Truro, Massachusetts.